PRAISE FOR THE NOVELS
OF KENDRA LEIGH CASTLE

For the Longest Time

"A delightful story filled with endearing characters and laugh-out-loud humor."
—*USA Today* bestselling author Katie Lane

"Sweet and sexy character-driven romance!"
—Fresh Fiction

"A great romance story . . . yummy sparks and heated passion."
—Stuck in Books

"*For the Longest Time* adeptly shows that even misfits and dreamers can go home again."
—Heroes and Heartbreakers

"Characters you love to love and a few furry ones who will melt your heart. This has everything."
—Open Book Society

"If you're a fan of Jill Shalvis or Kristan Higgins, you're going to want to pick this one up. . . . Definitely on my must-read list from here on out."
—Fic Fare

"I devoured it . . . beautifully written small-town romance."
—Under the Covers

"Castle's Harvest Cove promises to be worth repeated visits."
—*Publishers Weekly*

Every
Little Kiss

The Harvest Cove Series

Kendra Leigh Castle

A SIGNET ECLIPSE BOOK

SIGNET ECLIPSE
Published by the Penguin Group
Penguin Group (USA) LLC, 375 Hudson Street,
New York, New York 10014

USA | Canada | UK | Ireland | Australia | New Zealand | India | South Africa | China
penguin.com
A Penguin Random House Company

First published by Signet Eclipse, an imprint of New American Library,
a division of Penguin Group (USA) LLC

First Printing, March 2015

ISBN 978-0-451-46759-1

Printed in the United States of America
10 9 8 7 6 5 4 3 2 1

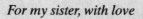

For my sister, with love

Chapter One

Breaking up a wild party in his own neighborhood wasn't Seth Andersen's idea of a fun Saturday night, but he found himself trudging up the walk toward the door of 121 Juniper a little after midnight anyway. It wasn't a big deal. When the call had come in, he'd nearly been home, technically off-duty but still in uniform, and Jess, the dispatcher, knew he'd take it. Harvest Cove was a small place. He could manage what would probably amount to nothing more than a "knock it off" conversation with the guy who lived three houses down. Hell, the sight of a uniformed officer at the door was usually enough to drive the point home, and he'd had an impromptu cookout with Aaron Maclean only a week ago. This shouldn't be a problem.

He sure hoped not, because right now, all he wanted was his bed. He'd learned to sleep through the sounds of artillery fire out in the desert, but he'd rather not have to try to sleep through Pitbull's praising of his woman's booty, over and over and over to a beat that could wake the dead.

Judging from the noise coming from the little Cape Cod, Seth figured that the house, not too different from his own, had to contain a couple hundred people more than it ought to fit. He was halfway to the door when it opened on its own. At first he thought Aaron had seen him and was coming out to save some time, but there was nothing masculine about the figure that stumbled through the door and nearly toppled into the bushes. Nothing masculine, Seth realized, but everything familiar.

It was just a little sad that he had the curves of a woman he'd never spoken to so thoroughly memorized.

"Emma?"

He blurted her name before he could think better of it, and the blank look she gave him as she shoved her hair out of her face only confirmed what he'd suspected: He'd lived in Harvest Cove for six months, and Emma Henry still had no clue who he was. Maybe it was the time he'd spent in the army—he'd gotten good at blending in with the scenery when he had to. But Seth thought it was more likely that Emma just didn't notice anything not already on her to-do list. She sure seemed that type, and nothing he'd heard about her had ever changed the impression. Everything from her tailored suits to the way she clipped around in those sexy heels screamed all business, all the time.

Not tonight, though. Turned out she owned a pair of jeans after all—and from the smell, he thought she might be wearing as much beer as she'd imbibed.

"Something wrong, Officer?" Emma straightened, shoved her long, dark hair out of her face again, and put on what he expected she thought was an innocent expression. Not a bad effort, but her inability to stay still while maintaining her balance was kind of ruining the effect.

"Nothing too bad, Miss Henry," Seth replied, remembering his manners this time as he ambled forward. He was just some random cop to her. Probably just as well.

"We've had a few noise complaints from the neighbors. I came by to let Mr. Maclean know that he needs to either calm things down or break it up."

"Oh. Are we that loud?"

He tried not to smile, since she seemed sincere.

"Yes. Yes, you are."

"Wow. I'm really sorry."

Her eyes rounded. The light out here was dim, but Seth knew from his previous almost-encounters with her that they were a startling forget-me-not blue made even more striking by her fair skin and dark hair. Usually she had all that hair pulled back, but he liked it this way, with the thick waves down past her shoulders. Some of the ends were damp, though, and Emma was having a hard time keeping it out of her face. She shoved at it again, frowning, her full lower lip plumping further when she stuck it out to concentrate.

She was cute. And really, really drunk. It seemed so utterly out of character for her that he had to work at suppressing his amusement. As he got closer, he could see that her shirt was even damper than her hair, the dark fabric clinging to her breasts. He couldn't help but notice—her curves were impossible not to notice, even at his most distracted. Still, her bedraggled, slightly bewildered appearance left him feeling more protective than turned on. She needed to be home, tucked in and sleeping this off, not wandering outside at this hour. Bad things happened everywhere, even in the Cove.

Seth sighed inwardly. His bed was looking farther away than he'd hoped.

"Do we know each other?" Emma asked, wrinkling her nose and looking utterly confused.

"No."

"How'd you know my name, then?"

"The Cove's not that big, Miss Henry," he said. "You run the party-planning business down on the square. I've only been here for six months, but knowing who's who is part of my job."

That seemed to satisfy her, at least well enough to change the subject. "Oh. Well, Officer . . ."

"Andersen."

She blinked and appeared to mull that over for a moment. "Okay," she finally said, and Seth knew she had tried—and failed—to place what should have been a familiar last name. "You're not going to arrest anybody, are you? It'll ruin my sister's party if you do."

"Your sister's party?"

One dark brow arched. "She's getting married." Even as drunk as she was, the "you idiot" on the end was strongly implied. He had to swallow a laugh. Not everyone could be wasted and beer-stained, and still pull off "haughty" this well.

"Ah," Seth replied. Now her presence at the house party—not to mention her condition—made sense. "Bachelorette party, then."

"Yeah."

Seth's eyes went to the door, considering it. "Please tell me there aren't any strippers in there."

She snorted. "If there were naked people in there, I would know. I mean, I think. I hope there aren't any naked people in there."

Her small smile hinted at the promise of an absolutely gorgeous full one. He'd never seen her smiling. But he'd certainly like to.

Jesus, Andersen, just get this over with and go home.

He cleared his throat. "Well, whatever the stripper situation is, I need to speak to Mr. Maclean, Miss Henry. Are you heading back in?"

She hesitated, then turned her head to look at the house. "I guess."

His eyes narrowed. "You weren't planning to drive home, were you?"

"No! Why would you think I'd do something that stupid? I don't even have my keys!" The words were slightly slurred, but they were loaded with real offense. He wanted to believe her. He didn't want her to be the kind of person who did the sorts of things that so often left behind devastating messes for people like him.

Seth didn't know why it mattered to him. It just did.

"It's not an unreasonable question, Miss Henry. You wouldn't be the first person to make that mistake."

Emma glared at him a moment, then closed the distance between them, weaving a little but maintaining her bearing until she was glaring up at him, close enough to reach out and touch.

"Listen, Officer Am . . . Alf . . . Amster . . . whatever," she said, waving her hands dismissively before settling them on her hips. Seth tried not to let his eyes linger, but it was tough. He was a sucker for an hourglass figure, and hers was just about perfect.

"*I* am a *respectable businesswoman* in this community," she informed him, the picture of angry, wounded pride. "I don't know who the hell you are, but just because you get to carry a gun and handcuffs and whatever doesn't give you the right to—to impugn my integrity."

He found himself caught between wonder and gut-busting laughter. It took everything he had not to give in to the latter.

"I'm not impugning anything, Miss Henry," he answered while struggling to keep a straight face. He wondered what other fifty-cent words she liked to throw around when she was mad. The woman was probably a veritable dictionary when pissed off and sober. He found the idea ridiculously sexy. "I'm just concerned for your safety. I don't want you to get hurt."

The change in Emma's expression was instant. Her eyes widened, anger vanishing to become innocent surprise. Her lips parted, just a bit, as she looked up at him and became the picture of vulnerability.

"Really?" she asked.

Seth blinked. He'd dealt with plenty of drunks in his line of work, but he was having a hell of a time finding his footing with this one. She'd been surly and sweet in equal amounts, shifting between the two fast enough to give him whiplash. Right now, though, there was something winsome about the way she looked up at him, something that pushed a few buttons he hadn't expected to have pushed tonight, or any time soon. Those buttons had gotten pretty rusty, but it seemed like they were still there.

He guessed he should be glad he could still feel an attraction like this, like a hot punch straight through his chest. Maybe he would have been, if the sensation had ever foretold anything but trouble.

Since she appeared to be waiting for an answer, Seth nodded his head. "Really," he said.

She swayed for a moment, her gaze inscrutable. Then she smiled, that big smile he'd been waiting for that crinkled her nose. For a few long seconds, all Seth could do was stare. Whatever he might have imagined, this was better. As beautiful as she was, that smile was like someone had turned a light on inside her.

"You should smile more often," he said softly, realizing too late that the words hadn't stayed in his head where they belonged. At least they didn't seem to faze Emma, who simply shrugged, nearly losing her footing in the process. Seth moved on instinct, reaching out to catch her beneath the arms before she went down on the walk. Her hands gripped the front of his shirt as she regained her balance. When she looked up at him this time, her face was only inches from his. He caught the faint smell of her perfume, something light but musky, a whiff of exotic smoke. Its sensuality was a startling contrast to Emma's normally buttoned-up image. A hint, maybe, of the woman beneath.

Do. Your. Job. Andersen.

"You have pretty eyes." She sighed, fingertips running down the front of his shirt to his hips. His stomach muscles flexed in reaction, and his breath caught in his throat. Parts of him stirred that had no business stirring when he was working. And that was what this was—part of his job. This would be a good time to remember that.

"Thanks," Seth replied, forcing out the word while removing his hands and stepping back. "I need to—"

"Will you take me home?"

It took him a few seconds to close his mouth. "What?" His voice sounded hoarse to his own ears. She couldn't possibly have said that. If she had, she couldn't possibly mean it. And if she did, there was no way he could say yes, because that would require a level of awfulness he was nowhere near considering.

Emma looked up at him with those big luminous eyes, and he wondered whether he'd somehow taken a wrong turn and landed in hell.

"I want to go home. I can't drive. Can you take me?"

"Uh . . . why don't you just . . . Hang on a sec," he said. "Stay here." This was not his problem. This was Aaron's problem, because it was Aaron's party. He walked away quickly, trying not to run and thinking of every unappealing thing he could to erase the wildly erotic images trying to cascade through his brain. He blamed his fatigue. The last few nights hadn't been good ones, sleepwise, and it seemed like that had caught up to him all at once. How else to explain his reaction to her? She was a beautiful woman, sure. But while he might not be Channing Tatum, he hadn't exactly had a hard time finding a date when he'd wanted one.

The front door opened again just as he reached it, and Seth was relieved to see his neighbor emerge, purple-streaked hair and all. It was a wonder they got along as well as they did. The only art Seth had ever spent much time looking at was World War II pinup girls, and Aaron had been very up-front about the feminine form, outside of a basic aesthetic appreciation, not being his thing.

As long as Aaron kept his lawn mowed and wasn't a complete jerk, Seth didn't much care who the man brought home.

"Emma?" Aaron looked past him at first, beyond to where Emma had just been standing. "Are you okay? Zoe said that somebody told her you didn't feel good and—oh. Hey, Seth." He watched Aaron take in the uniform, then wince. "Oh. I guess it's Officer Seth tonight. This is about the noise, isn't it? Sorry."

"Yeah." Seth shifted his weight from one foot to the other and thought again of his bed. His body was telling him it would actually stay asleep for a solid block of time tonight. That was, if he could ever get to his bedroom. "We've had a few complaints. I said I'd stop by on my way home to let you know, since I didn't think you'd have a problem taking care of it."

Aaron shook his head with a sigh. "No, of course not. This got to be a little bigger than I was expecting. We started at the bar, and I think the bar followed us home."

He swept an arm at the cars parked up and down the street. "Guess it's what happens when you throw a big party in a small town. The whole world shows up. It was supposed to be ladies only, but we've gotten a few infiltrators."

Seth snorted. "Uh, you might want to look in a mirror."

"I do. Frequently," Aaron replied with a flash of a grin. Then he shrugged. "I'm the host. I get a free pass."

Lucky bastard.

"You want me to help clear everyone out?" Seth asked, relieved when Aaron immediately shook his head no.

"Nah, I can handle it. Sam and her friends are staying over. Everyone else can leave the same way they got here. I was starting to worry about what was going to get broken first anyway. House parties are a lot more fun when they're not at *your* house, you know?"

"I can imagine."

Aaron arched an eyebrow, a smile playing at the corners of his mouth. "Not a partyer, Officer?"

"Very funny. And no, not so much. Used to be, but I guess I kind of outgrew the appeal."

"Hmm. You're kind of young to sound like such an old fart." Aaron tilted his head, regarded him with a fair amount of curiosity, but then returned his attention to the woman farther down the walk. "Emma, why don't you come back in?" Aaron called. "I don't think sleeping on the concrete is a great idea."

Her unintelligible mutter had Seth turning back to look. Emma had apparently decided that standing up was too much work. She was now lying down in the middle of the walkway, curled into the fetal position. That told Seth all he needed to know about her current state.

"You realize she's going to puke," he said.

Aaron pursed his lips and exhaled loudly through his

nose. "Yep. Look, I hate to ask, but can you watch her while I kick everyone out? Even if you can just get her into the grass so no one steps on her . . ."

"He's taking me home."

Her voice was so clear, it took Seth a moment to register that it had come from Emma. He looked sharply at her, seeing Aaron's startled look out of the corner of his eye as he turned his head.

"Miss Henry—"

"Emma," she interrupted him, just as clear. Her head lifted ever so slightly though her hair covered most of her face. "An' you said you would."

"I didn't say that! I just told you not to go anywhere." He knew he sounded defensive, but the last thing he needed was for his neighbor to think he'd been hitting on his drunken friend on his way to telling him to shut down his party. He looked beseechingly at Aaron. "I didn't say that."

Aaron simply waved him off. "I'm sure you didn't. She's just channeling Jose Cuervo right now. It's kind of like speaking in tongues, but with a lot more sexual innuendo."

Relieved, Seth laughed and shook his head. "Been there. Do you have a way to get her home? She seems stubborn enough to try to walk there if she manages to get up again."

"Oh, she'll be fine here."

"No, I won't," she insisted. "I don't feel good. He said he'd take me home. He's a—a policeman." She gave a woeful-sounding hiccup. "I have beer on me. I want my bed. I hate the ground. This sucks."

Seth arched a brow when he returned his attention to his neighbor. "You sure about that?"

Aaron frowned and sighed. There was enough alcohol

in the puff of air that wafted by Seth's nose to confirm that Aaron wouldn't pass a breathalyzer right now, even if he was pretty coherent.

"No. If she really wants to go, I'm sure there's somebody who can . . . well . . ." His brow furrowed, and Seth knew he was mentally going through the list of people sober enough and trustworthy enough to deliver Emma home. He waited, suddenly certain that the list would be short to nonexistent. Finally, Aaron sighed. "Shit. I drove back here, but I'd be over the limit now. I'm not putting her in some random person's car and hoping for the best. And not to sound like an ass, but she doesn't have a lot of friends, anyway. Emma's kind of . . ." He trailed off, seeming to consider his options, and finally chose a word. "Independent."

The simple statement struck an unexpected chord with him. Independent could mean a lot of things, but he was pretty sure Aaron didn't mean it as an insult. He understood not being close to many people, whether by choice or simple temperament. Maybe he and Emma had some things in common after all. Didn't seem likely, but neither did finding her drunk as a skunk and hanging on to the earth to keep from falling off it. Anything was possible. And the solution to this particular problem was inevitable.

"I'll take her."

Aaron seemed surprised. "That's really nice, but you don't have to do that."

Seth lifted a shoulder. "I know. But she seems to think I do, and I can manage a detour before I head home."

"Aaron, quit arguing with him," Emma groaned, her voice more muffled now. "Officer Ambi . . . Officer? Just take me home. I don't feel so good." Emma's voice drifted over to them from where she lay, curled into herself.

"Em, you're staying here, remember? With your sister?" Aaron said, leaning to the side to speak to her. "Your things are in the house."

"Then give them to Officer What's-his-face."

"Seth. It's *Seth*," Seth told her, hoping to avoid further butchery of his last name for one evening.

"Seth. Whatever. I want to go *ho-ome*," she moaned. "Everything is spinning. God. Why did I drink so much?"

Aaron cringed. "Those are the words of doom."

"Impending doom," Seth agreed. "I won't leave her until I'm sure she's settled in for the night."

He could see his neighbor was uncomfortable with it, and he didn't blame him. But if Emma really wanted to go home, which she seemed to, he was her only option. Oddly enough, he didn't mind the imposition. Aaron, however, was going to need more convincing. They were friendly, but they hadn't quite made it to "friends" yet.

"Look, I don't sleep much," Seth admitted. *Even though I would have tonight.* "I can stay up awhile longer."

"It's not that," Aaron said. "I'm more concerned about leaving her alone. She's going to be sick."

"Shut up. I can hear you!"

"I know, Em." Aaron rolled his eyes, then lowered his voice. "Seriously, though."

Seth shifted his weight from one foot to the other, leaned his head to one side to stretch muscles tight from a long day, and chose his words carefully so that Aaron would understand he had nothing to worry about. Being a soldier and a cop didn't have to mean anything, but he was a guy who took the honor inherent in both professions seriously.

"I have a twin sister," Seth said. "I've pulled plenty of hair-holding duty. It takes a lot to faze me, so if she needs a keeper until her stomach settles, I guess I can do that, too. Like I said, I don't sleep much. This is at least as interesting as anything on TV at this hour."

Aaron chewed his lower lip for a moment. "It would be flattering to think you were doing this to win my favor, but I'm pretty sure that's not the case, so . . . why? You don't even know her."

"Sure I do. Emma Henry, local force of nature, right?"

That made Aaron laugh. "That's one way to put it. And this is . . . chivalry?"

Seth couldn't help the slow grin. "The lady demanded an escort. I am but a humble public servant."

Aaron laughed again, shook his head, then rubbed the back of his neck with one hand.

"Okay, Officer Lancelot, go sweep her off her feet while I get her bag and start kicking people out. I'll put my number in with her things so you can text when she's settled. Be good. Hands to yourself except where warranted, or I'll unleash hell on you, standard disclaimers, et cetera."

Seth felt a stiffness he hadn't been even aware of begin to leave his shoulders. Why it was suddenly so important that he be allowed to see to Emma's well-being, he had no idea. But his instincts had rarely failed him, and he didn't question them now. "Understood. She'll be safe with me. You have my word."

Whatever Aaron heard in his voice, it seemed to satisfy him, and he nodded. "Okay. And you've got mine that I'll have everyone but the people staying over gone within a half hour or so. Thanks for being a neighbor about it instead of, ah . . ."

"A jerk?" Seth supplied.

"You said it, not me," Aaron said. Something told Seth this wasn't the artist's first encounter with cops breaking up a party, and that it probably wouldn't be his last. Still, the guy was hard not to like, and he obviously took care of his friends. Good qualities, even if he was occasionally prone to get in a little trouble.

Hell, so was he. Or he had been, once.

"Back in a sec." Aaron jogged up the walk and headed inside. Seconds later, the music stopped, and a strong, clear voice rang out. "Ladies and gentlemen, local law enforcement has just stopped by to let me know that it's closing time at Maclean's watering hole, so like the song says, you don't have to go home, but you can't stay here." There was a chorus of groans. "Yeah, well, considering most of you just followed me home anyway . . . Jesus H. Christ, Al, where are your pants?"

Seth chuckled to himself as he walked to where Emma lay and crouched down beside her. All that thick, dark hair was in her face, and he reached down to brush it aside with a couple of fingers. Her eyes were closed, long spidery lashes twined together, but he doubted she was asleep. Probably wishing for sleep, though. She took in deep gulps of air, a telltale sign that the nausea was in full effect.

Her night of fun was definitely over.

"Miss Henry?"

"Ung. Emma. Might as well call me Emma."

"Okay. Emma. Can you get up?" He kept his voice low and soothing.

"Don't wanna."

"You still want me to take you home?" he asked.

"Uh-huh." She kept her eyes shut, staying very, very still. "Carry me?"

His eyebrows lifted, though he shouldn't have been surprised. Drunk didn't cure bossy, which she certainly seemed to be. "You sure about that?"

"God yes. No standing." A pause, then a small and oddly attractive furrow of her brow as she sighed. "Please?"

Her voice was plaintive, and defeated, and he couldn't have denied her if he'd tried. So, carrying it was. He slid one arm beneath her knees, the other beneath her shoulders. "Here we go," he said, and lifted. She was light in his arms, and turned her face into his chest as he stood, making a soft unhappy sound. He tried not to think about how right she felt, tucked up against him. For all he knew, the woman was hell on wheels when she was sober, and as far from his type as humanly possible. Right now, though, her soft vulnerability tugged at him.

He was the kind of guy who'd been born to protect things. It was just in his nature, same as the need for a certain amount of order. Right now, he wanted to protect *her*. And he had a bad feeling that instinct would wreak havoc on the order he'd finally achieved here, in this quaint little town where the fact that nothing ever happened was a large part of the appeal.

As his guests began to depart, walking down the street back toward downtown or piling into cars, Aaron hurried outside again.

"Here," he said, lifting the small overnight bag so that Seth could grip the handles. He followed Seth's gaze to some of the cars, then met his eyes with a knowing look.

"The ones leaving in cars have designated drivers," Aaron said. "I keep a good eye on things, and I take keys. I'm not interested in being even a little responsible for somebody wrapping themselves around a tree because they shouldn't have been behind the wheel."

The grim look on Aaron's face, so at odds with his sunny personality, told Seth he was cautious from experience.

"Okay," Seth said.

"Okay," Aaron echoed, then sighed. "Well, thanks. She lives in the apartment over her business, down on the square. Entrance is in the back. Have fun with the stairs." He gave Emma's hair an affectionate ruffle. "'Night, sweetie. Call me tomorrow and we'll coordinate getting your car back to you, okay?"

Emma's reply was an unintelligible mumble against Seth's shirt, but Aaron seemed to take it as an affirmative.

"Text me," he said again to Seth, then turned and walked back toward the house, bidding people good night as he walked by them. Seth didn't miss the soft laughs as people caught sight of Emma in his arms, or the whispers as people speculated. He brushed it off. People would talk—they always did. It didn't bother him much, though he suspected Emma wouldn't feel the same. For her sake, he hoped the situation was obvious enough that it wouldn't prompt much gossip. She seemed like a woman who put a lot of value on her image—which in her case was "cool and professional."

"I've got your things," he told her, "so let's get you home."

"'Kay," she sighed, snuggling further into him, her fingers tucked into his shirt between two buttons. "I like you."

He smiled, surprised. "I like you, too. How's the stomach?"

"Mmph," was the only reply, and it sounded negative. He thought of his nice clean cruiser and felt a sinking sensation.

"Emma, I realize we don't know each other, and you don't owe me a thing for this, but if you don't mind, can you not puke in my car?"

One bleary eye opened to look up at him. "No promises."

Seth nodded to himself as her eye shut again. Whatever happened, he was all in now. Only one thing was certain—after this, Emma Henry would definitely know who he was. And whether or not that turned out to be the extent of their acquaintance, they'd probably be able to agree on one thing.

It had been a hell of an introduction.

Chapter Two

Emma woke up slowly, the way she always did. She breathed in deeply as her body adjusted to the light streaming in the window and hitting her closed eyelids, becoming aware of the sensation of her limbs sunken into the soft mattress, the soft sounds of birds chirping outside.

The taste in her mouth like the floor of a truck stop.

She opened her eyes slowly. Her eyelids were sore. As a matter of fact, her entire body was sore. And her *head* . . .

"Oh. God." It took an obscene amount of effort just to lift a hand to her throbbing head. The strands of hair that caught between her fingers were hopelessly tangled. Her thoughtless bliss upon waking vanished, to be replaced by memories of the night before. Hazy memories, but they were enough. The part where she'd driven to Aaron's was clear. The champagne at his house was clear—obviously a bad idea, but she remembered it just fine. Then they'd headed to the Harvest Cove Tavern, and that was where things got a little scattered. There'd been beer. And . . . tequila. And—

"Dancing. Oh *God*."

Her voice was little more than a croak, and her throat

felt like she'd been gargling with razor blades. Emma gingerly raised herself to a sitting position, though that made her throbbing head a thousand times worse. She squinted around her room, which looked perfectly normal. That was great, except she had no idea how she'd gotten here.

No . . . wait. . . . There was a guy. A cop, I think. Was he at the party?

That's right. There had been a cop. Somehow, she didn't think he'd been an invited guest, though she was pretty sure they'd had a lengthy conversation. And she was more than pretty sure that her ride home had been in a squad car. A fragment of that ride returned to her.

"Okay, Emma, you look really green. We're almost to your place. Can you hang on just a few minutes longer?"

"If you drive faster, maybe."

He hadn't just driven her home. He'd come in. To help. Because she'd been a complete disaster. Dread curled in the pit of her much-abused stomach. Emma's eyes shifted to her nightstand, upon which sat a glass of water and a bottle of aspirin. On the floor was her wastebasket, helpfully lined with a plastic bag. It was blessedly empty.

Whoever this guy was, he'd taken care of her. She was deeply grateful and deeply embarrassed all at once. She didn't like owing people for things. And she didn't like making a spectacle of herself. It looked like this time around she'd managed to do both.

A familiar feline form wound around the corner of her half-shut door and sauntered in, greeting her with a soft, high-pitched meow utterly at odds with his size. His tail was curved into a furry question mark, as though he was wondering what on earth she'd been thinking last night, too.

"Hey, Boof," she rasped. He quivered his tail at the

sound of his unusual name, which her sister's fiancé had invented for him. Jake had gotten a kick out of the big kitten's penchant for headbutting, and he enjoyed adding sound effects when he was around to watch. "Boof" was used frequently. As it turned out, it was also the only thing resembling a name that the cat would answer to. Emma had fought it, but Boof, in true feline fashion, had seemed determined to thwart her.

She was pretty sure that Jake was still gloating.

It was a surprise to see her cat up and about. He usually slept with her. Then again, she wouldn't have wanted to sleep with herself last night, either. Boof gave another squeaky meow, then sat looking expectantly up at her. Looking for breakfast, no doubt. He loved her, but for the feline, food came first.

She slid her legs over the edge of the bed, steeled herself, and stood. Her legs were wobbly, but functional. Though her feet were bare, she was still wearing last night's clothes, the scent of which now wafted up to her and had her feeling sick all over again.

Stale beer. Mmm.

At least her shirt was dry now. And her hair. The way they had gotten wet in the first place was a part of the evening she wished she didn't remember, but she did. Not with perfect clarity, but well enough.

Emma tottered to her dresser, stripped off the offending clothes, and dumped them in a fragrant pile. Then she pulled one of her worn old sweatshirts and a pair of flannel pants out of her drawers, sighing with relief when she put them on. *Better.*

She walked slowly out of the bedroom, feeling more like an old woman than someone standing on the cusp of thirty. As much as she wanted to stay in bed and hide beneath the covers, something told her she needed to check the rest of the apartment ... just in case. The bedroom across the hall, the one she used as an office, was empty, as was the bathroom. Everything was neat and organized, exactly the way she liked it. Nothing seemed dangerous except for the big brown medium-haired tabby winding between her legs as she walked. But something nagged at her, though it took her a few seconds to identify what. Then it hit her.

It was a new smell.

She paused right before heading into the open living area when she caught it, faint but recognizable even through the still-unpleasant scent of her hair. She'd always had a sensitive nose, a thing sometimes useful and occasionally annoying. Right now, it was simply ... illuminating. And mortifying. Because that smell, a subtle, clean, slightly woodsy scent, was the cop's cologne. The first whiff of it reminded her how much she'd enjoyed breathing it in as he'd carried her to his car. Then from his car. Then up the stairs. And she knew, just *knew*, that she'd told him how amazing he smelled. At length.

Right before puking her guts out.

I'm never going out again. Ever.

Emma closed her eyes and mouthed several epithets before starting forward again. There was a brief moment of relief when her quick, initial glance around the room showed her nothing. Then she heard the deep, sleepy sigh from her couch, only the back of which was visible from where she stood.

Her feet propelled her forward even though her angrily throbbing brain was screaming at her to go back to bed before it was too late. Still, in a matter of seconds, Emma found herself standing at the corner of her big comfy couch, staring down at the semifamiliar figure of last night's savior. Her hero.

Perfect. I need a hero like I need a hole in the head.

And yet here he was, looking every inch the white knight she didn't need. Emma had remembered his scent, his uniform, and a vague sense that he was cute. Apparently, the booze had clouded her vision as well as her thoughts, because in the harsh and sober light of morning, "cute" didn't even begin to cover it. Not even the hangover from hell could do much to dull her appreciation of this particular sight.

The man was hotness incarnate.

He was still in uniform, stretched out with one arm bent across his chest and the other tucked behind his head, giving her a full-length view of a long, lean body that she could tell was in excellent shape just from the way his clothes fit. He'd untucked his shirt, and the top couple of buttons were undone, so she could see the white neck of his undershirt, a marked contrast to his olive skin. His face, relaxed in sleep, was a study in angles—sharp cheekbones, square jaw, a slim, sharp blade of a nose. His mouth was wide, generous, with soft-looking lips that were parted gently. Thickly lashed eyes tilted slightly down at the corners, closed beneath dark, heavy brows. His short, dark-brown hair was tousled, probably from sleep, and it just made him that much more beautiful.

He was absolutely, completely, horrifyingly gorgeous. And while she stared, trying to figure out whether it was possible to get him out of her apartment without him actually seeing her, the feline in her life decided to indulge one of his favorite—and her least favorite—habits.

If she liked, needed, or was working on something, Boof would inevitably park his big furry butt on it. Too late, Emma realized that she'd stared at the cop long enough for the cat to decide he was of some import to her. In the blink of an eye, Boof was sitting on him.

Emma's eyes widened. "No!" she hissed, her voice a ridiculous stage whisper. "Damn it, Boof, no!"

The cat looked at her placidly from the center of the cop's chest, seemed to consider her for a moment, and then bunched himself up to lie down. Emma was positive that if he'd had a middle finger, Boof would have given her one.

"Boof!" she whispered again, a harsh rush of air that the cat had plainly decided to ignore. He gave her the slow, sleepy blink that her sister, Sam, assured her was feline for "I love you." Emma thought it was probably more like "Screw you, stupid human." Especially right now.

The cop woke up just as Boof started to knead his chest, purring loudly.

He hissed in a breath. "Ouch!"

Emma stiffened, ready to shout as his hand moved to, presumably, swat at her cat. Instead, he settled it gently on Boof's back, then rubbed the cat's soft fur with his fingers.

"Hey, big guy. Watch the claws." Big warm eyes the color of her morning coffee opened, hazy with sleep. And of course, they found her right away.

"Hey," he said again, easily, as though it was the most natural thing in the world that he was here, a stranger who'd cared for her through a bout of epic vomiting and then slept on her couch. When she said nothing, he breathed in deeply, stifled a yawn, and pushed himself up into a half-sitting position while steadying Boof with one hand. He kept the hand beneath the cat to cradle him against his chest, then used his fingers to begin rubbing underneath Boof's chin, against his cheeks, behind his ears. All the favorite places.

Her treacherous cat was immediately in heaven. The cop, on the other hand, quickly returned his focus to her.

She wished she could remember his name. She wished she could think of something, anything that wouldn't make this worse than it already was. Her hair was probably making it worse already.

"You feeling better this morning?" he asked. "Sorry I didn't split before you got up. I was waiting to make sure you were, um . . . finished," he said, gesturing vaguely toward the bathroom, "before I left. Guess I dozed off."

His voice was low, with just a hint of roughness that buzzed along her ragged nerve endings. She fought off a shiver, irritated that she was having any kind of a reaction at all to this guy. He didn't belong here. He shouldn't still be here. The need to have him gone was so strong that she would have scooped him up and carried him over the threshold, reverse bridegroom style, and then run back inside to lock the door if she could have managed it. He looked pretty solid, though. And he'd probably struggle.

Please let him not try to make small talk. Please.

Emma crossed her arms over her chest and tried to give him her best intimidating glare. The cop just looked back at her, his dark eyes far more serious than his words had been. The quiet intensity she saw in them messed with her resolve, threw her off balance.

Well, maybe it was the hangover that was doing all that. But still.

"You brought me home last night," she said, her voice sounding like something dredged up from one of the deeper pits of hell.

"Yes, I did."

She held herself a little more tightly as several more details surfaced in the morass of last night's memories. "You held my hair. When I was sick." And rubbed her back while she'd cried about what an idiot she was in between. She would tell him never to speak of it, except that she had no intention of acknowledging it had ever happened in the first place.

The cop licked his lips, a distracting little flick of his tongue as he finally looked away for a second. Knowing this was a little embarrassing for him, too, made Emma feel a tiny bit better. Not much, but it was something. Of course, it hadn't made him get off her couch yet.

"I did that, too, yeah."

Emma shook her head, staring at this odd and handsome creature who apparently offered full-service rescue for blindingly drunk women. "Why?" she asked. "Why would you do that?"

His dark brows rose a little. "Because you were in rough shape when I got you back here, and I didn't want to leave you alone? Plus, you asked me to stay." He moved his shoulders restlessly. "I just didn't feel right leaving you like that. Bad things can happen. You'd be surprised."

"Oh." She couldn't argue with that. He'd probably seen plenty of those bad things firsthand, given his job. It wasn't an explanation she could argue with—she hoped she would have done the same, in his position. Of course, she would have been gone like a thief in the night before things got all weird and embarrassing.

This guy didn't seem to have any qualms about it.

"Does Aaron know that—"

"He knows," the cop interrupted smoothly. "I was under strict orders to keep him posted."

"You're . . . friends, then," Emma said, frowning as she tried to remember the connection. Mostly she just remembered lying in front of Aaron's house. That there was a connection at all, though, eased her mind a little. It was better if this was a friend of Aaron's and not just some random cop who'd been driving by and taken pity on her.

"He and I are neighbors," the cop said. "Though after this, I think 'friends' works, too. He did say he owes me dinner." He angled his head down, tilting it to one side. "You sure you're okay? You're still pale, and you were pretty sick. Want me to grab you some juice or something before I take off?"

"No," Emma said, a quick denial that was forceful enough to make him blink. "No," she said again, trying to soften the sound of it. "I . . . appreciate it. And everything. I just need to, ah, recover. I guess." She closed her eyes and gave a short, rusty laugh. "I feel like something somebody scraped off the bottom of a shoe."

His grin revealed perfect, very white teeth. "Yeah, you mentioned you don't get out much."

She managed a rueful half smile. "Not like that, anyway."

The cop's serious eyes softened, and some small, stupid part of her wished, just for a moment, that he was here because she'd brought him, not because she'd needed a babysitter. It was a stupid wish, and she banished it as quickly as she could. Guys like him were not for women like her. That was a decision she'd made a long time ago.

No jerks. No loose cannons. And definitely no heroes.

"It's not a big deal. Nobody's perfect," he said, drawing her out of her unpleasant thoughts. Emma could see he really believed that platitude. He obviously hadn't been in the Cove very long.

I'm supposed to be perfect. It's all I've got. But that's not something I'm going to stand here explaining to you.

"Hmm," was the best reply she could manage. She wanted a shower. She wanted her coffee. . . . Well, maybe weak tea would be better this morning. What she really wanted was the Hot Arm of the Law here to clear out and pretend they'd never met. To his credit, he finally seemed to get that. He swung his legs over the side of the couch, set Boof gently on the floor, and began to put on the shoes he'd set neatly beside her coffee table.

As she watched her cat flop onto his back and demand belly rubs as a plot to keep the cop's attention, all sorts of questions occurred to her, most of which she wasn't all that sure she wanted the answers to right now. But with a little effort, she finally remembered one important thing.

"Seth," she said, and he looked up at her while he tied his shoe. "Your name is Seth. I'm sorry I don't remember the rest of it."

"It's okay," he said, flashing that killer smile again as he reached over to give Boof's belly a quick rub. "You never really got the hang of it last night. Andersen. New guy in town. I know you're Emma Henry, though."

"Yeah," she said, a silly smile curving her lips before she banished it. Totally inappropriate to be smiling at a guy you wanted out of your life ASAP. It would help if he didn't seem like he was enjoying her company. And that had to be an act, because guys didn't tend to enjoy her company even when she had her shit together. And that was always.

Make that *almost* always.

"Well," she said as he finished tying his shoes and stood. She hated being at a loss for words, but she couldn't blame Seth for it. This miserably awkward situation was all on her. With luck, this would be the end of it. "Thanks," she said, "for, you know, everything. I appreciate the help." *And let's just pretend we've never met each other from here on out, okay?*

"Not a problem," he replied. He picked up his duty belt from the coffee table and put it on, then grabbed his keys. A small inscrutable smile crossed his lips before

Seth turned to go to the door. God knew what he was thinking.

Emma watched him walk away, hating herself a little for taking a second to admire the way his pants hugged one very nice butt. She had to stop herself from offering a more tangible form of thanks—dinner, a bottle of wine, something more than just a lame "see you around" for having put up with her at her most pathetic. But though her instinct toward politeness was strong, her sense of self-preservation was stronger. Seth was too interesting to see again. Even if she'd been looking for a guy, which she wasn't, he was completely unsuitable. The sight of the badge on his chest and the gun at his hip just drove that home.

Still, manners dictated she follow him to the door, if for nothing more than to bid him a final farewell and provide a visual reminder that no, he wouldn't ever want to go out with a woman capable of looking this bad.

"Bye," Emma rasped. "Thanks again. I'll make sure Aaron makes good on that dinner offer. You've earned it."

He turned his head to look at her, and for a brief instant she thought he was going to do something terrible, like ask to see her again. Instead, he just said, "It was nice meeting you, Emma. Hope I'll see you around."

It was exactly what she'd wanted. And she felt a nasty slap of disappointment anyway as Seth gave her one last devastating smile and shut the door.

Emma looked down at Boof, who had come to rub against her leg.

"Aaron was right. I really am a hot mess," she said.

In response, Boof gave an irritable meow and headed for the kitchen. His breakfast was late. And really, shouldn't she and her cat both have more pressing concerns than Officer Seth Andersen? She told herself that the answer was yes as she locked the door, then headed for the kitchen.

And she was still telling herself that as she pulled the curtains aside just enough to watch him get in his cruiser and drive away.

Chapter Three

She was sitting quietly at her desk Monday morning, minding her own business, when the sense of impending doom that had been circling since the day before landed on Emma with a resounding thud. The thud, in this case, sounded a lot like the text alert on her cell phone. And the bearer of ultimate doom was her assistant, Brynn.

You might want to see this.—B.

No. No, she really did not. But Emma clicked the video Brynn had linked anyway, then watched silently as someone who looked a lot like her used every rusty skill remembered from childhood dance lessons to wow the crowd down at the Harvest Cove Tavern. Every wobbly pirouette, every random butt wiggle, had been captured for posterity in a shaky video some enterprising soul had taken on his or her phone.

Emma made a soft, pained sound. "The robot? I did the *robot*?"

Yes, she had. It was on YouTube. It was probably on Facebook.

It was bad.

And since the name BigPimpin372 could have belonged to any number of local jerks, she had no one to chase after to demand the video be taken down.... Though when she calmed down a little, she fully intended to try anyway. She just needed a minute. Maybe more than a minute.

Emma rubbed absently at the increasing ache in her right temple as the woman in the video threw herself into a chair, tossed her head back to pose dramatically, and upended a pitcher of beer onto herself to the cheers of the crowd. It was a serviceable *Flashdance* homage, she guessed.

"Well. Wow."

Apparently her sister wasn't the only one with a flair for the dramatic. Who knew?

Emma made it through the ending, a brief clip of herself singing Katy Perry's "Firework" into a microphone that had been cut short because the cameraperson hadn't seemed too steady on his feet at that point, either, and then started to read the YouTube comments before remembering that one should never, ever read the comments. Especially when they were about oneself. A glance at the time stamp told her that the video had been up since early yesterday, probably before whoever took it had fallen into bed. She carefully set her phone down on the desk.

"I have a nice singing voice," she informed the empty shop. "So there's that."

After a few long minutes spent staring at the phone as though she could will it and its contents out of existence, Emma blinked rapidly and straightened. It was time to get back on track. She pulled up the proposal she'd been working on and typed a few words. When she realized they didn't make much sense, she erased them, then propped her chin on her hand to study the work she'd done so far. The words kept jumbling together, though, and there was a tightness in her chest she couldn't seem to get rid of.

It had been a long time since she'd had this feeling, but it was one she never really forgot. If she wasn't very careful, she was going to wind up with a full-blown panic attack.

Minutes went by, slipping into half an hour, then forty-five minutes. Emma tried to remember the techniques she'd once used to calm herself down, focusing on her breathing, the steady inhaling and exhaling. She found she could at least be grateful that it was a slow Monday, and that she had no appointments until early afternoon. Emma closed her eyes, visualizing a quiet meadow, a gentle breeze, solitude.

Breathe in. Breathe out. It's okay.

The bell above the door tinkled, but the fact that she was no longer alone didn't really register until her sister's voice filled the quiet of the shop.

"Hey, it's alive!"

Emma's eyes flew open, startled, and the look on her face must have revealed everything. Sam hurried forward, bootheels clicking on the wood floor, concern etched across her lovely face.

"Jesus, Em, are you okay? You're as white as a ghost! Did you eat today? Are you sick?"

"No, I'm fine! I was just—just resting!" Her hands flew up defensively, and Sam stopped just short of her, looking uncertain. Things were better between them, but there were still boundaries, old ones, that had yet to be crossed.

"Are you sure?"

Not really. Part of her wanted to grab her sister and cry

on her shoulder until Sam's pretty blue tunic was soggy with tears. The rest of her, however, the bigger part, would never allow that. Comforting her shouldn't be Sam's job. She could handle it herself. That was what she did, after all. Emma Henry, Woman of Steel. It wasn't exactly a superpower, but it would do.

Emma collected herself as best she could, despite the uncomfortable squeeze of her rib cage around her lungs, and pretended everything was fine.

"I'm not dead yet, anyway," Emma said, keeping her voice neutral and managing a thin smile. Not great, but better than looking terrified. "I'm just putting together a package with some options for the McKendricks." She gestured at her computer screen. "This seems more like a sweet sixteen party than a baptism, but if they want to go big, who am I to judge?"

Sam hesitated, and Emma could see her debating whether to continue to press. Finally, though, Sam offered up a small mischievous smile. "There aren't, like, ice sculptures involved, are there?"

Emma let out a breath she hadn't even known she was holding, and when she smiled again, it was warmer. "Not this time, no. But you'd be amazed at some of the things I've had to set up."

"This is why I couldn't do what you do. You have to keep a straight face," Sam said, moving to perch on the edge of the desk. It was a not so subtle way to make sure her sister couldn't dismiss her easily, Emma knew. An effective one, too. Despite all the years they'd orbited each other only distantly, they understood each other well.

Sam had come to check on her for a reason. There would be no avoiding the conversation.

"It's easier to keep a straight face when getting paid

depends on it. Trust me," Emma said. When Sam simply sat there, looking at her expectantly, Emma folded her hands and tried to steel herself for what was coming. "Look, I have kind of a lot going on today, so . . ." She drew the word out, letting it hang in the air like a question. Sam gave her a look that clearly indicated doubts about her sanity.

"Really? That's it?"

"*What's* it? I'm not trying to run you off, Sam, I'm just busy." She tried to keep the edge out of her voice—the one she knew very well had crept in over the years. Her tough shell had been the price of staying in the Cove, with all its baggage and memories. Sam understood some of it . . . better than anyone else in her life. But her little sister had gotten to run away, and had stayed gone for nine years before coming back last fall. Emma had gone to college, but she'd gone only as far as Boston. She'd never really left. She hadn't felt she could.

Whether the benefits outweighed the drawbacks was an open question, since the answer changed daily.

"Yes, you are trying to run me off," Sam said, tucking a lock of pale blond hair behind her ear. "And you know very well what *it* is." The cheerful veneer fell away again. "When I walked in, I wasn't sure whether you were going to throw a knife at me or keel over. I know how you are, Em. Seriously, are you okay?"

Emma organized a stack of papers into an even neater stack of papers. "You mean about my local film debut? Not my best work, but I'll live."

Sam sighed, with an expression that said she wasn't buying it. Not that Emma had expected anything different. "It's just a stupid little video," Sam said.

"You saw it, I guess?"

"Yes. It was better live."

Emma sighed. "I doubt that."

"Okay, so it's three and a half ridiculous, kind of funny minutes that could have been a lot worse," Sam said. "Most people aren't making a big deal about it. I hope you know that."

Emma looked back at her blandly. "Uh-huh. 'Most people' meaning your friends, who definitely aren't everybody." She tapped one French manicured fingernail on her desk. "Look, I know it's making the rounds, Sam, and I know it's an even bigger laugh because everyone thinks I have the world's biggest stick lodged up my ass. So they can have their fun with it, and I'll ignore it until it goes away. End of story. You don't need to worry."

Sam looked surprised by her blunt assessment, and Emma took some pride in that. She'd worked hard at not showing much emotion over the years, and her work had paid off. How she felt underneath her reserve was a completely different matter, but she'd deal with that later. Alone.

"Well," Sam finally said, "I wanted to tell you that nobody who *matters* cares. And that the jerk who put it up in the first place already took it down."

That news brought a measure of relief she couldn't hide completely, strong enough to make her feel slightly light-headed. "Oh? How do you know that?"

"Jake saw Melody Northrup maybe half an hour ago. Her dog, Otis, had a limp she wanted looked at. And while she was there, Jake got an earful about her free-loading son and his online activities, which she wanted to apologize for. He called me right away."

"And you came right here." *Northrup*. Emma closed her eyes briefly, summoning the image of a guy right around twenty-one years old, snapback hat over stylishly scruffy hair, ironic T-shirt, cute in a douche-y sort of way.

For all that her memories were fuzzy, she remembered him. He'd been trying to grind on her before she'd told him to get lost in more colorful terms than she would normally use.

"Of course I came right here. Like I said before, I know you." Sam frowned, her blue-green eyes full of worry.

"Melody is BigPimpin372's mom, I take it. What's his name? Josh?"

Sam nodded. "Yeah. Josh Northrup. Jake says he's a total failure-to-launch. She went in to make his bed today once he rolled out of it, and he'd forgotten to log out of his account on his laptop. Luckily he's still afraid of his mom."

"I know Melody a little. He should be," Emma said, knowing the wave of relief she felt was an overreaction. That stupid video had been up all day yesterday, and from her small sampling of the many comments on it, the damage was done. Not to mention that she'd had quite a live audience to begin with—on Saturday nights in the Cove, the Tavern was the place to be. Still, at least the video was gone, even if the gossip wouldn't be.

"Good," she breathed. "That's good." The invisible bands around her chest loosened a little with the knowledge that no matter what anyone said, the evidence of her public display of ridiculousness was gone. It wasn't perfect, but it was a start.

And this, all of this, was a distraction she didn't need. As if yesterday morning hadn't been enough to throw her off. Seth's name surfaced in her thoughts just in time for her to try to stomp it back down.

"Thanks," she said to Sam, who was still watching her with that concerned look on her face, like she might spontaneously combust at any second. "Tell Jake thanks, too," Emma added. "I'm glad it's gone, and I'm glad you told me."

"Well, you're welcome. I'm glad I made you feel better."

"It's not going to be better for a while yet. Ask me how I feel in a month or two." When Sam's brows went up, Emma relented a little. "Yes, you made me feel better. I appreciate it."

Sam's bright smile was a reward in itself, but as much as Emma would have liked that to be the end of this particular visit, her sister stayed put. It wasn't hard to guess why. Emma bit the inside of her lip and mentally girded herself to run the rest of this gauntlet. The people who'd once tormented her sister as a quiet misfit had never seen this side of Sam—the stubborn, nosy side that came complete with the slightly bent sense of humor all the Henrys shared.

It was good to have Sam back—better than Emma had imagined—but today, she would have preferred to brood silently over endless cups of coffee. Finally, she gave in. "What?"

"The hot cop? I brought you good news. Can't you toss me a scrap of information? Anything?"

"I don't think Jake will be happy if I give you his number."

Sam swatted her arm. "Don't make me hurt you."

Emma rolled her eyes. "You want scraps? Fine. They're all I've got. For whatever reason, Seth decided to keep watch over my sorry, drunken butt until I sobered up. Apparently he's a nice guy. I wouldn't know much more than that, because I have no intention of seeing or speaking with him again unless I try to one-up myself and actually get arrested for public intoxication someday." She shuffled a few papers around on her desk. "It's nowhere near as interesting as people are saying."

"How do you know what people are saying? You're a mole person."

"I can guess." She looked away, her voice dropping when she muttered, "And I read the YouTube comments."

Sam winced. "Why? Why would you do that? Comments sections are the cesspits of the Internet!"

"You would have read them, too," Emma pointed out. "People think I used my feminine voodoo powers to have hot monkey sex with the cop who broke up your bachelorette party."

Sam looked less disgusted than intrigued. "So . . . did you?"

Emma's mouth dropped open. "No!"

"Oh, don't get all huffy that I might have wanted it to be a little bit true."

Emma felt her mouth twisting as her brows drew together. "Why would you say that? What kind of a sister actually wishes things like drunk sex with random cops on her loved ones?"

Sam's laughter soothed away a little of her annoyance, but not all.

"You make it sound so sordid, God! I'm supposed to be the dramatic one, remember? I want more fun in your life, is all. If that involves eighties music and sexy men in uniform for you, I'm not going to judge."

"Yeah, well, you'd be the only one," Emma grumbled, typing in the name of one of the venues she was suggesting to the McKendricks. As far as she was concerned, this conversation was over. Sam, though, was going to take a little more convincing.

"So . . . no sexytime at all?" The hope in Sam's voice was a direct blow to Emma's pride. Was she really that boring?

Did she really want the answer to that?

"He fell asleep on my couch," Emma said flatly. "Which I expect Aaron told you already."

"I was hoping that was the sanitized version. I wanted to hear it from you, butthead. Did you not get my messages yesterday? I think I left around twenty."

"Twenty-one. And I didn't feel all that well. I didn't figure you would, either, Tiara Girl." Emma gave up on the McKendricks' proposal again and leaned back in her chair. Sam didn't look remotely embarrassed. And she shouldn't, Emma thought, feeling a pang of envy. The tiara she'd worn the night of the party had suited her, just like her fiancé did.

Emma hadn't wanted to like Jake Smith—he was, after all, the guy who had shattered what small amount of self-esteem Sam had managed to cling to through high school. While Emma had perfected the art of "studious and serious" back then, Sam had been determinedly unique in a way that had made her a target for bullies. Jake had been a popular jock whose friends were some of the worst offenders. Improbably, he'd taken a shine to Sam . . . and then humiliated her when she'd just started to open up to him. Emma had nursed her little sister through the heartache and figured that would be the end of it. But when Sam had come back last October, Jake had seemed determined to make amends.

According to the diamond on Sam's finger, he'd done a pretty good job of it. And Emma had finally had to concede that, yeah, Jake had turned out all right after all. Of course, she'd made him work to get her to admit that. It was only fair.

"If I'm Tiara Girl, then you're the Dancing Queen. So did he get your number?"

Emma stared at her sister. "Yes. Because the first

words out of his mouth when he woke up were 'Damn, that hangover looks good on you.' Have you been painting in a closed-up room? Inhaling fumes? On purpose, maybe?"

"All the time. I like to be able to hear colors and feel sounds. Did you get *his* number, then? No, I don't even need to ask that. For a second I forgot who I was talking to."

"You're honestly looking at what happened as some kind of dating opportunity." Emma shook her head.

"I'm honestly looking at it as your having verifiable interaction with an eligible male. So, yeah," Sam shot back. "Aaron agrees with me, by the way."

That was right—they were neighbors, Emma thought, cringing inwardly at the thought of Aaron trying to help some sort of imaginary relationship along. That was one of the things about living in a small town—sometimes the whole place was a modern-day version of a Jane Austen novel, complete with pushy and incompetent matchmakers.

"Aaron needs a hobby," she said.

Sam arched a slim blond brow. "That's the pot calling the kettle black."

"I date sometimes," Emma said, feeling herself begin to bristle.

"I would *love* some proof of that."

"I don't need to prove anything to you. I don't need to go chasing after some guy who was nice enough to hold my hair back while I puked, either, just because he's cute and male. I'm comfortable with my life the way it is. Just accept it, okay?"

Just like that, their brief interlude of sisterly peace crumbled to dust. Sam pressed her lips together in a thin line, and Emma could see she'd thoroughly exasperated her sister. It had been this way since they were kids. Sam was a dreamer. Emma was practical. The two things didn't always mix well, no matter how much they loved each other.

"I could accept it if I thought it was true," Sam finally said. "Which I don't. I also don't think you should chase anybody. I think there should be herds of eligible men darkening your doorstep, vying for your attention by, like, flexing. And arm wrestling."

It was a sweet thing to say, and unexpected, and very Sam.

Well," Emma said, both flustered and flattered, "I don't think I'm in any danger of that happening."

"Only because people think you're scary," Sam said. "I actually think you enjoy that."

She couldn't help the small smile. "Maybe."

"Hmm. I know you think I'm being shallow, Em. I just don't like your being alone so much."

"I'm not alone when I'm working," Emma pointed out, touched by the admission. "And as you keep complaining to me, I work all the time. You're not supposed to give me concerned lectures, by the way. I'm older, so that's my job. Anyway, Mom lectures me enough."

"Like you didn't learn to tune her out years ago." Sam gave her a knowing look. "Maybe I'm just concerned because you look really tired and unhappy lately. And because you've been avoiding me since the party, which was awesome in large part because of you. Not just the crazy dancing thing, either. We had *fun*. So why are you miserable? Is it just the video? It honestly was more funny than bad, and it's gone. But you still look like you might kill someone if they looked at you wrong."

Because Sam was right. Emma took a moment and considered how best to explain.

"Here's the thing. I went to get coffee yesterday when I started to feel human again. A guy sang to me. *The song*, so he must have been there . . . or maybe he'd just seen the video. I didn't know it existed yesterday. But anyway, the barista winked at me. I know I heard the word 'cop' being whispered. Lots of knowing looks, a few laughs, more at me than with me. It's a great story, I guess. 'Uptight Party Planner Becomes the Wild Woman of Harvest Cove.'" She looked down at the keyboard. "I didn't answer you yesterday because I didn't feel like talking about it. It's *embarrassing*."

Worse, it was utterly beyond her control. And control was a thing she valued above all else.

Sam's hand moved to cover hers, an artist's hand, slim and elegant with nails done in sparkling black polish. Her voice was gentle.

"Oh, Em. So you let your hair down one night, after all these years of going for the Upstanding Citizen Award around here. So people saw you cutting loose. So what? You deserve a good time once in a while. This probably sounds weird coming from me, but you might want to think about loosening up. Just a little. If you stay this tightly wound, I'm going to worry about you even more than I do now."

Emma gave her a beleaguered look. "You know better than anybody how doing anything different around here comes back to bite us in the ass times three. Maybe we can blame that witchy ancestor we're supposed to have. Do you have any idea how long it's taken me to build a reputation as a boring hard-ass? Everyone here expects us to be flighty screwups."

Sam poked her. "We come from a long line of wonderful, illustrious flighty screwups. Take some pride in your heritage, woman."

Emma propped her chin on her hand, covered her face with her fingers, and groaned. "I don't want to be what everyone expects, Sam. I just want to be boring and dependable so people will keep paying me to be responsible for things. I want to be normal so people leave me alone."

Sam heaved what sounded like an affectionate sigh. "Two things. One, nobody's normal."

"Jake is normal."

"Jake is full of hidden weirdness, trust me. I wouldn't love him half as much if he weren't. Anyway, two: Em, partying too hard on a Saturday night *is* normal for people our age, at least once in a while. Do you even know what regular people do? I'm not joking. I feel like you walk around in a hermetically sealed bubble sometimes. The only way I'm sure we're related is that when the bubble bursts once in a while, all the awesome comes out."

"I thought that was tequila."

"Thanks for that visual." Sam's eyes narrowed with curiosity. "Did he really hold your hair back while you, um . . . ? Because that's really—"

Emma parted two of her fingers to peer up at her sister. "Can we *not* talk about Seth, please?"

"Seth. That's right. You said that before. It's a nice name. Seth what?"

A glare seemed like an appropriate answer, and Sam seemed to get the hint, sliding off the edge of the desk. "Fine. Sit here and brood about the horrors of seeming approachable. The tragedy of having fake hooked up with a gorgeous guy."

"The misery of having a sister who ought to know that there is nothing good about being the talk of the Cove and a Henry at the same time, yet pretends it's no big deal anyway."

That one hit the mark, as she'd known it would. Sam

looked wounded. "Yeah, I do know," she said quietly. "Sorry, Em."

"It's fine." All she really wanted was to close the blinds and curl up in her bedroom until she felt a hundred percent human again. Barring that, she would throw herself into work until she was too tired to obsess about anything but sleep.

Sam's arms went around her, another sweet surprise. Emma tried not to stiffen, but she always did. It had been reflexive for too long. After a few seconds, though, Emma relaxed into the hug, allowing herself a little of the comfort her sister offered. Sam dropped a kiss on the top of Emma's head.

"This will blow over, Em. It's just a little thing. Nothing's going to rock your world. People will find something else to talk about in a few days, and that'll be it. Henryness moment forgotten."

"I hope so."

"I know so. It might be different if you weren't more put together than ninety-nine percent of this town, but you don't need to worry about that." A soft chuckle. "You're still not normal, though."

"Hmm." Emma smiled, breathing in her sister's light scent, and for an instant they were children again, blissfully unaware of all the things life was about to start throwing at them. Then Emma pulled away. She needed to, before any of this sudden rush of emotion spilled over and escaped. Crying at work, much like crying in general, was not okay. Something about Saturday night had cracked her carefully crafted defenses, and she needed to shore them up before she found herself weeping over things like puppies and sappy commercials.

"I'm fine. Now go on back to work," she said. "I know this is blowing your lunch break."

Sam shrugged. "Nah. I told Zoe I'd grab soup and sandwiches from that new place across the square. Mulligan's."

"Tried it. The creamy tomato soup was excellent."

"Cool. I may have to get that." Sam started for the door, then stopped, shook her head, and turned. Emma watched, struck all over again by how much her sister had finally bloomed in coming back here, the last place anyone would have expected such a thing to happen. She could still remember Sam as the little girl who had crawled into bed with her for a full year after their father had died, afraid of the dark, afraid of being left alone.

Now, Emma thought, the only one still alone was her.

Way to be completely depressing. And to forget to pretend I know nothing about Mom sneaking around with Jasper Reed. Because, ew.

Sam hesitated, then said, "When you said you wanted to be left alone . . ."

She didn't finish the question. She didn't have to, and Emma immediately felt like a jerk for making her sister wonder just what she'd meant. No matter how strong Sam had turned out to be, this was her one weak spot. She didn't need to be accepted by everyone—but she gave the people she loved all the power in the world to hurt her.

Knowing she had the same weakness, Emma kept that list of loved ones as short as possible. Sam, however, would always be on it.

"You know I didn't mean you, Sam. You can bother me anytime you want." She paused. "Within reason."

Sam's grin was equal parts pleasure and mischief. "Good. As long as I get to decide what's reasonable, since we both know you're just a *little* uptight about your schedule."

Emma shook her head, looked down, and started typing again. "Mmmhmm." She really did need to get back to work. There was an appointment in half an hour she needed to get ready for, Brynn would be in shortly, and the day would roll along no matter what she did. It was better to try to keep up with it.

"I wouldn't want to get in the way," Sam continued. "Or distract you. Or point out that a police cruiser just drove by with a really hot guy behind the wheel. I think he's pulling in, actually. Is Seth a brunet?"

"What?" Her gaze immediately flicked back up. She hadn't been able to keep the panic out of her voice. The thought of seeing him again, now, whenever, was just—

"You're not even looking outside!" she cried.

Sam burst out laughing. "Gotcha."

Emma slumped down in her chair, feeling like her heart might beat right out of her chest. "Oh my God. Go *away*. Now, before my legs start working well enough to chase you."

"Fine. I'll tease you later when you come down off the ceiling. Love you." Sam looked inordinately pleased with herself as she walked out the door, leaving Emma with her computer, a considerable pile of work, her afternoon appointments, and her own thoughts—none of which involved a dark-haired cop with a gorgeous smile.

Almost none, anyway.

Chapter Four

The Harvest Cove police department was small, comprising the police chief, one sergeant, six full-time officers, and two part-timers. Together they managed to run herd on the town of roughly five thousand residents without too much trouble. Given the size of the department, there were no dedicated divisions for traffic or vice—the officers were expected to be able to handle all of it. Seth did, gladly. He'd always preferred to be a jack-of-all-trades, keeping both his mind and his body busy.

Unfortunately, nothing in Harvest Cove was going to keep him busy enough to forget about Emma Henry. And by the time he was heading home from his shift at close to four in the afternoon on Tuesday, he'd spent plenty of time thinking about her. What she was doing, how she was feeling . . . especially about that damn video. He'd thought it was cute. She wouldn't, though. And not just because he knew full well that any gossip about her would have a completely different tone than the good-natured ribbing he'd gotten about supposedly spending the night with a hot brunette.

According to Mark Salvatore, a fellow cop he'd gotten friendly with, some people around here would just love to see Emma fall flat on her face. It didn't surprise Seth.

That was people for you—they'd find a crack in your armor and lob in a hand grenade, just to see what would happen. Especially if the armor belonged to a woman no one seemed to know well, and who seemed to prefer it that way. Seth had heard her called "icy" more than once.

He thought of her standing there with her hair on end as she tried to figure out how to make him go away without offending him, and he smiled at the memory. Whatever she was, icy wasn't it.

That certainty, coupled with an inability to shake the images of her that kept wandering through his thoughts, had him swinging by Petite Treats on the square when he went off duty. He made a couple of guesses, then parked in front of Emma's storefront in one of the old buildings that lined the town square.

Everything here was wood and stone, most of it qualifying as historic and the rest built to look as though it was. A little bit colonial, a little bit fairy-tale, and charming in a way that drew in a fair number of tourists every year, Harvest Cove looked like an ad for small-town New England. They even had a legend about having been founded by witches, and as "proof" could point to the Witch Tree, one of the oldest oaks in the country, spreading its gnarled branches over the small park at the center of the square. It was a beautiful thing this time of year, with its leaves young and green, but it would be in its glory come October. Seth looked forward to seeing it.

It was nice to look forward to things again. He'd spent enough time numb to appreciate the difference.

With a small pink-and-blue box in hand, Seth pushed open the door to Occasions by Emma. There was the soft, silvery sound of a bell as he stepped inside. Seth looked around, curious about what the business Emma ran might look like. That she seemed to have gone with understated class didn't surprise him at all. The walls were painted soft gold, a warm contrast to go with the burgundy curtains that framed the big window that looked out onto the square. On the walls hung framed, professionally shot pictures of couples and families at various events—ones he assumed she'd planned. Some of the pictures had a card discreetly tucked in the corner, advertising for the photographer. Seth walked slowly across the wood floor, taking in the elegant furniture arranged into a seating area, the albums set out for clients to browse through, the small samplings of work from what he expected were the vendors she preferred.

It wasn't boring, nor was it overly busy, and the impression Seth got was one of quiet competence. From the look of things, Emma knew what she was doing.

A carved wooden desk, big but feminine, sat angled in the far-right corner with a pair of chairs facing it. Those were empty, but the desk was not. Unfortunately, it wasn't occupied by Emma, either. A pair of warm hazel eyes watched him with frank assessment.

"Hi. Can I help you?" Her red hair was pulled back into a long, curly tail, and even from here he could see the dusting of freckles across the bridge of her nose. She was charmingly pretty, but something in the way she looked at him, and at the box in his hand, suggested she had hidden skills in, say, knife throwing. Hand-to-hand combat. Something. He knew a gatekeeper when he saw one.

"Hi," he replied. "Is Emma in?"

"She's just finishing up with some new clients. Is there something I can help you with?"

Seth's eyes moved to the curtained doorway set into the back wall, and he heard the soft murmur of voices beyond it. She was busy. So much for spontaneity. He shrugged and hoped it looked nonchalant. He'd been smooth, once. This didn't feel smooth. Neither did the unexpected rush of heat to his cheeks.

Christ. So this was what months of celibacy did to you.

"No, I just thought I'd stop in and say hello on my way home. I, ah, brought her something." He gestured at the box in his hand and felt like a complete idiot. The woman tilted her head and looked at him with undisguised curiosity, then rose swiftly.

"If you want to leave it with me, I can give it to her," she said, walking forward. She extended her hand, and he wasn't quite sure whether to shake it or shove the cupcake box into it. After a quick internal debate, he chose the former. Her smile told him he'd chosen correctly.

"I'm Brynn Parker," she said. "Emma's assistant."

"Seth Andersen," he replied. "Nice to meet you." It occurred to him all at once that she probably knew exactly who he was. The look of recognition on her face said so, anyway. He wondered if Emma had mentioned him, or if the story had come from elsewhere. Hell if he'd be asking. Gossip traveled at the speed of light in this place, a fact he was still getting used to. He guessed he should just feel lucky that he'd managed to fly under the radar for as long as he had.

He started to hand Brynn the box. "If you could just tell her—"

He didn't manage to finish his sentence before four people emerged from the office in the back. Seth immediately recognized Bob Harding, who'd been the mayor of the Cove for years, along with his wife, Mary, and daughter, Penny. Bob, heavyset, balding, and good-natured in a way that struck Seth as more than a little put on, was talking in the only volume the man seemed to have—loud.

"Looking forward to seeing what you can put together. I'd rather use someone local, but this is Penny's day, so the final decision is up to her. I'm trying to pretend money is no object, but ..."

He looked a little pained as he trailed off—an expression Seth didn't think he'd seen on the man before. Mary and Penny were taking in the displays with critical eyes, their heads together as they murmured softly to each other. Mary was a thin, brittle-looking blonde, one of those people always wearing an expression like they'd just smelled something bad. Seth hadn't yet determined whether that was snobbery or just unfortunate genetics. Penny, her streaky brown and blond hair in a sleek bob, was a little younger than he was. A manager down at the bank, she was on the pretty side of average and seemed friendly enough whenever he'd encountered her, though short conversations about his checking account weren't a great way to get to know someone.

Emma emerged last, and seeing her again, here in her element, knocked the wind out of him. She clipped out in a sexy pair of heels, a fitted white skirt with black polka dots and a skinny black belt, and an aqua shirt that hugged her considerable curves. All that gorgeous dark hair, which he'd last seen looking like it had barely survived contact with an electric current, was caught up in a loose bun.

She looked just as sweet as the treat he'd brought her, with the same tantalizing hint of being more decadent than she appeared.

"I think we can offer a much better price for the same level of quality you'll find in a larger city, Mr. Harding. I've planned some beautiful weddings here, and I think when you ..."

The instant she spotted him, her voice died. It sounded smoother now, Seth noted. Not hoarse anymore. Her eyes were huge when they looked at him, the bright blue of the open sky. Her silence—not to mention her stare—drew everyone's attention right to him. As Seth waited patiently for Emma to remember what she was doing, he gave a small smile and a nod to the mayor.

"I—I'm . . . sorry," she said with a soft, embarrassed laugh, eyes darting between Seth and her prospective clients. "I just wanted to say that I think you'll all be very happy with what I put together."

"Well, we'll find out next Tuesday," Penny said. Her smile didn't quite reach her eyes, though they warmed considerably when she saw him. "Hi, Seth! What are you here for? Planning a party or looking for ones to crash? I hear you were busy with that this past weekend."

Emma didn't flinch, but her mouth tightened just a little. It had been a cheap shot. Penny Harding might be perfectly pleasant to him, but she didn't seem to care for Emma much. This visit, Seth guessed, had been her father's idea. The Hardings had money, old money, and lived out on the coast road called the Crescent where most of the original families had big historic houses. Still, Bob Harding was no multimillionaire, and, like a typical father of the bride, he was probably starting to panic about how much he was going to spend. Plus, as mayor of the town, bringing in a bunch of outside professionals for his only daughter's wedding wouldn't look very good. Local made sense, if there was someone in the Cove who could deliver quality.

He bet Emma could, but she was going to have to work at least twice as hard to convince the Harding women that she was up to it. That much was obvious. The dynamics were interesting, even if he didn't want to get sucked into them.

"It was a pretty quiet weekend, actually," Seth finally said. "No party crashing. Just had to help with a little party downsizing. It wasn't a big deal."

"Oh." Penny looked disappointed in the answer, or maybe just his lack of reaction to the question. Maybe she was mad because she hadn't been invited. Somehow, he doubted she'd been in attendance. If she wasn't in Emma's circle of friends—if such a thing even existed—Penny wouldn't be in Samantha Henry's, either. He was still sorting out the community he now lived in. It mattered to the job, even if he didn't get out much on a personal level. Getting everyone straight took time, though—people's connections were as intricate and complicated as a spider's web.

"Well," Penny said after a moment, "typical weekend in the Cove, then. I guess you probably didn't move here for the fun and excitement."

That made him smile. "Nope."

"That's right. You're Steve and Ginny Andersen's nephew," Bob interjected. "You're settling in well, I take it?"

"Very," Seth replied. "Thank you. This place is just what I was looking for."

"Well, that's what I like to hear!"

"So what *are* you in here for?" Penny pressed. She did it with a smile, prying but still polite. "Police department throwing a party of its own?"

He was suddenly very conscious of the box in his hand, and of the eager audience waiting to see whether he and Emma were actually involved, or semi-involved, or incriminatingly awkward. He wasn't a big fan of audiences. Especially when there was a decent chance he was about to get shot down in a big way. He did his best to sound casual.

"I've never been in here before. I was driving by and decided this was the day to come in and check it out."

"You're welcome to look around," Emma said, her smile forced and overly bright. She looked a little like she might bite him if he wasn't careful. "I'm just going to see the Hardings out."

He gamely pretended to be interested in a large photo album while she ushered the Hardings to the door. Flipping the pages, Seth was impressed with Emma's willingness to take on both the stylish and the slightly weird. He knew he wouldn't want to be responsible for pulling together a *Star Wars* wedding.

The best man had dressed as Chewbacca. That was friendship, right there.

While the Hardings said their good-byes in the background, Seth perused photos of weddings, a few corporate functions, family parties—things from small and intimate to grand. The range and quality of the work were interesting enough that he jumped a little when a voice sounded beside him.

"Can I help you with something, Officer?"

"Uh." A quick glance around told him that Brynn had vanished into the back offices somewhere. He was relieved to get the one-on-one meeting he'd wanted. Emma, however, seemed the opposite of relaxed. She was holding herself so stiffly, he wouldn't have been surprised to see her start vibrating.

"It's Seth," he reminded her, though he knew she hadn't forgotten. She wanted distance, and formality was one way to give him a push. He guessed she'd be disappointed when she figured out he wasn't that easy to move.

Remembering the box in his hand and the purpose it was meant to serve, Seth lifted it and held it toward her.

"Here. I was in the neighborhood, so I brought you something."

"Oh." Emma didn't just look surprised—she looked shocked. "I, ah . . . um . . . thank you." She lifted one hand, then jerked it away as though the box might burn her. Flustered, she tucked a stray lock of hair behind one ear, and with a series of short, jerky motions, accepted the gift. Seth worried a little that she might drop it, but she pulled it together once both hands clutched the box. At that point she simply stared down at it as though it were a foreign object.

Seth grinned. He couldn't help it. This, not the cool, competent businesswoman, was the woman he'd come to see. He was quickly discovering that Emma was completely, awkwardly charming when he knocked her off balance. That was something he seemed to be good at, so why not? Hadn't he moved to Harvest Cove to remember how to enjoy the simple things? This was pretty simple, and he was enjoying the hell out of it.

"You can open it," he prodded gently. "The box isn't the present."

"Right. Of course," Emma said, her cheeks turning deep pink. She breathed out a nervous laugh as she flipped the lid open, immediately rewarding Seth with a smile that was pure delight. In that instant, he was as genuinely happy as he'd been in ages. It was a feeling, both surprising and wonderfully simple, that he didn't have time to wonder over. She looked up to meet his gaze, eyes crinkled with amusement.

"Cupcakes?"

He lifted one shoulder in a shrug, a little flustered himself—not that he'd admit it. "Yeah, well, I wasn't sure what you liked, so I picked two. I'm not much of a judge. I'll eat anything."

Emma nodded as she examined the offerings. "Well, that's not a bad way to be. You've got good taste, too, because believe it or not, one of these is my favorite." She picked up the one sitting in a green paper cup, covered in shaved coconut and topped with a tiny slice of sugared key lime. "Key lime coconut. Yum." She was looking at it with too much anticipation to be faking it—and so far, she hadn't struck him as much of a liar. This was well worth the long minutes he'd spent agonizing over cupcake choices.

"What about the other one?" Seth asked, moving closer. "The one with the raspberries? I thought it looked good."

"It is. Larkin makes the best black-bottom cupcakes. They're little cheesecake-and-chocolate fat bombs." Her eyes flicked up to regard him curiously. "What made you pick these two?"

"Honestly? I didn't know things had gotten so much more complicated than chocolate or vanilla until I walked in that place. I just went with the prettiest ones."

"That's a risky selection method."

"Seems to be working fine for me."

"Oh." Her blush, Seth noted, was as pretty as she was.

They stood only inches apart, and he had to incline his head to talk to her. She was the perfect height, just tall enough to tuck her head beneath his chin if he slid his arms around her. The strength of the compulsion to do just that had him flexing his fingers nervously. He thought she was beautiful, and she was certainly fun to poke at, but he wasn't looking for anything beyond just that—light and fun. It shouldn't be a problem, considering he was fairly certain it would take Emma months, if not years, to get to where she'd even be interested in one of his arms around her, much less two.

Still, the attraction was strong enough to be distracting. She smelled good, too, like she had the other night beneath her "eau de spilled beer." He knew he'd carry her scent with him when he left, along with the image of her the way she was right now, surprised and pleased about something as simple as a cupcake.

"What are you doing tonight?" The question slipped out before he could stop it, and he knew right away it had been the wrong thing to ask. Her smile vanished, replaced by the cool wariness that seemed to be her default. How the hell had she gotten so good at it? he wondered.

"I'm busy."

Deeply ingrained stubbornness wouldn't let him drop it there. "Is this the kind of busy where you're actually doing something, or the kind of busy that lasts until I take the hint that you're always going to be busy when I ask you out?"

"Look, Seth," she said, closing the lid of the box and stepping back—safely out of touching distance, should he be so inclined. "I really appreciate what you did for me the other night, and you seem like a nice guy. I just have too much on my plate to be getting involved with anyone right now."

The rejection stung, even if it was expected. It was his own damn fault for asking in the first place, he thought irritably. His good mood wilted like a flower left too long in the sun.

"That makes two of us," he replied, and it was true. . . . Hadn't he decided a long hiatus from outside complications was in order while he built a life here? So there was no reason for him to feel this defensive. Not that knowing it seemed to help any. "I just thought you might want to grab dinner or something. I don't know that many people here yet. People are friendly, but I'm not local. It's taking some time."

It wasn't a play for pity, just the truth. He might not be interested in a whirlwind social life, but he missed having a few go-to people when he wanted company. There were a handful of candidates he thought might turn out to be good friends, but he didn't tend to dive into things all at once. That was a great way to end up with people in your life who made you want to hide when the doorbell rang.

"I'm sorry," Emma said, and the regret in her voice was clear. "It's not you, really—"

"Don't be sorry," he replied, cutting her off smoothly. "It was just an idea." She was having none of the interruption, though.

"You didn't let me finish," she said, an edge creeping into her voice. "It's not you. It's the situation. Even if I wasn't busy, if I went out with you, all it would do is keep people talking. You're not from here, so I wouldn't expect you to understand, but rumors about people in my family tend to snowball."

His eyebrows rose. "Snowball into what?"

"Small missteps become legendary screwups. For instance, the Henrys were one of the founding families of Harvest Cove. Guess which family has stories told about one of its female ancestors being a witch?"

Emma's obvious annoyance about that surprised him.

"That's just local color, though," Seth said. "People never take that kind of thing seriously. Normal people, anyway."

She looked at him intently, not even cracking a smile. *So serious.* He wondered why. He wondered a lot of things about her, for all the good it was doing him.

"How about this, then? One of the eighteenth-century Henrys married a Native American woman," Emma said. "They were apparently happy and had a bunch of kids, but that Henry—George, I think; there were a lot of Georges—was, in his day, blamed for everything from crop failures to bad weather to the occasional hangnail. He'd married a heathen, didn't make her convert, and so invited a good, old-fashioned smiting of the town from the powers that be."

"Okay," Seth said. "That's time-specific superstitious weirdness, but I see your point."

"Oh no," Emma said. "You really don't. There were Henrys who were famously unlucky, or famously stupid. Henrys who supposedly had a Forrest Gump–like influence on major events. If a thing went bad, a Henry had to have caused it. We're known for marrying badly, making money we don't deserve, and a general lack of dependability. We're like the human cooties of Harvest Cove."

That made him laugh, though he tried to stifle what he could because she looked so grim. "It can't be that bad. I haven't heard anything like that."

She arched an eyebrow. "You haven't heard that my mom is a tie-dyed hippie running a massive drug-dealing operation out of the house?"

"Um, well . . ." Okay, so he had heard that, and thought it was insane.

"Well, there you go. And my sister . . ." She trailed off, frowned, and then shook her head. "She had a rough time in school. Especially after Dad died. People can be really awful."

"Yeah, I know how people can be." He wondered what had gone on with her sister, but the look on her face said he shouldn't ask. As far as he knew, Sam Henry was a talented, respected local artist who was about to marry one of the town veterinarians. But the old stories and rumors were insider information. He was still just a curious outsider camping among the locals.

"What about you?" he asked, curious.

"What about me?" she asked. "I'm the boring one. I already told you that."

"No, I mean, why do you stay if it's so much harder for you here?"

She seemed surprised at the question. "It's home," she said simply.

"But if you don't like it . . ."

"I didn't say I didn't like it," Emma said, a faint smile curving her lips. "I just know how things work in the Cove. There's plenty of good to go with the bad, like anywhere else. How can I change the bad things if I leave?"

He had to appreciate her hardheadedness, even though it meant he'd be dining alone. Again. He'd been joking when he'd called her a force of nature the other night, but the steely glint in her eyes made him wonder if he'd really been that far off the truth. Still, with everything she'd said, and some of what she hadn't, Seth wondered if the town's perceptions were the only thing she was fighting.

She had a father who'd passed away, a mother who was thought of as eccentric, and a sister who'd been absent, from what he understood, up until last year. And yet here was Emma, rock solid and working her ass off to create something that would last. A lot of people would have run. She'd sunk her roots in deeper.

Hell if it didn't make her that much more fascinating. Not that off-the-charts stubbornness portended a healthy match, but she was so *different* from the women he was usually interested in. It occurred to him that this news would thrill his mother, a thought he shut down immediately.

Overpriced cupcakes and a dinner-date rejection weren't anything to call home about.

"So," Seth said, "the upshot of all this is that I'm probably going to hear a story about you, a tiger, and Mike Tyson at some point in the next few days."

Her eyes crinkled a little at the corners. "Probably."

"Real life should be so interesting."

She shook her head. "No, I'm really just as happy it's not."

He wondered if it was that awful to her, that people might think they'd spent the night together, and decided the answer probably wouldn't do much for his ego. He also decided that it was time to cut his losses and head out, living to fight another day.

"Tell you what. If I start hearing any tiger stories, I'll make sure to set the record straight."

That finally earned him a laugh, soft but genuine. "Thanks."

"Enjoy the cupcakes. And good luck with the wedding thing. I'll see you around," he said.

"Seth?"

He turned back to look at her just before he hit the door, already making silent promises to himself to just let this one go, to find some other way to occupy his free time. But the woman he saw, standing all by herself in her shop and looking a little like she'd lost her last friend, turned all his good intentions to dust. He couldn't shake the feeling that he was seeing the real Emma right now, not the image she'd so carefully cultivated and put on every day. If that was true, the real Emma was about as alone as he was.

It was just a single shared thing, one connection, but right that second, it felt like everything.

"Yeah?"

"Thank you. Again." She held up the cupcake box. "For these, and everything else."

He smiled, even as he wondered what he could possibly do to clear his head of her, and decided he might need a longer ride than usual. Like maybe to Alaska. Out loud, though, all he could do was tell her the truth: He was at her service.

"Anytime."

Chapter Five

"No, I . . . No, I didn't actually go streaking through the square. Where did you hear that? No, there wasn't a flash mob, either. Yes, I'm sure. It's . . . Wait, how is that disappointing?"

Emma pressed her fingers to her temple and rubbed gently while she held the phone to her ear with the other hand. Her mother seemed to think the tales of her daughter's exploits were hilarious, which figured. Andromeda Henry was a warm, giving human being, but she had a twisted sense of humor. Especially, Emma thought, when it came to yanking her elder daughter's chain. That was at least part of the reason why the beautiful old house Emma had grown up in was always sporting obnoxious colors on the shutters and mailbox. Last year they'd been purple for a while. Currently they were bright green, which was about the color Emma had turned when she'd seen them.

Sam thought it was funny. Of course, Sam would. And Andi's well-to-do neighbors on the Crescent liked it about as well as they usually did, which was to say, not at all.

Emma walked up Hawthorne Street, heading away from the square and the little harbor just beyond, with its rocky cove and strip of pebbled sand. The air was salty today, a strong breeze carrying the taste and scent of the sea. Emma breathed deeply, trying to focus on anything but the ridiculous story her mother was so amused by.

It wasn't Mike Tyson and a tiger, but that was sort of a low bar to clear.

"Oh, honey, I can hear you brooding," Andi was saying. "Come on. It's too ridiculous not to laugh at. I'm just glad you had fun at your sister's party. You ought to have fun more often."

"People keep saying that," Emma grumbled. "It's not like I'm a hermit."

"Not a hermit," her mother agreed. "More like one of those warrior monks who spends all his time training or meditating and never really interacts with people unless he has to kill them. For the greater good, of course."

"Mom," Emma groaned. "That's a horrible analogy! What have you been reading?"

"Things. And why is it horrible? Take away the shaved head and the body count, and I think it's pretty close."

Emma pressed her lips together as she walked past black wrought-iron fences and lampposts, past trees covered in leaves that were still the young green shade of spring. It was cool enough to warrant a light jacket, so she'd thrown on a plain gray hoodie, a piece of her wardrobe that she almost never took outside. Everything else had seemed too dressy for a simple walk — and she didn't usually take walks, so her active-wear collection was the pits. She also wore the only comfortable jeans she had, which were ancient and dotted with paint, and the sneakers she'd bought one of the times she'd pretended she was going to work out regularly.

She felt vaguely uncomfortable with the idea of being

out in public like this, but the urge to get outside and escape her thoughts had been overwhelming. Now she just tried to move quickly enough that no one would be able to identify her.

Naturally, her phone had started vibrating just as she'd locked the apartment door.

"Mom, we've talked about this," Emma finally said. "I'm fine. My life is fine. I'm not going to end up sharing dinners with Boof and crocheting doilies in my spare time."

"I know you're fine, Emma. I'd like you to be better than fine, but that might require some upheaval and you never did like much of that. I just wish you didn't take everything so seriously. I was hoping to hear you laugh about all this."

"I would if it were funny."

"The idea of you and Big Al streaking through the square isn't funny?"

"That's not one of the many words that come to mind, no." She was nearing the gallery where Sam worked and sold her pieces, a once-dilapidated little historic home that now shone like the gem it had been underneath the weathered siding and grime. The wooden sign that hung outside had TWO ROADS GALLERY etched into the wood and painted gold. A mud-spattered SUV was parked out front, a sight that piqued Emma's interest despite herself. She knew what the truck meant, and she had a sudden itch to see one of the epic battles Sam had described to her.

The only sticking point was her outfit, but she didn't think there would be many people milling around right before Zoe closed up for the day. Curiosity getting the better of her, Emma slowed.

"Mom, I'm going to stop into the gallery, okay? I'll give you a ring later."

"Are you actually outside? In the sun?" Andi asked.

"Yes. I haven't even burst into flames yet."

"Good. You know your sister isn't working today. I think she and Jake were going out on his friend's boat. The nice friend. Not the redhead."

That did make her chuckle. "Fitz, then. She said something about that. The not-nice redhead is probably with them, you know. Shane gets pouty when he's left out."

"Shane might make it to nice someday. But he's probably going to need a good ass-kicking to achieve it."

Emma snorted. Shane Sullivan was built like an NFL quarterback and was not likely to have his butt kicked by anyone. That was at least part of his problem. To his credit, he did openly admit to being a jerk, though he also seemed to think that exempted him from doing anything about it. Still, Emma figured he must have a few decent qualities, since when Jake had dumped most of his tight-knit circle of friends last year over their refusal to accept Sam, Shane had behaved enough like a true friend for Jake to keep him.

It was hard for Emma to picture, but Sam assured her that Shane wasn't always bad. Usually, but not always.

"I figured I'd stop in and see Zoe."

"Oh." Andi didn't bother hiding her surprise. "Getting out, taking a walk, visiting people . . . This is actually so unlike you, it's scary. Are you okay?"

Emma rolled her eyes. "I'm f—"

"Fine, I know," Andi finished. "I know. Okay, I'll let you go. You're still coming for dinner tomorrow night, right?"

"I told you I'll try, Mom. The wedding I'm handling that day has an early reception, so it's definitely possible, but I may be a little late. I'll call."

"Well, bring Boof so he can play with Peaches and

Loki," she added, referring to her own cat along with Sam's mischievous little black one.

"Yes, Mom." She stopped at the head of the walk that led to the gallery door.

"I can hear you rolling your eyes. Keep it up and I'll invite the Andersens' nephew."

It took Emma a few seconds to make the connection, but when she did, her mouth dropped open. "Don't you dare! How did you even . . . Just don't!"

"I'm your mother. I know everything. Have a nice afternoon, honey!" Andi did her best villainess laugh and hung up, leaving Emma to look disgustedly at her phone before stuffing it in her back pocket. *Great.* She knew her mother wouldn't actually invite Seth, but that wasn't the end of the teasing by a long shot. Andi was friendly with Ginny Andersen, because of course she was. And he'd obviously been woven into the lore developing around her. It was beyond thrilling.

She stalked up the walk to the gallery and opened the door. The sound of Zoe's raised voice greeted her, along with the sight of an uncharacteristic amount of dirt on the wood floors.

"Jason, I realize you think you're allowed to do what you like in here because you *occasionally* buy something, but I swear to God, if you think you're going to continue coming in here once or twice a week just to spend ten minutes dumping the great outdoors on my clean floor, we are going to have a problem."

Zoe Watson, hands on her hips, stood in the middle of the gallery's large front room, staring down a six-foot-ten man as though she were an angry giantess instead of a diminutive five foot two. Emma stopped short, not wanting to interrupt—in fact, a little afraid to interrupt. Sam might have told her about the ongoing war between Zoe and Jason Evans, Jake's grumpy park ranger cousin, but she hadn't properly conveyed the amount of tension the two of them gave off. The air was thick with it.

Jason scrubbed one hand lazily through his brown hair that was just long enough to show its loose curl. It would have added to his scruffy charm, if he'd been at all charming. "We don't have a problem. You have a problem," he said. "I'm just minding my own business. It's not my fault you're wound so tight that a little dirt makes your head explode."

Zoe's eyes flashed, the steely gray almost glowing. Emma wondered whether she really wanted to be a witness to whatever came next and took a step backward. Zoe's hand immediately shot out, palm up, in her direction.

"No, don't you go anywhere. I'll be with you in just a second." Her eyes never left Jason, but her tone was so commanding that even Emma knew better than to try to leave. Instead, she watched uneasily as Zoe took two steps toward the man glowering down at her. The contrast between the two couldn't have been starker. Jason was in ancient jeans and a battered jacket, neither of which disguised the fact that the man was built well, and the scruff that covered his jaw did little to soften the handsome angles of his face. He looked like a surly woodsman . . . which he basically was. Zoe, meanwhile, could have stepped out of a magazine. She wore riding boots and leggings, a long shirt covered by a light cardigan, and a loose scarf draped around her neck. Her hair, with caramel highlights woven into the tight curls that fell past her shoulders, was pulled partially back to expose a heart-shaped face that was strikingly lovely even though it was wearing an expression almost as surly as Jason's. Her chin was up—never a good sign.

"I'm putting my foot down. You bring a field in here on your boots again, you get to sweep it up."

He snorted. "And my incentive to do that would be ..."

"The ability to continue purchasing things in this establishment."

Jason looked unimpressed. "You'd rather have a clean floor than my money, huh?"

"It's not just your money. It's your charming company I'd be without. And yes, I prefer my clean floor. Believe it or not, I like to have a life beyond vacuuming."

They stared at each other for long seconds, and Emma had to give Zoe credit. Jason was intimidating—on purpose, no doubt—but she didn't even blink. Finally, Jason's voice rumbled into the tense silence.

"You don't even have a decent mat to scrape my boots off on."

Zoe's eyebrow arched, but her voice stayed cool. "All right. I'll tell you what. Just for you, I will personally put out a better mat. And if you don't use it, that mat is going where the sun don't shine."

Jason stared a few moments longer, then gave a soft grunt. Emma could swear she saw his lips twitch, though he didn't smile. "Deal," he finally said.

"Shake on it," said Zoe, her tone indicating this wasn't optional. She put out her slim, well-manicured hand. Jason's hand swallowed hers up, gave it a quick shake ... and then lingered before he pulled away. The tension in the air, Emma thought as she watched them wonderingly, had just shifted to something a lot more interesting. She didn't have time to gawk long, though, because Jason clomped past her.

"How's it going, Henry?"

He didn't seem to require an answer, since he kept on walking right out the door. Emma turned her head to watch him go, then returned her attention to Zoe, whose mocha cheeks were stained a deep pink. She stared at the door Jason had just stomped through, then shook her head as if to clear it and blew out a breath.

"Sorry about that," she said. "I swear these arguments have gotten to be like a weekly appointment. He probably has me penciled in on his calendar."

"He just might," Emma replied. She hesitated, then said, "Have you ever thought that maybe—"

"No," Zoe said, tipping her chin down to glare at her. "I get enough of that from your sister. Don't make me boot your butt out of here, too." Then her lips curved into a smile, banishing any impression of toughness. "So what brings you in, party girl? Sam said you've been in hiding."

"Not hiding," Emma said, joining Zoe when she moved to sit in one of a pair of carved wooden chairs, the handiwork of one of the local artists she worked with. "I'm just keeping myself busy."

"Busy doing things other than appearing in public."

"Exactly." Emma smiled. "So far so good."

"I wondered if you were undercover in your hoodie." Zoe crossed one leg over the other, tipped her head back, and sighed. "It has been a *long* day. And as usual, I'm going to go home and find out Idris Elba hasn't shown up yet."

"Maybe he lost your address," Emma said, slumping back in the chair. "I feel your pain. I'm looking at takeout, more work on my proposal for the Hardings, and my cat."

"The babe-a-licious Boof." Zoe chuckled. "I'm not big on cats, but he's different. He's like a big furry throw pillow."

"He moves. Sometimes."

"Pictures or it didn't happen." Zoe looked at her, curiosity evident in her storm-colored eyes. "So what brings you in? You don't usually pop in for visits. Not that I'm complaining."

"I just needed to get out," Emma said. "I'm a little sick of my own company. Brynn offered to close up, so I guess I was making her as crazy as I was making myself." She screwed up her lips and studied her newish sneakers, and made the sort of admission she wouldn't normally make. But this was Zoe, and it had been a long week. "I can be kind of a pain in the ass."

Zoe snorted. "That makes two of us. I understand the affliction. I like things done a certain way. So do you. It makes me like you, even though we should probably never live together."

"There would be blood over furniture arrangements," Emma agreed. When Zoe continued to look expectantly at her, she relented. "I don't know. I had a phone call."

"From . . . ?"

"A guy I gave my number to last Saturday, apparently."

Zoe's brows drew together. "You mean like a threatening phone call?"

"Oh no, nothing like that! Just a quick 'Hi, how you doing' followed by an invitation to the movies this weekend."

Zoe's relief was written all over her face. "That's good, at least. Are you going to—"

"No! God no." Emma felt a chill race over her skin just thinking about the potential disasters that might invite. "I barely remember what he looked like. Not to mention, I wasn't exactly myself at the time. I feel like he's asking out an entirely different person. Not, you know . . ." She swept a hand down her ravishing outfit. "Me."

"I was there. Pretty sure you were you. There was a lot going on, but no pod people. I'd remember that."

"You know what I mean. I was—"

"Enjoying yourself?"

"Drunk," Emma replied, her voice flat. She felt her phone buzz again, so with Zoe looking on, she pulled it from her pocket to look at the message. For the second time today, it wasn't one of the three people who normally showed up on her phone. "You've got to be kidding me."

"I hope you're going to share that," Zoe said. "I need something in my day that isn't annoying."

" 'Hey, Em,' " she recited, then groaned. "Em? Really? Not when I don't know you, I'm not." Emma tipped her head back, took a deep breath, then looked down at her phone again and continued. " 'Had fun with you last Saturday. Dinner this weekend? Let me know! Chris.' "

"Chris who?"

"I have no idea." She combed through fuzzy memories to no avail. She had danced with people. A lot of people. Their faces, however, eluded her. What was her taste like when she was drinking? It might be bad. She might get insanely thick beer goggles. The risk was too much to take, even if she'd been interested in a date this weekend. Which she wasn't.

A dark-haired vision in a blue uniform tried to butt into her thoughts right then to make a liar out of her, but she pushed it back as best she could. He was hard to forget, though, not only because she knew *exactly* how attractive he was, but because he'd checked up on her. And brought her cupcakes. *Cupcakes!* What kind of a guy did that sort of thing?

She shifted uneasily in her seat while Zoe considered her.

"I have to ask. . . . Why is this bothering you so much? You don't want to go, you say no."

"I'm bothered because I don't even know these people, much less like them."

"You must have liked them fine last weekend. Though I will admit, you loved the world last weekend. It was cute," Zoe said. "You're usually very self-contained. I just think you surprised a lot of people." She indicated the phone. "Like your new suitors there."

"It was ridiculous," Emma said. "I was a joke."

Zoe's brows winged up. "Who told you that? You weren't any different from anybody else. You laughed, had fun, cut loose, celebrated your sister. I mean, I'm no wild thing usually, but you did notice I was wearing a feather boa for most of the night, right?"

"And yet no one is telling stories about you streaking with the village idiot."

Zoe tapped her fingers on the arm of her chair. "Anybody who actually believes that isn't worth the breath it would take to correct them. You know this."

"I just . . . This isn't the kind of attention I want."

"Consider it free publicity. Party planner knows how to party," Zoe replied. "Anyway, give it a week or two and it won't matter."

"Yeah, no," Emma said. "A week or two isn't soon enough. I'm trying to impress Penny Harding with my business acumen, and all she wanted to do was embarrass me in front of her parents and Seth."

"Seth. The officer you didn't share a night of passion with?" Zoe leaned forward, her eyes bright with renewed interest. "Okay, *this* I need to hear. Why was he visiting you?"

"Nothing. It's nothing," Emma rushed on, wishing she hadn't even said his name. "The point is that it's just given the Hardings one more reason to hire someone else for Penny's wedding."

"Penny Harding, aka Petunia Fussybottom," Zoe said, rolling her eyes. "She's one of the biggest pains in the butt in the Cove, Emma. I would take her not wanting you as a compliment. You should have smacked her upside the head when she started in. Then you'd at least have some satisfaction, since you're right—there's no way she'd pick you. You're not on her Christmas party list."

Emma gave a small, rueful smile. The Hardings' annual Christmas party was always a big event, as was making the guest list. Her mother talked about how boring the parties had been back when she'd gone with her husband, but Emma still wondered what it might be like. She'd never find out, though. Her mother had been off the guest list as soon as her father had died, and any of the current crop of Henrys making it back on was unlikely at best.

"She wouldn't pick me on her own," Emma said, "but her father is getting twitchy about the cost. He knows I'll do it for less than what he'll find elsewhere. If I put together something amazing, he's going to push hard to keep everything local. Plus, he's the mayor, so it looks bad for him to be outsourcing."

"He's probably more twitchy about the possibility of it not happening at all. How long was this whirlwind courtship? Two months? I'm not saying I don't believe in insta-love, but . . . I don't believe in it. And who falls madly in love with *Penny*?"

"Don't know, don't care. I *need* this wedding, Zoe. I don't usually get to work with big budgets, and considering the guest list? There is no better advertising. Penny doesn't have to love me, but she can damn well have her socks knocked off by my work. I just need the chance."

Zoe stared silently for a moment. Then she said, "Sam's right. You get a little scary about your work."

"She says that about you, too, you know."

"And she's correct, though I'd be fine with some attractive gentlemen blowing up my phone once in a while. You'll land the wedding if you want it this bad, because I understand how you operate. We take no prisoners." Her lips curved in a smile that was more than a little self-deprecating. "It's that pain-in-the-ass thing we both have going on. But take it from somebody who had to learn to build in downtime for her own sanity—I think you need to try to relax a little. Maybe have some fun with your newfound notoriety." She shrugged. "A social life isn't the end of the world."

Emma snorted. "Says the woman whose work *is* her social life. The First Friday events you put on here don't count."

"Ah-ah," Zoe corrected her, holding up a finger. "I'm with people during them. They count. But I get out when I feel like it, now that I actually have a few friends around here. I'm cautious, not antisocial. I love my slippers and flannel pants best, but there are moments I need more. And anyway, I think I was allowed a settling-in period to figure out what works for me. You've been settled in here since birth. What's your excuse?"

"That I *am* antisocial," Emma shot back, which made Zoe laugh. Emma tried for a smile in return, but couldn't quite manage it. "I don't know. I try so hard to do everything just right, to be the one person in my family people can't laugh at, and a few drinks and a YouTube video later, people are looking at me funny."

"Not funny," Zoe corrected her. "Just differently."

"I don't like different," Emma grumbled, knowing she sounded sulky. She couldn't help it. It had been preying on her all week, this idea that she'd taken a sledgehammer to the Emma Henry she'd so carefully built to display to the rest of the world.

"Well," Zoe said, standing and stretching, "like it or not, the cat's out of the bag. You are not, in fact, a robot. And you have a great smile, which is probably one of the many reasons the phone has been ringing."

"I think my wet shirt the other night had more to do with it, but you never know, I guess." Emma stood, too, knowing that it was time for Zoe to close up. She didn't want to be underfoot any longer. "Thanks for listening to me," she said. "I would have dumped this on Sam, but she's busy with Jake today."

"Hey, you're wearing a hoodie. I knew it was serious."

As Emma grinned, surprised to find that her load had lightened a little just from talking it out, her phone buzzed again. The smile faltered, even as Zoe's widened. "I am apparently a very social drunk."

"There are worse things. You could have gotten in a bar fight."

"Granted." Emma's hand started to move to grab her phone, but she stopped it. She'd wait until she was outside. "See you, Zoe. Have fun picking up the debris field."

The sound that rippled up from Zoe's chest sounded disconcertingly like a growl. "First order of business once I lock up is to drive out to Home Value and get one very nice boot-scuffing mat. Then it's his move."

"Should be interesting."

"That's one word for it, sure."

Emma might have laughed, were it not for the glint in Zoe's eyes being a little murderous. Instead, she found herself trying to mask her growing anxiety when her phone vibrated again. And again. It was bizarre. After all these years, she was sought-after company by someone other than her mom. And though that would have made a huge difference to her once, right now, this was the last thing she needed. This was quiet, committed, nose-to-the-grindstone time. She'd explored her inner wild thing quite enough for one decade, thanks. Besides, she'd decided a long time ago that love and marriage weren't going to be for her. Why bother leading someone on? Why even take the risk of getting started? The only acceptable risks, in her mind, were business related. And she only undertook those very carefully.

Maybe it wasn't a thrilling life, but it was a comfortable one. A safe one. There had to be a way to return things to some semblance of normal. Like, now. She just couldn't quite figure out what that might be.

"You're welcome to come over later if you want," Zoe said. "I'm just going to make a pot of tea and watch movies. It's been a long week."

Part of her wanted to. Emma had approached Zoe with the same caution she applied to everyone else, softened only a little by her sister's affection for her new friend. But unlike most people, Zoe had waited out her standoffishness. Emma prided herself on a minimal need for socializing, but when she felt the urge, it was nice to know she had options.

Tonight, though, she was pretty sure her best option was flying solo. She had a lot to sort through, on top of the work she had.

"Thanks, but I don't think I should inflict myself on anyone else tonight. I have things to do anyway."

"Things like drink a pot of coffee and obsess about what other people are saying?" Zoe asked.

"Maybe."

"Well, you have fun with that. If you change your mind, I don't plan on leaving my couch, so I'll be home."

"We'll see. If not tonight, then soon." Emma gave a half wave and turned to go, feeling another vibration of her phone. She had a single, fleeting moment of temptation—what would it be like if she took Zoe's advice and tried to just enjoy the attention? But that impulse was gone almost as soon as it appeared. She had to stick with what worked. After all, doing things her way had earned her some measure of success, respect. . . .

And most of all, it had kept her safe. It had saved her the hurt her sister had endured, among other things. She hadn't been able to protect Sam, but she could damn well protect herself.

No matter how lonely it got.

Emma called out a final good-bye before walking back out into an early evening that was clouding up just like her thoughts had. Still, she didn't turn toward home, though the instinct to do just that was strong. For once, she knew there was plenty of time for work later—all the time in the world, it sometimes seemed. Right now was for thinking—and walking—until she got her head on straight and came up with a plan for how to move forward.

She cast a single, worried look at the darkening sky before heading down the sidewalk. At the rate things were going, she knew she could be walking a long, long time.

Chapter Six

By the time the sky opened up, Seth had weeded the front flower beds, planted a couple of young trees, and refilled the bird feeder out back. Some younger version of himself, still rattling around in his psyche, was horrified that he'd spent his day doing what he'd once considered "old people activities."

The rest of him felt tired, sweaty, and too good to care.

His house had been a little rough around the edges when he'd gotten it, but it was really starting to come together. The little Cape Cod had gotten a fresh coat of paint about a month ago, and the yard looked great. It would look even better once all his new plantings took hold and filled out. He knew himself well enough by now to know that he needed some kind of sanctuary to get away from the world occasionally.

The second he'd stepped into his house, he'd known this was it. He rarely had company, apart from the birds. That was fine by him—birds had a healthy respect for personal space.

The rain started all at once, like someone turning a shower on full blast. A single roll of thunder was all he got as a warning, but it was enough to send him into the garage just ahead of the downpour. He was about to close up when he saw a lone figure pounding on Aaron Maclean's door, already as drenched as it was possible for a person to be. Whoever it was, she was out of luck — his neighbor had been gone all day. He glanced quickly over the sodden gray hoodie, the torn jeans, the long and dripping hair. Then she turned her head so that her profile was visible, and he had to do a double take.

Emma. Of course it was. Because the instant he decided something was no damn good for him, it would magically appear at every turn. He had a brief, unpleasant urge to just shut the door and head inside, letting her sort the rain out on her own. It wasn't like going out of his way for her had gotten him anything but grief so far. But a combination of deeply ingrained politeness and the still-strong, if unwanted, attraction had him calling to her.

"Emma! In here!" He waved his arms at her when she looked around, and for once she didn't hesitate where he was concerned. She made a mad dash toward him, arms wrapped around herself as though that would somehow keep the rain off. The sky flickered, and another roll of thunder sounded, loud enough that he could feel the vibration. Emma ran into the cool, dry garage. When she looked at him, her eyes were enormous, her fair skin pale. She was completely soaked.

"Hi," was all she said. Water dripped from the pert little tip of her nose.

"Hi, yourself." He wished he could be a little less interested in kissing a few of those droplets away. He knew damn well the kind of reaction he'd get. The frustration, however, didn't mean he couldn't be friendly. "Did you walk all the way from the square?" She was a good three miles from home, and even if she was an avid walker, he'd never seen her out here before.

"Yeah." She looked sheepish. "I didn't notice how dark the sky was getting until it was too late."

"I can see that." He thought about driving her home immediately, then saw her shiver. She really was soaked through. And that miserable protective instinct, the one he couldn't seem to turn off where she was concerned, kicked in and took over his mouth before he could do much about it. "Come on in and dry off."

He took the fact that she didn't bother to argue as a mark of how miserable she felt. "Okay," she said, and offered him a weak smile. "Thanks." She scurried past him, her feet leaving watery prints on the cement floor, and let herself into the house. He followed, curious. Something was different about her today, and it wasn't just that she looked like she'd been swimming while fully clothed. Maybe it was just that this was the first time she'd actually run toward him instead of backing away.

The thought fascinated him—almost as much as it unnerved him. He knew that part of the reason he'd felt free to fixate on her a little, enough to try out his rusty flirting skills, was that she was safe. As in, he had no chance with her at all, which in turn meant there was no chance of him screwing things up.

Bet she'd love to know how good you are at that. Maybe just tell her why you picked a tiny town this far from home to move to. That'll send her right back out the door soon enough.

He shut down the nagging, taunting voice as quickly as he could, but his uncertainty stayed to hover like the rain clouds outside. Seth flipped the light switch on the wall when he walked into the house, the kitchen brightening instantly. Emma stood in the middle of the small room, dripping on the linoleum. She had been looking around, but focused on him immediately once he shut the door. They considered each other silently for a moment. She looked as though she didn't quite know what she was doing here. That made two of them, but wondering didn't change anything.

"Tell you what," he said. "I've got some sweats you can borrow. We can toss all that in the dryer, I'll make coffee, and when everything's dry, I'll get you home."

"You don't have to—"

"I know that," he interrupted her, hearing the snap of irritation in his voice. But could she just once accept something from him without making a big deal of it? "I'll get the sweats. Stay put."

Seth headed out of the kitchen and upstairs to his bedroom, where a quick look through his drawers netted him an old pair of sweatpants with a drawstring waist—necessary if anything of his was going to stay up on Emma—and a comfortably worn police academy sweatshirt. He grabbed a towel from the linen closet, carried everything back downstairs, shoved it all unceremoniously into Emma's arms, and said, "Bathroom's right by the front door. Bring the wet stuff out and I'll get the laundry going."

She blinked, but she didn't argue with him. Emma silently headed out of the kitchen, though he caught the single, confused glance she threw over her shoulder at him on her way out. He pretended to be busy getting out a pair of coffee mugs, though what he was really doing was attempting to get his head back in some kind of functioning order before she walked back out wearing his clothes, probably looking good enough to—

Yeah, might want to stop right there before your gutter brain gets noticeable, genius.

Seth bit the inside of his cheek and tried to focus. He knew he wasn't the only one who felt the tension between them, strong enough that it sometimes seemed about to start shooting sparks. For whatever reason, she didn't seem to want anything to do with it, and he was in no position to press her about it. But this was his house, she'd busted into his otherwise pleasant day off, and for once, she could at least do what made sense instead of making things more difficult. He didn't think that was too much to ask.

When he heard the bathroom door shut, Seth found his coffee-making interrupted by the insistent thought that Emma was peeling off her wet clothes, piece by piece, in his house. He braced himself against the counter, bowed his head, and sighed heavily.

Keep it casual and friendly. That's all you have to do. You've managed it with everybody else. . . . Why not her?

Right. She might be soaked to the bone, but right now, he knew he was the bigger mess. And there wasn't a thing he could do about it. So he locked away his heated thoughts as best he could, took a deep breath, and put the coffee on.

Funny, the things being cold and wet could make you do. For instance, getting naked in Seth Andersen's bathroom. That was one she hadn't seen coming. Then again, doing things she normally wouldn't seemed to be a trend lately.

Emma stripped off her sodden clothes, wrung the water out of her hair in the sink, toweled off, and found that she was too glad to be warming up and dry to feel all that strange about the situation. No doubt that would come later. For the moment, she concentrated on cinching the waist of Seth's sweatpants so that they would stay up on her, then pulling his soft, blue sweatshirt over her head. He was on the tall side of average, but slim, so while his clothes were too big, she wasn't completely swimming in them. But having his clothes against her bare skin, breathing in the light scent that permeated his house—his clean and very male scent—felt decadent in a way she'd never experienced. For a brief moment, she didn't feel as though she belonged wholly to herself anymore.

Her reaction, a shiver not from cold but a kind of raw desire so swift and fierce it took her utterly by surprise, made her bite hard on the inside of her cheek to try to clear her head.

This is not the time. Not now, not ever. Get it together.

It didn't work all that well, but it was enough to get her moving again. A look in the mirror was satisfactory, if not thrilling. Emma used her fingers to slick her wet hair away from her face, gathered up her wet clothes in the towel, grabbed her phone, and padded out of the bathroom on bare feet.

The warm, comforting smell of coffee brewing soothed her, as did the patter of rain against the windows. Emma looked around as she headed for the glow of the kitchen, taking in a house that seemed comfortable, if a little Spartan. A nice leather sofa and chair sat opposite a good-sized flat-screen TV mounted on the wall. There was also a small fireplace with a framed print propped on the mantel. The subject matter prompted a soft, silent laugh, and she shook her head.

This was definitely a guy's house. Even if he did have actual hand towels and scented soap in his bathroom.

She headed back to the kitchen and stopped short as soon as she entered. Seth's back was to her as he poured the coffee, and she let her eyes skim over him from head to toe. It was, she realized, the first time she'd seen him out of uniform. And the jeans he wore, faded and a little ragged, with wear marks on the pocket where she imagined he'd stuffed a wallet hundreds of times, fit him in just the right way to make her mouth water. Emma watched how the taut muscles of his back and shoulders shifted beneath the thin cotton of his T-shirt as he moved, and she realized, with a sinking feeling, that even the tanned back of his neck was sexy as hell.

What am I doing here? Dating him would be a bad enough idea even if he wasn't a cop!

Unfortunately, he didn't look like a cop right this second. All he looked was good.

He must have heard her approach because he spoke without turning around. "What do you put in your coffee?"

Emma licked her lips, sucked in a shallow breath, and tried to get her pounding heart rate under control. "Um. Cream and sugar. If you have it." Her voice sounded abnormally breathy. She needed to get a handle on . . . whatever this was.

"I think I can scrounge up a carton of milk and some sugar somewhere around here." He did turn then, walking toward her with all the casual grace of a jungle cat. "I'll take those. You might as well get comfortable."

Somehow, she managed not to melt when he took the pile of clothes from her, even when his warm hand brushed against hers.

"Great. Thanks." She managed to walk to the small circular table and sit in a chair, though she felt stiff and awkward and out of sorts all at once. Maybe it was that her face was on fire. Maybe it was the hint of a tattoo she'd seen on Seth's biceps when he'd taken the clothes from her. Or maybe it was just *him*.

Emma folded her hands in her lap, pressed her knees together, and tried desperately not to think about sex.

Seth was gone for only a minute or so, and Emma

heard the dryer start up somewhere else in the house. He was completely silent when he moved, she noted as he walked back into the room. It should have made her nervous, but he was so casual about it that she doubted he even realized how silent he was. *Probably helps him not get killed on the job,* she thought, and immediately felt her stomach start to knot.

His life isn't my responsibility. So can we fixate on something less upsetting while we're wearing his clothes, please?

He brought two cups of coffee to the table in heavy ceramic mugs, one a speckled royal blue, one that was a mix of autumn colors, shades of brown and red and green. She looked at them with interest, glad for the distraction from her own thoughts.

"These look handmade."

"They are," he said, liquid brown eyes meeting hers for a fleeting, electric instant before flicking away again. It helped to think he might find it as disconcerting as she did, though she knew it was just as likely he felt nothing at all. She'd shot him down once already. He'd probably moved on, no big deal. Unlike her, for whom obsessing over what would be "no big deal" to most normal humans was a full-time occupation.

"I was in Vermont a while back. Hand-thrown pottery seems to be kind of a thing there, so I brought back some mugs. They're nice and heavy, and I drink a lot of coffee, so . . ." He trailed off as he brought a spoon, a sugar dish, and a carton of milk to the table, then sat across from her. She noted he didn't put a thing in his own coffee, drinking it black. It made her feel fussy, putting her two teaspoons of sugar and a healthy splash of milk in her own.

She stirred, sipped, and decided it was pretty good

even without her favored vanilla creamer. Emma studied the swirls the milk had made in her coffee, feeling his eyes on her. Funny—it had stopped bothering her a long time ago when people looked at her. Seth, on the other hand, had unnerved her from the moment he'd awakened Sunday morning. The difference, she suspected, was that Seth actually seemed to be *seeing* her. And not at her best, for the most part. Or at least, not the way she wanted to be seen.

Steeling herself, Emma lifted her gaze to find Seth studying her. Their eyes locked again, and this time he didn't look away. She could feel the buzz of their connection like an electric current, surprisingly intense but not at all unpleasant.

Like Zoe, she didn't believe in insta-love, and found insta-lust more something to be suspicious of than to indulge in. But this feeling she got around Seth—this was something new. The kind of thing that happened to women decidedly less boring and considerably more beautiful than she was. She didn't know whether to revel in it or run before something terrible happened.

As a compromise, she did neither and tried to enjoy her coffee. But that was easier said than done.

"So," she said, forcing words into the silence in the hope of breaking this spell, "looks like I owe you for saving me again."

His grin flashed as he breathed out a soft laugh. "Yeah, well, you keep landing in front of me and needing help. I can stop if you want."

Emma looked upward as thunder shook the house again. "No. I'm good."

"Then drink your coffee and quit worrying."

The words startled her. "I don't. I'm not."

He tipped his chin down and raised his eyebrows.

"Emma, you've been wound up about something every time I've seen you. You also look like you're about to Hulk-smash my nice mug."

Her eyes widened when she realized he was right—she had the mug in a death grip, and probably had from the second she'd locked eyes with him. She slowly, deliberately pulled her hands away and flexed her fingers. If her cheeks got any hotter, she was going to just spontaneously combust. At the moment, it didn't seem like a bad option. It would be a respite from this weird, tense *thing* the two of them had. She tried, briefly, to fix it by reminding herself that she'd been comfortable enough with him once to demand he carry her into her apartment.

That didn't make it any better.

"So I'm a little tense sometimes," Emma said, her voice calm and even. "It keeps me on track."

"Uh-huh. You seem like you're hurtling down that track at about a thousand miles an hour most of the time," Seth replied, then took a sip of his coffee while she glared at him. Her irritation lessened a little, though not completely, when she saw the mischief dancing in his eyes. He was yanking her chain.

She sat up a little straighter in her chair. "I'm work oriented."

He looked unimpressed. "I noticed."

Her eyes narrowed. "What, you think it's a bad thing that I'm trying to get ahead?"

Seth put up his hands, palms out defensively. "No, I didn't say that." His half smile was rueful. "You're tough to play with, Emma Henry."

"No, I'm not."

Her denial was reflexive, and she knew she'd sounded sharp, but Seth just laughed.

"Exactly," he said.

He was making it difficult to do what she normally did with strangers, which was to hold them at arm's length until they gave up and left her alone. Maybe it was because, through his own determination, he wasn't exactly a stranger anymore. Not to mention he'd seen her in the least flattering ways possible twice now and still seemed interested.

What did you do with a guy like this? Hell if she knew. Her last steady boyfriend had been shortly after college, long-distance, and, ultimately, a complete failure. Her relationship with Ben had always been easy — which, as it turned out, had been a problem. For him, at least. For her, it had been a harsh lesson in the dangers of wanting things she couldn't be sure of, things that required more than her own hard work. She'd thought Ben was safe.

Talking to Seth was easier than it ought to be, but nothing about him felt safe. It worried her that that seemed to be part of the attraction.

He continued to watch her steadily. *You could just about fall into those big brown eyes,* she thought, then felt her cheeks flush with shame.

"You okay?" he asked.

"That seems to be the question of the day," Emma replied, then took a sip of her coffee to steady herself. "Am I giving off some kind of distress signal I don't know about? Is it because nobody ever sees me in sneakers? What?"

"You just seem . . . different," Seth replied. "Not just the sneakers, or that you walked all the way to my neighborhood with a storm coming in. I mean, both of those, yeah, but you also seem a little out of sorts."

"What are you, Oprah?"

One eyebrow arched. "No. Just somebody who likes you even though you don't seem to want me to."

He had a knack for pushing her off balance every

time she thought she was finding her footing with him. Emma frowned at him, though some secret part of her turned to goo at his words. He liked her? Really?

Why?

"You can't like me," she informed him. "You don't even know me."

He moved his head from side to side. "I bet I know more than you think."

"That's not creepy," she said, and he chuckled, a low, rough sound that flowed though her like hot liquid and pooled deep in her belly. No, there was nothing about Seth the Good Guy Cop that was safe.

"That's one thing I already picked up on. The dry sense of humor."

"And you have a weird one," she replied. "Don't think I didn't see the picture you've got hanging over your fireplace of George Washington riding a T. rex and carrying a lightsaber."

"That was a gift," Seth replied. "I had to put it in a place of honor."

"A gift? From a guy. It had to be from another guy. No woman would buy something like that."

"I've known a few who would," Seth replied. "But you're right. It was from a buddy of mine. Housewarming gift from when I had a place back in Jacksonville."

"Did he get you something for this place, too? Maybe a Monet but with velociraptors?"

His expression changed to one she couldn't read, and he fiddled with his cup. "No. He, ah, didn't come back from his last tour in Afghanistan."

Emma didn't think it was possible for her to feel any worse than she did in that moment. "Oh God. I'm sorry."

"It's fine," Seth said, though she couldn't tell from his half shrug whether it really was. "He was a great guy with a twisted sense of humor. And you're right. He probably would have bought me something involving raptors if he were still around."

This was the first time she'd seen Seth look uncomfortable, and the first time she'd found herself wondering about his past. With anyone else she would have let it go. But since he'd been pushing at her from the start, she suspected he could handle a single, simple question. Besides, against her will, she was curious.

"Were you in the army, then?"

"Yeah, I was. Six years. It was enough." His tone indicated that he had no interest in saying more about it, and Emma was protective enough of her own boundaries that she could respect that in someone else. Still, it left her wanting to know more. Seth had been in the army, and then in a big city. . . . Why come here, apart from the family connection?

"Where are you from, anyway?" she asked, and for some reason that brought back the grin she found boyish and impossibly sexy. *It's not wrong to admire it if I don't touch him. It's not,* she told herself. It felt like complete bull, but it was all she had at the moment.

"Wow," he said. "Was that an actual question about me? I think I might have heard it wrong."

"Funny," Emma said, but she couldn't stop the pleasure she got from having provoked that smile. "Don't answer me, then. Or make something up. I won't know any different."

"Too late. You're curious. I can tell. So here's the short answer: I'm from St. Augustine by way of Brooklyn. Moved right before middle school because my parents wanted out of the city."

"That's a big jump," Emma said. "And I thought I heard a little New York in your accent."

He shrugged. "I tried to shake it for a while when I was a kid, since I caught so much shit for it at school after we moved. Then I grew, got a little tougher, and quit caring. What I lost of it has just been time and distance, I guess."

"I like it," Emma said, and her eyes immediately widened. She hadn't actually meant to say that out loud. And if the way Seth was looking at her got any warmer, she was going to wind up nothing but a puddle on his linoleum.

"Thanks," he said, then eyed her cup. "You want another cup of coffee?"

"No, I'm good," Emma replied with a nervous laugh. She glanced out the window, where the rain had softened from a downpour to a gentle patter. "I should probably get back as soon as my clothes are done. I have—"

"Work to do. I know," Seth interjected. He didn't seem irritated, just resigned. It made her feel guilty, which was ridiculous.

"You don't bring your work home with you, I take it?" she asked.

"I try not to," he said. "It's the sort of thing that causes problems if you're not careful."

"Hmm." She drank down the last of her coffee, wondering whether he was passing some sort of judgment on her for working all the time. She'd certainly heard enough about it from Sam and her mother. He was still quiet when she put the cup down, but the tension between them had returned with a vengeance. Flustered, Emma tried to fill the silence.

"It's a good thing Harvest Cove is so—damn it!"

Seth blinked. "That's not a way I hear it described very often."

"No, it's my phone," Emma muttered. She grabbed it,

looked at another text from some guy named Ian, and set it facedown on the table with an angry little slap. "Sorry."

"This has something to do with what's eating at you, right?" Seth asked. "What is it? Ex-boyfriend? Bridezilla who hired you? What?"

"It's nothing." She wasn't in the habit of sharing her problems, and she certainly wasn't going to share them with Seth Andersen. Still, she felt that twinge of guilt again when he pushed away from the table and stood, his expression tight.

"Okay. Well, I'm going to go check on your clothes. Be right back."

Emma watched him go, knowing she'd managed to offend him. He wouldn't say so, of course. He just didn't seem the type. But she had a sneaking suspicion that there would be no more impromptu visits with cupcakes after today's chat. Her hard shell was functioning exactly as intended—he was tired of trying to crack it, so he would leave her be.

Rather than feeling triumphant, she just felt weary and empty. And she'd never felt less like the kind of woman who could happily consider her options, all of which included different flavors of men, for the weekend. All she wanted was peace and quiet, control and sanity. Was that too much to ask? Sure, in time she'd get it back, but she wanted it now. If only she could find a way to make herself look normal and boring again. She couldn't un-dance the *Flashdance* performance, but there had to be some way to pour water on the newly flickering flame of her notoriety.

Seth walked back in, carrying her neatly folded clothes.

"They're basically dry. The jeans might need a little more, but I figured you'd want to get going, so—"

The idea hit her hard and fast, and it made so much sense she could almost hear the click as the pieces of her problem fitted perfectly together into a solution. Not a great solution, but a workable one. She didn't want a boyfriend, but she could certainly use some cover.

"We should hang out," she informed him.

Something in her voice made him stop in the middle of the kitchen and look at her warily.

"Ah, what?"

"You and me. We should go out sometime. In public. Dinner, maybe." She thought about her schedule and decided that this could take precedence over family dinner night if it needed to. "What about tomorrow? Later, because I have a wedding, but I could fit it in. Are you free?"

"Is this a trick question?"

She furrowed her brow. "No. I'm dead serious."

It worried her that he looked so suspicious. Then again, the man caught criminals for a living. Of course he would know she had ulterior motives. "What is this? You're making it sound like a business appointment."

Emma tried to figure out an inoffensive way to explain it, failed miserably, then plunged in anyway. "I feel like it might be a good idea for me to get out more. You asked about dinner before. I'm willing as long as we keep it friendly."

"Okay," Seth replied. "I'm not sure where this is going, but I don't feel like anything big has changed since you shot me down earlier in the week." When her phone buzzed again, he eyed it, though she refused to look at it. It didn't matter. Understanding began to bloom anyway. And for as nice as Seth had been, Emma caught her first glimpse of the steel beneath his easygoing demeanor.

"Do you need to get that?"

"Nope." She shook her head and tried for a carefree smile. It felt like a grimace.

"Because it's been going off a lot, and I'd hate to keep you away from . . . work? Family?" he continued.

"Neither. Just something stupid. I'm ignoring it."

"Not all that well. You look like you want to throw it at somebody."

She shifted uncomfortably. It felt as though they'd shifted from coffee to an interrogation. "It'll stop. Eventually."

He considered her coolly. "This wouldn't have anything to do with last weekend, would it? Your maybe giving your number to some of the local party crew down at the Tavern. The stories about you and me. The video."

Her stomach sank. "You saw that?"

He did look slightly sympathetic about that, at least. "Yeah."

"Great. And *no*, why would this have anything to do with all of that?" But she sounded defensive, and she knew it. Emma prided herself on being good at what she did, but lying wasn't on her list of abilities. It was a problem that seemed to run in her family.

"Uh-huh. You're looking for a shit shield, not a date. I get it." His voice had dropped to a low growl, and he was looking at her with enough ice to freeze her solid. It was the first time he'd been anything less than kind to her, and the absence of his warmth made her feel surprisingly lost. She told herself it didn't matter, but the words rushed out before she could stop them. She needed to clarify. To explain. To make him stop glaring at her.

"I don't need a shield! I just . . . You already offered, and the stories are getting—well, I told you how they would get . . . and my stupid phone today will *not* stop ringing—" She felt her jaw starting to clench until she was nearly growling the words through bared teeth, but Seth cut her off.

"And you think maybe parading around and semiconfirming some of those rumors involving me will make the other stuff stop by what, magic?" When she said nothing, he shoved a hand back through his hair. "Jesus, Emma, seriously? That's not a date! That's . . . messed up!"

Her frustration, not all of it directed at him, bubbled to the surface. Maybe it did sound kind of messed up when you said it out loud, but Seth could have just not argued with her and gone along. Why did people always have to make things so difficult? She was competent, damn it! She knew what she was doing! Well, usually. This was new. But her track record with other things gave her hope.

Emma tried to keep her voice steady, even though she wanted to shout. "It's not messed up to want my life to get back to normal. I don't need all this distraction, and you're stable, and everyone already thinks we slept together. What's the harm in hanging out a little until things calm down? What would be so awful about people thinking whatever they want to think about us?"

He looked utterly astounded, and not in a good way. "Nothing, if you weren't just doing this to try to fix things so you can keep running your own little corner of the universe where nobody bothers you. This has nothing to do with me. And it sure as hell isn't about wanting to get to know me. I'm supposed to feel honored that you want to use me? I asked you for a date, not *this*!"

"I do want to get to know you." She blurted it out, then realized that she actually meant it. Maybe she should have just picked one of the guys who'd called her and tried to make that work until she was satisfied that the rumor mill had moved on. But that was a complete crapshoot, not to mention a definite waste of time, whereas Seth . . . Without knowing why, she was positive he was worth knowing.

Her revelation seemed to impress Seth a lot less than she'd impressed herself.

"If that's really what you want, trying to set me up as your fake boyfriend is the wrong way to go about it."

"I only asked if you wanted to go to dinner with me," she shot back. "A *friendly* dinner. I never used the word 'boyfriend.' Or the word 'fake.'"

"You didn't use the word 'excuse,' either, but that's what you'd be using me as. You also didn't use the words 'man whore,' which is what I'd feel like."

Emma wasn't quite sure how, but she'd utterly lost control of the situation. Now he sounded angry, which wasn't at all the reaction she'd been hoping for. Negotiating was something she excelled at—but it was only now that Emma realized she might have overestimated her abilities when it came to subjects that were a little more personal. This wasn't exactly the same as tangling with Annalise over centerpiece design.

"I'm not asking you to . . . you know . . . do *that*!" she said, her cheeks heating.

"And this is a selling point because why?"

She had a hard time cutting through the mortification to answer, but after a few long seconds, she managed. "You know, one more person being judgmental isn't helping." She chewed her lip. "What if I picked out some stuff for us to do and made it my treat? Would that be more appealing?"

He groaned. "Not helping with the whole man-whore thing, Emma."

She expelled a long, exasperated breath. "Fine! You

know, you helped get me into this mess. You could take some responsibility here."

Seth's eyes rounded. "How's that? I wasn't anywhere near the Tavern," he pointed out.

The week's frustrations spilled over, and then she was shouting. "You took me home! You stayed the night!"

"Okay, you demanded I take you home, and I fell asleep on your couch. But don't worry. That's the last time I'll do that. Problem solved!"

Rather than backing down, he'd simply shouted back at her. His frown was thunderous, and Seth's words sliced into her more deeply than they should have, considering how little she knew him. Maybe—just maybe—she was being unreasonable. But he wasn't intimidated by her, and the way he'd refused was a nasty blow to her pride. He seemed to find the idea of a platonic date with her not just undesirable, but offensive. As though the prospect of sex with her was all she had going for her.

It left a bitter taste in her mouth.

"Fine, abdicate responsibility," she snapped. "I handle things better on my own anyway."

Seth looked at her so intently that she could feel her skin warm where his eyes grazed it, and she wondered whether she was going to wind up walking home in the rain. At the moment, that didn't seem like such a bad option. Just when she was about to get up and grab her clothes out of his hands, though, Seth walked slowly to the table and set them in front of her.

"We don't really know each other, Emma," he said, "so I've got two things I think you need to hear: One, you worry too damn much about what everybody else thinks. And two, if I ever *do* take you out, there won't be anything fake about it."

Emma stood, disliking the advantage his height gave

him as he loomed over her. She faced him down, planting one hand on her hip, and fixed him with the glare that usually sent people scurrying away.

"Why does it always have to be about sex? Why can't men ever just be happy with what's being offered and quit pushing?"

Seth leaned down until his mouth was only an inch away from hers, and Emma's breath stilled in her throat. *Is he going to kiss me? Seriously? He'd better not! I think. Well, maybe. Wait, what?* Her confusion was only intensified by the charge that passed between them, lighting up every nerve ending until she felt as though her skin might start sparking. His breath fanned her face, and when his nose rubbed hers, she tilted her head back, eyes slipping shut.

Terrible idea, she told herself. *I'm going to regret this. Later.*

A single breath left her, almost a moan. And then he spoke, breaking the spell and making her terrible, horrible, no-good, very bad week complete.

"That's why," he said. "But until you figure it out, I think we're done here. Now get changed and I'll take you home."

Chapter Seven

Of all the things Emma might have asked him to do, pretending to date her was probably last on the list of things he would have guessed. Hell, it hadn't even been on his list. Who asked a guy something like that?

Emma Henry, that was who. And it was somehow more irritating to know that she was just as attracted to him as he was to her. Being so close to her, watching her eyes close and her lips part, had confirmed that. He'd almost taken advantage of that moment of surrender. But her voice kept playing, over and over again, in his head.

I don't need all this distraction.

Yeah, well, neither did he. But at least he could accept that he wanted his hands on her no matter how inconvenient it was.

Damn it.

Seth ignored the plaintive looks she kept shooting him as she made her way to the bathroom and back, then when she handed him the clothes he'd lent her, and finally when he led the way into the garage to get in the car. The sight of his motorcycle did seem to distract her, at least. He caught her eyeing it the way a duck might eye an alligator sharing its pond.

It was hard not to smile, but he managed it. The thought of Emma in one of her snappy little outfits on the back of his cherry red Indian Chief was—well, it was pretty hot, actually. Until he pictured the way it probably would play out, which involved her hanging on for dear life and screaming. While he did maybe thirty miles an hour.

It was almost worth going on a fake date with her for. Almost.

She didn't speak until he was backing into the road, and then it was stiff and formal. A glance showed him posture so rigid, she looked like she might snap in half.

"I'm sorry if I offended you." She didn't sound it, but he expected that. She was just sorry he'd refused. His temper, which had a long fuse to begin with, had already cooled.

"I'm not offended. I'm annoyed. There's a difference."

"Oh." Emma folded her hands in her lap and looked out the window. Apparently that was her last word on the subject. Seth drove in the silence. Her silence should have been a relief, he guessed, but he felt his own shoulders stiffening up the longer they were together without speaking. She was a complete puzzle to him. Self-contained, serious, but with a sly sense of humor she let slip out sometimes and some seriously screwed-up ideas about relationships. He wondered if she'd always been this uptight or if she'd just been born that way.

At this rate, chances were he was never going to find out. That was probably a good thing. He'd get around to feeling that way eventually.

You're not looking for a serious relationship, either, he reminded himself. Except there was a lot of area between "serious relationship" and "so opposed to dating that you'd rather just hire somebody."

They hit the light before the square, and Seth finally turned to look at her while they were stopped. He knew he should just let well enough alone, but this afternoon had put a sizable dent in his pride.

His staring caught her attention almost immediately. Emma looked back at him, and in this light her eyes were startlingly blue. Her still-damp hair fell in waves around her face, dark against her fair skin. She was completely, frustratingly gorgeous. He had no idea why she was so against even a simple, honest date, but there seemed to be a lot going on beneath her prickly exterior. *"I handle things better on my own anyway."* Wounded, angry ... It sounded unnervingly familiar. He couldn't let himself get sucked in by Emma.

But hell if that glimpse of some deeper issue didn't make him want to fix it for her. He hadn't met Sam. Was she like this, too? he wondered.

"What?" she asked.

"What is it with you? Was it a bad relationship? What?"

"You know," Emma said flatly, "you already said no. Can we just leave it at that?"

"No. No we can't," Seth replied. "Because I'd like to understand why your head is in the place it seems to be."

"And where do you think that is?"

"Up your ass."

She pressed her lips together, drew in a breath, and for a moment Seth regretted being so blunt with her. He'd never been great at talking to women. Guys were easier, more basic. There wasn't any guesswork involved. Women, though ... They were impossible puzzles to solve. And this particular woman appeared to be one of those giant puzzles that most people never finished, the ones with the billion tiny pieces.

"My head is fine, but thanks. I already explained. I thought, since you seemed interested, that we could try being friends. Friends *only*. That it would be mutually beneficial."

"You get very eloquent when you're mad," he said, trying not to find it charming. She made it hard, sitting there so elegant even in her hoodie and old jeans.

"Thank you."

"I'm not sure it's a compliment. It makes you easier to read, at least. Tell me something—what do you see me getting out of this mutually beneficial 'friendship that looks like more'?"

Emma hesitated. "Well, you said you hadn't really gotten to know many people. I could be kind of your entry into Harvest Cove society."

"Uh, even if that kind of thing interested me, which it doesn't, you're a loner. You've already told me everyone thinks your family is crazy, and I don't think this place *has* anything you could call 'society.' Try again."

Her eyes narrowed, just a little. "The light's green." It sounded like an accusation.

Seth drove through the light and hung a right onto the square. Once he pulled into a spot in the lot behind her building, Seth slammed the car into park, determined to finish the conversation. That was, unless Emma stormed off, but she didn't seem inclined. She wouldn't have gotten where she was without being a fighter. Like him.

Of course, right about now he wasn't thrilled to think about what they might have in common.

"This is pointless to argue about," Emma said. Her chin lifted, and she tucked a lock of hair behind her ear. "I asked you to a friendly dinner, which was perfectly reasonable, and you said no. I don't think it needs any further discussion."

He heard her phone vibrate in her pocket, and he noticed the way she didn't answer it. How many guys, he wondered, had been absolutely thrilled last weekend to discover that the gorgeous ice queen in their midst might not be so icy after all? He didn't think she had any idea how appealing she was, even now. She'd probably been awkward, once. She was still kind of awkward, but it worked on her. That explained her discomfort with the attention, but not her outsized reaction to being sought after. That seemed to bother her more than the video had, and he was sure that had bothered her a lot.

I shouldn't care. But he couldn't shake the way she'd snuggled into him, the way she'd looked standing there in her pajamas the next morning, her hair sticking out at odd angles. She seemed to need somebody, even if she didn't particularly want anybody. Not that she'd admit, anyway.

Seth exhaled loudly through his nose. His afternoon had started off so well—this turn of events hardly seemed fair. Emma played her fingers across the top of the door, looking around the parking lot. Anywhere but at him. From what he'd seen of her, she was too polite to just dash out of the car. Maybe she just didn't know how to end the argument.

That made two of them.

"So . . . thanks for the coffee. And the clothes. And the ride," Emma said. "I guess I'll see you around."

"Sure."

He watched her open the door and couldn't miss the relief on her face before she turned away. Seth sat there in the idling car and watched her start to walk away. It took a good ten seconds before he slammed his hands on the steering wheel.

"Damn it."

He yanked open his door, leaving the car running, and got out, walking quickly toward Emma's receding back. "Emma, hang on a second."

She stopped, tensed. He could actually see her considering her options before she slowly turned around just as he reached her. She eyed him warily.

"I'm not fighting with you about this, Seth."

"I'm not interested in fighting about it, either," he said, glad she couldn't hear his pulse starting to race. Then she really would be running.

"I'm also not bargaining," she said. "There's nothing to bargain over. I don't want a relationship. You don't want my friendship."

"No," Seth said, "I don't." He noted how she refused to back away from him, even though they were basically toe-to-toe. She was used to getting her way when she pushed. So was he. Maybe that was why he couldn't quite let this go.

Now she looked exasperated. "Then what do you want?"

He took a deep breath, hoping he wasn't as rusty as he felt, and moved in before she knew what was happening. His arms slid around her, up her back, and he felt her instinctively arch into him the way a cat did when stroked in just the right way. Then he pulled her close, and was surprised to find that Emma didn't even tense. Instead, she closed the rest of the distance between them, though he wasn't sure whether she did it consciously. When her body pressed against his, Seth couldn't bring himself to care. Her head tipped back, and he saw a blend of confusion and longing that resonated with him in a way he hadn't expected.

But then, nothing about Emma was expected. So Seth didn't think. He just plunged.

The first taste was sweet, like sugar that still carried a hint of the coffee they'd shared, and incredibly soft. He'd intended nothing but a swift, gentle kiss to give her food for thought. Instead, he felt her lips part against his almost immediately, opening to tease his tongue with hers with a sensual promise that banished every rational thought. The parking lot disappeared around them. Everything vanished but Emma, her body rising against his while he pressed his hands into her back, holding her to him. Her arms slipped around his neck, fingers toying with the hair at the nape of his neck as though she'd just been waiting to touch it. The gentle movement sent hot little sparks of pleasure across his skin.

Deepening the kiss wasn't a conscious decision. He barely realized it was happening, angling his head to taste her more deeply, feeling her wrap around him until they were tangled together so completely that he felt surrounded by her scent, her warmth. Emma gave a soft, breathy moan, and slow burning desire shifted gears into hot, aching want in the blink of an eye. His hands tightened on her waist, hers on his shoulders, and she rose up, fitting herself against him so that his fevered imagination could conjure them perfectly in this position, except horizontal. And minus the clothes.

A car horn sounded nearby, pulling Seth back to reality with a nasty jolt. He tore his mouth away and sucked in a breath, trying to kick his brain into gear again. But with Emma against him, her eyes hazy and her lips swollen from his kisses, it was impossible to think straight. What the hell had he been trying to prove here? That she wanted him? And here he was, rock hard and making out in a parking lot without a care in the world apart from getting Emma naked. Which he guessed proved that he was a sex-crazed Neanderthal and not much else.

He needed to get out of here, before he promised Emma as many fake dates as she wanted, maybe even throwing in his soul for good measure, if he might get to touch her again. Because she didn't just taste as good as she looked. The woman kissed like heaven itself.

"I've gotta go," he said, pulling back abruptly.

Emma blinked owlishly at him, looking as though she needed a few minutes to collect herself, too. That was good—it delayed her inevitable shouting. And her politeness be damned, he was pretty sure she would shout about this.

"I . . ." She frowned a little. "What—"

He'd planned to tell her to think about it and then swagger off like James Dean. Smooth. Classic. She'd be left fluttering in his wake, right?

"I'll see you around. Later." He ground out the words, knowing they probably sounded more like caveman grunts than anything else, and hurried back to his car as well as he could, given his uncomfortable condition. He could feel Emma's eyes on him, but he couldn't meet them. Not when he put the car in gear, and not when he drove away.

Wanting her was one thing. But whatever this was, this heart-pounding, palm-sweating need for her, was more than he'd bargained for. Emma wasn't the only one who liked to have some control, and right now, his was just about gone.

Seth allowed himself a single glance in the rearview mirror, and he saw Emma staring after him. *That's it. Enough. I'm not going looking for her again.* She was so damn stubborn that it might at least buy him time to cool off and get his head on straight. He needed that time, even though some insistent voice inside his head had pointed out how much time he'd already had.

Not yet. But the thought of Emma lingered long after he'd left her, and, much like the woman herself, that thought refused to let him be.

Chapter Eight

She kept her head down and worked through the rest of the weekend. It was easy not to think when she had a wedding to deal with each day, which kept her, Brynn, and the two part-timers she affectionately called her Weekend Warriors hopping. By Monday evening, Emma wasn't thinking about the posting on YouTube, unwanted date offers, or the flaming wreckage of her own reputation. She also wasn't thinking of anything remotely business related. Her feet ached, her brain was tired, and all she wanted was to let her mind drift. Which it did. Except it was more like circling a single point of interest.

Emma sat on her couch, staring off into space while Boof lolled in her lap, purring loudly. Every once in a while, she'd lift a hand to touch her lips, which she could swear still tingled. A glass of wine sat on the coffee table, forgotten, as did her laptop with the notes for Penny Harding's wedding proposal up on the screen. Normally she'd still be going over it, making sure everything was perfect for tomorrow's presentation. Nothing seemed all that pressing right now, though. Not since that kiss.

That mind-bending, completely consuming kiss.

She'd always thought that romance novel descriptions

of that sort of thing were overblown. It was so much bullshit, the idea of addictive kisses that made you forget your own name while they were happening. At least, it had been. Until she'd gotten one planted on her. She still didn't know what he'd been thinking, and from the shell-shocked look on his face afterward, neither did Seth.

Emma rubbed absently at Boof's fluffy tummy, wondering what the hell she was going to do. "Stay away from Seth" seemed the most obvious answer. So why did she keep turning it over in her mind? And why had she found herself scanning the street for passing police cruisers all weekend? She'd even seen him once. Well, she was pretty sure she'd seen him. She'd nearly crashed her own car while craning her neck to see. That would have been one way to get his attention, she guessed.

Sadly, considering every other interaction they'd had, she didn't think he'd be surprised.

She looked around her apartment, as tidy and boring as it always was, then looked at the clock: seven p.m. Not too late to get away from her own company. She scooped up the cat and stood, eliciting an irritated little "mrrr" from Boof.

"Let's go do something," she said to him, trying to force some excitement into her tone. He didn't look impressed. "Sorry, Boof. You're kind of my social life. It's why we have the special kitty carrier. So we can be *all-the-time friends*." Her cheerful voice hadn't elicited much of a reaction, but her purposely creepy one got her a plaintive meow, the one that said, "Help me."

"Oh, knock it off. You know I only take you to Mom's or Sam's. You can eat all their kitty food and act superior."

Emma considered her options, decided on the most

obvious one, and despite Boof's loud protestations, got ready to go.

It was a warm evening, so Emma drove her little roadster with the windows down. Boof was in the passenger seat, secure in his bright blue soft-sided pet carrier and making quiet unhappy sounds. Nine times out of ten he was happy with their destination, but their occasional vet visits were enough to make him permanently mistrustful of her motives for bringing him along.

She drove up Hawthorne, out of the square and past Two Roads Gallery, then hung a left onto Crescent Road. The road cut through a well-manicured neighborhood of small, older homes before it curved and began to trace the shape of the cove. The trees became bigger, and enormous houses with long drives vanished behind them. Some peeked through the trees, but many were only indicated by the mailboxes lining the road. This was the Crescent she'd grown up on, with old names like Owens and Pritchard and Harding. The Sullivans, parents of Shane "Not the Nice Redhead" Sullivan, were out here. And there, glowing like a beacon, was the violently green mailbox of the Henrys.

Her reactions to it varied with her mood. Today, it made Emma smile. Not that she'd ever admit that to her mother.

"Let's go see Peaches, Boof. You can let your sister beat you up for a while."

Emma felt better as soon as she saw the house, and wondered why she'd been so determined to stay away Saturday night. It might have done her some good.

Behind the trees, the Henrys' land opened into a verdant lawn that rolled all the way down to the rocky edge of the land that met the sea. This land had been with the Henrys since the beginning, but the current house, built in the 1800s, was its glory. The sprawling white Victorian was a study in slightly faded elegance, with its wrap-around porch and tower room, its arches and angles that had hinted to Emma when she was a child of all manner of secret places to explore. There had been plenty, she remembered, found on her and Sam's adventures. Some their father had shown them, and some he'd let them discover on their own.

Then he'd died, and the adventures had stopped. Sam had retreated inward, and Emma had . . . Well, she'd . . .

Emma tightened her jaw at the melancholy that wanted to curl around her like a comfortable old blanket. *Not doing this today. Look at Mom's flowers. Look at something good for a change.* She was glad to see Andi's roses were in full bloom all around the base of the porch. They were red and soft pink, making the house as pretty as a Valentine's postcard. Her mother didn't hold with too many traditions, but the roses were one she had always adored. That, and filling the small, glassed-in greenhouse off the back of the house with fragrant herbs and whatever flowers had struck Andi's fancy. Horticulture had apparently been a favorite pursuit of the Henry women for generations.

Somebody in there had had a black thumb, though; Emma knew because she'd inherited it. Every time she gave in to the urge and bought a plant, she felt like she should apologize to it for sealing its fate.

She cruised down the drive, hearing the comforting and familiar crunch of gravel beneath the tires. It took her a moment before she finally noticed the extra car in the driveway beside Andi's sunny yellow Beetle. It was instantly recognizable, a classic Austin Healey convertible. She didn't know exactly what year it was—1960-something—but it had been around town forever and she'd always loved it. The owner was a sweetheart, too. Even if he was putting the moves on her mother.

"Man," Emma grumbled. She didn't really want to know what Jasper Reed and her mom were up to in there. She pulled in beside the Austin Healey, weighed her chances, and had just decided she would risk hysterical blindness by knocking at the door (no way in hell was she just walking in under these circumstances), when she heard the unmistakable growl of a motorcycle's engine coming up the driveway. She frowned, then turned her head to watch a vaguely familiar-looking bike closing the distance between them. The rider was more than familiar, in his beat-up jeans and leather jacket. The helmet hid his face, but she knew his body. Somehow, in a very short period of time, she'd become well-versed in the contours of Seth Andersen's form.

Emma knew it was sad, but nobody could judge her for it if she kept it to herself.

Her stomach dropped, then felt as though it exploded into butterflies as she stared. She wanted to move. In fact, she really wanted to turn the car back on and floor it down the driveway. Instead, she ruthlessly stomped out the flight instinct and got out of the car, wondering what he could possibly want. Had he followed her here? He didn't seem like that type, but anything was possible. Maybe he was secretly creepy. That would banish the weird guilt she'd been feeling about springing her "let's go out but not" idea on him.

Then again, she didn't have that kind of luck.

"What are you doing here?" she asked, cringing inwardly at the way her words had come out. Seth took his time replying, pulling off his helmet to reveal appealingly tousled hair and a wary expression she didn't much like. It wasn't like she'd gone all ninja and kissed *him* in a parking lot!

"I got invited. Nice to see you, too." He tucked the helmet under his arm.

Emma stiffened. "Invited? My *mother* invited you out here?" She heard the bitter snap in her own voice, loathing it even as she couldn't control it. "What, is she going to try to butter you up so you'll agree to take her poor, workaholic, socially stunted daughter out? Is that what this is?" It was a horrible thought, one she hated the instant it appeared even though it made an awful kind of sense. Andi worried too much. She knew all about the wild stories that had sprung from Sam's party, knew about Seth. Sam had probably fed her information while the two of them talked about how to push her into whatever they thought she needed in her life. Directly intervening with Seth seemed kind of extreme, but she couldn't discount it.

Not until Seth gave her a look that made her wonder whether she'd suddenly grown an extra head.

"No. And you might want to calm down, because that steam pouring out of your ears seems like a bad sign." He arched a brow, his expression reproachful, before he started to walk toward the house. "Just a suggestion."

Emma stood staring after him for a moment, completely at a loss for words. Only a mix of curiosity and anger got her moving again. She took Boof's carrier out of the passenger seat, slung the strap over one shoulder, and set off after Seth. She didn't understand it, but she was thrilled and infuriated to see him, both at the same time. It took until he was almost to the porch steps to catch up, and by then another car was pulling into the drive, a nice silver sedan. Seth turned his head to look at it, then lifted one hand in greeting.

"You didn't answer my question," Emma said, falling into step beside him.

"No, I didn't. Anything you've come up with is bound to be a lot more interesting than the truth." He looked down at her bag when it mewed piteously. "Tell me that's not some kind of cat purse. Like the things people carry those tiny dogs around in."

"It's just for short trips," Emma said. "He likes it." She didn't know why she always felt so defensive around Seth, but she couldn't seem to help it. His skeptical expression right now wasn't helping.

"Yeah, he looks thrilled. Isn't he kind of big to be in there?"

"It's just his fur. He fits fine."

Seth shook his head. "Only you would stick a giant cat in a color-coordinated purse to go to your mom's house."

"It's not color—oh." Emma glanced down at herself and realized that the stripe in her thin boatneck sweater perfectly matched the carrier. As did the ballet flats peeking out from beneath her wide-legged denim trousers. It hadn't been a conscious decision, just habit, but she still felt her cheeks grow hot. "It's not a crime to dress well. I'm just not a 'T-shirt and leather jacket' kind of girl."

She realized as soon as she'd said it how he was likely to take it. Sure enough, his expression hardened. "Yeah, I got that," he said.

"I . . . That's not what I meant!" Emma snapped, clutching the strap of the bag as she hurried up the steps behind him. "Way to jump to the worst possible conclusion, Seth."

"Wow," was his only response as he reached the door and turned to face her.

If at all possible, her cheeks felt even hotter. Not just because he was right about the idiocy of her statement, but because being this close to him brought back every hot second of his kiss. It would have been bad enough before. Now, though, knowing exactly how good he felt, and tasted, and smelled . . . Unable to adequately describe how she felt, she simply gave a guttural growl.

"You're driving me crazy!" she snapped. That finally prompted a glimmer of humor in his eyes, and in the slightly rueful curve of his mouth.

"Welcome to the club," he said just as the door swung open.

"Honey!"

Emma managed to tear her gaze away from Seth to look at her mother, who looked like she'd just gotten a particularly wonderful present. She was under no illusions that it was just because of her. Seeing her obstinately single daughter and Seth standing here together was exactly the kind of thing that would make Andi's day.

"Hey, Mom. I didn't know you were busy, so I brought Boof for a visit."

Andromeda Henry looked between them with more shrewdness than her proud eccentricity and usual Bohemian attire might indicate. She looked good, Emma thought, taking in the bright blue eyes that matched her own, the dark blond hair pulled up into a braided bun, the loose, flattering dress accented with natural amethyst and peridot beads at her ears and throat. Actually, she looked even better than usual, and she knew her mother had aged well by anyone's standards. But there was a . . . a *sparkle* to her that Emma had almost forgotten.

Jasper. There couldn't be any other explanation, though it was strange to associate the kindly bookseller with the twinkle in her mother's eyes lately. Emma didn't know if they thought they were being sneaky or what, but they weren't doing a great job of it. It was one of the few things on which she and Sam completely agreed.

Andi clucked her tongue. "Don't be silly, Emmie. You know you can come whenever you want to. I'm just glad you finally came out of your cave. We missed you Saturday." She rubbed a finger against the mesh Boof's nose was pressed to. "Missed you, too, big guy." Then she turned her attention to Seth, and any wild theories Emma might have conjured about his presence here tonight crumbled immediately to dust. Really embarrassing dust.

"Nice to finally meet you, Mrs. Henry," Seth said, putting out his hand. Andi shook it, smiling.

"Seth! I didn't think Steve and Ginny were ever going to get you to come!"

"I felt a little weird intruding on their social life. They're just really persistent," Seth replied with a grin. "Plus they said you've got the best sunsets in the Cove right here."

"They're right," Andi replied. "And I'm glad they finally prodded you into coming out. It's such a nice evening, we thought—I thought—I'd throw together some munchies and invite friends to enjoy the evening."

"We," Emma said, "meaning you and Jasper."

"I, um, yes, I invited him, too."

It was a rare thing to see Andi look panicked, and Emma had to bite back a laugh. She patted her mother's shoulder as she walked inside, hearing Steve and Ginny Andersen calling out their greetings.

"It's okay, Mom. But just so you know, Sam and I are getting kind of tired of you two putting off Jasper's 'meet the daughters' dinner. He's got to run that gauntlet sometime, you know."

Andi's startled, throaty laugh followed Emma into the house. She stopped in the foyer, unzipped the bag, and hauled Boof out. He immediately trotted off in search of his sister—or more likely, her food dish—while Emma dumped the bag and her purse on a chair by the staircase. Andi stepped onto the porch, leaving the house quiet enough that Emma didn't realize anyone had followed her in. Seth's voice, low and warm, sounded near her ear just as she started to head back to the kitchen, and it made her jump.

"What did you say to her?" He only sounded curious, but Emma felt the rough buzz of his voice ripple over skin already sensitized by his nearness. And when she turned around to speak to him, he was far too close.

"Just teasing," Emma replied. In the dim foyer, Seth's face was shrouded in shadow, but there was no missing the way his eyes dropped to her mouth when she spoke. Nor was there any denying the way her body responded to his nearness. Everywhere. She swallowed hard.

"About me?" There was a hint of vulnerability in the way he asked the question that surprised her.

"I wouldn't joke about you."

"I guess I figured that. Look," Seth said with a sigh. "About the other day. You made yourself really clear, and I'm s—"

Oh God, not sorry. Be anything but that.

"No," Emma rushed on. "It's fine. Really," she added for good measure when Seth simply stared at her. How was she supposed to say that she hadn't stopped thinking about it? That if there was one thing she didn't want him to be sorry for where she was concerned, it was kissing her that way? She knew it didn't make any sense, not after she'd been so adamant about not wanting to head down that road with him. But Seth had managed to touch a part of her that she kept hidden from almost everyone, doing it with a sheer stubbornness that rivaled her own.

And she didn't want him to be sorry.

"What's fine? Kissing you?" He sounded as confused as she felt.

"Yes. I mean, it was. It isn't, normally, but it was. Really, very extremely fine. At the time." She wished she could just sink through the floor and disappear. Quickly. Forever.

"So you don't want me kissing you again, but it was pretty amazing the other day, is what you're saying," Seth translated, and Emma thought the hint of amusement she heard in his voice was uncalled for.

"I didn't say that."

"That you didn't want me kissing you again?" His smile was completely distracting. Emma glanced toward the door, where she heard Steve and Ginny coming up the steps as her mother chatted happily with them. This wasn't a conversation she wanted to have within earshot of their families.

"No. I mean, yes. Wait." She closed her eyes and frowned, wishing he wasn't standing so close to her. Why did he have to smell so good? She touched a hand to her temple. "We'll have to talk about it later. They're coming in." She opened her eyes to find Seth watching her closely, and the warm interest she'd missed outside was back. He hadn't been lying, she realized — he actually did like her. She had no idea why, all things considered, but it was easy to see. In fact, he'd been up front from the start.

The rush of affection, entirely separate from the lust she didn't seem to have any control over, took her completely by surprise. It was silly, she told herself, to feel even remotely attached to someone so quickly. Especially when he kept seeing her at her worst—drunk, or drenched, or just generally ornery. Except that was part of why she felt this way. That, and the smile playing at the corners of his mouth while he watched her deal with him.

Damn. I like him, too.

Right that second, it didn't seem to matter that he was exactly wrong for her in every way possible. All that mattered was feeling, quite unexpectedly, part of a unit instead of her usual solo. It had been so long, she hardly remembered it. It was so sweet and lovely that it banished every trace of her confusion and frustration.

Seth glanced toward the door. "Sure. When do you want to—"

She rose up and pressed a quick, hard kiss to his lips, silencing him before he could finish. Emma heard his sharp intake of breath, but he didn't pull away, staying perfectly still even when she lifted her hand to trail her fingertips lightly over the shadow of stubble along his jaw. His lips were still as soft as sin, silken and pliant beneath her own. She gently kissed his lower lip before drawing back completely and lowering her heels to the floor. His eyes opened slowly to look down at her with the kind of heat that made her grateful they weren't completely alone. He'd be impossible to resist, and she wasn't even sure she was ready to progress past, say, hand-holding. And yet here they were.

Seth looked as though he might be about to say something, when the door opened and everyone came in, clomping merrily down the hallway and into a discussion—she guessed it could loosely be called a discussion—that she really wanted to finish.

"Come on," Andi called. "Jasper's got the fire pit go-

ing. Well, that or he's singed his eyebrows off, but hopefully the fire's going."

Steve and Ginny, a sweet couple who'd been friends
of her mom's for years, greeted Emma on their way by.
Ginny already had her phone out and was promising to
show off pictures of their new puppy, a Pomeranian
named Spike who was apparently a handful. Emma was
glad to see them, and gladder to see her mother in such
a good mood. Not that she was ever very moody, but that
new sparkle to her was impossible to miss. Maybe Jasper
was the real deal. It was about time, Emma thought.
Andi had been an amazing mother, but she'd never
stopped missing her husband. It was time she had someone to share things with again.

"You ready to go out?" Seth asked. The discussion
had been tabled, but there was no question he was still
thinking about it. She nodded.

"Sure. There's probably a bag of marshmallows out
there, too. Mom's a s'mores junkie."

"Then she and I are going to get along great," Seth
replied with a grin.

They headed for the French doors that opened onto a
stone patio that had seen plenty of parties, plenty of
friendly cookouts . . . and plenty of sunsets. It was one of
the good places in the Cove, Emma thought. One of the
places where she'd made lovely memories to turn over
and over in her mind, like a stone carried for protection.
Emma stepped outside, eyes on a sky streaked with
peach and pink and wild crimson, edged with just a hint
of lavender.

"Beautiful," she murmured. This was one of the reasons she stayed. Practical though she was, deep down,
Emma thought there was a kind of magic here that ex-

isted nowhere else. Skies like this were a gift, but they were also a part of the odd and beautiful package that was Harvest Cove.

"It is beautiful," Seth said. And when they walked out toward the fire pit, and the tall, lanky man muttering curses at it, she felt Seth's hand at the small of her back. It was a light touch, but it spoke volumes.

What have I started? she wondered.

It was both worrying and wondrous that this time—just this once—she thought she might allow herself to find out.

Chapter Nine

After everything he'd been through, and everything that had driven him to run all the way from Florida to Massachusetts, getting involved with someone was the last thing he should be doing. Seth knew it, and he had the memories of a few bad decisions back in Jacksonville to prove it. But when Emma perched on one of the low, semicircular stone slabs that served as seating around the fire pit, his feet immediately overrode his mind's objections and made a beeline for her.

When she looked up at him, fingers threaded together between her knees and her toes pointed inward, he found himself hopelessly charmed. It didn't seem to matter that the woman was by turns confusing, abrasive, suspicious, and rude. Because she was also sweet, surprising, and completely adorable just as often . . . and she seemed to have no clue she was any of those things, which only enhanced their effects.

Maybe it's time to give it a shot. For real this time.

Seth hesitated as the thought occurred to him, even though some part of him had known he was heading in this direction since the first time he'd spotted Emma clipping along the sidewalk in a pair of heels that matched the umbrella she'd been carrying. Both had been yellow, the color of sunshine despite the cold November rain. He'd smiled when he saw her, the first real smile he'd experienced in a long time.

And now here she was, scooting over so he could sit next to her, making him a part of a scene so cozy that even a month ago he wouldn't have believed he could be involved in it.

Seth sank down beside her, the stone beneath him cool like the evening air. He'd heard that summer took its time getting to Harvest Cove, and that was fine. He missed his family, but not the sweltering heat. And there was a piece of his family here, a fact he was grateful for every day. If it hadn't been for Uncle Steve and Aunt Ginny, he wouldn't have known where to go.

Emma's mother had put out a small spread of snacks on a low table nearby. When he sat down empty-handed, she leaned around her daughter to admonish him.

"I don't know if anyone's told you this, Seth, but if you want to come to my house, you're basically agreeing to let me feed you while you're here."

He raised his eyebrows, amused. "Meaning grab a plate or suffer the consequences?"

Her blue eyes, a deeper shade than Emma's, sparkled with good humor. "Exactly. And since the consequences involve helping Jasper with the fire, you're going to want to get eating."

"Hey," Jasper said, feigning hurt. "I got this one going, didn't I?"

"Sure. You've also got a couple of new burn holes in your jeans."

Seth didn't miss the look the two of them exchanged, one that spoke of a history of teasing and private jokes . . . and more. A glance at Emma told him she hadn't missed it, either, though she seemed more intrigued than unhappy. That was good, he decided, standing again to obey the lady of the house. He preferred to see Emma happy. She seemed like someone who hadn't experienced a lot of happiness, whether by choice or chance.

Not that he knew her well enough to know that, not really. But his need to find out—to find out everything, including what made her tick—was rapidly swamping all of his misgivings.

God. I'm really going to get myself into this. As if there had ever really been any question. The more pressing one would be what he intended to do if and when things went south. That, however, was a subject he'd leave for some three a.m. insomnia-fueled brooding session. Right now, it would be nice if he could just concentrate on sitting around a fire with good company and a beautiful woman who'd kissed him. On purpose, even. And who seemed interested in doing it again. Seth nudged Emma's shoulder.

"Want anything?"

She shook her head, looking up at him with her lips curved into a wry little smirk. "No. I'm saving myself for the s'mores. They're my favorite."

He was filing that information away when Andi began to laugh. "Just not the entire bag this time, Em."

Emma clucked her tongue and rolled her eyes. "*Mom.*" Her blush, Seth decided, made her eyes even bluer.

He didn't quite manage to hide his grin as he grabbed a heavy stoneware plate and loaded it with a little of everything, from puff pastries stuffed with something or other to little barbecued meatballs in sauce to some kind of pizza roll. He made note of the unopened bag of marshmallows, the chocolate bars and graham crackers, and the long metal skewers for spiking a marshmallow into the flames. He was looking forward to the s'mores himself.

"So," he said, settling himself back beside Emma. "Whole bag of marshmallows, huh?"

Her eyes slid back to him, slightly narrowed. "Maybe. Once."

"How'd that end for you?"

"About as well as you'd expect."

"You must have been little at the time."

Her gaze went elsewhere. "Umm . . ."

"Seriously?" Seth started to laugh. "Don't tell me this was last week or something."

Emma frowned at him. "No. I was seventeen. And Sam bet me I couldn't." Her chin lifted. "So I proved her wrong."

"Yes, she did," Andi interjected. "If I remember correctly, you won ten bucks and a night of severe nausea for your trouble."

"And bragging rights," Emma added. "You can't forget those. They're very important."

Andi rolled her eyes, but Seth could see the love there. They didn't look much alike—he supposed Emma must look more like her father—but there was something that marked them as mother and daughter nonetheless. After some of the stories he'd heard, it was nice to discover that Andromeda Henry was far more of a friendly earth mother than an aging pothead, and one hell of a cook besides. He liked picturing Emma growing up here, and wondered what she'd been like. Still serious, he'd bet. But she had visibly relaxed since they'd arrived, and given the marshmallow story, he'd also bet that there'd been more humor and love in her life here than her usual cool facade would suggest.

It was good, Seth thought, to come from a home like that. So had he. But the ties Emma had to hers hadn't been frayed and damaged the way his had. He tried to brush aside the pang of regret that thought produced. Things were okay now, he told himself. Much better than they had been when he'd been close to home. Hell, he talked more to his parents and sister now than he had when he was there. Things were better. He was better.

Even if he worried that he'd become a man who was best loved at a distance.

Emma's nudge jerked him out of his brooding, which he was grateful for. The concern on her face surprised him, though it probably shouldn't have. She had a lot going on beneath that prickly exterior.

"Are you okay? You look like that pastry has destroyed your will to live. You probably shouldn't eat things that make you feel that way."

Her teasing did a poor job of masking her worry, but he managed a smile even though that tone in her voice was one that gave him a sinking feeling in the pit of his stomach. The last thing anybody needed to be doing anymore was worrying about him. And it was a reaction he was awfully tired of inspiring in others. Especially because, for the first time in a long time, he was genuinely okay. Okay enough to be sitting here wondering when he might get Emma alone to finally enjoy an uninterrupted kiss and see where it went.

He had a lot of ideas about that. None of which he needed to be thinking about in polite company.

"The pastry's great," Seth assured her. "And I'm fine. Just trying to work out how much I can eat and still have room for s'mores. They're delicate calculations, you know."

"Sorry for breaking your concentration," Emma replied, looking anything but as she plucked a pizza roll off his plate and popped it in her mouth.

"Yeah, I can see that. Food thief."

"Sharing is caring," she informed him. "Also, this is my house. So it's my food. Technically, I'm sharing with you. Be grateful."

Her grin was so distracting that it took his aunt Ginny to remind him what he was supposed to be looking at.

"Look at that sky." She sighed, and the group fell silent as all of them did. Seth lifted his eyes to take in the glowing streaks of peach and rose, flame and violet that turned the scene above and around them into a painting of exquisite mastery. It hardly looked real, but the warmth of the woman beside him kept him grounded, reminding him that he was really sitting here. A glance around showed him his aunt snuggled into the side of his uncle and Andi and Jasper not quite touching but angled into each other in a way that made them a unit. A couple.

Normally, this wouldn't have been his scene. Working as a solo act suited him better. But as conversation started up again, he found himself drawn into the warmth that these people created. Even more because he could see that Emma belonged right where she was, a part of this place and secure in the knowledge that she belonged here. He'd asked her why she stayed, but it seemed like a silly question now.

Then she turned her head to catch him watching her, and instead of dropping her eyes or blushing or pretending to be interested in something else, she held his gaze and lifted one corner of her mouth in a soft smile. In that instant, he felt something terrible and wonderful flicker to life deep in his chest, and he understood something.

No matter how much he worried that his relationships were always going to be a painful exercise in futility, he'd known for a while that he was never going to be sure until he tried with someone worth the effort.

And when she smiled, he felt the final piece click into place, letting him know that he'd finally found her. All that remained was the effort. And all he had to lose was everything.

Emma startled him by pulling the plate out of his hands. "Okay," she said. "No one should look that unhappy over food. You obviously need a marshmallow."

She was up and walking away before he could think of anything to say, and he heard the soft laughter from the others. Jasper, a tall, lanky Brit he'd encountered at the used bookstore on the square, caught his eye.

"She's a bossy bit of goods," he said with a smile. "Like her mum." That earned him a smack in the arm from Andi. Seth grinned despite himself, feeling his uncle's eyes on him. When Seth turned his head to look, Steve looked pleased, giving him a small nod. His father's younger brother was a quiet man, with close-cropped gray hair and the bearing of a soldier—probably because he'd been one, had retired as one . . . and understood what it was like to come back from a war with wounds no one could see.

His uncle's urging had brought him here. And every time he saw Steve's contentment with his life, this place, Seth knew that the move was one decision he'd made the right call on. His aunt Ginny looked in the direction Emma had gone, then at him, and gave him a wink. Seth felt his mouth curve into a silly grin and felt as ridiculous, simultaneously embarrassed and pleased as he had the first time he'd brought a girl home to show off. That was either a good sign or a really sad one, and he wasn't going to sit here trying to figure out which, just in case the answer was the unflattering one.

He might be a little screwed up, but he still had a healthy ego.

Emma reappeared with what looked like all of the supplies from the table, handing out the skewers to everyone before shoving one into Seth's hand. "Here," she said. "I'm assuming you know how to toast a marshmallow."

He tipped his chin down to give her a look. "I was a kid once, too, you know."

Emma snorted. "This isn't kid stuff. Proper marshmallow toasting is serious business."

Steve chuckled softly. "Careful, Seth. I've been watching this girl around campfires for years now. You do it wrong, she'll go after you with the skewer."

"I've never resorted to violence," Emma said primly, opening up the graham crackers and snapping off a few pieces of chocolate before fishing in the bag for a marshmallow and then carefully impaling it on the metal. "Just lectures."

"Which may prompt others to violence," Andi added. "My daughter is nothing if not thorough."

"Damn right," Emma replied. Then she looked at Seth expectantly. "Well? Let's do this thing."

She was being so easy with him that he didn't offer even a token objection. It was too much fun to see her so comfortable, so in her element . . . and running the show was definitely her element. Seth obligingly dug out a marshmallow and shoved it on the end of the skewer, making Emma wince.

"What?"

"It's just all mushed. . . . Never mind." She exhaled softly through her nose, then smiled. "I can get this to a perfect golden brown, just melty enough. Watch and learn."

"Don't need to," Seth replied, shoving his skewer into the flames. "I'm good at this."

Her brow arched. "Oh yeah?"

"Oh yeah. Check it out." He felt her watching while she carefully toasted her own marshmallow. He kept an eye on it, his lips curved at the way she methodically turned the skewer to get the entire surface, as promised, a uniform golden brown. He wasn't as careful, only concerned with making sure the marshmallow didn't get so mushy inside that it slid off into the fire.

"Done!" Emma pulled her perfect marshmallow off the skewer, stuck it onto the graham cracker and a square of chocolate, mashed another graham cracker on top of it, and bit into the s'more with a moan that nearly made Seth drop his own skewer. The cry of distress that almost immediately followed, however, saved both his marshmallow and his sanity, at least for now.

"It's on fire! What are you ... Blow it out—you'll ruin it!"

"No way. Watch and learn," he said, grinning as she chewed her s'more and watched his burning marshmallow in horror.

"Nice," Steve said. "That's gonna be a good one."

"Why?" Emma asked. "Why would you incinerate it?" She was laughing, but he could tell she felt he'd violated one of the cardinal rules of the fire pit. Instead of answering right away, he pulled the skewer away from the fire, watched the marshmallow burn to a uniform black, and then blew it out.

"Don't knock it until you've tried it," he said when she wrinkled her nose. "Come on." He pulled the charred mass from the skewer and held it in front of her. "This is perfect. Just try it, okay? Trust me."

"It's burned," Emma said.

"It's excellent," Steve interjected. "That's an Anders-en-style marshmallow right there."

"It's true," Ginny said. "Gross and amazing all at the same time. Pure Andersen."

Emma laughed. "Um."

"It's going to get cold. You need to eat it now, hot out of the fire. Come on. Just open your mouth. You don't have to touch it." When she just looked at him, he repeated, "Trust me."

Emma rolled her shoulders, licked her lips, glanced at her laughing mother, and then opened her mouth with a look that indicated she might just hurt him. Seth popped in the charred marshmallow, feeling Emma's lips close over the tips of his fingers before he could completely remove them. That brief feeling of suction, of her lips and tongue on his skin, made him forget to breathe as his chest tightened right along with every other part of his body. He kept his expression purposely blank, even though it was a struggle, but when Emma's eyes locked with his, he knew she could see exactly what he was feeling.

What he didn't expect was the flash of heat he saw, turning her eyes electric blue for a brief, heart-stopping second before she looked away to chew thoughtfully. Seth picked up one of the napkins she'd brought over to clean off his fingers, trying very hard not to imagine what it would be like to let her lick them clean. Around him, the others chattered on, seemingly oblivious to the fact that his flaming marshmallow had sparked an entirely different sort of combustion.

"Well?" Jasper asked Emma. "Do you like it, or are you going to be sick?"

Emma finished chewing, blinked, her eyes wide, and then gave a soft chuckle. "It was charred and gooey and pretty destroyed, but . . . it was really kind of awesome."

There was some amused cheering and clapping as Seth put his fists in the air. "Success!" he said.

"Hmm," Emma said with a wry smile. She ate the rest of her original s'more, then grabbed another marshmallow to skewer. "It's just a burned marshmallow. Don't get too excited."

"Hey, that's only the tip of the iceberg. I know all kinds of cool things. You just wait and see."

"Uh-huh," she said. "I hope those cool things don't involve fire, because a marshmallow is about as far as I'm willing to go with that."

"You'll just have to find out," he told her, waggling his eyebrows. She winced.

"Well, that's unnerving."

"Yeah? I was going for that."

"Well, mission accomplished," Emma replied. They looked at each other a moment, then laughed. Emma gave his knee a gentle shove with her own and shook her head. Seth grabbed another marshmallow as he let himself slide into the group's conversation, settling into the evening with a degree of comfort he hadn't expected, but fully welcomed.

Tonight had been full of surprises, but it was Emma who had provided the biggest one—that no matter what had brought him here, it might just turn out that in Harvest Cove, he wasn't so alone after all.

Chapter Ten

"**D**id you spike your own coffee or something this morning?"

Emma looked up from her desk to find Brynn staring in at her, then looked around. "What?"

"I heard you singing to yourself all the way at the front of the shop. I didn't know you listened to LMFAO." Brynn grinned, and she was instantly transformed from a classy businesswoman into some sort of piratical faerie. It was a side of her assistant that Emma was never quite sure what to do with. They were friendly, but Emma had kept firm boundaries in place. It kept things running better, she reasoned. Even if it got awfully quiet in here sometimes. Every once in a while, though, Brynn would try to jump the breach. Letting her know about the video had been one such occasion. It looked like this morning was another.

For once, Emma was in too good a mood to shrug her efforts off. Last night had been . . . good. Maybe the best night she'd known in a long time. And though she hadn't managed to catch Seth alone again, he'd whispered in her ear as they'd all said their good-byes.

"I want to see you again. Soon." Whether that was a demand, a promise, or both, it had carried her into the

day with more enthusiasm than any time in recent memory. This was something new. She didn't normally like new things, tending to view them with suspicion, but that kiss last night had been her decision. Hers. She'd always had good instincts. And though it went against everything she'd been telling herself for years, it looked as though she might need to trust her instincts here, too. So far today, that seemed to be working just fine. As her mother was always telling her, it wasn't always a bad idea to just roll along and let it be.

Andi could never resist the opportunity to insert a Beatles reference.

"I guess it's a 'Sexy and I Know It' kind of day," Emma said, smiling.

Brynn laughed. "Those are my favorite kinds of days. You all set for the Hardings?"

"Ready as I'm going to be," Emma replied. "I've got pictures, samples, prices . . . and I'm completely taking a shot in the dark, because all she gave me to work with was"—she batted her eyes dramatically and affected a higher voice—"'I sort of thought, like, a fall thing. But it's close to the holidays, so maybe, like, a holiday theme. Oh, but I saw this Hollywood wedding show where they made the reception look like a harem. So maybe that!'"

Brynn wrinkled her nose. "She wants belly dancers and shirtless eunuchs?"

"Wearing Santa hats, apparently," Emma said. "And elephants frolicking with reindeer near the open bar." They looked at each other, then burst out laughing.

"Please tell me you did that. Please," Brynn said.

"Sadly, no, because I want the job. But I thought about it," Emma replied with a smile. Brynn only looked slightly disappointed. Emma took a sip of her cooling coffee and studied her assistant, who lingered in the doorway. When she'd hired her three years ago, Emma's first impression of Brynn had been that the younger woman seemed charming, if a little puppyish. It was only afterward that she'd discovered that Brynn could be as much a rottweiler as she was a golden retriever. She'd been dying for the job, a fact that Emma still puzzled over, and she worked her ass off, making herself quickly irreplaceable.

The fact remained that she didn't know Brynn all that well. It wasn't something that had ever bothered her, but it struck her with a surprising amount of force as she watched her assistant wait for . . . well, Emma wasn't sure. But she was definitely waiting. And then she realized that she'd kept everything about the Harding proposal completely to herself. That was just what she did with bigger jobs, at least in the planning stages.

It hadn't even occurred to her that another set of eyes might be useful. It was a little late for that, but it couldn't hurt to share, she supposed.

Emma raised her brows. "Did you want to see what I've got? We've got a little time before they get here."

Brynn bounced, as did her long red ponytail. "Yes!" she cried, then widened her eyes and looked away. "I mean, as long as you don't mind."

Emma smiled, surprised. "I didn't know you were so excited about it."

"I just know it's a long shot, which means you'll pull out all the stops. You always come up with a way to sweeten the pot enough that you win the clients over, and it's always something different. I want to know what you think will hook Penny Harding. I mean, apart from gratuitous butt-kissing."

"That's the only thing I can't really offer," Emma admitted. "I want this, but I've got my limits." She picked up one of the folders stacked neatly at the corner of her desk and offered it to Brynn. "Here, have a look. Tell me what you think."

The grin she got was worth it as Brynn all but bounded over to grab the folder. She opened it and began to skim through the proposal while Emma watched, curious. "Ooh, you're thinking the Bellamy Farm?"

Emma nodded, folding her hands beneath her chin. "She wanted seasonal. The grounds are beautiful, the barn they've converted into an event area should be more than adequate, spacewise, for the numbers they gave me. And since the main house is a B and B, she and her groom can stay right there. Faith worked up a great sample menu for the catering, and I've got samples of Annalise's bouquets and centerpieces with similar themes to show them."

"It's perfect," Brynn said, lifting her eyes, "but . . ."

"But?" Emma frowned. Dissent wasn't what she was expecting, but that was what she saw in Brynn's expression. Her instincts were normally to nip such things in the bud and go on about her business, but something told her to listen this time. Her assistant looked nervous, as though she worried Emma might decide to chase her out of the office while snapping at her heels, so Emma tried to look and sound as nonthreatening as possible. She took a deep breath.

"What is it? If I've missed something, I need to know."

"It's not that you missed anything," Brynn rushed on. "Not at all. This would be a beautiful wedding, completely perfect. I'm just . . . a little concerned about Penny's reaction to the barn."

"Why? It's rustic, spacious, decorates beautifully. Not to mention it's pure Harvest Cove. Do you remember the Nightingale wedding we did there last year? It was gorgeous!"

She heard the defensiveness in her voice and tried to tamp it down, but it was hard. She'd put a lot of thought into what might wow the Hardings, and this was it. It had to be. Penny was local. Her father had been the mayor forever. . . . Why not evoke what was beloved about their home?

Brynn shifted her weight from one foot to the other and looked as though she wished she hadn't brought it up. "You're right. Never mind."

"No," Emma said firmly as Brynn started to turn. "If you know something I don't, I'd rather know what I was walking into. What is it?"

"Penny is my cousin," Brynn said, looking away. "I don't know if you knew that."

Emma sifted through her memories, vaguely recalled something about the Parkers being related to the Hardings, and knew she'd discarded it as irrelevant where Brynn was concerned. There didn't seem to be any strong ties there. "Okay," Emma said. "And?"

"She hates it here," Brynn said hurriedly. "She always has. She just won't say it in front of her parents, because they'd get upset. So while this would be a beautiful Harvest Cove wedding . . ."

"Oh God," Emma said, picking up a proposal and staring at it. "Why didn't I know this?"

Brynn winced sympathetically. "Because you don't like each other. And I didn't think to say anything. It's my fault. I'm so sorry!"

"No, no, of course it isn't," Emma said, stunned that this bit of information had so thoroughly escaped her. But a sharply critical voice whispered through her mind, the voice that had pushed her to always do better, do more, focus harder.

Of course you didn't know. You don't really know any-

one here. You barely know yourself. And you know perfectly well who you designed this wedding for.

She felt sick. In the absence of any information about Penny beyond the obvious, she'd created the perfect Harvest Cove wedding . . . for herself. This was exactly what she would want, and since she didn't expect to ever marry, Penny's "give me a fall-themed wedding" request had provided a blank canvas for her own desires. It had never even occurred to her that she was putting together a display of everything Penny hated. And now it was too late to fix it.

Emma carefully placed the proposal back in the folder and closed it. "Oh God," she said again. Her hands felt cold. When she looked up at Brynn, she was startled to see that the woman was almost in tears.

"I'm so sorry, Emma. I honestly didn't realize you were heading this direction. I expected, you know, frilly and pretentious, since that's basically what Penny is. Maybe it'll be okay. Maybe she's changed her mind—"

"Is that why she's getting married so fast? To get out of here?"

Brynn nodded miserably. "We don't talk all that much, really, but that was the impression I got. She feels trapped. Greg is a way out, and he really does seem crazy about her. There's somebody for everybody, right? He just got a really great job in Silicon Valley. It's all she talks about when I've seen her lately."

Dozens of new options presented themselves, ways to work the California theme into the wedding instead of the New England fall. Ways to *really* hook Penny. And she couldn't use any of them, because the Hardings would be here in ten minutes. Bob and his wife would probably love what she'd done, but it was small consolation. Emma knew she'd already lost. And Penny, being Penny, would be thrilled to reject her so easily.

All because she was so determined to work alone. She knew best. Because she was so very good at making executive decisions lately.

"I should have said something." Brynn's voice shook.

Emma pulled herself out of her thoughts, looked up at her normally vibrant assistant, took in the abject misery, and sighed. She stood, walking over to where Brynn stood, and gave her arm a pat.

"Why would you? I didn't ask. I never do." She laughed hollowly. "You probably have all sorts of ideas you haven't shared, right?"

Brynn looked distinctly uncomfortable. "Well. Sometimes. But yours are always better."

"And I'm scary, right?" Emma offered a small, knowing smile.

"Sometimes also that," Brynn admitted. "But you really do great work. I'm happy to play support and learn."

"Hmm." Emma stated to chew her lip and stopped herself. Making her lip bleed right before the Hardings showed up wasn't going to improve the situation. They'd probably think she'd been in a bar fight or something, considering. "I think," she said slowly, "that I'm going to have to reassess some things."

Brynn looked stricken, and Emma immediately knew why.

"I'm not going to fire you," she reassured her. "This isn't your fault. This one's on me, okay? I just mean that, going forward, some things should change. I think it's clear I need more . . . you know . . ." How sad was it that she could barely get the word out? She knew her face was all screwed up when she finally managed it. "Help."

"Oh," Brynn said. She looked as though she was caught between laughing and crying. Emma grabbed a tissue from the box on her desk and handed it over.

Brynn accepted it and dabbed at the corners of her eyes, then laughed softly. "Damn mascara."

"Exactly." Emma looked at her a moment, impeccably put-together Brynn so very close to completely losing it in her office, and wondered why she'd never noticed how much her assistant cared about her job. Maybe it was because Brynn treated it just the way she herself did.

Maybe because the two of them seemed to be more than a little alike. Brynn was just friendlier. It was a revelation Emma hadn't expected—though it explained why she'd known Brynn was right for the job almost from the moment the woman had walked into the interview. Like called to like, she thought. Sometimes in strange ways.

"Why don't we talk about it?" Emma suggested. "After work, if you're not busy. We can get food and figure out how to improve things around here so we never have to repeat this impending disaster."

"Oh, I don't think it's—"

"We both know it is." Emma looked wistfully at her neat little stack of folders and thought of her amazing PowerPoint presentation, which was going to go completely to waste. "We should go someplace with fried food. Lots of it. And beer."

"You drink beer?"

Emma tipped her head down to look down her nose. "You can't be serious."

Brynn gave a sheepish shrug. "I mean, I heard about you wearing it. I just didn't know you drank it. I figured you for more of a fine-wine girl."

"Both. I'm also a snobby microbrew girl." *She doesn't really know you, either, Emma. Nice going. She's only worked here for three years.* "What do you say? Misery loves company."

Brynn appeared to think about it, though it looked

more like she still wasn't sure Emma was serious. Still, after a moment, Brynn nodded. "I think . . . that would be good. Beltane Blues?"

The Cove's restaurant and blues bar was exactly what Emma had been thinking. "Perfect." She blew out a breath. "Okay. Let me just . . . get ready to deal with this."

Brynn's hazel eyes were full of sympathy. "You got it. I'll just be, you know, out there." She started to leave, but she turned at the last second. "Don't give up," she added. "You never know."

No, Emma thought as she nodded and watched Brynn go, her stomach knotting up even as she wondered whether the day might turn out to have a tiny bit of good in it despite what was coming. *You never do.*

It wasn't quite as bad as she feared, but it was certainly a lot worse than she'd hoped for. Brynn had been right — the look on Penny's face the moment the words "Bellamy Farm" were spoken told the tale.

Bob seemed to love it, and even his wife, Mary, looked excited — as close as she got to excited, at least. But Emma kept her focus on Penny, and by the end of the meeting, she knew there was no way in hell she'd won her over. And because she hated to lose, Emma spent the rest of the day working twice as hard on the events she'd already scheduled, winning over a woman who wandered in shortly before closing to ask about arranging an upscale birthday party for her husband. By a little after five, she was running on fumes and lacking the energy required to keep ducking the little black cloud following her around. She almost begged off on dinner, but it felt like letting Penny Harding win the day completely. That was a defeat she refused to concede even if she did just want to go home and curl up in a ball with her cat.

She and Brynn drove separately to Beltane Blues, a building with weathered siding and neon lettering just a block from the harbor. Previously a pizza joint famous for both its sauce and the rumors of roaches in the kitchen, it had been transformed into what Emma considered the Cove's strangest business that had actually managed to succeed. It had never occurred to her—or to most locals, from what she knew—that what the Cove really needed was a blues bar.

Apparently, they'd all been wrong.

Emma parked, then headed inside, ready to dive face-first into a plate of onion rings. Brynn had already grabbed a table and was working on a steaming basket of hush puppies. A few people looked at her as her heels clicked across the gleaming wood floor, but she was too hungry to glare or say hello—and too tired to figure out which was warranted. She'd been too much of a wreck to eat lunch, and she was paying for it now.

"Hey!" Brynn said. She, at least, seemed to have recovered from their earlier disappointment. For once, Emma appreciated it. Some days needed a smile or two. This was certainly one of them.

"Hi," Emma said, dumping her purse on the floor and sliding into a seat. "Hang on. I can't talk until I've eaten a few of these." She grabbed a hush puppy, dunked it in honey, and shoved the entire thing in her mouth. Brynn just watched incredulously.

"Somehow," she said, "I always imagined you as one of those clean-eating types. Grilled lean meats, veggies, that sort of thing. You always eat a soup or salad for lunch."

Emma held up a finger, finished chewing, and then said, "That's so I can pig out at dinner." She took a sip of the glass of water that had been waiting for her, flipped open the menu, and looked over her options. She couldn't quite meet Brynn's eyes when she asked, "I know you probably think of me as an uptight, anally retentive, no-fun buzzkill, and that's okay. But I have to ask. . . . Am I awful to work for? Be honest."

"No!" Brynn was so vehement that Emma looked up. The younger woman repeated herself, but softened her tone. "No. You're a great boss, Emma. A little hard to get to know, maybe, but great. None of what you just said about yourself is true. I mean, apart from being uptight, though I'd probably just call it being really put together at all times."

Emma made a soft noise. "You mean boring. I am completely, indisputably boring. *And* uptight."

"As opposed to what? Exciting and unstable? The world needs competence."

That made Emma laugh, which in turn left her feeling a tiny bit better. "I want that embroidered on a sampler and hung on my wall." She shook her head. "I don't know. I thought I liked boring. Lately, though . . ." She stopped herself, waving her hand. "I don't know." This was what it came down to, she thought. Spilling her guts to her employee at a blues bar. This was her life. The music coming through the speakers, a gravelly voiced singer lamenting something or other while his guitar wailed plaintively, matched her mood completely.

"What is it?" Brynn was watching her from across the table, head cocked, eyes shrewd. Another reminder that as sunny as she was, her assistant was no ball of fluff. Emma fiddled with the frayed corner of her menu and looked around at the dark wood and leopard print that dominated the interior of the place. *Boundaries,* she reminded herself. But tonight, she was sorely tired of bumping up against them. The waitress made a quick

stop to take their drink orders, and Emma chose a strawberry beer from England that was not only yummy, but
came in a rather large bottle.

"You really want to hear this?" Emma asked when
they were alone again. "My problems are as dull as the
rest of me."

Brynn surprised her by rolling her eyes. "Emma.
We've worked together for three years. And all that time,
I've been waiting for you to decide that maybe, possibly
it would also be okay for us to be friends. I mean, I see
you almost every day, we both love the business, and I'm
under the impression that your accessory fetish rivals my
own. We've finally made it as far as dinner, so . . . lay it on
me. I'm happy to listen."

It wasn't remotely what she'd expected to hear. She
also saw no evidence in Brynn's expression that she was
just sucking up. "Wait. I thought we were friends. I mean,
sort of," Emma said.

Brynn shook her head. "We're friendly. Not friends.
It's different."

She was struck with a pang of guilt, though she
couldn't completely sort out why. She'd always treated
Brynn well—but she'd also mentally filed her under
"employee" and acted accordingly. It had seemed like
the best option. But Emma had to admit, if only to herself, that it had also been the easiest option. No muss, no
fuss, no extra issues to deal with. Just like everything else
in her life.

"I don't see how it's that different," she said, but it was
a lie, and it sounded like one. Brynn didn't let it slide.

"Emma, have you ever seen me outside of work? And
working off-site is still working."

She didn't have to think very long about it to realize
Brynn was right. It was strange, realizing how few people

she *did* interact with outside of work-related issues. Sam had brought her new friends into the mix, and for that she was grateful, but still . . . piggybacking off her sister's social life wasn't really something to point to as a badge of honor. It wasn't as though she was so socially inept, she couldn't make friends, too. She hoped.

"You already have friends, though," Emma said. Didn't people run in packs? Like hyenas?

Brynn simply sighed. "Emma, your rigid definitions of things need some bend in them. Are you going to tell me what's eating at you? You've been off since Sam's party."

The waitress arrived with their drinks, and Emma was glad for the momentary distraction. She placed her order, which included a burger covered in an unsettlingly large pile of fried jalapeños, and handed off the empty hush puppy basket with a request for more.

"Okay," Emma said. *What the hell.* "It has occurred to me lately that it may not be that I love being boring so much as that I'm terrified of being anything else. Does that make any sense?"

She poured her beer into a glass, took a sip, and sighed at the perfect blend of strawberry and hops. Brynn watched her with what looked like amusement. She nodded.

"Yes. Especially because you're one of the most type A people I've ever met. Which is completely fine," she added hurriedly. "I'm type A, too. I make stacks of my stacks of things, and asymmetry is my mortal enemy. But you *really* like order and control. Works great for some things, probably not so much for others. Like, um . . ." She was searching for an example, but Emma already had one.

"Like having a life. Yeah."

Brynn thought that over, then grinned. It was only a little apologetic. "Maybe. But if nothing else, your You-

Tube moment proves that you're capable of making questionable decisions just like the rest of us. And it was definitely *not* boring."

Emma thought about it. "No," she said, lifting the glass back to her lips. "It wasn't."

"And you survived in one piece," Brynn pointed out. "So you don't really have anything to be afraid of."

"The gossip isn't fatal, no," Emma admitted. "I don't like it, but it isn't fatal. I honestly thought people would stop coming into the shop. Just . . . stop, you know? That doesn't seem to have happened yet, even if my sources tell me the rumor about Big Al and me streaking refuses to die. And even if I just heard a new variation where the house party was so wild that Aaron got arrested and I slept with Seth to avoid the same thing. Because I'm diabolical, apparently."

"I like that one," Brynn said. "It shows grit."

"Aaron likes it, too. He's the one who called and told me."

"From what I've seen of him, that doesn't really surprise me."

Emma sighed. "I just wish it would run its course already. I'm still getting texts from a couple of guys. *Still!* Is it that hard to take a hint? I work weekends. I don't go out. That night was like unicorn-sighting levels of unusual."

Their food arrived then, and Emma had to force herself not to just start shoveling the food in her mouth. She was irritated, unhappy, and starving. At least the company she'd chosen had turned out to be something of a comfort. That was a surprise, but a nice one, for once.

"You're discounting the thrill of the chase," Brynn said, wagging a French fry at her. "Some guys like that."

"And some guys are intolerable douchebags."

Brynn blinked, then burst out laughing. Emma realized how odd that had to sound to someone who only ever saw her "proper and buttoned-up" work persona. She tried to picture herself the way her sister teased her about being—like Mary Poppins without the sense of humor—and joined in the laughter when she imagined Mary herself calling random people douchebags.

"Well," she finally said, "it's true."

"No argument there. Though I've seen firsthand that you don't have a problem with *every* guy around here."

She felt her cheeks flushing. Why could she not maintain a normal face temperature whenever Seth came up? She could battle everyone from restaurant owners to the most wretched mother of the bride without even a twinge. But if Officer Sexy was mentioned? Flames.

Emma realized she'd just mentally called Seth "Officer Sexy," which didn't improve the situation.

"Why are you turning purple?" Brynn asked.

"I'm not," Emma replied, fanning herself with a napkin. "So, what are you referring to here? You mean that cupcake thing?"

"That," Brynn said, looking smug as she swirled another fry in ketchup, "and the very public display of 'I want to rip your clothes off' in the parking lot last week."

Emma had a sudden urge to crawl under the table and hide. *That's what happens when you make out in public, you idiot. Don't you remember the people who used to gross you out in high school? Honestly.* "Oh. You saw that?"

"I stayed late at work because of the rain. Don't worry—I ran back around the corner when I saw you. And waited. And *waited*." Brynn looked awfully entertained as she took a sip of her margarita. "Well done, by the way. He's hot."

"Um. Thanks."

"And you don't want to talk about it," Brynn said. "So we don't have to. Sorry," she said, looking anything but. "Just . . . it's nice to see you getting out a little." She laughed. "Maybe it'll rub off. The last couple of guys I went out with have been fails of epic proportions. One guy spent most of the evening explaining how his life plan involved living with his parents for at least another five years. I'm twenty-six. I don't have time for this shit."

"Seconded. It's worse at thirty." Emma raised her glass, and Brynn clinked it against her own.

"To not wasting our time," Brynn said. "Carpe diem, carpe noctem, and basically carpe whatever we want."

"No prisoners," Emma agreed, then drank deeply. When she lowered her glass, she regarded her assistant with fresh interest. "Tell me something. When I interviewed you for the job, you wanted it more than anyone else by a mile. Why? I'm a small-town event planner. We're growing, but we'll never be huge. What was the appeal? You gave me some canned answer at the time. I've always wondered what the answer really was. Especially because, despite your talent, you stayed."

Brynn appeared to think that over, tapping a fingernail against her glass. Finally, her big hazel eyes returned to Emma. "The reason I gave you was half of the truth. I love it here. It's home. The opportunity to stay and do what I love meant a lot."

"Okay. And the other half?"

"Honestly? I've been admiring your fashion sense for years. Anyone who can be as intimidating as you are while wearing both polka dots and a matching teal belt and shoes is a born leader. If I was going to learn, I wanted to learn from the best. And maybe pick up a few shopping tips."

"So, as long as my shoes stay fabulous, you'll follow me anywhere?"

"You got it."

Emma laughed softly. She knew it was a joke—sort of. But she also knew that Brynn wouldn't still be here if she didn't value the experience. Not only was that flattering to see so clearly; it was also a signal that if she wanted to keep her, she was going to have to stretch a little outside her comfort zone.

It was slightly less terrifying than usual. Probably because she seemed to be doing a lot of stretching lately.

Emma took a big bite of her giant burger, savoring the stinging heat on her tongue. Once she was finished chewing, she looked across the table with the most serious expression she could muster. It was enough, since Brynn paled. It made her wonder just how intimidating she usually came off, even when it was just the two of them. Then she thought she might not want to know. Emma forced herself to soften the expression.

"Two things," she said. "One, I think it's time to start letting you take the lead on some things. Not *everything*," she added hurriedly, "but I take on a lot of the workload when I don't have to. And I don't share well. I know this." She folded her hands, unfolded them, and then started playing with one of the fresh hush puppies.

Brynn, on the other hand, looked thrilled. "That would be amazing! I mean, if you're comfortable with it. Because I understand about the sharing thing. And if we're just doing the friend thing tonight, I can absolutely agree with you. No, you are not good at sharing."

Emma gave a snort of laughter. "Fair enough. I'm not comfortable with anything, really. Not at first," she admitted. "But this is something that needs to happen. So we'll work on it."

Brynn's red ponytail bobbed with her vigorous nodding. Her assistant's excitement would help her let go of the control a little, Emma told herself. At least, it had better, or this would be an ugly exercise in futility. "Second," Emma said, holding up a finger, "how do you feel about shopping?"

"Shopping? Like, clothes shopping?"

"Yes. If it involved someone who was maybe a little controlling but incredibly classy. And has good taste. And wants to go buy some summer dresses in the near future."

Brynn stuck her hand out across the table. Emma looked at it for a second, puzzled, until the other woman waved it up and down. "Are we going to shake on this or what? It's a deal."

It wasn't what she'd expected. None of today had been. But as Emma grasped Brynn's hand and shook, she wondered why she hadn't attempted these small steps outside of her comfort zone before. Not all the results had been good, but for the first time, she was forced to consider whether the benefits in taking a risk once in a while might not outweigh the potential for catastrophe. For all that losing the Harding wedding had been a gut punch, it had also been a wake-up call.

She just needed to muscle past the fear. She wasn't there yet . . . but it felt like she was making a start. Emma thought of Seth, and of his whisper—*"Soon"*—and decided that as long as she was on a roll, it might not be a bad idea to take one more risk today. Whether that conversation ended up being a triumph or a complete debacle, at least she'd wake up tomorrow knowing where things stood in the Amazing Life of Emma Henry.

"Deal," she said, then pulled her hand away, feeling a strange sense of triumph. Even a small change in her world was a big deal. A risk. She knew just how much she had to lose, and she knew what it felt like to have holes left in you that refused to heal. Still, nothing that had happened since her now-legendary performance at Sam's party had turned out to be the world-ending event she'd expected. The rumors were ridiculous. Today's rejection had stung, badly. But she'd met Seth, who seemed interested in her despite her horrible romantic instincts. And as Brynn's cheerful chatter about an upcoming sale at a favorite upscale clothing store washed over her, Emma had to admit that this didn't feel dangerous or scary, either.

It simply felt like moving forward, a sensation she'd nearly forgotten.

And better, it felt like gaining a friend.

Chapter Eleven

He'd almost forgotten what it felt like to have a day this bad.

Seth slunk into his kitchen, popped a couple of aspirin, and wandered back out to the family room to flop in his favorite chair and stare blindly at the television. His cheek and eye throbbed, and the tenderness told him he was going to have one hell of a black eye in the morning. That alone would have made it a less than stellar day, but the e-mail he'd had waiting for him after work had been the icing on the cake.

He looked up at the ridiculous picture above his fireplace, remembering a different day, a phone call. *One more gone. Shit.*

He wasn't sure how long he sat there as the room grew dark, staring at the flickering images on the television without really seeing them. Everything he'd held at bay, the sorrow, the anger, the guilt, settled on him like a comfortable old overcoat. He let it stay, having learned that sometimes, you just had to sit with the feelings and let them have their way with you awhile before you could put them away again.

The knock at the door echoed through the quiet house like a gunshot, and he hit the floor without thinking. A split second later he'd shoved his face into his hands, feeling foolish. He'd been too deep in his own head, in a place thousands of miles from here, and had the old reaction. All things considered, it could be a lot worse. The war had changed him, but it had left him basically intact, with a few odd little quirks thrown in for good measure. He knew he was lucky.

But that hadn't banished the guilt. Especially not on days like today.

Seth got quickly to his feet, turned off the TV, and glanced out the window on his way to the door. The streetlights had come on, and the sky bore only a faint, final trace of the sunset. A sleek little sports car, one he knew well, was parked in his driveway. It made his steps falter. As much as he wanted to see her, as curious as he was about what had brought her to his door, a part of him just wanted to drift in his own melancholy for a while and then go to bed. He was tired. Maybe too tired for another round with Emma the Inscrutable tonight. She might surprise him with another kiss. Then again, she was just as likely to tell him to stay the hell away from her if he couldn't keep his paws to himself, no matter that she'd been the instigator.

In the end, his own impossible attraction won out. He took a deep, cleansing breath and opened the door.

She stood on his doorstep in a small circle of light, her hands folded uncomfortably in front of her. She was in one of her classy work getups, a little gray suit with a flared skirt and a skinny red belt that drew his eyes right to her tiny waist. An equally red pair of heels made her legs the next destination for his attention before he lifted his gaze back to her pale heart-shaped face. Her eyes seemed enormous, the bright blue of the ocean on a calm, clear day.

"Oh my God, what happened?"

"Hazards of handling a domestic dispute solo. His wife got it worse." He shrugged, but his response didn't seem to satisfy Emma, who started to lift her hands to his face before stopping halfway, biting her lip, and shoving her hands behind her back. It was just as well—he wasn't sure that her touching him was a great idea right now, mostly because he wanted her to so badly. Last night had been fun, not to mention surprisingly easy. He wasn't in the mood for fun, though, and Emma was nowhere near as comfortable with him on her own. The last thing he needed tonight was more frustration.

"Does it hurt?" she asked.

"Yeah, like a son of a bitch," Seth replied. "I had some ice on it afterward. Took aspirin. I'll live." He looked down at her, curious. Her hair was down, falling in dark waves around her shoulders. For him? Or just for comfort? She never wore it down to work. He hated himself a little for knowing that . . . and a little more for immediately imagining plunging his hands into all that thick, soft, silken hair.

Not a great night for this, Andersen.

"What can I do for you, Emma?" he asked. "I'd invite you in, but I'm pretty beat."

"Oh," she said, "that's okay. Um. I'll just . . . I'll catch you a different time. I just thought . . . You know what, never mind. You're hurt. I'll just go."

Her hands fluttered around her as she spoke, her cheeks turning a deep pink, and Seth sensed that sending her away would amount to a missed opportunity he'd be kicking himself for tomorrow. Turning up here on her own wasn't something he'd expected from her. It might not be something he'd get again if he sent her off. He knew he made her nervous, and he also knew that wasn't Emma's preferred state of being.

Seth sighed, relenting. "Emma. Come inside."

"I don't want to bother you if you need to rest, Seth. It's fine."

"No, I'm just a little grumpy. Getting punched in the face will do that to you. But if you can deal with that, then come on in. Maybe some company will be good for me."

She didn't look entirely sure about that, and he didn't blame her, but he also knew she wasn't apt to run from a challenge. When she took a small step forward, Seth knew he'd been right.

"Okay," she said. "But don't feel bad about telling me when you want me to take off."

The corner of his mouth curved up. "I won't. Come on in."

Emma knew something was off the second he opened the door.

It wasn't just the black eye, which looked painful. It was the expression on his face. Seth looked tired, almost haunted. She'd gotten used to his smile, she realized, and the sense that whatever was going on around him, he tended to keep a sense of humor about it. Tonight, though, dressed in a ratty old pair of athletic shorts and a T-shirt that looked like it was only barely hanging on, Seth no longer seemed like the affable knight in shining armor.

Maybe giving in to impulse and coming here had been a mistake. She'd been cruising on the good vibes from her dinner with Brynn, somehow sure they'd overflow onto the rest of her evening, whatever she chose to do with it. This wasn't what she'd been hoping for . . . but it was too late to turn around and bolt for the car.

"You want a soda or anything?" he asked, flipping on a light. Emma looked around, unsettled. Had he just been sitting here in the dark?

"No, I'm fine," she said. "Seth, really, I can go—"

"Stay," he interrupted her. He must have heard the harsh edge in his own voice, because he softened it when he spoke again. "Really. I'm not enjoying my own company tonight, but there's no reason I can't enjoy yours."

He looked so lost, she thought, startled as she was by the force of the feelings that barreled into her. She wanted to know what was wrong, and she wanted to fix it. Now. Because in here, with just the two of them, his sadness seemed to fill up all the extra space. As she watched, Seth sank onto the couch and settled in, stretching out his legs. One of the legs of his shorts rode up enough to expose a muscled thigh, which flexed as he got comfortable. The sight of such a small bit of skin immediately began doing some interesting things to her ability to breathe.

When she lifted her eyes to his, he was watching her intently, and she was sure he knew exactly what she'd been staring at. She felt herself flush, the heat rushing through her system like wildfire. It was different now that he'd kissed her. Now that she'd kissed him. The tension between them was heavy with the sorts of possibilities Emma had been determined not to entertain where he was concerned.

But somehow, here she was. And she'd come to him.

It made her question her sanity, among other things. And this time, she couldn't think of a single, plausible excuse.

"Why don't you sit?" he asked. His mouth curved in a ghost of a smile. "I don't bite, no matter how bad I look."

Emma laughed nervously and tucked a lock of hair behind her ear. "You don't look bad. Just injured." *And you look like you'd happily take a bite out of me. What worries me is that I think I might like it.*

She looked at the couch, then at the leather recliner near it, had a brief debate about just how much of a chicken she was going to be, and finally hurried to the couch to perch at the far edge of it. She felt like an ass, but it did prompt the first flicker of genuine amusement across Seth's face. He shook his head and chuckled.

"You're something else, Emma."

"What's that supposed to mean?"

"You know exactly what I mean." He shifted, wincing a little. His face had to hurt, Emma knew. Sam had given her a black eye once when they were kids, when Emma had decided that one of Sam's masterpieces really needed stick people added to it—in black paint. Sam had ended up grounded, but Emma was pretty sure Sam had never regretted getting even.

Flustered, Emma cast around for something to talk about besides her own obvious apprehension. Her latest disaster seemed as good a starting point as any. "I didn't get the Harding wedding," she said. As a distraction, it worked like a charm. Seth frowned, made a soft, pained sound, and then settled on an expression that was more polite concern.

"No way," he said. "I figured you had that in the bag."

"Nope. I went down in flames. Didn't ask the right people the right questions."

That seemed to surprise him. "Yeah? I thought you knew everything about everyone around here. More of a party oracle than a party planner. No?"

She bunched up her fist at him. "Keep kicking me while I'm down. Really."

Seth tilted his head at her. "Actually, you seem like you're in a pretty good mood. That's why I'm surprised you didn't get the job. Something else happen to cancel that out? Lottery win, or maybe you finally went streaking with Big Al for real?"

Emma wrinkled her nose at him. "Getting naked and running around downtown wouldn't put me in a good mood."

"I hear it's therapeutic," Seth replied. He flexed his fingers absently against the leather of the couch. "So don't leave me guessing. This is two days in a row I've seen that smile. You seem to save that for special occasions, so . . . a diabolical plot to take over the world, maybe? Or were you eating burned marshmallows before you got here?"

"No!" But she laughed. "I did think about the marshmallows, but . . . no. The Harding thing stinks, honestly. I'll probably obsess about it later. But I had a nice dinner with Brynn. I'm giving her more responsibilities, and we're going shopping. It was productive." She lifted a shoulder, smiled. "It was also fun. I'm not sure why we didn't do it before. Apparently I'm not that approachable. Who knew?"

That finally got a real smile out of him. "So you gave her more work, and she wants to hang out. Obviously this was meant to be."

"I guess. It'll be fun. Hopefully. I don't do things with other people much. I mean, non-work-related things. You know." She breathed deeply, looked around the room, and tried not to stiffen up. She wished she could stop saying things around him that would make normal people walk quickly away in the other direction. Maybe she should just get a button that said HI, I'M SOCIALLY IMPAIRED! TALK TO ME AT YOUR OWN RISK! and be done with it. At least then people would know what they were getting into.

"No, I get it. I'm like that."

Emma looked sharply at him, eyebrow raised. "You? I watched you last night. You're completely friendly. And you don't stick your foot in your mouth every time you open it."

"So we have stylistic differences."

Emma rolled her eyes. "Right. 'Awkward loner' is a style, then?"

"You weren't either one of those things last night. You're not awkward when you're working, either," he pointed out. "You're cool and collected. And from what I hear, a little scary."

"That's competent, not scary. And I'm good at work. It's the one thing I *am* good at."

Seth snorted softly. "Wrong."

"No, I'm not," Emma replied. She dug the toes of her heels into the rug and propped her elbows on her knees, resting her chin on her fist as she frowned at him. She must have looked funny, since she got another smile, not broad but warm. Still, she couldn't shake the feeling that something was wrong.

"So why are you having such a bad night?" she asked.

Seth looked at her blandly. "It's not obvious? My face hurts. And no jokes—I heard enough of them at the station."

"I know. That's not what I meant, though. You seem down. That's all. I wouldn't think some jerk punching you would bother you so much."

She was right. She knew it when he looked away from her. There was more; he just didn't want to share. And why would he? They hardly knew each other, and she hadn't exactly been easy to talk to since they'd met. Not about anything important, anyway. She nibbled at her lower lip, wondering how to draw him out. This was her annoying compulsion to fix things, she knew. But she couldn't help it.

"Well, I'm not always Mr. Sunshine. Sorry."

Whatever was wrong, he hadn't been lying about one thing: He was grouchy. Part of her wanted to snap back at him. The other part was relieved that perfect, gorgeous Seth Andersen had some flaws, too. For some reason, rather than putting her on edge, it helped her relax. Flaws were comforting. She had plenty of experience dealing with her own. Seth winced again and closed his eyes with a pained sigh. Emma watched him, utterly sympathetic. There was a cut by his eye, probably from a ring. It couldn't be helping. She tried to think of something she might be able to do. It only seemed right, considering what Seth had done for her. Fuzzy though the memories were, she did remember him holding her hair, rubbing her back, and consoling her while she was violently ill.

"How's your neck?" she asked. There was only one thing she could think of, and given his mood, there was the distinct possibility he would tell her to take off. Still, while soothing wasn't her forte, she knew firsthand that in some ways she was capable enough.

"Stiff," Seth replied, his voice grittier. "Kind of like the rest of my face right now. Maybe you should go, Em. I'm just going to end up hurting your feelings or pissing you off, and you deserve better than both."

Hearing her nickname out of his mouth startled her, but in a way that left her with a sweet warmth that made her even more determined to help him. It didn't matter what his problem was. It only mattered that she could likely help him, if only a little. She was nervous about touching him, but that was her problem. She'd deal. This wasn't about her, and for once, she was glad of it.

"I can help," she said. "If you let me."

He opened one eye to look at her. "How's that?"

"I can rub the stiffness out of your neck and shoulders. I'm good at it," she added hastily when he opened the other eye to regard her with a look she couldn't fathom. "I used to do it for my mother all the time when Dad was sick. She said it helped. I have strong hands, I . . ." *Way to leave an opening, Emma.* "Please don't make fun."

To his credit, he looked surprised that she would even think that was a possibility. "I won't," he said. He looked at her hard for a moment. "Really? That would be great, but don't feel like—"

"I wouldn't offer if I didn't mean it," she said, more sharply than she'd intended to. It was habit, this reaction to being questioned, and one she knew she needed to work on. Especially where Seth was concerned. At least he didn't seem to take offense.

"Okay," Seth said, looking around. "Well, ah . . . where do you want me?"

There was a quick flash of the smile that melted her, sending her mind directly into the gutter. *Oh, you have no idea.* Out loud, however, she tried to cling to her dignity as best she could.

"You could sit on the floor in front of the chair," she said. "Or grab a pillow and lie on the floor. Either wa—"

He was off the couch and out of the room before she could finish her sentence, which she supposed was enough of an answer. "If you've got muscle ointment, you might want to bring that, too," she called after him as he disappeared upstairs. She slipped off her heels while she listened to him fumbling around upstairs, her heart quickening just a little.

This is completely innocent. You're doing something

nice for him because he's hurt, she thought. Unfortunately, she was as bad at lying to herself as she was at lying to anyone else. She really did want to help. She also really wanted to touch him without looking like she was all about touching him, so this was perfect.

Seth hurried back downstairs with a pillow tucked beneath one arm and a tube of ointment in his hand. When his eyes met hers, he smiled, and it was the first time she'd seen him genuinely happy since she'd arrived. Apparently he was really easy to please.

"That was quick," she said.

"You're going to understand why when you start," he said. "I've been putting off finding a masseuse around here, but I really need to. I had one back in Florida."

He dropped the pillow in the middle of the rug, and without an ounce of hesitation dragged his shirt over his head. Emma forgot to breathe. She may have forgotten her own name for a few seconds. It was one thing to ogle good-looking guys in movies, but this was a living, breathing male now shirtless just a few feet away, and in her opinion, he was completely perfect. His gold-dusted skin rippled over lean, tightly corded muscle as he moved. Emma drank him in, savoring the way his chest tapered down to a narrow waist, the dusting of dark hair from his navel to somewhere beneath the waistband of his shorts. Tattooed on his right biceps was a raven in flight, simple and black and beautiful.

Seth seemed oblivious to the admiration. He crouched down and lay on his stomach, burying his face in the pillow.

"Ready when you are," he mumbled from deep in the fabric.

Emma looked at him, prone and completely at her mercy, and wondered how exactly she was supposed to get through this without dying of embarrassment. She'd never given a guy a back rub. She never gave anyone back rubs. It involved a lot of touching, which she tended to be reserved about with all but those closest to her. Still, this had been her idea, and Seth was certainly enthusiastic about it once she'd insisted. After a moment of consideration, she got up, walked over to him, and hiked up her skirt to sink carefully down on her knees beside him.

She picked up the little tube lying beside him and opened it, rubbing the mint-scented ointment over her palms while she tried to come up with a plan of attack. She'd come this far. Running wasn't an option, so she supposed there was nothing for it but to follow through and hope she didn't burst into flames from shame, lust, or some unholy combination of the two.

Tentatively, she put her hands on the tightly bunched muscles between his neck and shoulders and began to knead. Seth groaned, and she knew right away why this had appealed to him.

"How do you walk around like this?" she asked. "You're completely knotted up!"

She dug her fingers in and began to work at the knots, grateful to have a problem to focus on. It kept her from thinking too deeply about her hands being on his bare skin. He muttered something unintelligible.

"What?"

Seth turned his face to the side, his eyes remaining closed. "I get kind of tense."

"You hide it well," Emma replied, rubbing circles into the back of his neck with her thumbs. The muscles snapped beneath them. "If this hurts, I'll let up."

"No," he said quickly. "This is good. It always hurts before they loosen up."

They fell into a silence that was surprisingly comfortable, Seth's breathing slow and rhythmic while Emma worked on him. With tension like this, it was no wonder he used to go for regular massages, she thought. It was hard to believe that all this could be from stress—he always seemed so calm. Much calmer than she was. It made her wonder about him, all the parts of his life before this. She'd gotten a little of the abbreviated version, but it had told her almost nothing that she really wanted to know.

Her hands moved over him, kneading, rubbing, her hands warming to the task. Seth hissed when she found another nasty knot in his right shoulder.

"*Shit*. Right there. Don't stop."

His voice was a little slurred, and his words, spoken in the haze of some combination of pain and pleasure, sent Emma into a fit of giggles she couldn't seem to hold back. She tried. Desperately. But after biting her lip nearly hard enough to break the skin and hoping the shaking of her shoulders wasn't something he'd notice, a few breathless gasps of laughter escaped anyway. One eye opened to look at her.

"What's funny?"

"You."

A half frown. "Hey." But he didn't seem offended, only vaguely amused. "I'm just lying here."

"I just thought, you know, if someone came to the door and heard you . . ." She pictured it and started laughing again. "Another chapter in my new life as a shameless harlot."

Seth's eye closed, but she got a big smile in exchange, along with a soft huff of laughter. "You have a dirty mind under all that polish. I knew I liked you."

She flushed, but her smile remained.

"You're good at this." He sighed. "Hands tired?"

"No." In fact, she thought she might be able to do this for hours as long as it was Seth. He made her nervous enough normally that she hadn't expected to ever feel powerful around him. But that was exactly how she felt, unsure though she was of her actual talents in this area. He responded to every nuance of her touch, his muscles tightening and then relaxing, soft hisses and relieved sighs escaping his lips every now and then. She knew it was foolish, but right here and now, just the two of them, Emma felt as though Seth was hers in a way no one had ever been. Hers to touch. To take care of. To keep.

No. Look at his eye. He's got a dangerous job. That little injury is just the tip of the iceberg. You can't fix everything, Emma. And some hurts can't be healed.

Her smile faded, and she dug her fingers in a little harder.

"Ouch!" Seth flinched. "Could you, ah, just a little lighter right there. Ow."

"Sorry." Emma immediately gentled her fingers. "Forgot what I was doing."

"It's okay." He shifted a little, and she moved her hands slightly farther down his back, kneading taut muscles that gave a little more readily as she worked them. "You said you used to do this for your mom?"

"Yes. My dad had cancer. We had hospice come to the house, near the end, and Mom sat with him all the time. She was so afraid he'd leave without her being right there." The memory could still make her ache with the old sadness. As long ago as it had been, she remembered it so clearly. Everything in their house seemed to have become muffled, every sound, every feeling—there had been a sense of stillness all the time, of waiting, accompanied by a faint medical smell that still made her avoid hospitals like the plague. "Anyway," she continued, "Mom was so tired, and she used to fall asleep in chairs and things, despite being under more stress than I could even comprehend. I didn't know how to help. I didn't know how to do anything. But one day her neck was in complete misery, and she asked if I could get at this one spot she couldn't reach." Emma remembered it well, how happy it had made her to be able to do even a small thing that could make her mother smile. "I was hired. And that was that."

"How old were you?"

"Twelve."

"That's pretty rough."

"Yes. It was." It was odd to talk about it. She didn't think she'd said so much on the subject for years. After everything, after the funeral, and the grief counseling, and the endless condolences, she, Sam, and their mother had just . . . put it away. The grieving had been so exhausting that there had come a day when they'd all just wanted to change the subject. Not that the pain hadn't lingered. There'd just been nothing left to say.

"And you're the older child, right? You probably looked out for your sister even before all that."

"Sam would call it 'bossing,' but yes, as much as she'd let me. She was stubborn, though. We have very different ways of dealing with things." She looked at his closed eyes, his dark lashes twined together. "Why?"

"I'm just interested." His eye opened just a bit to look at her. "In you."

Just like that, she was flustered all over again. How she could stay completely cool in combative business situations but be unable to deal with a compliment from a good-looking—okay, hot—man was one of her life's greatest mysteries. Though in her defense, she didn't get a lot of interest from hot men in the first place. It wasn't like she could practice.

"Oh. Well, um, what about you?" she asked, wanting the spotlight off herself. "Any personal tragedies I can pry into to discover the inner you?"

He chuckled, his back moving beneath her hands. "No."

"Can you at least tell me why you were so upset tonight?"

He went quiet, and Emma had just decided he was going to ignore the question when his voice rumbled up from where his face was half-buried in the pillow. "An old army buddy of mine killed himself. I got an e-mail from his sister."

Her hands stilled. "Oh. I'm sorry, Seth."

"Me, too. We were never great about keeping in touch, but it was always good when we talked. I knew he was dealing with some things. I just didn't think ... I don't know." He exhaled heavily and fell silent.

She chewed at her lip, completely at a loss for what to say. One of the things about having been a relative hermit in her personal life for so long was that she'd avoided having to deal too closely with other people's feelings—particularly the bad feelings. Parties were happy events, by and large, even if the planning could make people less than pleasant sometimes, and in any case, she was just the woman behind the curtain. Her level of emotional investment was different.

With Seth, she was reminded of exactly how little she could do in the face of someone else's pain. A part of her, a part she was instantly ashamed of, wanted to run away from it. But a different part, one she was surprised to find existed, pushed her to stay. To try, even if she had no idea what she was doing.

"Do you want to talk about it?" she asked quietly.

Seth rolled onto his back, rearranging himself so that he looked up at her from where he lay on the pillow. She'd lifted her hands away, but he took them gently in his and brought them down again, holding them against his chest. She could feel the steady beat of his heart as he studied her, his eyes dark and serious.

"Not really," he said.

Emma pressed her lips together and exhaled, frustrated. Being here like this, kneeling beside him with her hands against his heart, somehow felt like the most intimate position she'd ever been in with a man. But despite that, and despite the way he'd prompted her to tell him about one of her oldest, deepest wounds with so little effort, he was going to hold back. That it annoyed her was her own problem, not his, Emma thought. But it also made her realize something, something she would have thought impossible even a week ago.

I want more.

More of him. More from him. Just . . . more. And though it was as terrifying a thing as she'd been confronted with in years, Emma knew herself well enough to understand that it wasn't something she could just banish. And because she apparently had a masochistic streak, Seth seemed like he was going to be more like Shrek than Prince Charming— layered, like an onion.

A fixer-upper. Great.

She really wasn't sure her fixing abilities worked on humans. They hadn't worked at all on her.

"What are you thinking about up there?" Seth asked, drawing her back into the moment. At least it was a good moment, she decided. Half-naked man, her hands on him, no company. Bad for strategizing, but good for other things. Things she really needed to consider before jumping onto—er, into anything.

"I was thinking that I'd like to see you again," she said.

One eyebrow quirked up, as did a corner of his mouth. "Oh yeah? Like an actual date? Not just for public consumption?"

She gave him a self-deprecating smirk. "Yeah. The fake-date thing was a bad idea."

"The hell you say."

She liked him this way, playful and sweet. She just wished he'd let her see the rest of what was underneath, the bone-deep sadness she'd seen when he'd opened the door. She understood that feeling, even if he wouldn't say much about what had inspired it.

Patience, she thought. Too bad she'd never had much.

"Well, as my sister would say, I'm practically perfect in every way . . . but every once in a while even I can screw up."

"Your sister thinks you're Mary Poppins?" Seth asked. He looked her up and down so thoroughly that Emma felt like he'd stripped every shred of clothing off her. Her skin heated, but she tried to keep her tone light.

"Minus the sense of humor. And the magic carpetbag."

"I kind of like the idea of you in a petticoat," Seth replied. "You should try that."

"I'm starting to think you have some weird fetishes," Emma said, trying to pull her hands away. He tugged them back, and a hazy memory surfaced of copping a cheap feel of Aaron's chest at Sam's party. This was so much better.

I'm never going to get anywhere with him if all I ever do is react to him, she thought. It was just hard to do anything *but* react when he was spread out before her like this. Strategizing would have to come later. When she could think straight.

At this point, that might be *much* later.

"No weird fetishes," Seth said, mischief glittering in his eyes. "But you know what I do have a thing for?"

She knew she was playing into his hands, but Emma shook her head. "No."

"Classy little suits," he said, letting go of one of her hands to lightly grasp one of her lapels and run his hand down it, the back of his knuckles grazing her breast. Her heart stumbled in her chest, then began to quicken.

"Oh?" she asked innocently. Seth nodded.

"Suits," he said. His hand moved to toy with the ends of her hair, sliding it through his fingers. "Brunettes," he continued, giving the hair a light tug. Emma hesitated for only a moment before obliging him, leaning down so that her mouth was just a breath away from his, her hair sliding over the bare skin of his chest.

In for a penny, in for a pound.

"Suits and brunettes," she said softly, one hand braced beside his head. "That's a little weird, but not too bad. Anything else?"

Seth nodded, and the look in his eyes was strangely uncertain even as his lips parted in a fleeting smile.

"Yeah. You."

"Now that is definitely weird," Emma said, hardly believing that she was taking such a risk. "But I'll see what I can do."

Chapter Twelve

It was the second time she'd kissed him on purpose, but Emma knew from the moment her lips touched his that this kiss carried an entirely different meaning. The stolen kiss in her mother's hallway had been innocent—well, mostly innocent.

This one was anything but.

Seth's lips parted beneath hers instantly, his tongue darting out to tease hers. She played along, light tastes, flickering strokes of her tongue against his. It was gentle, playful, but with her hand still trapped against his chest, Emma could feel the beat of Seth's heart pick up to match her own. She felt his hand tuck her hair behind her ear, then trace a path down her cheek. It was a light touch, and heartbreakingly gentle. It made her wonder what he felt, whether he would ever tell her. There was time, she thought.

Except sometimes there wasn't. She knew it well, and that knowledge had colored every aspect of her life. Even now, as she flattened her palm against his chest, as he allowed her to slowly slide it down the length of his torso without letting go, she felt the same wild desperation that had always driven her to either hang on so tight it hurt, or to run while she could.

Instinct said run. But he was so warm, and the kiss was the kind of bliss she had only imagined. Emma couldn't pull away.

She sank into it, savoring the way his breath caught when her fingers played over his stomach, down, then up again. She loved the way he was built, slight but strong. And she'd spent far too much time imagining what he would look like, feel like, if she ever got brave enough to see beneath his uniform. Seth released her hand to hook a finger in her belt and pull.

"Come down here with me," he murmured against her lips. "Wouldn't want you to get uncomfortable."

She smiled. "Very chivalrous of you."

"You're lucky I was good at English or I'd think you'd just insulted me."

"Hmm," she said, shifting onto her side, unfolding her legs, and stretching out alongside Seth on the floor. Knowing he watched her, she took an extra few seconds to adjust her skirt, then offered an amused smile. The new position was more comfortable . . . at least in some ways. "I think you like my vocabulary. I think it's an aphrodisiac."

His soft laugh rippled over her skin, making her shiver while he made room for her head on the pillow beside him. "Sure. Your having your hands all over me for the last half hour had nothing to do with it."

"Shh," Emma said as she snuggled up against him, pressing a finger to his lips. "Don't shatter my illusions, please."

She could feel his smile, and he kissed her fingertip. It was a small, sweet gesture that managed to silence every doubt she had. They would no doubt return in force at some point, but for now, there was only silence. Emma wanted to enjoy it while she could.

Now that he had her where he wanted her, Seth pulled her in close, taking her mouth in a series of long, languid kisses that captured Emma more fully with every beat of the slow and sensuous rhythm they created. One of his hands slid up to brush against her hair, down her neck, his touch excruciatingly light. Emma pressed into him, offering what she hoped was silent encouragement. She stroked over his waist, up his back, tangling her fingers in the brushy softness of his hair. Every time he drew in a sharper breath, every time he moved against her, she waited for Seth's touch to lose its gentleness. Instead, his tender, teasing assault on her senses continued until it was all Emma could do not to writhe against him and beg for his touch.

Desperate, she managed to unbuckle her belt and undo the buttons on her jacket, stripping both off quickly to reveal the thin camisole beneath. Her breasts felt fuller, tighter, the nipples taut little buds that sent tiny shocks through her system each time they rubbed against Seth's chest. When his breathing grew a little harsher, she nearly growled in triumph. Her clothes chafed her skin, demanding to be shed despite Seth's apparent disinterest in removing them.

Maybe I'm moving too fast. Maybe I'm losing my mind. Maybe celibacy has actually destroyed some brain cells.

When her patience with him was stretched to the breaking point, Emma decided that nonverbal communication was getting her nowhere. She pulled back from the kiss, rose up on one elbow, and found herself staring into eyes so hazed with need that she wasn't sure whether to kiss him, kick him, or start removing his pants to save them both further agony.

"Are we going to have sex?" she demanded breathlessly.

"God, I hope so," Seth groaned, his voice strained.

"Okay," Emma said. "Because I'm going to start ripping off my clothes soon, and I didn't want you to get upset."

Seth's laughter was hoarse. "I didn't want *you* to get upset. You can take off anything you want to. I think I might die. Jesus."

"Why would I get upset?"

"I don't know. It's new. I didn't want you to leave. Can we analyze this later? I can see it was a bad decision now, and I'd like to get back to the clothes-off thing."

Leave it to her to find the last white knight on the planet. Desire pushed her to be more blunt than she would ever have imagined being in this situation. "Seth," she said, cupping his flushed cheek with her hand, "just so we're clear. I want you. Hard. Bad. Now."

He made a soft, strangled sound in the back of his throat, and Emma had only a split second to wonder what she'd just asked for before she was on her back, Seth covering her completely. Emma barely had time to gasp before his mouth was on hers, and this time the kiss held nothing back. It was everything she'd demanded, hard and hot, until there was no doubt left about what he wanted to do to her.

Emma had visions of coming off as a sex goddess, but she managed to get tangled in her cami while attempting to pull it off. To his credit, Seth didn't miss a beat when he got her out of it, and he managed to toss her bra across the room with it just a second or two afterward. Emma heard it hit the window, and she laughed into the kiss.

"I should have asked sooner."

"Next time just jump me. I'm good with that." He pulled back to cup her breasts in his hands, his breath ragged as he teased the tight buds of her nipples with his thumbs. "You really are perfect." Emma couldn't muster a comeback, instead just arching into his touch, her head falling back. This was what she'd wanted, she thought. This sweet ache, building into even sweeter oblivion.

Then his mouth closed over one nipple, beginning to suckle her. One hand slipped between her legs, pushing aside the thin fabric of her underwear to toy gently with the swollen nub beneath. When his tongue began to flicker against her skin, moving in time with his talented fingers, Emma's mouth opened on a wordless cry as her first orgasm arrowed straight through her. She surged against him, hips quivering as she rode out every hot pulse of her climax. Seth raised his head to watch her, his expression one of wonder.

Stunned and shaken at her body's reaction to him, she could only muster a single word: "Please."

He vanished, silent as a cat, and it seemed like only seconds before he was back, though it was just long enough for her to regain some semblance of rational thought. There was a small wrapper in his hand, and his pants had vacated the premises. Emma let her eyes roam freely over every glorious inch of exposed skin, glad that even her fantasies had paled in comparison to the real thing. His skin was the same gold-dusted shade all over, his thighs tightly corded muscle. And there was no question how badly he wanted her.

She slid her skirt off, glad to finally be rid of it, but when she started to do the same with her black silk panties, Seth held up his hand. "Wait." He shook his head, and she'd never felt so beautiful as she did when he looked at her. "I really like you in those, so just . . . wait."

He knelt between her legs, kissing each knee, then pushed them apart and lowered himself over her.

"Oh," she breathed when his hips pressed against her once, and then again, the hot length of his cock sliding against the silk and creating a delicious friction between them. Seth echoed her on a shuddering moan. Braced above her, his eyes closed, lips parted, he was the embodiment of all her wildest fantasies, lost in her just as she was lost in him. He continued to move, thrusting against her, varying the rhythm while Emma lifted her hips into him. The thin scrap of fabric between them was both barrier and enticement, facilitating the sweetest torment Emma could have imagined. Every tight circle, every long, hard thrust had her swelling tighter and tighter, pulsing against him. And he watched her; she knew he did. She could feel him taking in every whimper, every gasp—and she was too far under his spell to mind.

He took her to the precipice again, until she was shaking. When he moved away, Emma opened her eyes enough to watch him sit back on his knees and tear open the little package. When he was done, she looked at him and slowly, deliberately slipped the panties off, tossing them aside. Then she spread her legs wider, an invitation.

"Now," she said. *Please, now.*

Seth entered her in one swift thrust, burying himself so deeply that she clenched around him, crying out. He tensed and went still, though Emma could feel the tension pouring off him in waves. His voice was halting, choked.

"God. So tight, Emma. Need a minute."

When he looked at her, his eyes full of the strain of clinging to control, she realized that it had been a while for both of them, not just her. And knowing that, knowing this wasn't something he was taking lightly, undid a hard knot of tension she hadn't even realized she'd been carrying deep in her chest. She didn't want to be alone in the feelings that raced through her system like wildfire. She wanted this to matter to him—because he mattered to her.

He dropped his head to her shoulder, taking in deep breaths. She tried not to move, but her entire body now seemed to throb with the beat of her heart, so close to flying. Slowly, Seth withdrew, then sank into her again with a groan. Emma began to urge him on, sliding her hands down to his hips, letting him set the pace but asking, not so subtly, for more. His pace quickened, quickened until Seth was driving into her, shoulders tense, making the sexy little sounds in the back of his throat that pushed Emma right back to the edge.

She fisted one hand in the rug, while the other dug her nails into his hip. Emma lost all sense of anything but the two of them—all of her thought and feeling seemed to have narrowed down to a single, onrushing point of light. She arched, seeking release, and looked into Seth's face as he strained to hold back, to let her find her pleasure first. He was, in the moment, the most beautiful thing she'd ever seen.

Mine, she thought, as something deep inside tightened painfully, then began to crumble and fall away. She didn't have time to worry over it, though—not now—because of Seth's shaken voice.

"Em. Now. Right now."

He slammed into her hard, and she cried out his name as the world exploded into tiny fragments of light, leaving nothing but the sense that nothing existed but the two of them, clinging to each other in the heart of a perfect storm.

*   *   *

Seth wasn't sure how long he lay there on his floor. It could have been hours, days even. The only thing he was sure of was the woman draped across his chest, her head tucked beneath his chin, breathing deeply.

He'd dozed after sex, then was startled to awaken and find her still there. Apparently, some part of him had been convinced he'd invented the evening as an escape from the day's misery. But no—Emma was very much present. And while he held her, trying to figure out exactly how they'd gone from dancing around each other to naked in the middle of his floor in the space of a few hours, she started to snore lightly. Seth looked down at the top of her head and laughed softly. She was unlike any woman he'd ever been with. And as he'd suspected, she looked amazing naked.

Whatever had shifted in the universe to allow his day to do a complete one-eighty, he was grateful for it.

Seth gently stroked her hair, long and silky. Emma didn't wake up, though she snuggled in a bit deeper. He'd grabbed an old afghan from the closet in the immediate aftermath and thrown it over the two of them. It was plenty warm, though the floor had ceased to be particularly comfortable. Or at least, he was once again capable of noticing that the floor was kind of hard. His face was starting to throb again, too, another unpleasant reminder that he couldn't stay in this nice little bubble forever. No matter how much he wanted to.

With a healthy amount of regret, he kissed her head and then gave her shoulder a squeeze. "Em. Emma. Emma? Earth to Emma?"

She didn't stir. Yet another piece of information to file away about Emma Henry—the woman slept like the dead. Seth considered his options, then slowly eased out from under her, settling her head gently on the pillow once he'd extracted himself. He pulled the covers over her, wondered whether he should try to put her on the couch, and then decided she looked cozy enough for now.

Seth hunted down his shorts, tossed carelessly in a corner, and pulled them on. Then he padded into the kitchen, his restlessness returning as his body woke up. The clock read midnight, which he noted as he got out the aspirin and poured a glass of water. He had to be at work at five, which meant that unless he managed to settle down again pretty soon, insomnia was going to win this round. He briefly considered taking Emma up to bed, curling himself around her, and allowing himself that much comfort. Maybe it would help him sleep. Maybe it would keep any nightmares, less frequent now but never completely gone, at bay.

Maybe he should chill the hell out before he decided to make Emma the centerpiece of a life he was finally starting to rebuild. His staying power was anything but a sure thing at this point, and she had enough to deal with, something that had become very clear to him tonight. So they'd just . . . take it slow. Enjoy where they were. Wasn't that the point of being in the Cove in the first place? Remembering how to just live in the moment again? He'd been doing a pretty good job of it.

But then, the last time he'd talked to Dave, his old friend had been doing a pretty good job of it, too. Reconnecting, getting help, starting to live life again. And now he was gone. Seth knew he was lucky to have escaped having either the basic wiring or the experiences, or both, that might have made suicide seem like an option. He wanted desperately to stay alive, to keep living.

Seth sighed, slid into one of his kitchen chairs, and

looked in the direction of the room where he could still hear Emma snoring lightly. He wanted this—wanted her. But for right now, it was better for both of them if they kept things as simple as possible. Until he was sure his past, and his problems, would stay his own.

Chapter Thirteen

Emma woke up to a number of unfamiliar sensations, all of which took her a few confused moments to sort out. First, the sun was in her eyes, though it shouldn't have been. Second, she seemed to be lying on . . . leather? Was that leather? And third, apart from the blanket on top of her, she was buck naked.

*What—*what—*what* is *this?*

She opened her eyes, blinking rapidly, then threw an arm over her head and rolled over. The leather couch crumpled softly beneath her, and Emma found herself looking at Seth's family room lit in the golden light of early morning. She pulled the afghan she'd been covered with up over her breasts, pushed up on one elbow, and looked around. Apparently she'd spent the night. But on his couch? Alone?

Puzzled, and beginning to have the unpleasant sensation in the pit of her stomach that usually signaled she'd screwed up somehow, Emma listened for any signs of life in the house. There was only silence, however. Frowning, she drew the blanket around her and stood, wearing it like the world's ugliest dress as she wandered into the empty kitchen, then back out into the family room, then up the stairs. Nothing seemed strange, though the comforter was rumpled in his bedroom and a book—some alternate history thing involving the Napoleonic Wars, according to the cover—was propped open, facedown on the bed.

He hadn't slept with her. She wasn't entirely convinced he'd slept at all. It was just another piece of the puzzle Seth was turning out to be, and Emma wasn't sure what to think. So she went into the bathroom to splash some water on her face and used his comb to work the worst knots out of her hair. If she had to do a walk/drive of shame home, she could at least look like she hadn't just rolled out of bed. Or off the couch.

Still, despite this morning's weirdness, Emma had to admit that it had never been as good as it had been last night. Just thinking about it had desire curling deep in her lower belly again, and she felt her lips curving into a satisfied little smile despite herself.

"Good" was actually an understatement. Of course, further testing would be required to make sure that this would be the rule and not the exception. Which would be easier if he hadn't slipped away without even saying good-bye. Her smile faded quickly as doubt crept in. Had something been wrong? Was he sorry they'd done it?

Could she maybe not invent a dozen more problems for herself before breakfast?

Back downstairs, she finally noticed the note he'd left, scribbled on a Post-it and stuck to the coffee table. She snatched it up to read the scratchy, masculine scrawl. Not that there was much of it.

Had to work early—didn't want to wake you.
Call you later, Snoring Beauty.

                                                    Seth

That, at least, made her smile. "I do not snore," she grumbled, putting the note back on the table. So maybe things were fine, and she was just borrowing trouble. She knew she had a tendency to do that. Still, something felt off. If she'd awakened in his rumpled bed, she wouldn't have felt so odd. But having been left on the couch while he slept elsewhere made her feel like an interloper.

She was in the middle of picking up her clothes from the various places they'd landed when there was a knock at the door. Hand in midair, she froze, crouched in the process of picking up her bra, which had somehow migrated behind the television set.

A thousand mortifying scenarios played themselves out in her mind in a matter of seconds, each worse than the last. It was one of his friends. It was one of her friends. It was one of her enemies. It was *all* of her enemies. It was all of the above, plus the mayor.

Instead, she heard the rumbling of a motor as a truck started in the driveway, and a quick look out the gauzy curtains showed her nothing but the delivery truck, heading back out after the driver had dropped off a package with a cursory knock. With a noisy gasp, Emma started to breathe again. Seth thought she cared too much about what other people thought. This was probably true, but old habits died hard, and she'd just as soon keep the fact that she'd spent the night with him under wraps until she knew where exactly they were going to go from here. She hurried to find the rest of her clothes and dressed quickly. Just before leaving, she flipped his note over and scrawled her number on the back of it. She wasn't sure he had it, which made her feel even less certain about last night. Something that had felt so completely right shouldn't have left her this way only a few hours later.

It only drove home the fact that she didn't really

know him. Not yet. But she wanted to. That was the one thing she was certain of, and what she held on to as she locked up and walked out the door.

"Something's weird."

"Just one something? That *is* weird."

Emma leaned against the trunk of the Witch Tree and shot her sister a dirty look. Sam was sketching a few feet away with the world's most innocent expression on her face, which meant she was being a jerk on purpose. Emma carefully put the remains of her picnic lunch to the side, scooped up a handful of sticks and dirt, and threw it at her sister.

"Hey!" Sam shook the dirt off her sketch pad. "I'm being sympathetic!"

"No, you're being a brat. Would you listen for a second, Georgia O'Keeffe? This is serious."

Sam sighed, looked resigned, and put the pad aside. Then she scooted forward until her knees were nearly touching Emma's. "Okay. Lay it on me. But if you're going to go into some sort of shame spiral because everybody knows you're sleeping with Seth Andersen, you might want to think about not parking your car in his driveway all night when you get a booty call."

Emma blinked. "When I get a— Damn it, Sam, could you find something else to call it? It was *not* a booty call! It was a ... a ..."

"Unifying experience? Night of transcendent physicality?"

"I will cut you. Don't think I won't," she warned her giggling sister. "You suck. That isn't the way I talk."

"It is in my head when I'm mad at you," Sam admitted, not looking the least bit guilty. "Oh, stop. I'm just teasing. But I did figure that's why you wanted to have lunch. Though I appreciate the fancy picnic spread and lack of pudding cups. I keep telling Jake they're made of chemical sludge, but he just can't quit them."

"That's because he's kind of a big five-year-old," Emma replied. "And no. Believe it or not, I don't care that people know we slept together. You know Jenny, the barista at Brewbaker's? This morning, she asked me if he had any single cop friends I could fix her up with. Apparently she loves men in uniform."

"And you didn't turn volcanic red and run away?"

"No. I said I'd ask him. Then I paid her and left."

Sam's blue-green eyes widened. "Oh my God."

"I know." Emma hunched her shoulders and sighed. "Seth thought I was crazy when I asked him to pretend to date me, but I was right about what it would do: no more random guys texting me, no new versions of my party story, no more random passersby singing 'What a Feeling' to me. Now it's just 'Hey, guess they must have liked that one wild night of passion because look, more sexytime,' and I really don't care."

"Wait. You asked him to pretend to date you?"

"Once. He said no."

Sam dropped her face into her palm. "Em. Honestly. That's so . . . you."

"I'm just going to pretend you mean it was a logical and simple solution to a nagging problem and move on."

"Whatever floats your boat." Sam folded her arms on top of her knees and watched Emma with renewed interest. "I wondered why I hadn't heard from you. Sorry I've been so busy, Em. I know I tease you, but you don't usually have actual problems. Just the imaginary problems you like to obsess over until you destroy them with your mental laser beams."

Emma pressed her lips together. "You could at least *pretend* you don't think I'm a spaz."

Sam smiled. "You're a lovable, extremely competent spaz. And you hide the spazziness well from the general public. How's that?"

"It'll do." Emma shifted, stretching her legs out in front of her. "It's okay that you're busy, Sam. You're getting married in a month, you're with a gorgeous guy who's crazy about you, you have a cool job and, you know, a life. I know you'll find me when you need me." She hadn't meant to sound so sad about it, but it seeped through anyway. While she kept her head down, nose to the grindstone, everyone else was passing her by, including the little sister who'd always needed her for support, even when they bickered otherwise.

Sam placed a gently reassuring hand over one of Emma's. For once, Emma didn't stiffen at all. She needed the comfort, however small.

"*Em.* I'll always need you. I was glad you wanted to have lunch with me out here today, no matter what it was about." She tilted her head to study her sister more closely. "Something *is* wrong. I can see it. What happened?"

"Nothing. Everything. I don't know." Emma blew out a breath and looked up into the gnarled branches of the Witch Tree, green dappled with golden light. "I haven't seen him since Tuesday night. You know, the infamous booty call."

Sam's eyebrows went up. "It's only Friday. I mean, has he called? If not, that's a dick move, and I will personally go beat him up, but otherwise ... I mean, he works weird hours, right?"

"Sometimes. He's not on nights right now."

"But you've talked to him, at least."

"Oh yeah, he calls. We talk. Sort of." Emma ground the heel of her shoe into the dirt and frowned at it. "He's actually very easy to talk to."

Sam looked at her curiously. "You know, normally you'd welcome a guy who was making a concerted effort to *not* crawl up your butt immediately. I'm not sure I'm seeing the problem here."

Emma rolled her eyes, wishing she could articulate this better. That had always been one of her strengths, being able to use words as tools or shields or even weapons. But this thing with Seth—she couldn't put her finger on it. It just didn't feel right. And it was more than just waking up on the couch Tuesday morning. . . . It was the unshakable feeling that he was tiptoeing around her for reasons that had roots in the vast, unknowable space that was his past.

"I talk. He asks questions. I talk some more. I'll bet you he could now answer all sorts of questions about me. I even . . . We even talked about Dad, a little."

Sam looked taken aback. "Oh. I didn't think you did that."

"I didn't. I don't. That's what I mean. He's so . . ." She sighed, then growled. "He won't talk about himself, Sam. I barely know a thing about him. He'd just found out that a friend of his had killed himself when I showed up on Tuesday, and he had nothing to say. He looked terrible, but it was off-limits. Which I understand to an extent, but it isn't just that. Where he grew up, how he grew up, his parents, his time in the army—*nothing* is fair game. I get a hint of information, and then he changes the subject."

Sam appeared to mull this over. "Well, it's early days yet, right? Despite the, ah, booty call. Are you sure I don't get to call it that? You called it that."

"I was being facetious. No."

"He's probably just really reserved. Not that—oh, look at you blush. I guess he wasn't reserved in bed, huh?" Sam flashed a delighted grin before her expression softened again. "Really, though, you might just have to give him some time. Maybe there's an evil ex. Maybe it's a soldier thing. Or maybe it's just him. If you like him, though, keep working at him. You're good at wearing people down. Like the ocean. Or a natural disaster."

"Such flattery." Emma arched an eyebrow, but Sam looked unrepentantly amused. "I *know*," Emma continued with a groan. "I know it could be anything. I'm just not used to this. He wanted me. I decided I was on board with that, which was kind of a huge deal. So what's the problem *now*? Why does it have to keep being complicated?"

"I think the problem is that people *are* complicated, and you're used to your work relationships, which are a lot more . . . transactional."

"You're not a work relationship," Emma pointed out, "and we do just fine."

"Em, you're my older sister. If you don't know me after all these years, after growing up in the same house, you have unfixable problems."

"I made friends with Brynn!" Emma said. "We took off and went shoe shopping after work yesterday!"

"Well, you're not sleeping with Brynn, to my knowledge, and also good for you! She seems fun, and you both have an unnatural love of girly suits." Sam patted her hand. "Look at my baby, all grown up and making friends."

Emma pressed her lips together. "Did I mention I'll cut you? I think I did."

Sam snorted. "Empty threats. You'd hate jail." Then

she sighed. "You really like this guy, don't you? I've never seen you so twisted up over someone."

Emma hung her head. Admitting it felt like waving a white flag, which was something she wasn't normally inclined to do. But there was no avoiding the truth. "I do like him. I don't really want to, but I do."

"You think if you fall for him, he'll leave." It wasn't a question. Sam knew her better than anyone. Emma nodded.

"Or worse. He's got an awful black eye right now, and it was just some routine thing. He's a cop."

Sam's eyes were full of understanding. "Yes, he is. And he's a good cop, or you wouldn't like him so much. But his having a dangerous job doesn't mean you couldn't keep him. It doesn't mean you'd lose him."

Emma flinched. "I've known him for two weeks. I have no idea whether or not I'd want to keep him." She knew she sounded defensive, but Sam, being Sam, had cut through all of the bull and gotten straight to the heart of the matter.

"You don't expend this much energy on anything unless you're serious," Sam said. "I can't imagine this is any different. You really like him, and he scares the hell out of you."

She nearly denied it, then decided not to bother. If she couldn't be honest with Sam, what did she have? "I don't know if I can do this," she admitted. "I know it's irrational. Not everyone up and dies terrible deaths for no reason, or screws you over and leaves."

"He's not Ben, Em. He's nothing like Ben. That much is obvious."

Emma wrinkled her nose. "You've never even met Seth. How would you know that?"

"Because you thought Ben was perfect from the

get-go, and that scared the hell out of *me*. He was always too good to be true. The fact that you recognize this one's issues is promising."

"I just wasn't . . . enough . . . for Ben." The words came out sounding stiff, but talking about her ex had that effect. She was over him, but not the implications of their breakup.

"Oh, bull," Sam snapped. "No one is ever going to be enough for him. And it'll never be his fault—just ask him. You weren't the problem."

Emma simply shrugged. As far as she was concerned, the jury was still out on that one. "That's old news anyway. I'm just not much good at getting close to people. I don't like the risk. It's not usually worth it."

"But sometimes it is," Sam said gently. "I took some convincing, but Jake managed it."

"I'm not sure which of us needs more convincing, me or Seth," Emma said. "And making people feel comfortable with their relationships with me isn't really my area. Unless they're paying me, which is different." She sighed and looked away. "Well, that sounded bad. With my luck, that'll be the next chapter in my imaginary saga. 'Emma Henry, Small-Town Hooker.'"

"Nah, that's Kimmie Talbot, over on Nightshade. I think that might actually be true, though." Sam leaned in. "You going to be okay? I really think it'll be okay."

"I have no idea," Emma said, beginning to gather up her things and place them neatly in her little two-person picnic basket. She looked up at her sister with a small wistful smile. "But talking about it helps. At least you understand all my messed-up Henry baggage."

"It's our gift and our curse," Sam replied, picking up her sketch pad and getting to her feet. She wore a long, shimmering shirt that looked like fine silver mesh over tight black leggings and a pair of strappy heels, and her pale blond hair shone nearly as bright as her shirt. Emma smiled at the sight of her beautiful little sister, finally comfortable in her own skin and living a life that fit her like a glove. She'd found her place in the world.

Emma felt as though she'd been close to finding that same sort of contentment for years now, having made her peace with so much of the past. But pieces were missing. The thought that she might be on the verge of finding one was tantalizing . . . but being wrong would cost her. She just didn't know how much.

The thought that Seth might somehow be in a similar position was cold comfort.

"I want to meet this guy," Sam said as they walked together from the sheltering shade of the Witch Tree into Oak Shadow Park, which sat lush and green at the heart of the square. "Are you going to bring him to the wedding? Since I'm making you be maid of honor and not letting you try to run everything, no matter how much you whine."

"I haven't whined. And I hadn't even thought about it," Emma replied, though the thought made her happy, in a nerve-racking sort of way. "Probably. If he can."

"And the rehearsal dinner. You should bring him to that, too."

"Mmm."

"Oh!" Sam spun, her eyes bright. "I know! Let's go out this weekend, the four of us. Jake and I can size him up, and then maybe I'll know how to help!"

Emma considered it as they left the wrought-iron fence at the edge of the park and crossed to the shops lining the square. Hers was just a little up from where they stood, which meant she had very little time to make a decision. She'd rather analyze it to death, but there wasn't time. There never seemed to be anymore, at least in her personal life. Things just kept *happening* before she could take the time to figure them out.

"Saturday's bad for me," she said. "As usual. And I think he works days this weekend. Let me see if I can pin him down for next weekend, okay?"

Sam gave her an incredibly feline smile. "You do that."

Emma gave her a playful swat as they stopped in front of Occasions by Emma. Brynn waved at them from the desk inside. Sam returned the wave, then refocused on her sister.

"Call me and let me know, okay? It'll be fun. And don't worry so much. Some people just take a little more time. Don't be afraid if he needs some work. I mean, we all do, right?"

"Most of you do, yes," Emma replied, and darted inside just in time for Sam's foot to miss her rear end. Sam stuck her tongue out and flounced off as Emma smiled sweetly and waved good-bye, feeling immeasurably better just for having been able to share. It had taken her a long time, but she was getting better at it. Not that she could have gotten a whole lot worse, but . . . baby steps.

"Emma! Good! Mrs. Charles has decided to go to war with Larkin over the cupcakes for the shower, and both of them have called to shout at me."

"Larkin shouted? She never shouts."

Brynn looked at her blandly. "This is Rowena Charles, Em. She could make Mother Teresa shout. Anyway, Ms. Party Coordinator, Mrs. Charles wants you to coordinate Larkin into agreeing to change everything she's baking for the shower in two days—at no extra cost, of course— and Larkin wants you to coordinate Mrs. Charles into a hellish vortex from which she'll never return. Thoughts? I tried, but they don't want me."

"Be grateful," Emma said. But she headed for her office with a smile, because no matter how bad things got, she knew she'd find a way to make things work. That was just what she did.

And for the first time, she had to consider that because of it, a future with someone might not be out of the question. She'd spent so much time arranging wonderful moments for other people.

All she needed was the nerve to give making her own life something wonderful one more try.

Chapter Fourteen

"You're holding out on me."

"I am not." Seth took a sip of coffee and stretched out one of his legs while he lounged on the couch, exactly the kind of start to a Saturday he liked. He'd been glad to hear his sister's voice this morning—after his initial annoyance at the phone waking him up—but he didn't think he was quite awake enough for the interrogation he was currently undergoing. One of the things about being a twin that was both a blessing and a curse was the deep connection they shared. And though he liked to pretend Kira didn't have a love life, she always seemed to know when something was going on with his.

"Are, too. You think you're so smooth. It's kind of sad, really."

Seth snorted. "The only sad thing is that you've never appreciated my awesomeness."

She laughed, a sound he didn't think he'd ever get tired of hearing. Not after he'd made her cry so often. He'd been determined that the last time would be just that—the last time. So far, so good.

"It's because I got more of the awesomeness," she said. "I just spend most of my time feeling superior. Sorry—it's just genetics. You got a raw deal, being male and all."

"Ha." He took another swig of coffee. "So how are things in sunny St. Augustine?"

"Believe it or not . . . sunny. And full of tourists. And you're trying to change the subject. So who's the girl?"

"I didn't say anything about a girl," Seth replied, hoping she couldn't hear the smirk that he couldn't quite help. No such luck, though.

"I hear you smiling, you jerk." Kira heaved a long-suffering sigh. "This is what I get. I shared a womb with you, I played army men with you, I let you hit on my friends, and you hold out on me. Fine. I see how it is."

He rolled his eyes. She could probably hear that, too. When he was younger, he'd been convinced his twin was psychic, but it turned out that she was just extremely perceptive. It worked well with her natural gift for snooping. He'd tried to push her into police work because of it, but she seemed just as happy being a journalist.

"So much drama," he said.

"As if I would pretend to be deeply wounded just to get information out of you," she replied, and because her mood had lifted his own, he relented just a little.

"There might be a *woman*. Not a girl. Someone I'm starting to see. Happy now?"

The squeal was deafening. He jerked the phone away from his ear and winced. "Seriously?"

"That's great! Who is she? What's her name? What does she do? Is she nice?"

"Of course she's nice. Jeez, Kira. It's not like I've been living under a rock. You had to do the screech?"

"I had to do the screech," she replied. "It was necessary. Quit sounding so grumpy about it, Seth. I'm just happy you're starting to get out again. You know . . . to reconnect."

His smile was wistful. "Not like back at home, you mean."

"Well . . ."

"It's okay, Kira. I know what a pain in the ass I was before I left." The burying himself in work even though he hated what it was doing to him, avoiding his family because he didn't have the emotional bandwidth for, well, anything. It hadn't been bad at first, right after he'd gotten out of the service. But by the time Uncle Steve had thrown him a lifeline, he'd felt as though he'd fallen into a pit with sides made entirely of slippery, shifting mud.

"You weren't a pain in the ass," she said firmly. "You were just . . . lost. I only wish you'd mentioned you were looking for jobs elsewhere before you blew town."

"I knew I needed to go. You all would have tried to get me to stay. It was for the best."

"Hmm. Leaving here, maybe. Not saying good-bye until you were halfway to Massachusetts, not so much. I know you've got some noble idea you were sparing us, Seth, but I think it was just easier for *you*."

He winced. "Kira—"

"It's fine," she said quickly. "You did what you needed to, and believe me, I'm just glad it seems to be working out." Her voice brightened as she quickly shifted the subject away from his hasty departure. Seth appreciated it, but his guilt lingered. He knew he should have said good-bye. He'd just been afraid that if he had, he would lose his nerve, and staying would have been the worst thing he could have done. He'd been losing himself.

It wasn't an easy thing to explain. Words weren't his favorite medium of expression. But here and there, he'd tried. It had helped immensely, though he knew Kira hadn't quite gotten all the way through forgiving him yet. Soon, he hoped. But not quite.

"So I'm hoping to get up there for a visit this summer," she said. "If that's okay. I know you wanted some settling-in time, but frankly, it's been six months and I have no patience."

Seth laughed. Yeah, she'd just about forgiven him. "Anytime," he said, and was glad to find that he really meant it, that the thought of seeing her filled him with excitement instead of dread. "Just let me know when you're coming so I can have more than three cans of soda and, like, half a package of cheese in the fridge."

"Really? *Yes!* Because I kind of already put in for time off next month, so . . . you were going to find me on your doorstep regardless. I miss you." All the humor vanished from her voice, leaving only the simple, sweet truth.

"I miss you, too," he replied, meaning it just as much. They'd been a unit since before they'd been born. They'd banged each other up from time to time over the years, but that bond had never been broken.

"Aw. So now I don't know what I'm more excited to see. This amazing no-name town that you and Uncle Steve are so in love with, or the girl—sorry, *woman*—who finally got you to break your dating moratorium. I'll make her love me. Just you wait."

Seth groaned. "And that's terrifying. Thanks, Kira."

"Hey, it's my job to bring joy into your life. I'm the good twin, remember?"

"Is that why you were always the one in trouble when we were teenagers?" he asked.

"I was unappreciated in my own land," she said. "And you were just quieter about your inherent badness. Plus I had better ideas."

"Yeah, I remember," he snorted. He thought a moment, tested out the idea in his head, and decided it wasn't just time to invite his sister to come see what he was making of his life up here. He'd waited, maybe too long . . . but he'd wanted to be sure this place was the right one first. He was a little surprised that his parents hadn't used Steve and Ginny as an excuse to come up already, but some part of him knew that Steve would have told them to wait.

He was only beginning to understand just how worried they'd all been.

"I need to get Mom and Dad up here, too," Seth said, and was treated to another screech. "Jesus, Kira!"

"Sorry. I just . . ." It stunned him to hear his devil-may-care sister on the verge of tears. "You really are better. I mean, you sound like your old self again. Is it the place, or the job, or . . . What's made the difference? What was missing here?"

Seth sighed softly, hating that she was still determined that he'd left because his family was somehow lacking. "You know it wasn't you, Kira. You and Mom and Dad are the only things I miss about being down there." He tried for a laugh. "Guess I never really got the north out of my system."

"But it's cold. And no palm trees."

"It's beautiful. Even when it's cold," he assured her.

"It's so *far*, though," Kira said. And it was, but . . .

"Some places just call to a person, I guess. I used to dream about places like this." He remembered the phone call from his uncle, right at the point when he'd basically decided to head for a job out in Washington State. He'd figured his father had put him up to it, but his normally quiet uncle had been surprisingly passionate in his argument for Seth's coming up to Harvest Cove instead. Ginny was a local, they'd been there for years, and he was friendly with the chief. A place could be made for him almost immediately with little fuss, and besides . . .

Steve wanted him there. Because he understood. And sometimes, just having someone around who got it was enough.

That had been the deciding factor, with the small size and purported beauty of the Cove coming in a close second. Seth had been positive that the descriptions of the town had been overblown, but no. It was exactly what Steve had promised. Maybe Kira would understand when she came up.

Not if, but when. The thought made him smile. The invitation had been long overdue.

"Well, I'm definitely curious. You make it sound so quaint. And *romantic*." She drew out the word in a ridiculous voice, then chuckled. "Don't do anything stupid before I get there, okay?"

"Hey, you know I wouldn't do anything stupid without you."

"That's what I like to hear," Kira replied. "All right, I have to go try to get coherent answers out of a politician now. May your day be better than mine."

"Sounds like it will be," Seth said. "I've got the day off."

"Loser."

"Love you, too, Sis."

He heard that funny catch in her voice again when she replied, "Oh, you know I love you. No matter how big a buttface you are. Later."

She hung up, leaving Seth with the bittersweet knowledge that he was still making his sister cry. It was simply for happier reasons.

He'd just stood up to get himself another cup of coffee when his phone rang. He figured it was Kira again, calling back with either some forgotten scrap of information or one more insult. He was used to both. But a quick look at the number made him glad he hadn't picked up and tossed out a "What do you want *now*, butt nugget?" without thinking.

"Emma," he said. "What's up?"

He had a brief instant of worry that she'd finally decided to confront him about waking up alone on the couch Tuesday morning. He hadn't explained about the intermittent insomnia yet because . . . well, because. But it was eating at him a little, enough that he was holding off asking her to come over. What if he couldn't sleep again? What if she woke up alone again and asked questions? It was bound to come up eventually.

Not today, though. When Emma spoke, it surprised him to hear the tension running through her voice. It was like listening to the ominous hum of a live wire.

"I need help. I've got an engagement party tonight that's turning into a slow-motion disaster. Both of my part-timers are down with the stomach flu their kids brought home, Brynn stepped off the curb and fractured her foot on her way into work, and I don't have enough hands to get the gallery looking the way it needs to by seven. I know this is probably the last thing you want to do tonight, but—"

"When do you need me there?" he asked. She paused for a moment, as though genuinely surprised he'd already agreed. It made him wonder, not for the first time, what kind of guys she must have dated before.

"Five," she finally said. "I'll meet you at the gallery at five. I've roped Sam and Zoe in, too. I think they're both scared to work with me, but I'm kind of desperate. Do I sound desperate? Because I'm really pretty desperate." Her laugh was slightly maniacal.

"I'll be there right at five," he assured her. "It'll be fine. You've probably dealt with worse than this."

He heard her blow out a long breath. "Not in a while.

And I've never had all my help taken out in one fell swoop. I told Brynn to stay away, but I'm worried she's going to hobble in and try to help anyway."

Seth remembered her and thought Emma was probably right. "If she shows, we'll shoo her out. Or at least tie her to a chair. Do I need to dress up for this?"

"Maybe. Probably. Yes."

"Done. Don't panic. I'll see you at five."

"God. Thank you. I owe you," she said, and he put a stop to that notion before it could take root.

"You don't owe me anything, Em," he said, deliberately using her nickname. "I'm coming because I want to. I was hoping we could get together tonight anyway. Okay?"

Her voice was tired, relieved, surprised . . . but pleased. "Okay."

They hung up a few moments later, and Seth stretched, reaching one hand up toward the ceiling. It seemed like today was going to bring him all sorts of signs that he was making a life here. Getting dressed up for polite company—not to mention Emma's sister—was just one more.

Hoping he still had a pair of decent khaki pants, he headed for the kitchen and one more cup of coffee to start his day.

By the time the tables were set up and artfully arranged, the buffet table was loaded with steaming hors d'oeuvres and smelling like heaven, and the entire gallery was draped in gauze and bathed in candlelight, Emma didn't care what anyone said.

She didn't just owe her emergency crew drinks; she owed them a seven-course gourmet meal. And if any of them tried to complain, she would have to stab them. In the most profusely grateful way possible, of course. After which they would have to go to dinner anyway, because she said so.

As jazz played softly through the speakers and the partygoers mingled in groups, Emma circulated a tray of spanakopita and chatted up the guests. Faith, the caterer, was shorthanded thanks to the stomach plague as well, and this was an easy way to pick up some of the slack. The setup was always more stressful for Emma than when the party was in full swing, by which point she no longer felt like climbing onto the ceiling and staying there wailing until the Party God arrived to magically fix everything.

Luckily, she hadn't needed divine intervention. And once she'd slipped into her simple black 1950s-style cocktail dress, one of her favorites, she'd felt fully in control.

When she walked back to the buffet table with the empty tray, sharing a relieved smile with Faith, Sam was waiting for her.

"Hey," Emma said, guiding her sister into an unoccupied corner to talk for a moment while scanning the room for anything that might need doing. Faith's two servers seemed to be covering the crowd just fine for the moment, and Zoe had vanished, probably pulled into a conversation somewhere or other. Seth was holding a tray of drinks and laughing with a couple of guys he worked with who'd come as guests. Emma let her eyes linger on him, unable to help herself. It wasn't just that the man wore khakis and a button-down shirt better than anyone had a right to—and she'd nearly had to pick her jaw up off the floor when he'd walked in. He'd been invaluable as they'd set up, moving quickly, doing exactly as she asked, and somehow spurring everyone else to work in the same fashion.

It was the first time she'd seen the soldier in him. And

despite years of swearing off men who preferred to run toward danger than away from it, being this up close and personal with one was more of an aphrodisiac than she'd imagined.

"You look like you want to eat him up with a spoon. Not that I blame you," Sam said, drawing Emma's attention back to her. Emma raised her brows.

"I'm surveying the room. It's my job."

Sam grinned, sleek and lovely as always in a simple black jersey dress. "You're surveying Seth's butt, too."

"That's one of my perks." When Sam laughed, she smiled. "Everything okay? If you need to go . . ."

"No, no, I'm completely fine. Tempted to dive face-first into those little ham things, but fine. I just had to tell you that—"

She stopped in midsentence, eyes widening as she looked past Emma's shoulder. "Oh. Uh-oh. Is that the bride-to-be?"

Emma turned, already pulling out her mental list of "common bridal problems and solutions" before she even caught sight of Elaina Morrow's tear-streaked face. Once she did, the problem was obvious. The solution, however, might take some doing.

Zoe escorted Elaina over, hand at the small of her back, making sympathetic noises while the woman hiccuped.

"This poor thing's future father-in-law made some modifications to her dress," Zoe said. Emma bit her lip and surveyed the damage. The beautiful cream silk sheath was now splattered with deep red wine, some of it still dripping on the floor. It had been a direct hit and then some.

"I kn-know he didn't mean to, but . . . he always drinks too m-much, and I don't know why h-he couldn't just *once*—"

Sensing a teary rant of epic proportions looming, Emma looked Elaina over, estimated a couple of things, and gave a small nod. She stepped forward, put a hand on Elaina's arm, and used the voice she always did with clients who, for whatever reason, were on the edge of a complete breakdown. Not that it wasn't completely justified in this case. Leo Davison was a letch and a drunk. But his son, Max, was a sweetheart, as was Leo's wife, Lauri, and Elaina's family members were good people. There was always at least one problem guest at a party. Part of Emma's job was not letting that one person ruin it for everyone else. Especially not for the ones who should be celebrating the most.

"A good cleaner can probably get that out, and I'm happy to take care of that if you like. But for now, you're going to need to change."

Elaina's eyes began to fill again. "But—"

"I don't want you to have to miss a second more of this party than you have to, so here's what I can do. You sit tight, and I'll drive right down the street to my apartment. You're about an eight, right?"

Elaina nodded and sniffled. "Yes."

"Well, so am I, and since dressing up is part of my job, I think I have just the thing to go with those shoes. Can you give me ten minutes? Sam will get you a glass of champagne and set you up in Zoe's office so you don't have to walk around in a wet, stained dress."

Elaina hitched in a breath and nodded vigorously. "Really? You would do that? I'm so sorry. Tonight was supposed to be wonderful, but—"

"Tonight is still going to be wonderful," Emma said firmly, and saw the hope spark in Elaina's eyes. She wasn't ready to give up on her night . . . and that meant it was going to be just fine. She exchanged a look with Sam, who nodded and quickly ushered Elaina away and taking a glass of champagne off a tray.

Emma sprang into action immediately, all smiles as she headed out the door, as if nothing were wrong in the world. Once she hit the sidewalk, though, she ran as fast as her heels would carry her. She opened the door to Zoe's office, dress in hand, exactly ten minutes later, and helped zip Elaina into the cream chiffon cocktail dress, breathing a sigh when it fit like a glove.

Elaina actually laughed as she twirled in the full skirt. "I love this! It's so *girly*!"

"And it looks fabulous on you," Emma said with a smile, while Sam and Zoe gave the thumbs-up. She handed Elaina a wipe to fix her mascara, then opened the door. "Ready to go enjoy your party?"

She was, but not before throwing her arms around Emma to give her a hug and whisper, "Thank you. So, so much. I'll make sure to stay away from Leo so I don't need to borrow another dress!"

Emma laughed, enjoying the sounds of the guests oohing and ahhing as the bride-to-be made her reappearance, then turned to find Sam and Zoe watching her with identical expressions of amazement.

"What?" she asked, and sipped at the remainder of Elaina's champagne to celebrate her triumph.

"You," Zoe said, "have nerves of steel." She shook her head, then walked past her, pausing to pat her on the shoulder before heading back out into the party. "I think I need some of that champagne," she said.

Sam remained, watching her with something like awe. Emma shifted uncomfortably. "It wasn't that bad," she said.

"Yes, it was. You just *acted* like it wasn't. It was . . . You're kind of amazing, Em. Did you know that?"

"Of course I do." Then she laughed and shook her head. "It's just my job, Sam. I'm only glad I was close to home, because otherwise it would have been a much bigger problem. We got lucky, that's all."

"There was definitely a little luck. And a lot of grace under fire." Sam screwed up her mouth, the way she always had as a kid right before she'd confessed to doing something she shouldn't. Emma lifted her brows.

"Sam, don't get funny on me. It's all okay. Crisis averted. I'm not magic—I'm just an event planner. The rest of the night should be fine." But her sister surprised her by stepping forward, wrapping her hands loosely around her waist and resting her head on Emma's shoulder. Emma rubbed Sam's back lightly, confused. "Are you okay? Are you having a prebridal moment?"

Sam laughed, but she didn't break the embrace. "No. I'm having a 'really freaking proud of my big sister' moment. I always thought you just, you know . . . bossed people around."

Touched, Emma chuckled softly. "Well . . . I mean, I do."

"You do a lot more than that. You work your ass off to make things special. And you really care. You're like a fairy godmother."

Emma frowned down at the top of Sam's head. "Were you into the champagne already?"

Sam lifted her head to give her a disgruntled look. "No. I'm giving you a compliment, butthead."

"Oh. In that case," Emma said, giving her sister a squeeze and a kiss on the cheek, "thank you. Because it really means a lot." And it did, to have the little sister she was so proud of acknowledge the work put into her own dream. They might be different, but they were still, in so many ways, the only two people on earth who would ever understand each other so well.

"Now I wish I'd let you boss me around about my own wedding," Sam said, sounding suspiciously teary.

"Believe me, I've been watching. If you weren't doing a good job, I'd be chewing at you." She paused. "I'm probably still going to be bossy that day, though."

"It's allowed, as long as you have fun," Sam said, pulling back with a single, suspicious sniffle. Neither of them was big on crying, but then again, after all this time, the occasional sisterly moment seemed worth a few tears. "Come on. We should probably go back out before somebody sets something on fire."

"Been there," Emma said, earning her a horrified look from her sister before they both headed back into the fray. As soon as they emerged into the main room, Seth made a beeline for them. Emma heard Sam's low, approving chuckle before she returned to the buffet table to see what Faith needed.

"By the way . . . I wanted to tell you before, but you've got great taste. I like him. And quit worrying. He's crazy about you." Sam dropped a sly wink and walked away just before Seth reached her, his brown eyes full of warmth and concern.

"There you are. Zoe told me what happened. Crisis averted?"

"Crisis averted. That one, at least. The night is young."

Seth grinned and shook his head. "You're really something. I had no idea these things were so much work. You would have made one hell of a general."

"Oh yeah? I didn't realize soldiers were prone to wine-stain crises." She shrugged. "Maybe I'll go sign up."

"Nah," Seth said. "You shouldn't deprive the world of

the sight of you in these dresses. It would be wrong." He looked her over with an intensity that had heat rising to her cheeks. "If I didn't mention it already, you look beautiful tonight. And very, very hot."

The look in his eyes, combined with the lingering adrenaline, made her feel bold. She stepped close to him, rising up on her toes to whisper in his ear. The scent of his cologne enveloped her, the pull of his warmth irresistible.

"I'm hotter out of the dress. Maybe if you're nice, I'll let you see."

His laugh fanned her neck, making the skin tingle. "Baby, I'm prepared to beg if necessary."

Emma looked up at him, letting her lips curve into a seductive smile even as her heart stumbled in her chest. She might never understand why the two of them set off sparks like this, but tonight, she saw no reason not to enjoy the fire that resulted. It might be more complicated than she would have liked . . . but then again, not *everything* about this was. She saw Faith trying to catch her attention from across the room and knew she needed to get back to work. The night was far from over . . . but for once, she knew she wouldn't be alone at the end of it.

"You won't have to beg," she said, and saw the playful twinkle in his dark eyes.

"What if I want to?" he asked softly, and Emma felt her womb clench at the thought.

"Then I'm sure we could arrange . . . something," she said. Then, before she ruined her night of triumph by spontaneously combusting, Emma turned on her heel and sashayed away.

Chapter Fifteen

It was midnight by the time she walked outside, the gallery as neat as a pin and everyone but her, Seth, and Zoe already headed home. Zoe locked up, and they all walked to their cars together, so tired that there were only a few scraps of friendly conversation before their good nights. As Zoe drove off, Emma breathed in the night air, weary down to the bone but alert in a way that told her she'd be up awhile yet. She always was after a successful event.

She would have liked to hang on to the triumphant fearlessness from earlier, but that was the one thing that seemed to have gone. In its wake, she'd been left with nothing but restless arousal and the nerves that cropped up every time she was alone with him.

What if he's just exhausted and wants to go home? What if he's just waiting for me to let him off the hook?

What if I'm being a complete idiot like usual?

"I realize it's pretty late," she began, though her train of thought crashed into a tree as soon as he turned his head to look at her. He'd ruffled his hair with his hand as they'd walked outside, and his eyes were adorably sleepy. She almost felt guilty for wanting to do so many wonderfully bad things to him. Almost.

"Did you need to go to bed?" he asked, and she thought—she hoped—that was disappointment she heard in his voice. It was all the encouragement she needed.

Emma shook her head. "I'll be up for a while yet. I just thought ... You were such a huge help, and you're probably beat."

"I'm used to being up late," he said. "Am I still invited over?"

Emma's mouth went dry, so she simply nodded. Her reward was a slow, suggestive smile. "Okay. I'll meet you there."

She managed the quick drive without crashing into a lightpost, despite the barrage of butterflies in her stomach. Even after they'd spent the evening firmly in her element, she couldn't quite get a handle on her nerves. She knew what was coming—hell, she *wanted* what was coming—but the thought of being able to have Seth whenever she liked was still so new, she hardly believed it might be possible.

They didn't speak on the way up the stairs to her apartment, or as she fumbled with the locks on her door. What normally took her one thoughtless attempt now took her three, plus a clumsy key drop.

Didn't I basically seduce him the other night? Come on, Emma!

Her reaction to her inner pep talk was to open the door too quickly and stumble inside, nearly landing on her face. Boof gave her a pitying look and then immediately went into his most shameless "pet me" theatrics for her company, wrapping himself around Seth's legs and wailing piteously before flopping over on his back. Seth chuckled and crouched down to rub Boof's belly, and when he looked up at her, it was with such innocent pleasure that she felt her heart constrict painfully in her chest. This wasn't lust. It was something else entirely, already enhanced by having watched him help and mingle and generally be a good guy all evening.

When he stood, Emma pulled apart the hands she'd been wringing awkwardly and tried to play it cool. It wasn't her forte, but she tried. "So. Um, why don't you come on in and sit? I can get you a drink. Or something." She gave him her most winning smile before turning to head for the couch, wondering what they were going to talk about before they got around to taking each other's clothes off. The weather? The food at the party? It wasn't weird at all, doing that when just a couple of hours ago she'd basically told him she'd like him on his knees.

She heard Seth mutter something behind her. Emma started to turn, but found herself pulled into his rough embrace instead. She went instantly limp, melting against him while he tangled one hand in her hair and buried his face in her neck. His breath was hot on her skin, and he felt so good in her arms that she wondered why she ever bothered to be anywhere else. She wrapped her arms around him, tipping her head to the side when he began to nuzzle kisses into her sensitive skin. The only sound in the apartment was that of their ragged breathing.

Emma cupped the back of his head, his hair soft through her fingers. Seth was wrapped around her, one hand at her shoulder, the other at her hip, and he moved his mouth to nip and then suck at her ear. The sensation nearly took her knees out from under her.

"I missed you." She sighed, her eyes closing. It was all she could think, the only thing to say. Something had caused a seismic shift in her universe in the last two weeks, and that something was right here in her arms. Here, where he felt so exactly right that a few days apart felt like years.

Seth lifted his head and pressed his forehead to hers, rubbing his thumb across her cheekbone. He didn't say anything, but he didn't need to. Instead, he used his mouth to return the sentiment, claiming her mouth in a deep, drugging kiss that left her clinging to him. Emma tilted her head to change the angle of the kiss, tasting him more fully, sliding her leg up to hook over his hip and open herself to him. Seth slid his hands beneath the skirt of her dress and cupped her backside, pressing into her with a sexy little gasp. Emma answered with her own soft moan when she felt the rigid length of his cock straining against his pants. His kisses grew hotter, harder as they fumbled together. Emma couldn't seem to stop touching him, couldn't touch him enough. All she knew was that if they didn't get horizontal pretty quickly, they were going to fall over. That wasn't an awful thing, but she wanted to experience something other than the floor with him.

It took a painful amount of effort to disentangle herself, but she managed it, loving Seth's aroused expression and hazy eyes. She'd done that. She hadn't known she was capable, but the evidence that she was flooded her with a purely feminine sense of power. She hooked a finger into one of his belt loops and pulled him forward as she stepped backward, toward the bedroom.

Seth obliged her by following, one dark brow arched. He never took his eyes from her.

She brought him into her bedroom, which was tastefully done up in black and white and teal, neat as a pin, and realized that he was the first man to cross its borders. It was the last thing she wanted to think of, and deeply embarrassing besides. She knew it had been a while. . . . She'd simply been too caught up to remember how long until now.

"Hey, don't get shy on me now," Seth said, pulling her

to him again when she felt her cheeks go hot. He kissed her cheeks, her nose, her chin. "You're supposed to make me beg, remember?"

"I just . . . remembered exactly how girly it is in here." It was an obscure, roundabout way of putting it, but it was all she was willing to say. Seth didn't seem to understand or particularly care. He cupped her breast, playing his fingers over fabric that covered deliciously sensitized skin.

"You're girly. I like girly. Every time I saw you in this dress tonight, I wanted to drag you away to some dark room so I could take it off with my teeth."

Her laugh was breathless and caught in her throat when he squeezed. "I'm glad it wasn't just me. Sam caught me staring at your butt. Repeatedly."

Seth grinned. "Not much to look at. I'm too skinny."

Emma arched a brow. "Please. You have a great butt. You have a great everything."

"Yeah, well, the feeling is mutual." He reached around her, deftly found the eye hook above the zipper, and then unzipped the dress. A gentle tug, and it slid to the floor, leaving her in nothing but scraps of crimson silk.

Seth exhaled softly, drinking her in. "Red. Wow."

One corner of her mouth curved. "I was hoping you'd like it."

"You have no idea." He lowered his head to kiss her, taking her mouth in a kiss that grew steadily deeper, more insistent as Emma fitted herself against him. It felt incredibly decadent, being wrapped in his arms nearly naked while he remained fully clothed. It was impossible to feel self-conscious now—not when Seth was telling her how much he liked her this way with his mouth, his hands. He began to move, backing her against the bed until she had to fall onto it. She went obligingly, situating herself so she could look up at him while Seth stood at the edge and took off his shirt, then started to unbuckle his belt. He moved quickly, but not quickly enough for her. She rose to her knees to help him, though "helping" quickly turned to covering his chest with kisses. He gave a soft laugh and stopped trying to undress, letting Emma explore his heated skin with her hands, her mouth. She managed the button and zipper of his pants more deftly than she'd expected, then wrapped her hand around the hot, silken length of him.

The sound he made banished any lingering embarrassment. She stroked slowly, lifting her head to watch Seth close his eyes and start to give himself over to what she was doing to him. A tiny crease formed between his brows, and his breathing started to come in short, harsh pants as she varied the rhythm, quickening, then slowing, kissing and licking at the taut skin of his chest and stomach as moisture pooled between her thighs. Right now, his pleasure was hers. It was empowering, holding him like this, his hips moving with her every stroke . . . erotic in a way she'd never experienced.

When he began to quiver, his eyes flew open.

"Not yet," he growled. "Not like this." She let him strip off his shoes and pants, slipping quickly out of her bra and panties while he worked, then scooted back onto the bed as he crawled in after her. He was beautiful, she thought as she watched him. All lean, sinewy muscle, his dark eyes turned almost black by the light of her single, small lamp. He looked so confident, so dangerous, exactly the kind of man she'd once avoided. And now here he was in her bed.

Exactly where he belonged.

The way he looked at her was almost reverent, and his gaze lingered on the parts of her body that had always irritated her—her breasts, her hips. But rather than judgment, she saw something like adoration.

"I think I told you this, but your body is incredible," Seth said. "You should be naked all the time."

She started to lift up her knees to cover herself a little, suddenly shy. "I've heard I run around that way at parties sometimes. Downtown, even."

His smile was lazy, sensual. "If people knew what you looked like under those little suits and dresses, you'd be hearing a lot more about it. But I think I'll just keep you to myself."

From anyone else, those words might have rubbed her the wrong way. Apart from the standard youthful fantasies about princes, warriors, Vikings, and the occasional spandex-clad superhero, she'd never wanted to belong to anyone but herself. But she already knew Seth didn't want to own her. She wasn't even sure he'd take the pieces of herself she was able to give, should she decide she was ready to offer them to him.

Who do I think I'm kidding? I already want to give him more than just pieces.

"I'm all yours." She tried to sound playful when she spoke, in case he didn't want to hear the truth beneath the words. If he did, it didn't bother him, because he proceeded to lavish each breast with so much attention that she soon was arching against his mouth, asking for more with each broken cry. His fingers dipped between her legs, between her slick folds to toy with the swollen nub of her sex. Emma moved with him, urging him with her hips to pick up the pace, to grant her release. But he seemed to enjoy pushing her ever so slowly to her limits, never letting her reach the place where she would come apart. She writhed beneath him, worry and doubt vanishing in the face of overwhelming need.

"Seth." It wasn't a request, but a demand. He pressed a long kiss to her lips, then whispered what he wanted against them.

"Ride me, Emma. I want to watch you."

She nodded, unable to catch her breath, and Seth rolled onto his back, pulling her over him. Emma rose above him, straddling his hips and sinking down onto him slowly, prolonging the pleasure for them both. For as fearless as she'd had to be in her professional life, letting a man see her like this, both powerful and vulnerable as she took him, had always been difficult for her. With Seth, though, the experience was heady, erotic. She tightened around him, inch by inch, until he was deep inside her. Through the thick sexual haze now enveloping her, Emma realized that Seth wasn't the only one benefiting from her position. She loved seeing him beneath her, his hands on her hips, his eyes half-closed. The way his lips parted soundlessly when she began to move, rising up only to plunge again and again.

His hands were all over her as she quickened the pace, squeezing him tight while he gripped her hips, caressed her breasts, telling her with groans and heated words exactly how much he liked it, how much he wanted it. Emma's head fell back as she rode him hard toward the edge, everything within her coiling tighter, tighter....

Emma paused at the edge, stilling so she could look at Seth spread beneath her, his every muscle tensed. His dark eyes caught her, held her, and she knew that she wasn't the only one who'd been ensnared by what they created together. Seth rasped a single word, flooding her with a heady mix of power and desire.

"Please."

She began to move again, crying out as her orgasm

slammed into her. She bucked against him as violent waves of pleasure crashed through her, taking her to a place she'd never known she could reach. Emma shuddered, then peaked again as Seth thrust up into her, the world dimming for a moment as he climaxed beneath her. She could feel his hands on her skin, his body joined with hers. . . . They gave her something, someone to hang on to as she came back to herself in a long, slow descent that left both of them shaken and spent. They breathed in time with each other, harsh, shallow breaths, as Emma finally slumped on top of Seth to feel his heart pounding through his chest. His arms came around her, and her first coherent thought was that she'd never felt so safe.

It shouldn't have been like this between them so fast . . . but it was.

"Em." His voice was harsh. "Holy shit."

"Mmm," was the only response she could muster. Sensing that she was the only one of them capable of it right now, she tugged weakly at her comforter until she could get it over the two of them. Seth didn't move a muscle, but once she was comfortably snuggled against him, he began to stroke her hair, gently. Her eyes slipped shut at his touch, and she felt all the cares of the day leave her. Every care but one.

"Stay," she murmured. "Please stay."

She felt the momentary tension in him, and then the easing of it as his breathing deepened, as his strokes slowed. It was all the answer she needed. Tonight, neither of them would be alone.

Emma's lips curved into a sleepy smile, and she let herself drift down into the quiet dark.

He hadn't intended to stay at Emma's all night Saturday. Or all night Sunday, for that matter. In fact, once they'd made love three or . . . five . . . more times and split the remains of a box of cereal Sunday morning, he figured he'd just go home, maybe get some work around the house done, and play it by ear. But while she was off making sure a baby shower ran like a well-oiled machine, something strange happened.

He missed her.

It wasn't just a wistful "looking forward to the next time we get together" sort of thing, either. It was an actual, physical longing that kept showing up to beat him over the head when he least expected it. He had the weekend off. It was supposed to be awesome, spent doing manly things around his house and then making a bunch of noise on his bike, and then maybe eating an entire pizza by himself before passing out in front of the TV.

Instead, he stuck around her apartment for a while after she left, playing with the oddly named Boof, whom he liked even though Boof was a cat. And he thought of Emma. And he went home and did some yard work, during and after which he thought of Emma. And he tinkered with his bike, and he thought of Emma even more, spending a fair amount of time on the classy little mint green dress she'd sashayed out of the apartment in. She'd looked like a Mad Men–themed wet dream. How did anyone concentrate on celebrating when she was around? He sure as hell couldn't concentrate on his Sunday.

Not until he'd brought her Chinese food for dinner. Then he'd found all sorts of things to concentrate on. Like getting to remove another one of her impossibly sexy dresses.

The woman was like a drug. On some level, it worried him. At least, when he wasn't busy just enjoying her company. It wasn't just the sex, though, that was mind-blowing. She was funny. And sweet. And clever. He felt comfortable with her in a way that should have taken far longer to achieve, if it happened at all . . . and even the thought of her made him smile.

Of all the things that might have made him feel like Harvest Cove might really be home, a woman was the last thing he'd expected. The cynical part of him insisted that this couldn't end well. Once the shine wore off, once they really had to start dealing with each other's baggage, the magic would end. But it was tough to concentrate on potential trouble when a beautiful woman was making him breakfast and wearing nothing but a fuzzy bathrobe that kept slipping off one slim, lovely shoulder.

Seth sat at Emma's little two-person table, mouth watering at the scent of sizzling bacon, and decided he felt about as good as he had in his entire life. Maybe it was the sleep. Maybe it was the sex. Or maybe it was just Emma, the whole gorgeous, neurotic package. That possibility was going to make his "let's take this day by day" strategy for handling relationships a little more difficult, but he felt so damn *good* for a change. Why try to fix what wasn't broken?

The cat leaped into his lap, fixed Seth with a look that dared him to try to remove him, and then settled down into an enormous furry lump, waiting to be petted. Seth obliged him and was rewarded with immediate and very loud purring.

"What kind of a name is Boof, anyway?" he asked, scratching the cat behind his big furry ears. Emma turned her head to look at the two of them, and Seth caught her amused smile before she went back to tending her scrambled eggs.

"Well, originally I wanted to name him Galahad."

Seth angled his head to look at the cat. "And Boof won out how, exactly?"

She laughed. "Well, Galahad was voted down, and he wouldn't respond to Henry—I mean, granted, he's a cat, so I took that into consideration—and it didn't seem to suit him. Even as a baby he had a habit of jumping onto my chest when I was lying down and either headbutting me or batting me in the face. Gently, at least, which was good because his claws are something else. Jake, Sam's fiancé, saw it one day and thought it was hilarious. He decided sound effects were in order, and then he started calling him 'the Boof,' which I told him sounded like the name of a bad professional wrestler."

"I guess it stuck anyway."

"Immediately. He answered to it from the get-go. Not that he'll necessarily come when you call, but he at least looks at the person calling him. So Boof it was, whether I liked it or not."

"Boof," Seth said. The cat blinked at him and twitched the end of his tail. "It's fun to say, at least."

"It's an original, just like him." Emma carried two plates to the table, each covered in bacon and scrambled eggs. She set one down in front of Seth, the other at her own place, and then went to get herself another cup of coffee before settling in across from him. He tried not to get overly distracted by the amount of skin the deep V of her robe revealed, but it wasn't easy. Considering the weekend the two of them had had, it seemed like he ought to be able to quit thinking about sex for a *little* while. Especially because he had to work in a couple of hours. So far, though, no luck.

Seth shoveled some of the eggs onto his fork and popped them in his mouth. Immediately, he knew he'd discovered something else about Emma. She could cook. "What did you put in these?" he asked, digging in.

"Garlic, onion, turkey, cheese, salt and pepper . . . and

whatever else seemed like a good idea when I opened up the spice cupboard." She shrugged. "Sam and I can both cook. We're not gourmet chefs or anything, but Mom decided it was something we needed to be able to do." She picked up a strip of bacon and bit off an end. "What about you, Chinese takeout guy? You don't look like a fast-food junkie, but I've been wrong before."

"I don't cook much," he admitted, "but I try to eat the healthy stuff that comes in boxes. Usually."

"Hmm. You're thirty, right? That's a lot of years to live by the grace of Chef Boyardee."

"Yeah, well, I had somebody else feeding me for most of them." He realized his mistake when he saw her interest sharpen, and he regretted it immediately. Quietly, he braced himself for the onslaught.

"That's true. I guess you would have. You said you were in for . . . six years?"

"Six."

"What did you do?"

"Shot at things." When her eyes narrowed, he amended that to, "I was a captain. Infantry."

"You went to college, then?" she asked. The surprise in her voice made him surlier than he might have been when he answered.

"Yeah, why? Did you think I didn't?"

He saw her jaw tighten and knew they were headed into unpleasant territory. He wanted to avoid that if at all possible, and he began grasping around for way to defuse the situation. He'd been prickly about the subject for so long, it had become habitual, but he knew it had been the wrong reaction to have with her.

"I didn't know if you had or hadn't," Emma said flatly. "In fact, I'm starting to think it's a little weird that I know nothing about you. You're a cop. You're around my age. You're from Florida and New York. You've mentioned a family, so I guess you didn't magically appear on earth out of thin air. And that's it. The end."

"That *is* the end, though. It's just not that interesting, Emma," he said, wishing she'd let it alone but knowing she wouldn't. "I did ROTC. Got a criminal justice degree. Did my thing in the army, got out, and after a while I found my way here."

She breathed in deeply, and he could see her trying to decide whether to press him further. What else could he say? The idea of divulging more made the hair at the back of his neck stand up. That six-year period hadn't been all bad, but it was a chunk of time he had such mixed feelings about—and that he'd been asked about so much whenever he'd gone home—that he would rather just let it be. She didn't need to think he was perfect, but he wasn't into showing off his scars. He didn't know if they would matter to her. More, he still didn't know whether they should. And in any case, it was too early to dump all that on her.

The chemistry they had together had been one of those unpredictable things, taking him completely by surprise. There was attraction, and then there was . . . this. It was damn near explosive. It also made trying to take the rest of it slowly a lot harder. Seth sighed, wishing the woman didn't like words so much. He'd much rather stick to physical expression when it came to how he felt.

Flustered, and feeling guilty both for putting uncertainty in Emma's eyes and for creating this sudden distance between then, Seth cast around for something he could say to close the rift again. It wasn't wrong, he told himself, to want to keep his time with her enjoyable. To hold off on the heavy stuff that might permanently change the way she looked at him.

"So, I got to make an interesting traffic stop the other day. Forgot to tell you."

He saw the momentary hesitation, then the acceptance in her small smile. "Really? What was that?"

Relief hit him hard and fast, leaving him almost lightheaded. He tried to keep his expression neutral. "Yeah, that guy you supposedly went streaking with? Al Piche?"

"We just call him Big Al, but okay. You pulled him over?" He'd caught her interest, and that was good. Just enjoying the moment was good. So much better than another tense conversation about what he'd been through, how he'd dealt with it. He couldn't erase the past, but he was awfully tired of the many ways it had found to keep him in its shadow. Pushing his frustration aside, Seth kept his voice light, knowing this would entertain her.

"I had to pull him over. He'd borrowed his friend's ice-cream truck."

"Borrowed." Her eyes crinkled at the corners, which was even better. "Did the friend know this?"

"No." He grinned at her, watching her eyes light, and something that had knotted up tight inside began to loosen again. "Mike Woodard owns it, you know, to make some extra money in the summer. He didn't want Al arrested, just wanted the truck back. I guess this has happened before?"

"Probably. His family has money, you know. So he has a lot of time to indulge his love of fun and his complete lack of shame. Someone told me he's a Mensa member, which is terrifying if it's true. Anyway, was the truck okay?"

"The truck, yes. The ice cream . . ." He lifted his hand and made a seesawing motion. "I found him covered in sticky wrappers, cruising along at about ten miles an hour and being chased through a neighborhood by a herd of disgruntled kids."

Emma burst out laughing. "What. The hell."

"He didn't seem to have a problem with being caught, so there's that, at least. Mark swears it's a rite of passage, having to take care of a Big Al problem. Guess I can officially join the club now."

Emma pumped her fist. "One of us! One of us!" Then she collapsed into laughter again, and the sound was like music. When she looked at him, her eyes danced with humor, and he knew everything was right between the two of them again. For now.

"You'll be a townie before you know it, Seth Andersen," she said. "Just watch."

"Could be," he replied. Suddenly he knew it was what he wanted. More, he realized, than he'd actually dared to hope for. Until now.

Until her.

And though he tried, the spark of hope that gave him was impossible to put out.

Chapter Sixteen

By Thursday, the weather had turned warm and muggy, and her brain had gone to complete mush. Emma didn't know whether to blame it on her nagging feeling that Seth was keeping her at arm's length, the humidity, or the fact that Boof had horked up three hairballs this week, all in places she'd be sure to step in them. But for the first time in months, she found herself struggling through the day instead of cruising efficiently along.

It had made her unfocused, which made her cranky. And though Brynn had gone to get them caramel frappés for lunch, the afternoon didn't show much improvement. By the time the bell above the door rang and a familiar, incredibly tall redhead walked through it, she was considering bailing out early and putting herself in an adult time-out with a box of cookies until she felt like herself again.

"Hey, Henry. Got a minute?"

She looked up, saw Shane Sullivan darkening her doorway, and sighed. Of all the people she didn't want to have to find some patience for today, he had to be near the top of the list.

"Hi, Shane. What can I help you with?" She could hear Brynn fiddling with the coffeemaker in the back office and knew her assistant would find an excuse to stay there until Shane had gone. She'd mentioned more than once that she found him both intimidating and seriously attractive.

Emma supposed there was no accounting for taste.

"Heard you saved the day at Max and Elaina's engagement party," he said. "Nice one. I was supposed to be there, but we had that stomach thing go through the office." He grimaced. "Definitely would rather have been at the party."

Emma blinked, unsure where he was going with this. "Well, it was a good one. Sorry you had to miss it."

He was an acquaintance, not a friend, and trying to make small talk with him felt seriously odd. She expected he wanted something. His continued rambling just confirmed it.

"This is nice in here," he said, looking around. "Have you ever done one of the firm's annual parties?"

"No, your father handles those himself."

"Which explains why they're so boring. I'm going to push for him to hire you this year."

Emma watched him wander the shop, looking at the framed photos, picking up cards, and putting them back down. He was well over six feet tall, built like an NFL quarterback, and yes, Emma supposed, very handsome. But he wasn't her type, and she had better things to do than stand here watching him beat around the bush.

"Did you want something, Shane? I'm kind of busy."

That got his attention, at least. "You're not as nice as your sister." He looked absurdly pleased by this.

"No, I'm not."

"Okay," he said, and incredibly, her bluntness seemed to relax him. "Here's the thing. I need a date for Sam's wedding."

The question was so out of the blue that it took her a few moments to process. Once she did, it still didn't make any sense.

"What?"

He grinned, dark blue eyes crinkling at the corners. "No, not you, don't worry. I heard you're into uniforms these days."

"You want me to find you a date?" She stared at him, wondering whether she'd dozed off and was dreaming this.

He nodded, and the pain when she pinched herself was real enough. "Basically, yes."

"Shane . . ." She paused, trying to understand what on earth might have driven him to ask her, of all people, to help him with this, and decided it had to be extreme desperation. "I'm your best friend's fiancé's sister. I barely know you. You *have* to have better resources than me." The dejected look on his face, however, said otherwise. "Have you really annoyed every eligible woman in the Cove to the point that you have zero date prospects? Is that even possible?"

"Maybe." He looked around. "The eligible ones I know well enough to talk to, anyway." He returned his gaze to Emma, and the determination in his eyes was a little unnerving. He really meant this.

Oh God. Why me?

"See, this is what I figure. You work with a lot of women, right? The baker. The florist. That cute redhead who's your assistant or whatever."

"Could you try not to be a pig while you're asking me for a favor? Please? Her name is Brynn. The other two you mentioned are Larkin and Annalise. And I'm not sure I'd inflict you on any one of them, since I'd like to retain my relationships with them."

He sighed heavily. "I'm trying. I'll try. Okay?"

"Mmmhmm."

"Anyway, I'm pretty sure those are the last three good-looking women in the Cove I've never talked to. Which means none of them has ever told me to go to hell. And two of them are from out of town, plus the cute red—er, Brynn's family moved away for a few years, so I have a fighting chance."

"You know, if you were going to stay here, you might have wanted to consider how being a serial dating jock with a big mouth and minimal empathy would affect your dating prospects later in life."

He winced. "Ouch."

"Well," Emma said, "it's true."

"I know. I just . . . I didn't actually plan on staying here. That's just sort of how things worked out." The expression that briefly flitted across his face was something far deeper than dejection, and Emma found herself feeling something unexpected for Shane: sympathy. Sam had warned her that he was like a big, slightly dense, mostly untrainable puppy sometimes, which made him tough to hate. How a guy could be bright enough to be a lawyer and dumb enough to get himself into his current predicament was beyond her, but Sam was right. Shane didn't seem very hateable.

Of course, she doubted he was dateable, either, good looks and desperation notwithstanding.

"I'm not a matchmaker."

Shane waved his hand dismissively. "You're a problem solver. This qualifies." He fixed her with that pleading look again. "I'm the best man. I just want somebody there to dance with when my best friend gets married. Come on, Henry."

It was hard to argue with that. Emma tapped her foot,

suddenly certain than Sam had heard about this hare-brained plan of his. It would have been nice to get a warning. And now here he was, with his big sad eyes, being weirdly endearing. She'd never set someone up in her life. This wasn't the way she would have preferred to start. In fact, not starting at all would have been good.

"Can't Sam hook you up? What about Zoe? She's single."

"Already been shot down there. She says she has a date."

"Oh." She frowned, considered her options—which at the moment amounted to letting Shane try to argue her into submission or just giving it a shot—and sighed. She wanted that quiet, peaceful box of cookies, not a lecture on the relative merits of finding Shane Sullivan a wedding date. "Well. I guess I could tr—"

"Great, excellent, you're a lifesaver," Shane rushed on, his miserable expression switching to a big grin in the blink of an eye. "Hook me up and I'll owe you big. Make me sound good, okay? Discounted legal fees if you ever get in a situation. Whatever you need. Awesome. Later, Em!"

He strode out, looking like he was on top of the world, and Emma stared after him, feeling like she'd been had. And what was with everyone calling her "Em" now? How had she attained "casual nickname" status with so many people?

You acted like an idiot in public, dumped beer over your head, and told people to call you Em—that's how. The stories might fade, but the nickname's going to stick.

Brynn emerged from hiding almost immediately after Shane left, holding her coffee mug in both hands. Emma looked at her, knowing that she'd heard every word. Maybe they could get this over with quickly and painlessly.

"Well?" Emma asked. "I know you like him."

Brynn shook her head. "I want to, but . . . no. I've got a family reunion that weekend, and if I blow it off to have a one-night stand with Shane Sullivan, I will never stop hearing about it."

Emma would have argued, except that she knew it was true. She did give her a halfhearted "It wouldn't *have* to be a one-night stand," but Brynn just smirked and shook her head.

"I wouldn't pass up a chance to take a bite out of him, so . . . yes, it would. But I really do need to go to that reunion. They deliberately planned it around the one weekend we're off for Sam's wedding."

"Damn." Emma put her hands on her hips and blew out a breath, glaring into space. "This is exactly how I wanted to spend my afternoon. Pondering who to inflict Shane Sullivan on."

"Ask Larkin. She's really easygoing."

Emma shot her a skeptical look. "I know. But that's not the same thing as being a glutton for punishment."

Brynn's lips twitched. "No, but she can handle herself. You know this. Annalise would suffer through it for you, but Larkin will just make a party of it. Schedule's clear for the rest of the afternoon, so you could maybe possibly go take care of that and get yourself some goodies at the same time. If you felt like it. Goodies might make you feel better."

Emma rubbed at her temple. "I'm that fun today, huh?"

Brynn moved her head back and forth. "You just seem a little . . . tired."

"You mean grouchy."

"I mean tired," Brynn said, but her laugh ruined the attempt to be diplomatic.

"Yeah, okay," Emma finally said, accepting defeat. Then she managed a smile, already feeling slightly better at the prospect of getting out in the sunshine and hopefully out of her own head a little. "Thanks."

"Not a problem," Brynn said. "I'm not being completely altruistic, you know. I'm putting together a proposal for the Jamison wedding, and I'll be less nervous working on it if you're not around hovering."

"I don't hover!" Brynn only raised her eyebrows, so Emma amended that to "I don't hover *much*. I—I try not to hover much. Okay, I hover. What do you have so far?"

"Ah-ah." Brynn held up a hand when Emma tried to scoot around the desk to look. "You told me to do my thing with this one and then show you, which is what I'm going to do. Get thee gone. Go get a pastry and earn Shane Sullivan's undying gratitude. Let me create my masterpiece."

"Hmm." Emma screwed up her mouth, but she backed off. "Fine. I'll go see if Larkin has any of those little strawberry tarts. You want me to bring you one?"

"Yes, but I'd just get goo on the keyboard," Brynn said. "I'm fine." She typed silently for a few moments, then looked up at Emma, her eyes wide and questioning. "Emma? Hovering."

"Okay." Feeling dejected without knowing why, she clipped back to her office, grabbed her purse, and then headed for the front door. "I'm leaving, I guess."

"Don't sound so excited."

"I'm holding it in so you don't get jealous."

Brynn snorted and lifted her hand in a half wave as Emma walked out the door. A breeze drifted past to ruffle her hair, and she breathed in the fresh air. It smelled like spring outside today, green and alive and a nice reminder that there was, in fact, a world outside of her office. Boof would be up in his window perch, no doubt, either sleeping or watching the birds. He could spend hours doing that.

She wished she was as easily entertained.

Feeling completely at loose ends, she walked slowly down the sidewalk of the tree-lined square, wondering what the hell to do with herself. She reached into her purse without thinking, doing a quick check of her messages. There was nothing, of course. Now that her status as a *taken* bar-dancing party freak had gotten around, all her texts were either work or family related, Brynn, or Seth. And all of those potential texters were busy right now.

Strawberry tart and matchmaking. Joy. Well, it was something to do, at least. Emma turned and headed up away from the harbor, walking until she got to the cheery pink lettering that announced she'd reached Petite Treats. Not that she hadn't smelled it beforehand. It was like breathing spun sugar, with the added visual of customers relaxing at pink-and-white iron tables outside, enjoying Larkin's handiwork. Her mouth started to water. She couldn't help it.

A bell rang as she stepped inside, getting in line behind four other people while they all perused the offerings in the long glass display counter. The day's offerings and prices were written in brightly colored chalk on a blackboard hung behind the counter, and a girl with a curly mop of dark hair waited on everyone with a smile. Her smile brightened when she saw Emma.

"Hi, Ms. Henry! I'll be with you in a sec. Are you here to see Larkin?"

"If she's around. But I mostly came for one of those strawberry tarts."

"Excellent choice." She took care of the other customers with charm and efficiency, and Emma watched her, amused. Aimee worked after school most weekdays, and most weekends as well, by choice. She was a junior in high school, and made no secret of her worship of the town's most celebrated pastry chef. Larkin put that worship to good use, and told anyone who would listen about her protégée. Emma had watched long enough to know that Aimee was bound for culinary school once she graduated, no question. She knew where her passion lay. That was a gift, that knowledge, as long as it was put to good use. And apart from all that, she was a good kid.

"Do you want it in a box, or are you going to eat it here?" she asked.

Emma considered that, and then an idea struck her. "Actually, give me two. Separate boxes. I want to drop one to a friend." She owed Seth for the cupcakes he'd brought her. And it was a way to connect, even in a small way, after a few days of not seeing him.

"Nice. He'll love it." Emma arched a brow, and Aimee blushed. "Um, he or she. Sorry."

"Oh, you know very well it's a he. Everyone seems to." Emma sighed. That made Aimee laugh, and she got the tarts into their little pink-and-blue boxes before ringing her up. The door to the kitchen opened, and a head poked around the corner.

"I knew I heard you! Who set you loose? That slave driver you work for never leaves, I hear."

"Very funny. I blame you. I swear I can smell this place from inside my office." Emma watched tall, thin Larkin O'Neill emerge fully, wearing striped pants and an apron. She had flour on one cheek and mischief in her bright green eyes. Her honey blond hair was piled on top of her head in a bun, apart from the long, thick bangs that covered her eyebrows. At six feet tall, she would have been impossible not to notice even if she hadn't already been drop-dead gorgeous. Emma had sort of wanted to hate her when she'd first opened the shop, but Larkin made that tough. She was earthy, kind of messy, and she loved food.

And actually, Emma thought, Brynn was probably right. Larkin was one of the only people she could think of who might be able to have a decent time with Jake's obnoxious friend. She bit the inside of her lip, annoyed just remembering the way he'd played on her sympathies.

Might as well get this out of the way.

"I came for a tart. And to ask you something," Emma said. That piqued Larkin's interest.

"Oh yeah? Hang on. I'll come around for a sec."

Aimee handed Emma her bag and started tending to the next customer. Emma stepped off to the side, beside one of the little indoor tables. Larkin joined her, looking like she'd just stepped out of a bakery-themed photo shoot for a magazine.

"What's up?"

"Well . . ." Emma hesitated. The two of them had partnered up for plenty of events in the three years since Larkin had arrived, but though they were friendly, they'd never taken the relationship out of the work arena. *Like Brynn,* Emma thought, and wondered if this was another case of a friendship failing to fully bloom because she'd deliberately refused to allow it. Probably. She guessed they would see, because this was a friendly favor on steroids.

"Is this about what that Boston pastry chef the Hardings are bringing in said about me? Because that's sweet of you, if it is, but I'm fine. I've heard a lot worse. If they want to spend a fortune on some jerk who charges a premium just because he was on *Food Adventure* for a minute and a half like five years ago, they can knock themselves out. I'm busy."

"Oh. Wow. No, I didn't hear about that." She'd deliberately avoided asking anyone about the Harding wedding once she was certain she'd lost the chance to plan it. It helped that she'd had other things to occupy her thoughts, but it was still an open wound, if a smaller one than she'd imagined it might be. It didn't surprise her that Penny would choose people who were expensive and unpleasant. But hearing that one of them had insulted Larkin rankled.

Larkin didn't seem as bothered. She waved her hand. "Chefs are dramatic. And catty. Like I said, I've heard worse. How are things? Good? No more performance art?"

"Um. No." She felt her cheeks heat.

Larkin clucked her tongue. "Emma. It was cute. And funny. And now you have your own local legend, lucky. That naked flash mob downtown after midnight must have been really something. Or it would have been, if it had existed. Should have picked better music, though."

"What am I supposed to have danced to?"

"Spice Girls medley," Larkin said, then laughed when Emma gagged. "You should come to karaoke with me and Annalise. Seriously. We're really bad, so it's okay."

"Oh." The invitation wasn't one she'd ever expected. She couldn't help but be suspicious of its origins. "It's not just because—"

"No," Larkin interrupted, rolling her eyes. "Not because we want you to humiliate yourself in public. We always talk about asking you. I just wasn't sure you did things outside of work."

"Things?"

"Well . . . you know. You're kind of a grown-up, Emma. In a good way, I mean. But I thought maybe you'd think we were silly for going. So I didn't want to put you on the spot so you'd have to say no and pretend like you didn't think we were giant dorks. I mean it—we're *terrible*. But it's a lot of fun."

Emma's response tumbled from her lips without a thought. "I'd love to sometime. And I don't think you and Annalise are dorks. I just assumed you all thought I was boring. I mean, I am, kind of, but not that boring. But I mean yes. I'd love to. Sure." Then she dropped her face into her hands while Larkin watched, looking utterly amazed by the outburst. "Sorry. You're right. I don't get out much."

She felt a gentle pat on her shoulder. "Oh, babe. You're one of our people, trust me. You just didn't know it. Now what did you need to talk to me about?"

Emma looked up into Larkin's understanding expression and found that it was much easier to ask than she'd expected. "It's a favor. Sam's wedding. The best man needs a date, and he asked me to ask you because I don't think he's progressed much beyond high school in that department." *Or a few others.*

"Way to sell me on him, Emma." She looked amused, though, so Emma pressed on. How was she supposed to make Shane sound good when most of what she knew about him was less than appealing? Honesty, she decided, was probably best.

"Shane's all right. Not great, but all right. He's also desperate. On the upside, I'll be there, you're already doing the cake, and it'll probably be a good party."

"And the downside?"

"Well, it could be Shane. I'm not sure. It depends. He's

not evil or anything, and I don't think he'll paw you. He's just kind of obnoxious. It's fine if you call him on it, though. It's an issue he's aware of." Larkin laughed softly, and Emma was pretty sure that was a no. "Don't worry about it, Larkin. I'll tell him I tried and you were busy. You're probably better off."

"No, now hang on. This is Shane Sullivan, right? Tall redhead? Lawyer?"

Emma nodded. "That's the one."

Larkin gave a nonchalant shrug. "Okay, why not?"

Emma blinked. "Really?"

"Yeah, sure. I never get to be a guest at weddings, and I like Sam and Jake. Their cake is going to be gorgeous. I'm happy to go eat some of it. Besides," she added with a smirk, "the guy's eye candy, if nothing else."

It was hard to think of Shane that way, but objectively speaking, she supposed Larkin was right.

"Well, great. I'll let him know."

"Sounds good. Give him my number or something. Listen, I have to run. Call you about the karaoke, okay? Maybe ask Brynn, too. She's a trip. I'll see you Saturday anyway. Mason wedding. Cake made entirely of cupcakes." She gave her a big grin, two thumbs-up, and then headed back behind the counter and through the kitchen door. "Later!"

"Later," Emma echoed. And though she wasn't planning a repeat performance any time soon—or ever—she couldn't help thinking that in some ways, the ripples from her one night of spontaneity had brought her as much good as bad. Maybe more. It was certainly turning into an argument for not hanging on so tightly to her routine and learning to take a chance once in a while.

Though it would be best, she decided, if those chances involved as little alcohol as possible.

With a small smile and a spring in her step, Emma picked up her bag of treats and headed out the door.

He wasn't at the station, though a very nice sergeant showed her which desk to leave the box on. It was strange, getting a look at this part of Seth's life, and it served only to drive home the reality of how little of himself he'd shared with her. The station was small, and a bit cluttered, but everyone seemed friendly. It wasn't anything like the TV shows she sometimes watched, but since those were usually madhouses, that was actually comforting. His desk wasn't much to speak of, either, but he had a few things on it, papers and Post-its, and most interestingly, a couple of pictures.

Emma picked up the one that caught her eye first. If she'd wanted proof he had a family, she didn't need to look any further. It had obviously been taken a few years ago, but there was a younger Seth, with the same big smile, next to a pretty dark-haired girl who looked just his age—his sister. A twin? Anything was possible. On one side of them was a smiling man and on the other side a woman, looking relaxed and happy on some long-ago afternoon spent in the sun.

Things couldn't be too bad if he had a framed picture of them on his desk, she thought. Maybe he just didn't want to tell *her* about them. That was a pleasant thought. Frowning, she replaced the picture and picked up the other one. The background couldn't have been more different. This one was in a desert under a washed-out sky, showing Seth in his camouflage uniform goofing around with another soldier, a tall, good-looking guy with a smile as big as his. Seth's tongue was out, and they looked like they were having the time of their lives. His best friend, maybe . . . and she thought of the picture above his fireplace.

Emma put it down quickly, suddenly uncertain, and wrote a little note to leave with the strawberry tart before thanking the sergeant and walking out. They were just pictures, but she felt as though she'd been reading his diary or something. Looking places she shouldn't. Which was silly—everyone at work could see those pictures.

But she wasn't with him at work. She currently occupied a small corner of his life that didn't appear to touch any of the other parts. Hopefully that would change, she thought. But it needed to change soon, because the sick feeling in the pit of her stomach wasn't one she wanted to become that well acquainted with.

Funny, how meeting him had pushed her to start opening up, even though he'd remained such a mystery. Okay, not really funny. Just upsetting. She headed down the steps, deep in thought, and then started to walk to her car. His voice pulled her back into the moment.

"Emma! Hey!"

She looked up to see Seth jogging toward her and had to take a moment to remind herself that this was the same guy who'd been lounging in her bed all last weekend. Today he was all in sharply pressed blue, his badge gleaming on his chest. She had a fleeting, wonderful, awful impulse to drag him into a dark corner and remove the shirt with her teeth. She quashed that, berated herself for thinking it, and then remembered that such activities weren't actually off-limits once they were alone together.

The possibilities had her blushing before Seth even reached her.

"I hope your cheeks are pink because you're thinking dirty thoughts about me," he said.

"Oh, all the time." She laughed. *No, really, all the time. You have no idea.*

"What are you doing here?" he asked. "Is everything okay?"

"Yes, no, everything's fine. I mean . . ." She held up the bag from Petite Treats, still flustered as she tried to reconcile the conflicting feelings she was dealing with. Trying to push aside what she'd seen on his desk, and how that had made her feel, was as impossible as being angry at him when he was so pleased to see her. "I had to go to Petite Treats for something, so I thought you might like a strawberry tart."

"Awesome. It's in the bag?"

"No. This one's mine. They showed me your desk, so I left it there."

Was it just her, or did she see a hint of uncertainty in his eyes? Steeling herself, she pushed a little further to find out. "I saw the picture of your family. I guess you really didn't just drop out of the sky."

He laughed, but with an edge of discomfort. "No, I definitely didn't."

She could feel him closing down, and this time her temper flickered to life. She tried to hold it at bay, keeping her tone light. "Your sister looks just like you. Is she a twin?"

"Um, yeah," he said, starting to rub at the back of his neck. "Kira is my twin. Older twin. By like a minute. Hey, I've got to head in and get my paperwork together. Did you want to grab some dinner or something later?"

Her frustration bubbled to the surface. "Honestly? What I'd like to do is put my high heel up your ass right now. But since you're in uniform, that's out, I guess. Enjoy the tart, Seth. I need to go."

She stalked away, savoring the moment of silence as he digested what she'd said. Part of her looked on in dismay, but the stronger part, the take-no-crap part of her that functioned perfectly well in most areas of her life, bared its teeth in triumph. She needed that part of herself right now. Because for all of her feelings about Seth, allowing herself to be steamrolled into just accepting whatever scraps of himself he chose to throw her was ultimately going to make neither of them happy.

This wasn't exactly how she would have chosen to make her stand about it, but she'd work with what she had. Even if all she had was a damn strawberry tart.

"Emma? Emma!" She heard his footfalls, but she kept moving, digging her keys out of her purse. He wasn't the only one who could be quiet when he wanted to. Her simmering anger made speaking just now a risky proposition anyway. Then he was beside her, and she had to cling to her resolve when she heard the confused anger in his voice.

"What the hell was that for? All I did was ask you to dinner!"

She spun on him, keeping her voice low. "You know very well what that was for." She exhaled loudly and looked around, conscious of people walking around, of a potential audience. She didn't want that, for either of them. It allowed her to keep a handle on all the things she *wanted* to say. "Look, forget it. You don't want to talk to me, and I don't want to do this here. I'm tired, and I'm going home."

"Not until I know what I did to piss you off all of a sudden."

She gave him a dark look. "It has taken me almost a month to find out that you have a twin sister. And actual, living parents. We won't even get started on the other picture, because that seems to be off-limits, too. So until you remove some of the red tape, my bedroom? Is also off-limits. I don't want to be used like this. I'm not a convenience."

He looked horrified. "I would never—"

"It's my fault, too," Emma said, feeling clearheaded for the first time in weeks. It wasn't a pleasant sensation. "I let it happen. It's just going to stop now. If you want to talk about it, fine, but you have work and I need to cool off. This isn't the place."

"Em—" His voice had stopped sounding wounded and it took on a warning tone. All that did was have her yanking open the car door faster. He didn't try to stop her, but he didn't look happy.

"Later," she said flatly, shut the door, and started the car. Seth backed off, but he watched her go. She could feel his eyes on her the entire way down the street.

She was only glad that she managed to wait until the turn to burst into angry tears.

Chapter Seventeen

B y the time he finished his paperwork and was headed
home, Seth didn't want anything but the wind in his
face and a clear head. He knew he could have one of
them. The other, though, he wasn't so sure of.

Seth changed quickly once he was home, dumping his
uniform over the back of a chair, locking up his gun, and
throwing on his favorite jeans and battered boots. He
grabbed his leather jacket and helmet, then, after a quick
internal struggle, dug out his spare helmet and rubbed the
dust off it. Maybe she'd come and maybe she wouldn't, but
it didn't hurt to be optimistic.

He knew he'd screwed up. He was pretty good at rec-
ognizing it, even while he was doing it. He was just having a hard time not screwing up here. This was all moving
faster than it was supposed to. He didn't know what he'd
been looking for—he hadn't expected her to ever look
his way, honestly. But she had, and here he was, and she
was going to bolt on him if he didn't fix at least some of
what he'd broken.

Maybe it's better if she goes. The thought whispered
through his mind, and he stomped it out just as quickly
as it had appeared. He knew that voice. It wasn't his anymore.

He managed to wedge the extra helmet into his saddle-bag and took off down the road, trying to find some peace in the rumble of the engine, the feel of the machine beneath him, and the control he had over it. It had helped at a tougher time in his life, and he felt it begin to help now. Not enough, though. He needed more. That was new, and so were the fumbling and fear that came with it.

No wonder he was screwing up. And he'd seen the anger in Emma's eyes, real anger for the first time.

Seth pulled in behind her building, parked the bike, and headed upstairs with dread curling in the pit of his stomach. Maybe she'd be too angry to see him. Maybe she'd tell him to go to hell, that she didn't have time for an emotionally detached cop who was up here hiding from his old life. Except he didn't feel emotionally detached right now. If he was honest with himself, he hadn't felt that way in quite a while. Lately, it seemed like he felt every damn thing. But it made one hell of an excuse to keep hiding, not just from his family, but from her.

Knowing that, acknowledging that, didn't exactly make his night. But it was important, and he knew it.

Through the door, up the stairs, and then to Emma's door. Seth knocked, heard Boof meow and Emma mutter at him. Then there were footsteps, the turning of a lock, and she was in front of him. Her hair was down, tumbling in thick and unruly waves past her shoulders. She wore sweats and an old T-shirt, and she was holding a half-empty glass of wine. Her eyes were wary and slightly puffy. He couldn't have felt worse if he'd tried.

"Probably still not a good time," she informed him.

"It's what I've got," he said. "Just hear me out, okay? Please?"

The "please" got her attention, at least. And the attraction, still pumping between them like a heartbeat, would buy him time. Seth hoped it was enough. He was tired of doing this to people who gave a damn about him.

"I don't get you," she informed him, taking a sip of the wine. There was a coolness in her demeanor, one he was familiar with from watching her these past six months. That had been fascinating. This was anything but.

"I know."

Her eyebrows lifted. "Oh? Well, it's nice to know you were being deliberately obtuse, then. Thanks."

Obtuse. Yes, she was still angry.

"Not deliberately. I— Look, will you come with me? I want to take you someplace. And I'll explain what I can, I swear."

She eyed his helmet. "Come with you . . . on the motorcycle?"

"Yeah. Give it a chance. You might like it."

"I don't like putting my life at risk, but thanks," she replied.

"And I don't like knowing you're angry at my stupid bullshit when you won't let me try to explain why it's there."

She fell silent, her big blue eyes frank and assessing. "Come in," she said. "I'll change."

Seth walked in as Emma walked away, no invitation in the stiff way she carried herself, and he knew better anyway. He fussed over Boof while she changed her clothes, then looked up when she emerged from the bedroom. Her hair was in a long ponytail, and she wore a dark, dressy pair of denim pedal pushers with a pair of ballet flats and a light cardigan over a thin T-shirt. At her throat were pearls.

Seth recognized it, all of it, as her armor. It made him less inclined to fight her on the clothing, though one element needed to go.

"You're going to want boots if you have them. Sneakers if nothing else."

She fixed him with a glare, but after walking away, she returned with a stylish, low-heeled pair of boots that were in no way what he'd meant. They were a middle finger, of sorts, but they would work. He wished she had a leather jacket, but that wasn't an argument he wanted to start right now. He'd drive carefully.

When he walked out the door, she locked up behind him, then followed silently down to the parking lot. When they reached his bike, he pulled the extra helmet out, then had to fight back a smile when she shoved it on her head and crossed her arms over her chest.

Even now, she could find a way to lighten his mood. She didn't even know she was doing it, that just being with him was making everything better.

The thought shook him, and he tucked it away. It was nothing he was ready to say out loud . . . and nothing Emma would want to hear. Not right now.

"Okay," he said, slinging a leg over the seat. "Get on behind me."

He thought she might change her mind at this point and nearly had his fingers crossed as he willed her to come with him, but he needn't have bothered. Slowly, stiffly, Emma got on behind him. She seemed to understand that she would need to hang on, but the arms that went around his waist felt so rigid and brittle, they might break.

That would have to do.

Seth started it up and roared out of the parking lot. He heard Emma's muffled yelp and felt her arms tighten around him, which he tried not to dwell on as he headed out of town and along the shore. She did better than he'd have guessed, back in the beginning. Still, she had a ways to go to relax. At least she hung on.

He took a left off Hawthorne and headed out of town, keeping to the two-lane roads that hugged the coast. The wind smelled of the sea, the breeze that flowed over his skin cool without being cold. He could smell the earth and air, and finally felt himself steadying, centering. Emma held on tight, curling into the back of him. He was used to riding solo, but today, this was better.

About ten miles outside of town he pulled off into a small state park, which was still quiet on weekdays this time of year, before summer rushed in with campers and cookouts and groups of summer rec kids. A couple walked along the stretch of beach in the distance, holding hands. The gulls were in an ecstasy over something left behind on a picnic table, but there was little sound beyond their cries and the soft rhythm of the waves.

Seth parked the bike, feeling Emma's grip on his tighten for a moment, then loosen as she slid off. He pulled his helmet off, then watched her do the same. Her hair was mussed beneath, which matched her disgruntled expression. He didn't ask whether she'd liked the ride. In her current state, she probably couldn't have answered it honestly, and that was fine.

"Come on," he said. "My table's over here."

"You have a table?" she asked, carrying her helmet and trailing slightly behind him.

"Sure." He led her to a scarred old picnic table right at the edge of the place where grass turned to sand, stepping on the seat and sitting on the top to look out at the gray waters of the Atlantic. He set his helmet behind him, then looked at Emma and patted the spot beside him. "You can sit if you want."

She had to think about it, and something twisted painfully in his chest while he watched her do it. But after a moment, she sighed, dumped the helmet next to his, and climbed up. She left space between them, though, but that wasn't a surprise.

They watched the ocean silently for a few minutes, until Emma spoke. Her anger seemed to have gone, but that cool edge remained.

"Well? You wanted to talk."

He collected his thoughts, and then started. Slowly. "I know you feel like I'm not letting you get to know me. I know in some ways that's probably true. But I wasn't in a great place before I moved here."

She tilted her head to look at him. "Oh?"

"Yeah. After I got out of the military, I went home. Close to home, anyway. Jacksonville. Big police department, new opportunities. I thought that was what I wanted. It was what I'd wanted before I went to college, and I'd always figured, hey, ROTC, help pay for school, get out in the world, fight some bad guys, defend freedom, whatever, then come back and be a police officer. I'm oversimplifying, but I was young. And naive."

"So was everybody, once." She shrugged. "I take it Jacksonville didn't work out?"

"No. It wasn't the job. I mean, good group of people, busy as hell. But I couldn't find a rhythm. I was home, except it didn't feel like home anymore. Everything was the same and I was different, but people just expected me to fit right back into place. My parents, my sister . . . and it wasn't their fault, but they didn't know what to do. I had trouble sleeping. I wasn't interested in reengaging. Old friends called, and I blew them off. All I did was work and hang around my apartment. And ride." He looked at her, watching him with those inscrutable, impossibly blue eyes. "I got the bike after my third tour in Iraq. The doc I saw thought it was a great idea. Stress relief, as long as I didn't wrap it around a tree or anything."

"The doc. Therapy?" She frowned.

"Yeah. I spent four of my six years in the army in the desert, Em. It . . . You see things during war. It's not how anybody thinks. Long stretches of nothing, and then these short patches of hell. And you feel like . . . People back here just don't get it. I mean, they can't, I guess. And you come back and it's like you were off-planet for that year. People say nice things, and that's great, but they don't want to hear about how your buddy got blown up by an IED, or how you watched a car full of kids get shot up at a checkpoint because the parents were too afraid to stop. Or how you think you're helping people, and then politics go and screw up all the good you thought you did. So you come back, and some of your buddies can't flip that switch to reintegrate. They quit functioning, and you worry that it's going to happen to you, too. Especially because you feel numb a lot of the time. You have nightmares. You can't sleep."

"PTSD."

He hesitated. He didn't know why. Then he nodded. "Yeah." He knew there was no shame in it. But everybody had their own ideas about what that label meant, even though the reality encompassed a huge spectrum.

Emma appeared to be digesting this, but he didn't see worry or pity in her gaze. Only the quiet thoughtfulness he'd seen her exhibit on more than one occasion. "Did the therapy help?" she finally asked.

"It did." He nodded. "I was proactive, and I had a good doctor. And I was lucky. She's the reason I'm walking around with a clean bill of mental health, and I'll always be grateful for that. But recovery isn't a straight line, and nothing is perfect. Most of my symptoms are gone, but I figured out the hard way that I'm not quite . . . the same. I don't like the crush of a big-city PD. Some guys thrive on that, and I might have once. But it reminded me too much of combat sometimes, and I don't like kicking into that mode anymore. I do better with a small command, being able to make a visible difference in a community. Slower, I guess, but in a good way."

"Harvest Cove," Emma said. He nodded.

"That's what I was hoping, anyway. So far, so good."

She sighed and looked out at the sea. "Why didn't you just tell me all of this from the beginning?" she asked.

"I don't like talking about it."

Emma turned her head to regard him, and the corner of her mouth curved up in a wry smile. "You don't say?"

Seth gave a soft, embarrassed laugh and shrugged his shoulders. "I thought it would be better to *not* start with my problems. I'm flailing a little here, Emma. I wasn't expecting you."

She seemed to consider that. "Well," she finally said, "that makes two of us. So what about your parents? Are you not speaking, or . . ."

"No, no, nothing like that," Seth said. "They just worry. When I left, I didn't give them a lot of notice. They didn't want me to go. I needed the change. They watched me struggle when I came home from the war that last time, and I think they were scared that this time I was going to end up . . . I don't know, worse."

"Like your friends."

He breathed out, looked at the ocean. "Like my friends. I think the only reason they didn't come chasing after me was that my uncle is the one who convinced me that the Cove was the place. Steve had a little bit of a hard time when he got out, too. Different wars, same place. Having him around helps."

"I like your uncle."

"So do I, and so do my parents, which is a good thing.

I love my family. I'm not from a bad home or anything. They're pretty normal. I mean, except Kira, but we're used to her."

"You didn't want to tell me about them, though. About anything," Emma said. She'd gone from sounding cool to sounding sad, and Seth thought that was almost worse.

"I thought taking it slow and keeping things, ah, light would be better to start. And you're more interesting than I am." He gave her a small smile, but she didn't return it.

"So . . . wild sex and limited conversation. That's what you want."

Seth cringed. "Jesus no! I haven't had an actual girlfriend in over two years, Emma, and that relationship didn't end well. I'm rusty, not an asshole. Is that really what you think of me?"

"No." She chewed at her lip and looked away. "I'm not great with people, Seth. I never have been. So unless you spell it out for me, I'm probably not going to be able to figure out what you're after here."

That was the big question. And as he watched her, looking out at the ocean as the wind toyed with her hair, the only answer he could come up with wouldn't clarify a thing for either of them: *her*. He didn't want to lose her. Emma and her smiles and the sunshine she brought into his life. Emma, whose every little kiss made him want a thousand more. She'd turned a life that was quiet and gray into something unpredictable and new, and she'd turned a little town he'd taken a big chance on into a place where he might really belong, all of it so quickly that his head was still spinning. He just didn't know how to tell her. Not in so many words. Not when every move he made with her seemed to set the ground shifting beneath his feet. The fact that he didn't want to run from it was important. *She* was important.

Which was why right now, the thing that worried him most was hurting her.

"I want to keep seeing you," he said quietly. "I want to be able to have dinner together and sometimes breakfast together and play with your ridiculous cat. That's not me trying to use you. That's just all I've got for an answer right now."

She was quiet for a few moments. "All those things you said . . . That's why no girlfriend, right?"

He nodded. It was uncomfortable to talk about, but he guessed this was the day for uncomfortable things. "I wasn't really looking to get attached. I don't think I was capable."

She stared out at the water. "It's not just you," she said, and he frowned, not understanding.

"What do you mean?"

"Not being sure you could have a relationship. I told you I didn't want one, but I didn't tell you why."

He waited for her to collect her thoughts, tracing the fine lines of her profile with his gaze. This was one of the other things about Emma—her ability to surprise him. He wondered how she could possibly have existed in this town for so long with so few people discovering who she really was.

Then again, there were a million reasons to put up walls. He was familiar with more than a few.

"I was with a guy. Ben. Back in college, and then after. He was brilliant. I mean"—she laughed softly—"I thought he was brilliant. He was also a professor, which should have been a huge red flag, but . . . well, like I said, I'm not great at people. Finding someone who seemed to be on my wavelength was kind of a huge deal."

He could see it, prim, elegant, intelligent Emma absolutely knocking the socks off some professor. Who had obviously been a giant douchebag. He began to hope this story ended with Emma's fist connecting with this guy's face, but he thought he'd probably be disappointed.

"So what happened?"

She shrugged. "Lots of whirlwind romance and me being impressed. After I graduated and came home, I figured it was only a matter of time before we took things to the next level. He hadn't asked, but I was . . . stupid, I guess. Naive. I was comfortable, and being with him was always so easy. I felt safe." Her blue eyes fixed on him. "After losing Dad, and how rocky things were afterward, safe was the one thing I really wanted to feel."

Seth thought of how he must have looked to her, an ex-soldier, a cop—a guy whose job would always involve a willingness to risk his life—and he knew exactly why she'd tried to head in the other direction. She was taking more of a risk with him than he'd known. More than she'd known, too, though not after this conversation. The realization came with a surprising amount of pain. He tried to keep his expression neutral, though, wanting to hear the rest.

"Anyway, I finally got tired of waiting. I decided, what the hell, I'll go up, surprise him, and we'll have a big romantic weekend during which I'll profess my love and he'll obviously insist we move in together. It was perfect."

"Except it wasn't," Seth said.

"Nope." She kicked the bench with her heel. "He didn't want to be surprised. In fact, he took the opportunity to accuse me of being distant. Cold. Only concerned about my own needs while I ignored his. I was the one who'd moved right back to my crappy little Podunk town. I was the one who had abandoned him. I couldn't just show up on his doorstep whenever I wanted. He needed someone who really understood him. Somebody who was just . . . more than me."

"This guy sounds like a complete asshole, Emma. Please tell me you punched him."

"No." Her mouth curved into a small smile. "I cried. When he told me that I was manipulative, I kicked him in the junk. Then I drove home."

Seth didn't know whether to put an arm around her or high-five her. Yet she didn't seem to need comforting. The story had been told with the kind of distance that said she was over the man himself. Just maybe not the things he'd said.

"He couldn't have known you at all. You're not cold, Em. You're anything but."

She lifted her brows at him. "Maybe not cold. But I can definitely be distant. I never liked to get too close. I know myself pretty well, Seth. I know what I do with people."

"You can be prickly," he conceded, wishing he knew whether it was okay to touch her face, her hair, anything to reassure her—and himself. "But you let me in."

"People aren't usually as determined as you. Or as much of a Boy Scout."

"I have my good points." Seth watched the breeze toy with the tendrils of her hair, her cheeks still pink from the ride. "I wish you hadn't listened to him. Doesn't sound like he knew you at all." In a single month he'd gotten to know her far better than that.

"Maybe not. But some of what he said that day wasn't completely off the mark, either. I'm good at holding everyone at arm's length. Sam tried to let people in, and all she got was abuse. So I always figured, why bother? I'll just get hurt. And I'd had enough of that."

She breathed deeply and fell silent, seeming lost in thought. He couldn't blame her. On paper, he was exactly the wrong kind of guy for her. But she was still here, and that had to count for something.

"So," he echoed, "we've both got some baggage. Think we can work with it?"

Emma studied his face. "That depends. What are the odds of me ending up crying and kicking you in the junk at some point if I say yes?"

He laughed softly, suddenly sure he couldn't have had this conversation with anyone but Emma. "Low, I hope." He didn't want her to walk on him, but he knew Emma well enough now to know that she needed honesty. "I can't make you any promises. You don't get to come back from as much time as I spent in a war zone without some broken pieces. I'm mostly healed, I think, but I'm still feeling out my limits. This place, and you, have been good for me. I'd like to keep that going. You make me happy, Emma. That's what I know."

For once, he knew he'd said the right thing. She tucked a strand of hair that had come loose behind her ear when she looked at him again. "Thank you," she said.

"For what?"

"For telling me. All of it." She shifted, suddenly restless. "I should tell you that, much like I'm not great at people, I'm also not great at uncertainty."

His heart sank. "Ah." *This is the part where she leaves. This is the part where she says "thanks, but no thanks" and goes.* The thought flooded him like ice water, and his heart began to pound. He hadn't expected to feel this kind of terror, this kind of loss. The fact that her scent, seductive and sweet, still enveloped him made it that much worse.

Then her hand covered his, a simple gesture that banished all the ugliness roiling inside him as though it had never been there, the sun dispelling the storm.

"But," she said softly, "I want to try."

He exhaled, releasing a shaky breath he didn't even know he'd been holding. "Okay," he said. It sounded silly to him, but he couldn't think of anything else. "Okay."

"I don't do things halfway, Seth," she warned him. But the coolness was gone, as was the anger, and he could hardly see past that to hear her words. "If we're headed nowhere fast, I need to know before I—just before too long, okay? Be fair. And stop pretending you don't have a past, because we all do. I can handle more than you think. I already have."

He nodded. "Deal." Sitting there beside him, prim and lovely in her pearls—only Emma, he thought, would wear pearls on the back of a motorcycle—she was one of the loveliest things he'd ever seen. That mattered. Really, everything about her seemed to. She'd gotten him to take a step today that no other woman had. It was exhausting and exhilarating at the same time.

"Seal it with a kiss?" he asked hopefully, and her chuckle was low and warm as she leaned in. She tasted of strawberries and wine, and Seth knew that at least for a little while, everything would be all right.

He'd learned not to ask for more than that.

Chapter Eighteen

On a beautiful Sunday afternoon, Emma and Seth pulled up to the comfortable old Craftsman-style home Jake and Sam shared. The temperatures hovering in the midseventies made it feel like summer had already arrived instead of still being just around the corner. Emma wore shorts for the occasion, white and high-waisted, even though she worried that the color matched her legs a little too closely. Seth was in a pair of old jeans and a black T-shirt, and he'd conned her into letting him bring her on the bike, so she'd been over earlier to drop off Boof. The cat needed to move occasionally, and a visit with Sam's cat, Boof's sleek and diabolical sibling Loki, was as good a way as any to achieve that.

Seth looked good enough to eat, Emma thought as they walked through the fence gate into the backyard. And his hair was still slightly damp from his shower. Well, *their* shower. Which was why hers was up in a bun. He flashed a wicked grin at her as he shut the gate behind them, and she felt a funny, aching twist in her chest that she'd been afflicted with more and more often lately where he was concerned.

Just light and easy, she told herself for the umpteenth time that day. *Take it as it comes. Relaxed Emma, that's me. Here I am, going with the flow.* And then: *Oh God, I am so full of shit. Where's the sangria?*

The sangria, fortunately, was on the wrought-iron patio table with her sister, while Jake was playing with the big stainless steel grill Sam had gotten him for his birthday. He abandoned it briefly to come greet them, and any worries she'd had about Seth and Jake not getting along evaporated almost instantly. Jake had a knack for putting people at ease, and he shoved a beer in Seth's hand seconds before steering him to the grill to show it off. As introductions went, it worked. Emma settled herself at the table with Sam and poured herself a glass of sweet, fruity goodness. Sam was more interested in other things.

"Aw, look, they made a fire."

"Hopefully they won't make too much." Emma eyed Sam. "I can't believe you bought him that. He can barely manage ramen."

"I think he has a knack, believe it or not. Maybe it's the books. He's assembling an entire grilling library," Sam said, watching Jake with obvious adoration. "It's cute."

"Sure. It's cute until he tries to grill steak and turns your backyard into a scorched hellscape. At least Tucker can run fast."

The umbrella she and Sam sat under cast a long shadow on the grass. Tucker, Jake's spastic cattle dog mutt, sat hopefully beside the grill, thumping his tail on the ground every time Jake so much as glanced in his direction.

"To good taste," Sam said with a grin, nodding in the men's direction before clinking her glass against Emma's. Her sister looked perfectly at home here, Emma thought, lounging in a chair and wearing ragged old cut-off jean shorts and a Pink Floyd T-shirt. Her pale blond hair was in a ponytail, making her look almost too young for the drink in her hand. After all Sam had been through, seeing her happy was something Emma never got tired of.

"Good taste," Emma agreed, and took a sip.

Sam smirked and lowered her voice so the men wouldn't hear. "So how are things? Are you feeling better? You two look pretty cozy. Hand-holding and motorcycle rides and other things I'm slightly weirded out by you doing."

"Things are fine. Everything's fine," Emma said. "We're taking things slow. You know. Nice and easy." She tucked a lock of hair behind her ear and shrugged uncomfortably. Sam looked at her strangely.

"Nice and easy. Ah. That . . . doesn't sound like you." Sam frowned. "You sure everything is okay?"

Emma nodded. She had no intention of trying to explain it. How would she put it? *Well, you see, he's trying to figure out whether his lingering emotional scars will prevent him from having normal relationships, romantic ones included, so I'm kind of the guinea pig, and it's freaking me out, but really, I'm okay, as far as it goes.*

Yeah, no.

"Hmm. Well, he still spends an awful lot of time looking at you."

"I know. I am pretty hot."

Sam snorted and rolled her eyes. "You're still obsessing, aren't you? You're such a stubborn butthead, Em. You're so busy analyzing everything that you miss what's right in front of your face. Not everything in life is spelled out in ten-foot neon letters."

"It would be easier if it were." Emma looked over at Seth, watching the way he laughed easily with Jake, the way he moved, and felt a hunger for him so fierce that it shocked her. It wasn't just desire, either. Every bit of him fascinated her, both the shadows and light. It was the same problem she'd had from the beginning. She wanted more. More of him, all of him, more than the "maybe" she currently had. She was a big-enough girl to recognize that this was her issue and not his...but that didn't make it any easier to deal with.

She wished, not for the first time, that she could change her own intensity settings.

"Some men communicate better in the universal language of groping," Sam said, pouring herself more sangria. Emma couldn't help but laugh.

"I don't need to hear this. Especially not if Jake is a groper. You're still my sister."

"Jake's language of love is dependent on how many hours he's worked and the last time he was properly fed."

Emma toyed with her glass. "Filing that away under information I didn't want. And I'm not obsessing, for your information. I'm just trying to figure some things out."

Sam leaned forward, her expression concerned but interested. "Things?"

"Things," Emma repeated. "Like, how not to confuse the amount of hot monkey sex I'm having with the level of affection in a relationship."

Sam looked shocked, then burst out laughing and poked Emma with her flip-flop-clad foot. "You shameless hussy! Monkey sex? Mary Poppins isn't supposed to have that!"

"I'm not Mary Poppins," Emma informed her, and thought about the shower escapades of earlier. "At all. You called me a fairy godmother last weekend. Fairies are notoriously oversexed. I mean, look at Tinker Bell."

"Wow." Sam watched her over the rim of her glass. "There's a lot of non-work-related stuff going on in that practically perfect head of yours lately. I'm not sure what to make of it."

"That makes two of us," Emma replied.

"I find that scarier than you could possibly know."

"Good." At least some things in her life never changed, Emma thought. They smiled at each other, then sat in comfortable silence watching the two men bonding over a discussion about the art of barbecue. Sam was right, she decided. They were a good-looking pair, if a study in contrasts. Jake was a bit taller, and boy-next-door handsome, with beautiful hazel eyes and brown hair that was often spiked up like he'd been shoving his hands through it—which a lot of times, he had been. Seth was darker, leaner, and the hint of his tattoo peeking out beneath his sleeve gave him a touch of the bad boy. In some ways, it looked as though they'd each chosen their own opposites—the artist and the prince, the geek and the rebel. But underneath, Jake, at least, was exactly what Sam had needed.

Of course, Jake had wanted desperately to win Sam over. He'd been in love with her for years. Seth was . . . a different case. He seemed to need something, but Emma didn't know if that something was her. Unfortunately, neither did he. But at least he'd been honest about it.

There was the sound of car doors slamming out front, and Emma started, looked around, and then frowned at her sister. Sam looked overly innocent, which meant she was responsible.

"Who else did you invite?"

"It wasn't me," Sam insisted. "I said 'cookout' and Jake heard 'party.' By the time I figured out what he was up to, it was too late. It's not that many people. I promise." Her voice lowered. "I don't think he really misses his crappy ex-friends, but being social still makes him happy. I'm probably going to have to get kitchen items for actual entertaining. Just so you know, you're getting roped in."

"The horror," Emma said. "You just want to use me for my fancy hors d'oeuvres skills."

"You should use them somewhere," Sam replied. "You don't have dinner parties. You don't even like people."

Emma took a sip of her drink, unimpressed. "Neither do you."

"I like people. Sometimes," Sam replied. "I just also really like snuggling in my pajamas."

Emma sighed. "I'm with you there. So who got invited? Half the Cove?"

Her question was answered before Sam could speak as Andi stepped through the fence gate wearing a long sundress and a filmy scarf, her hair tied back with a simple elastic. She looked younger, Emma thought. And happier.

And alone, which was unacceptable. She didn't know if it was a side effect of dealing with Seth's reluctance for the past month, but her tolerance for intrigue was right at zero.

"Mom!" Emma called to her as Andi set what looked like a big bowl of potato salad on the card table Jake had dragged out. "Why didn't you bring Jasper?"

She heard Sam's coughing to hide her laughter as Andi gave her elder daughter a look that had once sent Emma running. Not anymore, though.

"Emma Lynn Henry. What exactly is that supposed to mean?"

"I know you're seeing him, Mom," Sam said. "You

need to stop worrying about it and call him to come over, or I will."

Andi's cheeks turned pink, and she made a strangled noise both girls knew well. It had once been the sound of impending doom, after which the phone, the television, and all fun things would be taken away. She gave Emma a murderous look.

"Hey, I didn't tell her," Emma said, holding up her hands. "She figured it out for herself. It's not my fault you're old and decrepit and forgot how to sneak around properly."

"I'll show you decrepit," Andi replied, her eyes narrowed. But she pulled her phone out of the knit bag she had slung over one arm and obliged them. "Hey, you," she said when he picked up. "Do you want to get together a little earlier than we planned? Jake's having a cookout, and the girls are insisting. Yes, they think they're awfully smart. No, don't start with the 'I told you so.'" She listened a moment, smiled, and then shot her daughters a smug, inscrutable look. "Okay, see you in a few." Whatever he said prompted a husky chuckle from her mother that was utterly unlike her. It was almost . . . *sexy.* Sam gave Emma a look.

"We may regret this."

"I think I already do."

Andi walked over to the table to sit down and poured herself a drink. She looked exasperated, but she didn't seem especially annoyed.

"Satisfied? Jasper is on his way."

"So we heard." Emma tilted her head at her mother. "Not really sure why you were sneaking around in the first place, though. We're not little kids. We won't be traumatized if you have a boyfriend."

Andi's smile turned wistful, and she looked away

across the yard. "Boyfriend. That's a strange word to start throwing around when you're my age, but I suppose it's better than . . . What else would you call him? My companion? That makes me sound ancient!"

"Or like Doctor Who. How about your *lovah*," Sam drawled, earning a swat on the arm from her mother.

"That's a hell of a way to send people running in the other direction. Though there are a few people I should try it with, in that case." She sighed. "I know you girls like Jasper. You've known him forever, and he made it clear a long time ago he was interested. I wasn't going to tell you two when I hadn't sorted it out myself yet. Took a while."

Emma frowned lightly. "It didn't take you that long. You've only been seeing each other for a few months."

Andi's eyebrows lifted, and she laughed. "Honey, I've been sleeping with Jasper Reed for over two years now."

The mouthful of sangria Emma had been about to swallow went down her windpipe. She spit the remains into the grass, then doubled over coughing while Sam went into gales of laughter. Andi thumped her on the back.

"Sorry, Emmie. I'm sneakier than I look."

When she could finally breathe again, Emma sat up and stared at her mother as though she'd never seen her before. *Two years?* How could she have missed that? She prided herself on never missing anything! Her mother's blue eyes were sympathetic, though she still looked amused.

"It's okay, honey. You wouldn't have known. It was just a physical thing for a long time. You wouldn't have figured it out unless you were staking out the house at night."

"Told you we were going to regret this," Sam muttered into her drink.

Andi's mouth twisted. "Please. I know I'm your mother, but I'm not dead."

"No. No you're not." Emma grabbed a napkin to dab at her mouth and noticed Seth watching her, sharp-eyed with concern. She waved and smiled, and he relaxed a little, his lips quirking into a small smile before he turned back to Jake. "It's just . . . I wasn't expecting that."

"Well, to be perfectly honest, neither was I." Andi sipped at her sangria and sighed contentedly. "It means a lot that you two support it, though, so thank you for that. Even though he'll be impossible now that he knows that cat's out of the bag."

Sam fiddled with the end of her ponytail and watched her mother curiously. "Don't you *want* people to know you're a couple?"

"Yes, mostly. A few of our friends already knew. Steve and Ginny, for two," she said, looking at Emma. "I think I'm ready to just fully couple up and be done with it. But it hasn't been as easy as you'd think, you know, giving up the idea of being odd Andi Henry, living in her big house all alone and puttering around with her horrible paint colors and gardening and knitting and possible drug-dealing operation." She winked. "I've gotten set in my ways."

Sam nodded, but Emma didn't think her sister really understood. *She* did though—or at least, she could see how easy it would be to get so comfortable flying solo that you didn't want to deal with anyone's baggage but your own. She'd been headed firmly in that direction. Seth had slipped through all her defenses.

And now she wanted something else.

"What made you change your mind?" Emma asked, watching Seth again as he spoke to Jake, his voice too low to hear but his eyes as intense as they always were.

She wondered what was so interesting, then forced her attention back to her family. Andi was looking at her curiously.

"What do you mean?" she asked.

"Well, you said you were, um, together, sort of but not really, for a couple of years. I guess I only noticed this was a thing in the last few months, so something changed. What?"

"Some things are just going to have to remain a mystery to you, nosy," Andi said. "And here comes the man of the hour. He got here fast. Maybe his ears were burning."

"Mine certainly are," Sam said as Jasper came in through the fence gate. Tall, lanky, with gray hair just long enough to pull back into a small tail, he had an elegance to the way he moved as he loped toward them. Emma could see the tiny flash of the little gold hoop in his ear, which she had always thought made him look like a pirate. He'd owned Jasper's Used Books on the square for as long as she could remember, and she'd loved to hear him speak in his British accent. She still did.

It was funny, how *not* strange it was to see him and her mother together. He looked at Andi the way her father had—as if she were the only woman in the world. The memory was sweet, and sad, but she smiled at Jasper when he reached them.

"Oh dear, a gathering of Henrys. Trouble must be afoot." His brown eyes were warm, and Emma didn't miss the way he brushed his hand across her mother's back before he pulled up a chair between Andi and Emma and sat down.

"Double, double, toil and trouble," Emma agreed. "Fire burn and oh my God here come about ten more people." Her eyes widened as the gate opened again, and this time Shane, Jake's friend Fitz, Aaron and his apparently on-again boyfriend Ryan, and Zoe walked in. Zoe was already bickering with Shane.

"Oh, come on, Zoe," Shane was saying. "I washed my hands."

"When, hours ago?" she asked, frowning as she examined whatever was in the large ceramic bowl she'd brought. "I thought you were supposed to be part of the upper crust around here. Did you miss the etiquette lesson about not sticking your fingers in other people's food?"

"I don't need etiquette lessons. I have manners. I just don't always choose to use them. Anyway, you wouldn't go to the wedding with me, so you can at least let me taste your broccoli salad."

"You can. With a fork. And I told you, my brother is going to be visiting. He's my date."

"I'd make a better one," Shane grumbled.

"I don't know," Zoe said, looking up at him. "He's got a few things going for him that you don't. Like being housebroken."

"Hey." Shane pretended to look wounded. Emma sighed. Sam's friends were an interesting crew. And she was going to have to tell Shane that Larkin was willing to put up with him for an evening. That ought to put him in a good mood, which usually meant trouble.

"We're outnumbered," she said. "Jake's going to get it." But she watched Jake introduce Seth to the friends he didn't already know, then saw Seth's polite smile turn into a raucous laugh when Aaron said God knew what to him. She couldn't help but smile herself. He'd said he wanted to be a part of the community. A bunch of it had just come to him.

"Careful, there." Jasper's voice near her ear startled her, and she turned her head to look at him. His long face was set in more serious lines than usual, though when their eyes met, she got a sympathetic smile. "He's a nice boy. But you're wearing your heart all over your face."

She was too surprised to argue about it—especially because it was probably true. She looked at Sam and her mother, who were deep in conversation about the wedding for the umpteenth time, before responding in a voice as quiet as Jasper's own. "I am?"

He nodded. "Does he know how you feel?"

Her mouth went dry, and her heart kicked into a wild rhythm. "I doubt it, since I'm not sure about that myself." This was the question she'd been circling around for days, getting close and then darting away again because she couldn't quite face it. Especially after she'd agreed to try to take things slow. It shouldn't even be an issue. People didn't fall in love this quickly. People were sensible and took their time, thought it through. Especially if those people included Emma Henry.

Of course, her recent activities had been decidedly un-Emma-like. She didn't know what was normal for her anymore.

"Well, you don't look unsure. You look besotted."

Well, that's not embarrassing. Was I drooling? Was my mouth open? God. Emma shook her head slowly. "No. No, definitely not besotted. Sorry." That word, "besotted." It made her sound like she was drunk on Seth. Which was a little too close to the truth for her liking. She'd done enough stupid things while inebriated to last for a while.

Jasper's laughter was warm, his eyes kind. "You're as stubborn as your mum, Emma Henry. What would you call it, then?"

"I think we've decided to call it 'liking each other in an exclusive but slow-moving manner,'" Emma said carefully.

Jasper burst out laughing. "You've got a way with words, I'll give you that, even if it is a bunch of shite."

She glowered at him. "It's not *shite*," she said. "It's a normal human relationship. We're taking it slow."

"Ah, I see." Jasper's smile turned wry. "Taking it slow. I may have been through a bit of that myself lately."

"You didn't want to? Take it slow, I mean?" As odd as it was to be talking about her mother's relationship, she found she really wanted to know.

Jasper actually looked surprised. "Me? No, darling. I'm a professional bookworm and a hopeless romantic. Too many times along for the ride on the hero's journey as a lad, I expect. Now, your mother, gem though she is, tends to be a bit more . . . stubborn."

"That's true enough," Emma agreed, glancing at Seth again. "I guess everyone has to move at their own pace, though."

"I think I detect a note of the hopeless romantic there as well." Jasper chuckled.

"What, me? No. I'm just practical and boring."

"Bollocks." His look turned serious. "I've been watching you your whole life, Emma. And don't forget, I'm quite well aware of your reading habits. I expect your inner life is anything but boring."

She flushed, realizing he was right. Her tastes had always run to the escapist, from historical romances to sweeping fantasy—provided there was a happy payoff in the end. Those stories were her secret pleasure. Well, almost secret. "Okay, maybe not completely boring. But practical."

"It's not a bad thing. And what about him?" Jasper asked, inclining his head in Seth's direction. "I enjoyed your Seth the other night. And he seems quite keen on you. He ought to be, by the way. That video was charming. Dancing your little heart out. I knew you had it in you."

Emma groaned. "Eveyone in the Cove saw it. Every-one."

"Probably," he agreed. "I liked the flourish at the end with the beer. Very artistic. It's good to see you getting out a little, Em. Making an actual life here, instead of just living here. I worried when you decided to stay, you know. You were always a quiet little thing, very solemn, taking on the weight of the world when your dad died. I thought this might not be the right place for you to figure out who you wanted to be, instead of trying desperately to fit into someone else's ideas about what you should be."

Emma smiled, touched. Jasper had been a part of her life for so long, but she'd never considered that he'd looked out for her and worried over the years. She wished she'd known, but telling her wouldn't have been his way. Besides, she might well have shoved him away like she had most people. Now, though, knowing that he'd been looking out for her was a balm for the ragged edges of her nerves.

"I'm figuring it out, Jasper," she said, and was surprised to find that she meant it. Everything in her life had started to change, all at once. And for the first time, she found herself lacking the will to fight it. Instead, she was curious about what might come next. Curious, and scared as hell. But not enough to try to go back to where she was before.

He patted her hand gently and leaned forward. "Good. And for what it's worth, I hope romance wins out over caution. Every romantic should get to be knocked on their ass by love and live happily ever after."

She couldn't help but laugh when he put it like that, though there had been nothing particularly romantic in the way her relationship with Seth had gone so far. *Girl meets boy. Boy nurses girl through alcohol-induced illness. Girl asks boy to pretend to date her. Boy refuses, so girl awkwardly seduces him. Girl wonders if stability is a reasonable trade-off for hot sex.* Not exactly a fairy tale. More like a boozy rom-com. Or a bad porno.

"He's been through a lot," she said softly. "I don't think either of us was looking for someone. Not really. So I'm not expecting the happily ever after."

Jasper frowned and shook his head. "Emma Henry. You've been through your own kind of hell, and your mother told me you were the glue that kept everything from falling apart. You deserve the happily ever after, so don't settle for less. The world's a dark enough place, but it's darker on your own. When you find someone you want to walk it with, though, it can change everything. We've got to carry one other through the hard parts. Every little kiss matters." He glanced meaningfully at Andi, then looked at Emma and winked. "I should know. They're what I had to make do with until *someone* finally let me knock her on her ass with love."

She looked at Andi, who was oblivious to the conversation, and felt an odd, aching pull deep in her chest, like the fleeting pain from an old scar. She'd felt so helpless when they'd lost her father. Knowing that she'd made a real difference to the people she loved meant more than she could say.

"Thanks, Jasper," she said, and he gave her hand a pat. He was still the sweetest pirate she'd ever known.

"For you? Anything. And now," he announced more loudly, "I'm going to take more than my share of the potato salad your mother brought. The scent of burning probably means the meat's about done." He leaned down to Andi, who looked at him with an expression

Emma hadn't seen in so long that she hardly remembered. "Get you a plate, love?"

Love. She'd given up on the idea of it, and now she was surrounded by it—Sam and Jake, Andi and Jasper. Happily ever afters. Just like Jasper seemed to think she should want—even demand—for herself.

Seth's laugh rippled through her as he sprinted out of the house with a couple glasses of water. There was a disturbing amount of fire coming from the grill, and Jake was taking all manner of grief from his audience. Seth caught her eye, his grin full of mischief. Something deep in her chest tightened painfully, then let go as her last defenses crumbled.

Pull it back. Be smart. Do what you do best and protect yourself.

But she knew it was already too late.

Chapter Nineteen

"You're not going to believe this."

Emma had her hands full of lunch when she shouldered the door open Wednesday afternoon, only to find Brynn bouncing up and down on the other side.

"What?" She passed her with a confused smile and headed for the desk with a cup of soup and half a sandwich for each of them. Maybe there was at least some decent gossip to be had, though she wasn't sure that would merit all the excitement. Then again . . . this was Brynn. If nothing else, she could be counted on for bringing enthusiasm to the smallest things.

"I heard the Harding wedding completely blew up this past weekend. Penny's plans went way over budget, and when Bob found out what his daughter and wife were up to, he hit the roof. Everything's canceled. Penny threw some kind of operatic fit when she found out. She's starting from scratch, *and*," Brynn continued, "my source tells me that we're back in the running. Bob is determined to take another look at all the options."

Emma blinked, trying to digest this. Of all the things Brynn might have told her, this was the last thing on her list. "Well. Huh."

Brynn rounded her eyes. "Don't just 'well, huh' me.

We still have a chance! We can show off the Cove as a great spot for scenic weddings, and we can show off what we do best in making those weddings happen! This," she announced dramatically, "could be our moment!"

"If we ever make a commercial, you're going to be in it," Emma told her, forcing herself into motion again to open the bag containing her lunch. She got out the napkin, spoon, wrapped sandwich, and covered soup container and set them neatly on the desk.

"Emma!"

"Okay, okay, I'm processing. Give me a minute." She sat down, opened the top of the Styrofoam container of soup, and took a bite of sandwich. Brynn stared at her, looking as close to murder as she'd ever seen her. Inside, though, Emma was already running through the possibilities, the things that would have to be changed from the initial proposal, what to pick Brynn's brain about— everything. And then, of course, there was the time issue. Sam's wedding was rapidly approaching, and every weekend was full. Not to mention that she had a few things planned with Sam before the big day, just the two of them. This was an excellent opportunity at the worst time possible. For her, anyway. But that didn't have to mean it couldn't come together.

When she was finally ready to speak, she discovered that what would have been impossible for her only recently now seemed like the only sensible option. "You said you knew what she wanted. How quickly can you pull something together? I'd love to be able to give the Hardings something by Monday if they'll agree to come back in."

Brynn looked ready to start vibrating, and emitted a noise that made Emma wince. "Sorry!" she yelped, seeing Emma's expression. "I just . . . Really? You want me to do this?"

"Not all of it, but I'm a little swamped, and you were right about this before. Plus, you did an amazing job on the Jamison proposal. Do you think you can handle it?"

Brynn clapped her hands and made another sound that Emma could only interpret as "yes" before dashing over to one of the photo books. "I had this idea—something really classic, like Gilded Age elegance. We could do the whole thing at Gibson House."

It was completely different from what she'd envisioned before, but Emma immediately saw how it could work. "Is that going to bother Penny, though? Gibson House is right down from them on the Crescent. It's like having a party at the neighbor's."

"Sure, if your neighbor is Jay Gatsby," Brynn replied, waving the concern away. "Trust me. It's not a cheap venue, but it's going to be much more reasonable than the plans that just got scrapped. And then the flowers! Annalise did these gorgeous centerpieces for a luncheon I went to, and I couldn't stop thinking how the design would be perfect for—"

"Hang on," Emma said, holding up one finger. If there was one thing she'd learned, it was to strike while the iron was hot. Waiting had never gained her anything. This was a truth she was having to willfully disregard on a daily basis right now in other areas of her life. This, though, she understood.

She picked up the phone, quickly looked up the number, and punched it in. "Mayor Harding," she said, "this is Emma Henry. Yes, good. How are you? I'm ... Well, I'm glad I called, too. I just wanted to touch base with you and see if there was anything ... Really? Oh, that's too bad." She grinned at Brynn, who gave her the thumbs-up. "Well, it so happens that after our last meeting, my assistant, Brynn Parker, came up with an alternate idea that ... Yes, she is, a very nice girl. Mmmhmm, she mentioned being related to you." She watched Brynn roll her eyes. "I'd love to. . . . Monday, we thought Monday if that might work. You are? Great. No, no, we'd still be right in the budget range you gave us. Well, let me know what time works for . . . I certainly will. All right. Talk to you soon."

Emma hung up, widened her eyes at Brynn, and said, "I don't think anyone has ever been that happy to hear from me. I swear that when I told him you already had something in mind, he just about cried. Especially when I promised he could afford it."

That was when Brynn did something that was at once completely surprising and somehow, the most natural thing in the world. She dashed around the desk and threw her arms around Emma, enveloping her in a big, affectionate hug. "Thank you so much! I'm going to knock everyone's socks off, I promise!"

"I have no doubt." Emma laughed, giving Brynn a gentle squeeze before letting go. She'd thought it would be too difficult to give up control over something like this. It was strange to discover that she was just as happy to advise and let Brynn run with it. She wanted to prove herself. And Emma wanted to let her. Far from finding it nerve-racking, all Emma felt in passing off some of the burden was relief.

We need to carry each other, Jasper had said. And wasn't that in a U2 song? If both Bono and Jasper agreed on it, it had to be true.

"Scoot," Brynn said, shooing her away from the desk. "You have your own desk to eat lunch at, and I need to get on this while the juices are flowing. So. Many. Ideas."

Emma chuckled. "Um, great? Just be sure the juices don't make a mess, okay? Napkins. They're not just for decoration."

"Go away. I need to impress my snobby relatives." Brynn wrinkled her nose, waved her off again, and dug her food out of the bag. Emma shook her head and laughed softly to herself as she slunk into the back, wishing she had a little more to do today. That would stop her from brooding, at least. She'd always prided herself on being the kind of person who could keep her work life and personal life separate. Of course, that was a lot easier when she didn't actually *have* a personal life. As it was, the presence of the one was starting to seriously affect the other, and she didn't know what to do about it.

She tapped her fingers on her desk, then rearranged her already-organized papers. That day at the park, Seth had asked her if she would be able to work with both of their baggage. His seemed manageable enough, now that she'd dragged it out into the light of day. He still wasn't a fount of information, but she didn't feel quite so much like he was hiding from her.

Not hiding . . . but still a long way from being forthcoming.

It'll change, she told herself. *Give him time.* Which would have been a perfectly workable solution if only she'd been an entirely different person.

If only she weren't completely, ridiculously in love with him.

Emma slid her hands into her hair and propped her elbows on her desk with a gusty sigh.

It was too much, too soon, and it didn't seem to make a damn bit of difference. This was the real thing. Her feelings for Ben had been different. Back then, she'd loved an illusion, one fueled by her need to find someone who could fill all the empty places inside herself. Seth was different. She knew she loved him, the whole sexy, wonderfully flawed package. It had been coming on since—well, since the beginning, really. But the pieces had only really clicked together at the cookout.

Jasper had seen what her heart had already known. Finally acknowledging it had only made it worse. She loved him so much that it ached. So much that she'd avoided him since Sunday to try to figure out how to get a handle on this, so he didn't notice, freak out, and lock himself in his house to keep clear of exactly the thing he'd warned her he wasn't sure he could give.

Seth cared about her—that much she knew. But she also knew, with increasing certainty, that it wasn't enough. She'd never been good at half measures. Seth was just feeling his way back into having real relationships, and that was completely understandable. But she was clinging to a ledge that hung out over some fathomless abyss, and her grip was slipping. If she fell, she fell alone.

And if she hit the bottom, she would shatter.

Way to embrace the joys of a perfectly good relationship, Emma. She sighed, picked up her phone, put it down, and then tried to get some work done. All that happened, though, was that she wound up staring at an estimate from Larkin for a baby shower she was planning. *Larkin. Wednesday. Larkin.*

Relief flooded her. Seth was working tonight, and she was going to be at loose ends unless she found something to do with herself. At some point very recently, going back to her quiet apartment had ceased to be an acceptable ending for every day. Sometimes, she needed people.

As it happened, she now seemed to have a few. At least, she thought she did. Might as well test out the theory.

Emma grabbed her cell phone and texted Larkin, and for once it had nothing to do with anything covered in frosting. The response a few minutes later made her smile. She now had plans for the night. With friends. Imagine that.

She eased back into work after that, finally able to relax a little. If falling in love with Seth meant that she was going to exist in a state of constant inner turmoil from now on, Emma thought, at least she now had people to share it with.

"I can't believe you did that!"

"Believe it," Emma said, tossing herself into her chair to her friends' peals of delighted laughter. And they were friends—that had been clear the moment Larkin had driven up in front of the shop in her ancient sedan, rolled down the window, and shouted, "Get in, hot stuff! We're on a mission!"

Part of that mission, apparently, had been to get Emma to the mic to sing something from the collected works of Britney Spears. After a cosmo, a lot of laughter, and watching Brynn and Annalise duet on "You're the One That I Want," it had been surprisingly easy to get up there and bust out her best "Baby, One More Time."

Larkin high-fived her. "That was a beautiful thing. You've even got a good voice. Not like these amateurs."

Annalise stuck her tongue out. "What we lack in talent we make up for with volume." Emma had always thought the pretty florist was friendly but shy. Either she'd been mistaken about the "shy" part, or this was just the effect that Larkin had on people. It was hard to be reserved around a six-foot blonde who kept threatening to grab the mic and rap. Badly.

Brynn took a sip of her own cosmo. "I love tonight. I love that I can sit here and eat cheesy bacon fries and not be judged."

"That's because we're all stealing them every time you turn your head to stare at the bartender." Emma was glad she'd invited Brynn along—she fit in perfectly. Of course, the biggest surprise was how much she felt like she fit in herself. Had she really thought she had no time for this kind of thing? It was exactly what she'd needed. Her problems seemed about a million miles away.

It helped that it was really too loud to hear herself think, too.

"I'm just going to say," Larkin announced, "that this needs to happen more often. It's not only fun, but we're giving back to the community."

"By singing badly in public?" Annalise leaned back in her chair and smirked, then swiped one of Brynn's fries.

"Look, between our jobs and outings like this, there are days when we spend a good eighteen hours bringing both money and entertainment to the Cove. We're huge assets."

"You mean huge asses," Annalise replied, then swatted Brynn in the arm. "Will you just go get his number? Larkin can probably figure out a way to frame that as community service if you need more reasons than a great smile and a cute butt."

"Maybe we should be recognized for being such givers," Emma agreed. "Don't know what they'd put on the plaque, though."

Larkin seemed to consider this. "Keep it mysterious, like in Harry Potter. 'For services rendered to Harvest Cove' or something. But we'd know."

"I don't know," Emma said, watching as a large, hairy man in splatter-painted overalls took the mic and launched into a rousing rendition of "Don't Stop Believin'." "Using that logic, Big Al should have a wall of plaques by now.

I'm pretty sure all he does is provide money and entertainment to the Cove." He caught her eye and gave her the thumbs-up. Emma flashed one back. It was hard not to feel some camaraderie with a guy you were supposed to have gone streaking through the downtown with.

"Right? There'll be a statue of that guy in town one day. Mark my words." Larkin replied, raising her beer in his direction. All around them, the crowd sang, and Emma wondered if Larkin was right.

Across the bar, Emma caught sight of one of Seth's friends and waved. He grinned and waved back, then leaned over to say something to the guy he was with.

"Who's that?" Annalise asked, craning her neck to see. "Don't hold out on me. I already heard that you hooked Larkin up."

Emma raised an eyebrow at Larkin. "She may come to hold that against me."

"That's Mark Salvatore," Brynn piped up. "He used to play soccer with my older brother. Now he's a cop."

"Seth and some of the guys shoot darts in his garage sometimes," Emma said. She'd been glad to find that Seth's personal life featured friends he'd made at work. He got together with them when he felt like it. He was just quiet about it.

He was quiet about a lot of things.

She frowned into her drink, but a poke in her arm stopped her from starting to wallow again.

"This is a no misery zone, Emma Henry. If you're going to be unhappy, I'm going to make you duet with me. And I promise you, it will blow your little *Flashdance* routine right out of the water."

Her voice was stern, but her eyes glittered with humor. Emma laughed despite herself. "Sorry. I'm just overanalyzing my relationship. It's like a hobby. A sick, twisted hobby."

"Ooh, I do that," Annalise said, leaning forward, her long golden brown hair swinging over her shoulder. "That's bad news. All it's going to do is give you Resting Bitchy Face and take your focus off the important things in life."

Emma couldn't resist. "Which are?"

"Good friends to play with and the fact that you have a very nice, very hot boyfriend you get to sleep with anytime you want. Like, *anytime*." Her eyes widened. "Did I mention anytime?"

Brynn snorted. "She has a point." She looked at Annalise. "Sounds like maybe *you* should hit on the bartender, though."

"Oh, honestly. It's not like the man is wearing a sign that says 'In case of emergency, remove pants.'" She angled her head. "Is he?"

They all laughed, and as Brynn and Annalise shifted from their discussion of the bartender's assets to a friendly competition over who'd dealt with the most difficult customer this week, Larkin moved closer, her green eyes curious.

"I was just teasing, you know. I'd pick a better song for the duet." She grinned. "You're good, though, right? I hope you're having fun. I like that we've expanded to a foursome—I mean, if you two decide to be seen in public with us again."

"Are you kidding? This," Emma said, lifting her glass and sweeping her hand around her, "is exactly what I needed. I know I'm not naturally outgoing, but I was getting seriously sick of my own company. And you're fun."

Larkin pointed a finger at her. "You're contributing to

the general delinquency, trust me." Then she tilted her head to the side, assessing. "Is this thing you're unhappy about a big thing, or more like garden-variety worrying?"

Emma shrugged. "Haven't decided yet."

"Hmm. Annalise is probably right, then."

"About the bartender's pants?" Emma asked, earning a laugh.

"Yeah, probably. And also about enjoying what you've got. Think about it. When we go home, you can go play with handcuffs if you want to." She waggled her eyebrows. "Naked."

"This shouldn't be making me feel better. Sex doesn't solve problems," Emma said. But she couldn't help the silly grin.

"Maybe not, but it's a hell of a lot of fun," Larkin replied. "Hey, a smile! We're back in business! You still want to do a duet with me? Pretend I never threatened it as punishment."

"For telling me I'm being an idiot in the nicest way possible, I think I can do that."

"Not an idiot," Larkin said firmly. "Just human. Stick with me, and I'll annoy the crap out of you with my gratefulness for the universe."

Emma was momentarily reminded of her mother, which was more than a little disconcerting. "Um, is this a California thing?"

"Can't tell you," Larkin replied. "Gotta indoctrinate you into my cult of personality first. You should totally join, though. For the cupcakes, at least."

As Emma let herself be pulled back to the karaoke machine, she realized that her friends were only telling her what she'd been trying to tell herself for days—she had a good thing going with Seth. So instead of spending so much time worrying that he would never return her feelings, maybe she should just get back to enjoying what they had together and hope that the rest followed. Besides, making things happen was her specialty. She needed to have some faith in that.

Larkin handed her one of the mics, her eyes dancing with mischief.

"Let's do this thing, Flashdance. Ready?"

Laughing at the nickname, Emma nodded. Then she took a deep breath and jumped in.

Chapter Twenty

Emma didn't usually call him when he was on duty—she seemed to feel very strongly that it was bad manners, which Seth had discovered were her kryptonite—but when she did, it was always a pleasant surprise. Tonight, especially, since the call was to ask if it was okay if she slept over.

He didn't know what had brought this on, and he didn't much care. Ever since Sam and Jake's cookout, it seemed like she'd taken a step back. Why, he couldn't figure out, but it was pretty obvious. Maybe it shouldn't have bothered him so much. After all, he'd said he needed to take things slow. That he wasn't sure what kind of relationship he was capable of.

Except he missed her. The thought of going home to Emma, warm and asleep and waiting in his bed, got him through the darkest hours of the night when very little happened, and none of it tended to be any good. Fortunately, the hours passed with little trouble, and by the time the sky was turning gray with the approaching morning light, he was walking in his front door, taking care to shut it quietly so he didn't wake her.

Seeing Emma's little car in the driveway made him smile the way he had the first time he'd seen her with that big yellow umbrella downtown. That rainy day, the sight of her had been just what he needed.

Now, it was just the same . . . only stronger. Maybe on a different day he would have questioned it, but right now, he was too tired to do anything but welcome it.

Seth found her in his bed, nothing but a dark tuft of hair visible above the covers she'd wrapped around herself. He smiled again at the sound of her soft snoring, silently going through his postwork routine and then leaving his boxers on to crawl into bed with her. There wasn't much comforter to be had, so he had to do some tugging just to get underneath. On the upside, she slept like the dead, so he didn't feel like he was disturbing her.

It took some doing, but after a few minutes Seth had managed to curve himself around her, one hand on her hip, knees tucked behind hers. He nuzzled into her hair, breathing in the coconut shampoo she used. She smelled like summer, his favorite season, and was as warm as the sun-kissed sand. He had a brief internal debate about whether or not to wake her—it was impossible to be this close without the attraction between them sparking to life, and knowing how good it was made the decision more of a struggle.

In the end, though, exhaustion won out, if not by much. And he let the feel of her, the scent of her, pull him into deep, sweet dreams.

Seth had no idea how long he slept. That, he had discovered, was one of the awesome things about a good night's sleep that he'd taken for granted back when rest was a sure thing. His odds were a lot better now than they had been, but he wasn't sure his appreciation for the good nights would ever dim.

Neither would the pleasure of waking up to a beauti-

ful woman. Even when she was tracing his tattoo with
the tip of her finger so lightly that he woke up on the
verge of giggling like a little girl.

He sucked in a breath as his eyes flew open, and his first
sight was Emma, propped up on one elbow staring very
studiously at his one piece of body art. Her finger brushed
once more, then stilled when she felt him jerk beneath her
touch. Her gaze flicked to his, a hint of uncertainty in it
that vanished almost as quickly as it had appeared.

"Morning," she said softly.

"Morning," he murmured.

"I was looking at your tattoo," she said. "I like it." It
took him a few long seconds to work out what she was
talking about, but it clicked while he was yawning.

"Oh. Thanks. I like"—another yawn—"it, too."

"I hope so, since this is permanent."

"Mmm." She was very awake. He didn't know why,
though he had the nagging feeling he ought to. It took a
few seconds for the wheels to start turning, but once they
did, he realized something odd. "You're still here."

"I'm still here," she agreed.

It was a Thursday. Emma didn't miss workdays unless
she was deathly ill. The fact that she didn't look ill, or at
all worried that she wasn't at work, was more than his
sleep-addled brain could handle. "Did work blow up?
Did you fire yourself?"

"Only for the day," she said. "I took today off."

"I thought that wasn't allowed."

Emma shrugged, beginning to trace her finger over
the skin of his biceps again. "It's good to be the queen."

Seth gave her a wide, sleepy grin. "If I corrupted you,
I'm very proud of myself right now." He grabbed her
hand, then pulled it to his lips. "Glad you like the raven,
but he's ticklish."

"I'll remember that." She narrowed her eyes playfully, and he knew that whatever had been bothering her the past few days was done. "You don't have to get all excited about being a bad influence, you know."

"Hmm," he said, pulling her to him. "Kind of hard when it's gotten you into my bed at whatever time it is on a Thursday."

"One," she replied. "It's one, and I don't even remember the last time I stayed in bed this long. Maybe when I was a teenager. Maybe before."

"Or maybe never, knowing you." Seth kissed her jaw, then her cheek. "Guess I'd better make this worthwhile, then." His body was completely awake already, hard and throbbing simply from having Emma so close. The desire in her eyes was both promise and invitation. So he made slow, sweet love to her, taking his time and kissing her to distraction while he explored every creamy curve with his hands. By the time he slipped inside her, she was quivering. Seth felt her squeeze him tight, and every thought vanished. Every thought but of her.

They moved together in the quiet of his room while the sunlight filtered through the curtains, the only sounds the creak of his bed, Emma's soft gasps, and his own harsh breathing as he drove into her while she tightened around him. Lying beneath him, her dark hair in loose coils around her face, cheeks pink with exertion, she looked like some dark and ravished goddess, Seth thought. Even her eyes seemed to glow, turning hazy as he pushed her pleasure to the breaking point. Seth's muscles tightened as he hurtled toward the edge himself, holding back only until he could watch Emma find her own release.

When her body bowed beneath him, eyes shutting as she cried out, Seth finally let himself go, pumping into her until he came, shuddering, inside her. He sank down onto her when the tremors had subsided, showering her face with gentle kisses, then rolling to his side to wrap her in his arms.

Emma tucked her head beneath his chin, nuzzling into his neck, and sighed softly. The same thing he'd felt when he'd come home to find her here flooded him, filling him up until he had no room for anything else—no worries, no restlessness. Just the sense that everything in his universe was exactly as it should be.

"We could just stay here all day," he said, eyes closed. "See, that way you don't have to feel guilty for being out of work. You can just tell yourself it was okay because you stayed in bed."

Her laugh was soft and warm. "I don't feel guilty. I did think of something a little different to do if you wanted to leave the house at some point, though."

"Oh yeah?" he asked, his curiosity piqued. All of this, from her wanting to be here when he got home to planning a day with him, was different. In a lot of ways, she'd been letting him set the pace of their relationship, giving him subtle nudges but generally handling his ever-shifting boundaries. And she'd never said a word about it, letting him have what he needed before she'd ever understood why. It reminded him of something Sam had said to him that night at the gallery: "Em's a fixer," she'd told him when he'd made some comment about Emma's ability to turn chaos into order. Then Sam had laughed. "We're all her projects. It started to drive me a lot less crazy when I realized that she only makes projects of people she loves."

People she loves. He waited for the usual fear the *L* word inspired, but it didn't come. Instead, he simply wondered. She couldn't be in love with him. Could she? He looked at her now, intensely interested in anything her expression might reveal, any hint of deeper meaning. But all he could find was a sexily rumpled woman with a Mona Lisa smile.

"Well," she asked, "are you game?"

He tried to brush aside an odd little pang that might have been disappointment. "Maybe. Should I be worried about getting sticks and stones caught in uncomfortable places if I say yes?"

Another laugh. "No. I said different, not kinky."

"Then yes, I'm game. Feel free to try me with kinky anytime, though."

"I'll keep that in mind," Emma said. "Did you want to go soon, or—?"

She let the question hang in the air, but Seth couldn't quite bring himself to let go of her yet. Having her here felt right, and he didn't know when she might decide to give him an entire day again. So instead of getting up, he buried his face in her hair, holding her close as she relaxed against him with a soft, contented sigh.

"Soon," he murmured into the dark silk. "But not yet." He wished everything in life could be so easy . . . but sometimes, like right now, holding Emma was more than enough.

By the time they made it out of the house and onto the Crescent, it was midafternoon. Seth knew he hadn't left them a lot of time to do anything before he had to start getting ready for work, but Emma hadn't seemed to mind. She'd simply grabbed the extra bike helmet and looked at him expectantly.

"Well?"

She wouldn't admit to actually liking the motorcycle yet, but he had a feeling it was only a matter of time. Maybe eventually she'd want one of her own. He started to entertain ideas about things they might do, places they could ride, before banishing the thoughts. It was supposed to be a fun, no-pressure day, and he was determined to keep it that way. Still, Sam's words wouldn't let him be.

Only people she loves.

What if she did? What would he do then? Not walk away. It surprised him how completely he rejected the idea the instant he thought of it. He was past running. And anyway, what if—

"Turn in up here," Emma shouted in his ear, interrupting his thoughts. Her arms were wrapped tight around his waist, and she'd actually worn the right kind of jeans and boots this time. The feel of her pressed against his back would have made this a successful adventure in his book regardless, but her directions surprised him.

"Your mom's house?" he asked.

"Yep," was all she said, so he obliged, turning in and heading up the long gravel drive to the Henrys' sprawling Victorian. Even though he'd already been there, the sight of it still took him aback. It was just so damn big, looking like something out of a movie about romantically inclined witches or children who found other worlds at the back of their wardrobes. The biggest surprise had been the feel of it, though—the small part he'd seen had felt cozy, despite its size. This was a home. Emma's childhood home.

But her reasons for bringing him here puzzled him.

Andi's old Beetle wasn't in the driveway, so Seth parked in the spot closest to the house, then killed the engine. Emma hopped off and fished in her pocket while he got off the bike. When he'd removed his helmet, he found her holding her keys.

"I thought you might like to see the house," she explained. "Everyone I ever knew in town wanted to come in and have a look. I think some of them thought we were keeping severed heads in the basement, but still. It's a great house." Uncertainty clouded her eyes, and he wondered whether whatever had been bothering her still was after all. "I mean, unless this seems beyond boring to you . . ."

"No," Seth said quickly, and found that he meant it. It wasn't every day he got a chance to see a place like this, and the thought of getting to poke around the house where Emma had grown up was fascinating. It just hadn't been what he'd expected.

Should be used to that by now, he thought, and smiled.

"Come on, then," Emma said, brightening immediately. She grabbed his hand and led him up the steps, through the front door and foyer, where they left their helmets, and into the hallway where Emma had kissed him. He thought about grabbing her for a repeat performance.

"Where's your mom?" he asked, teenage suspicions about being spied on by nosy parents tumbling out of old memories to haunt him.

"Working," Emma replied. "Which means hanging out with her friends while knitting and getting paid. Her friend Joanne owns Diamonds and Perls."

"Oh. That's the place with, ah . . . yarn."

She looked amused. "Amazing how fast your eyes can glaze over. Yes, yarn. I'm sure you have a few hobbies that would make my eyes glaze over, too, so don't judge."

"I'm not judging." He trailed behind her, then asked, "What hobbies?"

"Like I didn't see the action figures in your spare bedroom."

"Uh, they're . . . childhood keepsakes?" he said. "It's not like I play with them or anything. And toys are way more interesting than yarn."

She turned her head to look at him blandly. "Uh-huh."

Seth made a mental note to move the vintage action figures to a better spot and tried to change the subject. "The stove is very cool. And very bizarre."

"Try cooking with it. It takes some practice," Emma replied. The white AGA's design made it look a century old, but she offered a brief explanation about its function as a way to warm the kitchen as well as to cook. It sounded more complicated than Seth liked to get with his limited cooking, but he had to admit, it worked in this house. Actually, as Emma walked him from room to room, pointing out features of interest, Seth found himself engrossed in the place where the Henrys had lived for generations.

He'd never been in a house that had a glassed-in greenhouse worked into the design. It looked like Andi knew what she was doing with it, too.

"How do you even grow up in a place like this?" he asked, running a hand over the ornate woodwork of the fireplace mantel. "Were you allowed to run around in here?"

"You've met my mother," Emma said. "Can you see her running around behind us with a vacuum and floor polisher? She never freaked out about the house. And amazingly enough, we never broke much."

"Lucky she didn't have boys," Seth replied. "My friends and I went through so many screen doors at my house that Mom started making me pay for them out of my lawn-mowing money."

Emma grinned. "I said we never broke *much*. There

used to be more vases. I could also show you the walls that have been repainted."

He chuckled, trying to picture Sam and Emma running wild through the cavernous house, knocking over antiques. "What did you do to the wall? Chocolate? Marker?"

"Both. I was the chocolate. Sam was the marker. We've . . . kind of continued in that tradition."

"It was always dirt with Kira and me. And we grew up in a ranch-style house. Typical Florida stucco ranch, you know, so it was easy to cover a lot of area before we got caught. We were good at divide and conquer," he said.

Emma's brows lifted. "What were you trying to conquer, exactly?"

He shrugged, his mouth curving at the memory. "Different things. My parents' resistance to our having lizards as pets, for one."

She wrinkled her nose. "Ew."

"Yeah, we heard that a lot. Not sure Dad cared as much, but he traveled enough for work that Mom got the last word on it. We did finally get a dog, at least. Not a very doggy dog, but he was a good boy." He hadn't talked about Ming in a long time, but Emma's eyes sharpened with interest. And these were good stories, he thought. Ones he ought to enjoy sharing as much as he enjoyed the memories.

"Poodle?" Emma asked.

He shook his head. "Pekingese. He actually really, really liked dirt, so Ming made a good adventure buddy, even if he thought fetching was beneath him."

Emma looked charmed. "What?" he asked, unable to help the grin.

"Just picturing you with a little foofy lion dog hunting lizards with your tomboy sister. She had to be a tomboy."

"Hey, Ming was a man dog. A very small man dog. And Kira is still kind of a tomboy, but she likes dresses. She used to go through a *lot* of dresses. I guess the dirt didn't wash out that well."

"Neither does paint. That was the one thing that used to drive Mom nuts, but Dad always stuck up for Sam. He just knew she was going to be an artist." He caught the wistful note in her voice, saw her glance at the collections of photographs on the mantel. Sensing it would be all right, he picked up one that featured a young-looking, dark-haired man putting a wheel on a little red wagon and smiling at the camera. He knew that smile, and those eyes.

"This has to be him," he said. "You look just like him. Prettier, I mean, but . . ."

Emma nodded. "I know. I act like him, too. That's what everybody says, anyway, except he was quieter. Just as stubborn, though."

"You don't remember?"

She shrugged, and he saw the sadness in her eyes again. "Yes and no. I was twelve. You don't remember as much as you think you will. Or as much as you want to. Sometimes I'm not sure whether I actually remember something that happened, or if I've just heard the story so many times that I think I do."

"I'm sorry you lost him." It was all he could think to say, but he meant it.

"I'm sorry, too," she agreed, taking the picture and gently putting it back on the mantel. "He was funny. I do remember that. All the Henrys have a dry sense of humor, but his was hilarious. And he was smart. He loved reading Sam and me bits of things he was interested in, or taking us for walks to show us things. He was amazing with his hands, too. Always fixing or building something.

He made Sam this cool little art studio up in the attic. I was so jealous."

Seth stepped closer to her. "What did he think you'd grow up to be?"

She laughed, but she wrapped her arms around herself before she spoke again. Emma looked vulnerable in that moment, and it shook him. Before he'd known her, he'd never have guessed she was anything but supremely confident—invincible. But she had scars, like anyone else. Like him.

"He said I was going to make people happy for a living. I thought that sounded completely boring, because I usually wanted to be Supreme Empress of the Galaxy, and making people happy didn't get you an art studio, but I guess he was right. I get paid to bring the happy." One side of her mouth curved in a half smile. "And I can always go mess up Sam's art studio if I feel the need. It's big enough for both of us."

"He'd probably love what you do," Seth said.

"Oh, he'd probably tell me to lighten up. He was always threatening to cloud up and rain all over me if I didn't." Her cheeks turned pink. "He called me Sunshine. His way of teasing me because I was so serious half the time, I think."

Seth thought of her matching yellow umbrella and rain boots, and something twisted painfully deep in his chest. He understood her so completely in that moment, the need to keep little reminders of who she'd been, what she'd lost, even as she tried to move forward. It made him want to share a piece of himself, to let her know she wasn't alone.

"My best friend, Andy, used to like to make up stupid nicknames for people. Especially the ones he liked."

That caught her interest, at least. "Andy. Was he . . . ?"

"The masterpiece above my fireplace, yeah. That was him."

She tilted her head at him, her expression completely open. "Did he give you a nickname?"

Seth laughed softly and rubbed at the back of his neck, remembering. "Oh yeah. He called me Feathers."

Emma blinked, and he laughed again. "Feathers?"

He grinned, remembering. This was a story he hadn't told in a long time, but for the first time since he'd heard the news of his friend's death, sharing it didn't hurt. It just felt right. "Yes, Feathers. See, Andy and I met at college, did the ROTC thing together, even managed to get stationed together afterward, but that's another story. Anyway, we used to have all these obnoxious, half-tamed birds around campus. They'd do just about anything to get their claws on food, shiny things, whatever caught their eye. You weren't actually supposed to feed them, but it was kind of a moot point. I think they were smarter than a lot of the students."

"I suppose *you* fed them, though," Emma said.

Seth shook his head, remembering. "Nope. I'd just go sit out there and watch them sometimes. They were funny. And they were complete jerks about what they wanted to take, which made it funnier. Until one day when I got the bright idea to enhance my viewing experience by bringing along a loaf of bread. Because, obviously, it would be just like feeding ducks at the pond."

"Which you're not really supposed to do, either."

"Okay, Wildlife Management, do you want to hear what happened or not?"

When she smiled, he continued.

"Anyway, I sat down on the quad, opened up my loaf of bread, and tossed exactly one small piece to a nearby bird."

Emma's smile widened, and her nose crinkled up. "Oh God."

"Yeah. You're looking at the only guy ever mugged by a flock of birds at the University of Florida. Andy used to say he couldn't even see me running, just this huge mass of squawking birds flying across the quad. We won't even talk about the mementos they left me with."

Emma was giggling now, and he knew she was picturing it. He laughed with her, even though he still got twitchy in parks sometimes.

"And hence, Feathers," she said.

"Feathers," Seth affirmed, pushing up the sleeve of his shirt to show her his raven. "So now you know the story of the tattoo you like so much."

She came to him then, still laughing as she touched the design he'd spent months working on with a tattoo artist. "They have ravens at UF?"

"No, but I like ravens better than those jerk black-birds. And it reminds me without giving me flashbacks." He grinned. "I wanted to remember Andy. He would have told me to make it look cool. And he would have laughed his ass off that I'd commemorate him this way."

"But . . . Feathers," she said again. "That's quite a nick-name."

"If I start hearing it around, I'll know who ratted me out," Seth warned her. She reached down and squeezed his hand.

"You won't hear it from anyone. Except me," she said, a mischievous twinkle in her eye. "Don't expect me to be able to help myself *all* the time. Come on. I'll grab a bag of chips and we can go sit up on the widow's walk. Though after what you just told me, you might feel like you're taking your life in your hands. We do have gulls."

He shook his head, glad he'd vanquished her sadness

for the time being. "I'm feeling lucky. Let's do it. Just make sure you show me how to make a quick getaway if we need to."

"You got it, Feathers." When Seth looked down at her and opened his mouth to protest, he was treated to a quick, hard kiss and the flash of a smile before she set off for the kitchen. Seth followed, though not before a single, long look at the collection of photographs on the Henrys' fireplace. Her memories. He'd never expected that they would have so much in common. Or that she could make him feel even more grateful for the people he'd gotten to keep—his parents and sister. If he'd needed any more proof of all the healing he'd managed to do in the past couple of years, setbacks notwithstanding, the conversation he'd just had was it.

The past didn't always have to be an open wound. It could be just what it was—his past. At least, it was when he was with her. It was amazing, Seth thought, the progress a guy could make when a stylish high heel was kicking him out of his comfort zone on a regular basis.

Seth pulled Emma back into his arms just before they reached the kitchen, feeling like a weight had been lifted off him. He didn't know why or how, only that it had happened because of her.

"Thanks," he said. "For today. You've got a knack for figuring out exactly the right thing—you know that?"

She tilted her head to the side, and there was something in her eyes he hadn't seen before, something that made them seem fathomless as they searched his face. "Only because I ..." A faint crease appeared between her brows, but it was gone almost as quickly as it had appeared. She shook her head with a faint smile. "That's why they pay me the big bucks. I'm glad I made your day. It's just a big old house, but it's mine."

It was on the tip of his tongue to ask what she'd been about to say. But she was already walking away, and he didn't want to risk spoiling what was left of their afternoon by pushing her about something that might not have been anything at all. So Seth did the only thing that seemed to make any sense—he let it go, though he knew it would niggle at him the rest of the day. Instead, he carried the bag of chips she handed him to the roof. Then Seth sat on the widow's walk with his arm around Emma, looking out at the sea and feeling the bloom of a thing he hadn't expected ever to feel again.

Peace.

Chapter Twenty-one

"I'm an idiot."

Emma lay on her couch, fending off Boof's head-butts while she cradled the phone against her ear. A bag of chocolate eggs she'd hidden in case of emergency lay on her coffee table, torn open and half gone. She wasn't proud, but desperate times called for desperate measures.

"You're not an idiot."

"Yes, I am. I was standing right there, and he was looking at me like, like . . . I don't know. But it was a moment. And instead of telling him how I felt, I made some stupid joke. And then I got the potato chips, because that is totally a nonverbal way of telling a man you love him."

"Em." Sam had been very patient with her ranting, but Emma could hear the amusement in her sister's voice. "You're not an idiot. You got scared. It's allowed."

"Maybe it's better this way," Emma said, popping another chocolate egg into her mouth and chewing while she scratched Boof beneath his chin. "Maybe I should just wait for him to figure it out. I've got a few years, right? Until my looks start to go?"

"Emma, you're thirty."

"I know! But what if I start to fall apart in a couple of

years? And he's still hanging around figuring himself out, and my best years are behind me, and—"

"Oh my God. I'd forgotten how you get when something's really bugging you."

Emma frowned. "What is *that* supposed to mean?"

"You know what I mean," Sam said. "You. Conjuring worst-case scenarios, probably with a bag of chocolate nearby. Losing your damn mind. It's like the price nature exacted for making you so collected the other ninety-nine percent of the time."

"You're not funny," Emma grumbled, and tried to be quiet about it as she chewed another piece of candy. "I screwed up."

"How? Did you not have a good day?"

Emma opened her mouth, considered the actual answer, and then sighed. "No. It was a great day. Except for that."

"Which was a problem only in the scary confines of your own head," Sam said, and then her voice grew gentle. "If you really want to tell him, then quit worrying about it and just let it happen. There'll be another time. Maybe even a better time. I saw the way he looks at you. I genuinely don't think he's going anywhere."

"How does he look at me?"

"Like you're amazing. Which you are, with the notable exception of right this second. But you'll get through it."

Emma pressed her lips together and looked at Boof, who was perched on her chest doing his slow "I love you" blink while she rubbed his head. "I don't know. Maybe it's better if I just keep it to myself for a while. I feel like I'm running and he's walking. I don't want to dive in and then realize I've made a huge mistake again."

"Oh, I so know exactly how that feels," Sam said. "With Jake, I was the one dragging my feet, but that was exactly what I was afraid of. I was wrong, though. It would have been a huge mistake not to dive in. *Despite* past experiences," she said pointedly. "And mine were actually with him. Seth isn't Ben. We've discussed this."

"I know he isn't," Emma said. "I'm glad he isn't. But that still doesn't mean he's figured out where I fit in his life. He's just starting to open up. I need to figure out a way to put the brakes on before I crash into a wall or something." She flopped her head back and stared at the ceiling. "I knew. I knew that if I ever really fell in love, it would make me miserable."

"Great attitude."

Like you were all sparkles and rainbows when it happened to you."

"Fair enough." Sam was quiet for a moment, then said, "If you really feel that strongly about it, just tell him. Your head will explode if you don't, and anyway, at least then you'll know where you stand. The not knowing is why you're miserable."

"Yes. There's that."

"And? I'm hearing an 'and.'"

"And," Emma said, her voice growing softer as she found herself at a loss for the words that usually came so easily, "when I was there with him, I started to realize exactly what a huge step I was about to take. What I'd be risking, you know . . . what it could mean. . . ."

She trailed off and Sam started to speak again, but the noise outside drowned out most of it. Emma frowned, moving Boof off her chest and standing to look out the window.

"What's going on?" Sam asked. "I can hear the sirens here, too."

Emma peered out the front window, looking out onto the square, and saw a squad car go flying, sirens blaring, in the direction of Northside. She could hear others in the distance. And the wail of ambulances. Her breathing quickened, and there was a sick feeling in the pit of her stomach.

It could be anything. Accidents happen all the time. It could be anything.

"I'm going to see if I can find out," Emma said. "Call you back."

He knew when he got the call that it wasn't going to be good.

Seth pulled the cruiser up in front of the dilapidated little house in Northside, a part of town he'd become awfully familiar with. He'd gotten his black eye one street over, and he was called out to the neighborhood on a regular basis. There were good people here, like anywhere, just trying to mind their own business and get by. But there were also some problems, and those problems tended to be recurring.

This particular problem fell into that category.

As soon as he got out of the car, he heard the sound of glass shattering inside, a woman's voice shrieking in anger, followed by a man's bellow. A couple of neighbors milled around outside, looking worried. They were tired of the trouble, Seth knew. So was he.

"Hey, Officer Andersen," one of them said, jogging up to him. He was young, maybe nineteen, with a scruffy goatee and a hard look about him. But Seth knew the kid was working his ass off in community college here, determined to get out of the grinding poverty in which he'd been raised. Seth had already told him that if he needed help, all he had to do was ask. He'd seen too many of these kids not make it out because the deck was just too damn stacked against them.

"Hey, Paulie. Thanks for calling."

"No problem." His lean, sharp face was etched with worry. "They've really been at it tonight. We all tried to ignore it, but the whole 'I'll kill you, you bitch' thing starts to kind of worry you after a while." Jimmy Aldrige had been threatening to kill "that bitch," otherwise known as his girlfriend, Jenny Blankenship, for far longer than Seth had been in the Cove. Lately, though, it seemed like the calls had come more often, and Jimmy's ranting had taken on a wild, dark edge that made Seth uneasy.

"They both drunk?"

A roll of the eyes. "They ever not drunk when you've been out here?"

"Fair enough. Officer Salvatore's on his way, too. I learned my lesson with Jimmy's brother." He tapped the corner of his eye, and Paulie chuckled.

"Made you look badass, though."

"Sure. Maybe I could pay him to punch me once a week."

"Dude, that's putting money back into the community right there." Something larger shattered inside the house, and this time the woman's scream held a note of fear. Paulie's smile vanished as he looked toward the house.

"I'm tired of this shit. One of these times he's going to kill her. For real."

"Not tonight, at least," Seth said. He watched Mark's cruiser pull in, lights flashing, and was glad to see his friend step out. He walked over to him, and after a quick consultation they headed up the leaning, rotted front steps. Seth could hear the sounds of a television inside, muffled voices from a commercial. The light from it flickered through the dingy window.

This isn't gonna be good. He knew it, sensed it with every instinct he had. A glance at Mark told him he wasn't the only one who sensed it, like a sour tang in the air. Still, it was time to begin.

A hard knock on the door. "Mr. Aldrige? This is the police. We're going to need you to open up."

The house went eerily silent, but for the television. Jenny's silence was worrisome, but it wouldn't be the first time she'd turned around and backed Jimmy up after he'd beaten the shit out of her. Seth knocked again, his voice firmer. "Police! Open up!"

He heard footsteps then, slow and deliberate, approaching the door. Seth's fingers twitched, and he brought his hand to the butt of his gun. It was a small measure of comfort as the air around him seemed to thicken. For a brief instant, this night blended with another one, and he could almost smell the cool, dry desert night, the pungent stink of the village. On the other side of the door was a man who was responsible for the deaths of at least ten U.S. soldiers, and Seth could hear a baby crying.

It's time to break the door down. Let the baby not be anywhere near the bastard. Jesus—

He blinked, and it was just the Cove again, dingy yellow light spilling out onto the porch as the inner door swung open to reveal a potbellied man in his forties, clad in boxers and a stained T-shirt, his eyes red and rheumy, peering at them through a screen. He stank of booze. Seth tried to breathe. He hadn't had a flashback since before he'd gotten out. Why he'd have one now was—

"G'off my property," Jimmy growled. "I know who you are. I know."

"Mr. Aldrige," Mark started, and that was when Jimmy moved and Seth saw what he had in his hand.

"Shit," Seth said, and went for his gun. Mark shouted something, but it was lost in the muzzle flash and sharp pops that blew holes in the night.

*   *   *

When the handful of phone calls Emma made to try to find out what was going on produced no results, she was forced to do her least favorite thing—sit and wait. As minutes turned into an hour, and then two, she knew that Seth must be there at the scene.

It's probably an accident. Or maybe something bad happened and then the cops were called. He's fine.

It was a completely logical train of thought, but as time passed, Emma couldn't hang on to it. She paced restlessly, considered just getting in her car and heading toward Northside more than a dozen times. All she wanted to know was that he was safe, and she had no way of doing that without looking like she was completely overreacting to some sirens and flashing lights. Never mind that what she'd seen was out of the ordinary for the Cove. He was a cop. This was what he did. What did she think she was going to do—panic and hunt him down every time she saw a speeding squad car?

"I'm fine," she told herself out loud. "I can do this."

It was a tough sell to begin with. Then the phone rang.

"Have you heard from Seth yet?" It was Sam's voice, a rush of sound.

"No. No, why? Did you hear anything?" Emma tried to keep the edge of panic out of her voice, but it was an exercise in futility.

"I did." Sam cursed quietly. "There was a shooting over in Northside. One or two dead, and Fitz heard that there was a police officer down. I'm not sure—he didn't know—"

But Emma had quit listening. The world seemed to tilt beneath her feet, and the still silence of her apartment became overwhelming, oppressive. Any minute now, one of his friends would knock on her door to tell her. Or maybe they'd forget about her, just a girlfriend, until his parents had been notified and they remembered he had a life here, too. People who cared about him. Someone who loved him.

Her heart began to pound as her mind tried to wrap itself around the possibility that he was gone. In her mind's eye she was twelve again, being told that there was nothing more to be done, that the fight was lost and all that was left was to prepare for what was coming . . . to sit and wait and try to cope with her powerlessness to save someone she loved more than anything.

"Emma, listen to me. This doesn't mean it's him. You need to call. . . . Emma?"

"I have to go." Her voice was barely a whisper, but she managed to turn the phone off and set it down carefully. When she pulled her hand back, it was shaking. Terror, grief, fury were all circling. . . . She could feel them. But Sam was right. Until she knew for sure, she had to stay functional. She had to push through.

This is why I decided no heroes. Remember? Nobody who would make himself easier to lose. Nobody who would make me go through this again.

She walked to where her purse was on legs that felt wobbly and numb, slung it over her shoulder, and headed for the door. She wasn't exactly sure where she should go—the station? The hospital?—but she couldn't be in her apartment another second. Emma had just shut the door when her phone began to buzz again. She looked at an unfamiliar number, and her breath stilled. This would be the call. This . . .

She managed to get it to her ear, and she spoke even though it felt like someone had her chest in a vise, squeezing it tighter and tighter.

"Hello?"

"Emma."

Then she was sliding down to the floor on legs that were no longer interested in supporting her, resting her back against the door while she listened to a voice that was as strong as it had been when she'd heard it just a few hours ago.

"Emma, are you there?"

"I'm here. Seth. I thought . . . I heard there was a shooting. Are you—" Everything she wanted to say came out disjointed, a series of half-finished thoughts and questions. She still couldn't quite believe it was him on the phone, though as it sank in, the relief that crashed through her had tears welling in her eyes. She sniffled them back, wiping at her eyes with the heel of her hand. She didn't want to cry in her hallway. She didn't want to cry over Seth. She didn't particularly want to cry at all. The emotional tumult that sank its claws into her was horrifyingly familiar, and extremely unwelcome. She inhaled deeply, trying to come down, regulate her breathing, make her heart stop fluttering like a trapped bird.

"There was, but I'm fine. The bullet just grazed me."

She closed her eyes. "You were shot?" A number of images rose in her mind, none of them welcome, all of them frightening. Why would anyone try to kill Seth? But of course she knew the answer. He enforced the law. Being hurt or killed in the service of it was simply an occupational hazard.

"No. He tried. That's all. I'm okay."

"And him?"

A pause. "Not so much."

"You—you shot him." She tried to imagine that and found she couldn't. That was a part of himself he hadn't shared with her, the part that had gone to war, that was trained to kill if need be. It wasn't upsetting so much as it was simply alien to her.

"I did. The alternative wasn't so great. His girlfriend was already critical when he answered the door. We just didn't know." He'd shifted from sounding glad to hear her voice to sounding puzzled. "Are you okay? I wanted to catch you before you heard anything, but we had a mess here and they wouldn't let me go before the EMTs cleaned up my head."

She felt as though she'd been punched. "Your *head*? He tried to shoot you in the head?"

"That's where a lot of people aim, yeah. . . . Emma, it's not even that deep, I promise. I'm fine. I just want to wrap this up and see you. I couldn't find my damn phone—this is Mark's—but I didn't want you to worry."

Her laugh was nothing more than a harsh rush of air. "You could have died."

"No, this is what we train for." Then she heard it, his weariness creeping in, and the vise around her chest gave another squeeze. "Listen, I'm hoping I can get out of here before too much longer. Can I see you? Come there, tonight?"

The thought of seeing him right now was overwhelming. She wanted it so badly that it was physically painful. And that was the problem. There was so much adrenaline coursing through her system that she didn't know which end was up. Another couple of tears escaped from the corners of her eyes, frustrating her, and she swiped at them with a shaky hand.

"Is this going to happen again?" she asked.

"What?"

"You getting shot at. You nearly getting a bullet in your brain from some dirtbag. Me not knowing for hours whether you're okay, just hearing rumors about dead people and downed officers."

He swore softly. "Emma, I wish I'd gotten word to you sooner. The Cove doesn't get a lot of murders. There are things we had to do, and the time moves faster than you think it does."

"You didn't answer my question." She was beginning to sound foggy from trying not to cry, but there was nothing to be done for it. She was sure he heard it, and just as sure he had no idea what to do about it. Since she didn't, either, that was sort of satisfying.

"This is my job. It could happen again, sure, because it's my job. But you knew I was a cop. I work at being a good cop so I don't get killed. *I'm okay*, Emma."

"I know. This time." But she wasn't naive enough to think that coming out on top in a confrontation was always due to talent. Some of it was pure luck, and luck was a fickle thing. "I thought you were dead. I honestly thought you were gone. You know what that feels like." Her voice quavered, and she hated it. She hated this feeling, too, like she'd been scraped raw, every nerve exposed and completely vulnerable. Everything she'd built on the damaged foundation of the girl she'd been had crumbled in an instant, revealing the cracks and flaws.

He sighed, and she could hear all the activity in the background, other people cleaning up what sounded like a mess.

"I do know. I want to see you, Emma. There are some things I need to—I just need to see you. It was a rough night. Please."

She closed her eyes again, wishing she had some kind of defenses against what she felt for him. Anything. Instead, she knew that seeing him right now would wreck her utterly. Whatever he asked, she'd give, and more. Just being able to touch him would melt away all her misgivings. He wouldn't even have to profess his love—only his need for her. And at some point, she would get to go through this all over again. Or worse. Because however much she loved him now, she sensed that she had even more to give. And if he should go, he would take all of that love with him, leaving her empty . . . all over again.

She'd thought she could take the risk. But she'd forgotten how it felt to have her heart torn out—and this was just a taste.

"I can't." She forced out the words, her throat stinging. "I need some time. I forgot, Seth. I forgot what this feels like. I don't know if I can do this right now." *Or ever. I promised myself I wouldn't ever feel like this again.*

"You were scared. I completely understand, Emma. I know this isn't what you expected or wanted, but if you'll just let me see you. I need to tell you—"

"I can't," she said quickly, cutting him off. Whatever he'd meant to say, she was in no condition to hear it. She sensed that even the smallest endearment from him would steamroll her, and she had to be able to think instead of just feeling. All she could do right now was feel, and it made her want to crawl out of her skin.

"I'm so glad you're safe, Seth," she added softly. "You couldn't know how much. I just need some time."

Another long pause. And finally, quietly, he said simply, "I understand."

Somehow, she managed to tell him good-bye. Then Emma hung up, beginning to shake so badly that she dropped the phone. For a time she stayed where she was, crying softly in the hall, head in her hands, while her cat cried plaintively for her on the other side. Finally, though, she managed to get to her feet, going back in only to throw a few simple things in a bag and collect Boof.

By the time she got in her car, she was beginning to go numb. It wouldn't last, but Emma welcomed the numbness, hoping it stayed long enough to let her fall into the temporary oblivion of sleep. She was the girl who had never run away, but right now, that was all she wanted to do. She wanted to go anywhere she wouldn't have to deal with the fear she was feeling. Anywhere she wouldn't have to deal with herself.

Instead, Emma went to the only safe place she had left—her mother's.

She'd been so ready to hand Seth her heart, to expose the part of herself she held most closely. Maybe she should be grateful for the reminder of the sorts of wounds love could inflict, deeper than any weapon could achieve.

Once, she'd been a girl who had slept with her father's pillow, spraying it with his cologne so even the ghosts of his memory wouldn't desert her. But she'd grown up . . . and she never wanted to be that girl again.

Chapter Twenty-two

"We're staging an intervention."

Emma looked up from where she sat slumped at the kitchen island to see Sam and her mother watching her from the doorway. She didn't move, barely bothering to arch her eyebrow.

"There are only two of you. That's not an intervention. And I don't need one anyway." She tipped down the side of the pint of marshmallow fudge ice cream sitting at her elbow, realized she'd eaten it all, and heaved a gusty sigh. There was probably a blob of it on her sweatshirt, but she hadn't sunk that low yet.

She heard them approaching, heard the stools being scraped against the wood floor as they settled themselves directly across from her so that she couldn't ignore them. Emma looked up, resigned. She'd known this was coming, after all. You didn't go from being a go-getting entrepreneur to a listless slob in the space of a week without people worrying.

Especially when you'd basically moved back in with your mother because you couldn't handle being alone.

"Emmie," Andi started, "you know I love having you here. But what you're doing to yourself isn't healthy."

"I get up in the mornings. I go to work, and to events," Emma pointed out. "I eat. I'm bathing."

"Sure, you work. And the second you get home, you turn into . . . this," Sam said, indicating her sister with a bewildered expression. "I didn't even know you *had* a sweatshirt."

"I don't. It's yours," Emma replied, which earned her a disgruntled look.

"Honey," Andi said gently, "you normally love what you do. I know what happened the other night hit you pretty hard, but . . . you haven't even talked to Seth."

She flinched a little. No, she hadn't talked to him. Nor had he tried very hard to talk to her. One quick phone call to check on her Friday, and that had been it. Granted, she'd refused to see him that day, too, but she'd at least expected him to fight a little harder. To push her into seeing some benefit to being with a man she was constantly at risk of losing. As it was, she'd begun to think that she'd imagined what was between them, at least on his part.

That she'd fallen in love with another illusion.

The pain of even considering that was almost as bad as what she'd experienced Thursday night. Almost.

"Well, he hasn't made any more of an effort than I have, so don't just blame me," Emma said. Sam and Andi exchanged a look. "What?" Emma asked, annoyed. She loved them, but it had always made her crazy when they'd kept things from her.

"He may not be calling," Andi said, "but he asks about you."

At Emma's blank look, Sam elaborated. "He's been into Diamonds and Perls a couple of times to make sure you're okay. And into the gallery once."

She stiffened, though she couldn't stop the way her

heartbeat quickened, or the warmth that flooded her. Whatever he'd felt, it was strong enough to keep checking after her. So not all her feelings had been wasted. It was a struggle to keep her voice neutral. "He could have just called."

"Oh? Would you have talked to him?"

Emma hesitated. She wanted to talk to him. She desperately wanted to see him. But she wasn't a big fan of inflicting pain on herself, and what would she say? Asking him to get a different job was unfair. Being a police officer was part of who he was. Telling him not to get injured and killed was just stupid—he didn't want to have those things happen, either. And telling him she loved him now—what good would that do? He probably wasn't any more ready to hear it than he was a week ago. Besides, her love couldn't save him from the things that might take him away from her, no matter how much she wished it.

"I don't know," she finally said.

"Well, I do. You wouldn't have, because you're scared to death," Andi said. Emma looked up sharply from toying with the empty ice-cream container.

"You of all people should understand why," she said, hearing the edge in her voice. "He could have *died*, Mom. Just like that, for no good reason. And he's going to put himself in a position to have the same thing happen over and over and over."

Andi nodded. "Not if he can help it, but yes, he would do it again. That's the kind of man he is. Honey, he and the other officer are probably the reason Jenny Blankenship isn't dead. You don't think saving a life is a good reason to risk your own?"

Emma felt her jaw tighten as she stared down at the rustic wood of the island. She knew the answer. But that didn't mean she had to like it. "I just don't want him to risk his. I don't—I don't want to lose him." It was difficult to even form the words, but she needed to get them out, and her mother and sister were the only two people on earth she could bare herself to this way. "I knew when I met him he was a risk. I didn't want to take the chance. But I couldn't get him out of my head, and he was so easy to be with. So I let myself think nothing could happen here, that it was okay. And it's not. One day he could walk out the door and never come back."

"Any of them could," Sam said gently. "One of us could. Would you rather give us up completely, just in case?"

Emma rubbed at her nose. After years of avoiding it almost completely, crying seemed to be one of her new hobbies. It made her angry, but that never seemed to stop the tears. "No," she said, her voice foggy. "Don't be stupid. You're my family. It's different."

"Yes and no. You could choose to shut us out anyway. I'm glad you don't, so don't get any ideas, but it's always a choice," Sam said. "I remember losing Dad. I remember how long it took all of us to come through that. Just like I remember worrying that I might lose you or Mom, for a long time afterward. I *still* worry. You two are my anchors. I'd be devastated if I lost you. But my life would be so much poorer without you that not having you in it isn't even a choice I could make." She reached across the table to take Emma's hand. "It's the same with Jake. If I lost him tomorrow, I still wouldn't trade a second of what I've had with him."

"Yeah, well, he's more likely to get scratched or bitten at his job than shot or stabbed," Emma said, though she didn't pull her hand away. The comfort of that connection was something she needed—and she felt the truth of every word her sister said about being anchored by the love she had for her family. They were her constants, even when Sam had been physically gone from town. Just knowing she was out there, only a phone call away and always willing to talk, had been a balm when she'd needed it. And now that she was here, the distance between them bridged almost as if it had never existed, Emma couldn't imagine what she'd do without her.

"Em, bad things can happen to anyone, anytime they walk out the door. Dad is a perfect example. He didn't do anything that should have put him at risk, but the cancer happened anyway."

"I've been through what you're afraid of, Emmie," Andi said. "Remember that. You didn't just lose a father. I lost my husband. The love of my life. He was, too," she said with a sweet, sad smile. "He grounded me, supported me, loved me in spite of the sniping that lasted for years after we married because I wasn't a local girl, just some flighty flake he'd picked up at a ski resort. Typical Henry, they said." She laughed. "And he was. He went his own way, followed his heart. But Bill was steady as a rock. I needed that steadiness just like he needed my passion, and what we made together was solid, real. I loved him dearly, even when it wasn't perfect or easy. That love gave me a lot of good years, a lot of beautiful memories. It gave me the two of you." She looked pointedly at Emma. "Your dad scared me, too, honey. I was a free spirit. I didn't want to settle down. I thought it would be the end of who I was, all my dreams. But if I'd walked away, I would have missed out on all the dreams we made together. The family we made together. And even though I miss him every day, I will never regret loving him with everything I had." Her eyes, full of emotion, shimmered in the light. "I don't want to see you miss out on a love like that, Emmie."

Emma sat very still while her mother's words washed

over her, resonating even in the parts of herself she'd kept locked away in a desperate attempt to protect them. And for what? She was hurting right now because of things that might be, instead of hanging on to the things that already were, and reaching for all she might have if she was brave enough to try.

Her mother was right. The beauty and love that had come from her father's life far outweighed the pain. He'd been worth the risk Andi had taken. Just as Seth would be worth the risk she would have to take.

Emma let out a long, shaking breath. "You're right. You're both right."

Sam smiled. "Can I get a recording of that?"

Andi gave her daughter a look. "Sam."

"No, really," Emma said, giving her sister's hand a squeeze, and then rising to walk around the island and wrap her arms around her mother. She'd kept a lot of hugs to herself over the years, but this one felt right. Andi held her tightly, enveloping her in the warmth and scents of home. "I shouldn't have run. I didn't know what to do. I love him so much, Mom. I don't want to lose him, but I was so scared—"

"I know, honey," her mother said, stroking her hair. "I think he knows, too. He's been through enough to understand. But he needs you as much as you need him. When he came in the other day, that was clear. I know it's against your nature, but maybe just try letting yourself love him. The rest will follow."

Emma nodded, her head clearer than it had been in days, and pulled away to look at the two most important women in her life—her family. "I guess I did need an intervention. I love you guys. Really. So much."

"We love you, too," Sam said. "Which is why the intervention isn't over until you throw my sweatshirt in the wash, get in the shower, and then put on some pearls or something. I feel like the universe is out of whack with you like this."

Emma smiled, feeling immeasurably lighter. But there was more, a sense of urgency that pushed her to rush upstairs and start getting herself together so she could make things right. With the paralyzing terror gone, what remained was the overwhelming need to find Seth, to see his face, and put her arms around him.

To finally tell him what was in her heart, and let love take care of the rest.

Love notwithstanding, Emma was a bundle of nerves when she knocked on Seth's door. She had been ever since he'd picked up the phone when she'd called.

"Can I see you?" she'd asked. "It's important. There's a lot I need to say." She didn't want to do this on the phone, unable to see or touch him, and that was at least something he seemed to agree with.

"Can you come over?" he asked. "I've got something I need to show you. I can bring it there if you'd rather. . . ."

"No," Emma said, thinking of the potential audience. "I think alone is better. I'll be there soon."

The soft buzz of his voice had been impossible to read, though he'd sounded eager enough to talk to her. Emma hung on to that, hoping that she hadn't managed to break in a few days what she'd spent so long waiting for. That fear was banished, though, the instant he opened the door.

He was the best thing she'd ever seen, Emma thought, her chest tightening painfully and yet another wave of hated tears rising to sting her eyes, threatening to spill over without a single word. He had an ugly scab at his temple, the only visible reminder of his brush with death.

His hair was slightly mussed, and the eyes that met hers were full of both weariness and something more—an intensity she'd only glimpsed in him when they'd been wrapped around each other. His generous mouth didn't curve into a smile as it usually did when he saw her. Instead, he simply spoke one word.

"Emma."

She worried she might lose it right there on his doorstep. All she wanted was the reassurance of his touch, but the few feet between them could have been miles. Miles she'd created this time. Emma swallowed hard, brushing her hands nervously down her simple polka-dot sundress.

"Seth, I—" She hiccuped, and was mortified. "I'm sorry."

He sighed, and to her amazement, he moved to close the space between them. "It's okay," he said, and then his strong arms were around her, wrapping her in their comfort. Then she did cry, promising herself that this would be the last time for a while, dampening his T-shirt while he stroked her hair, her back as he held her close. "It's okay," he said again, dropping a kiss on the top of her head when the storm had passed, and she simply stood resting her cheek against his chest, listening to the steady beat of his heart.

This, she thought. *This is all I need right now.*

His voice rumbled against her ear. "Come on in. I want to show you something."

Emma lifted her head to look at him, but his expression betrayed nothing. Seth reached down to take her hand, then led her inside, shutting the door behind him. There was a large cardboard box sitting open beside the stairs, but the newspapers wadded up on top held no clue as to what had been inside it. Seth pulled her toward the couch, and when he sat down, she followed suit, curious. When she was situated, he picked up a large book that was sitting on his coffee table. Emma hadn't immediately noticed it, but when she did, it was recognizable enough.

"A photo album?" she asked. He nodded, the sharp lines of his face serious.

"I had Kira send me some things. You'll meet her soon. She's coming to visit next month. I mean, I'd like you to meet her. If you want to."

The uncertainty that crept into his voice sliced through her. Emma nodded. "Of course I want to meet her."

A faint, genuine smile. "Okay. Well . . . there was a lot in the box, but I managed a decent abbreviated version to start." He looked at her. "Open it up."

Slowly, Emma did, and found a page of pictures featuring a smiling young man and a woman holding two babies: one with a pink hat, the other wearing a blue one. His parents. His sister. Him. Emma looked up at Seth, beginning to suspect what he had done. The sweetness of it, and what it implied, humbled her.

"Your family?" she asked.

He nodded. "Keep going. Lots more mug shots where that came from."

Emma began to turn the pages of the thick album slowly, treated to photos of Seth toddling around with a stuffed pig, Seth wearing a birthday hat, Seth riding a bike. Seth with the famous Ming, an adorable little flat-faced dog who looked as though he smiled all the time. He grew older, making faces with his sister, playing soccer, then driving a beat-up old car. There was college, with pictures of him and a grinning young man he identified as Andy. And as Emma turned the pages, Seth talked, weaving the images together with brief anecdotes that together told the story of his life until now, everything he'd held close and been so reluctant to share.

"Here's my unit on my first tour in Iraq," Seth said as she turned another page. And now it was all uniforms and camouflage, men smiling in the desert sun, sometimes tired and dirty but obviously bonded. The stories changed—he put names with the smiling faces, and pointed out those he stayed in touch with along with those who hadn't come home.

"That's Pete Carlisle. The one I was upset about the first night you came over," Seth said, tapping a finger beside a tall, thin drink of water who was laughing while another soldier pretended he was going to kiss him. "He was a great guy. I wish I'd tried harder to reach out when we started to lose touch." Seth shook his head, and Emma knew these were wounds Seth was still tending. But he would heal. She could help him heal. The way he was helping her.

He walked her through more of his military career, moving into his law enforcement one. "You're skinnier here," she laughed, leaning into his side while he pointed out where the photos had been taken. "And your hair is so short!"

"Told you I'm too skinny," he replied with a smile.

She looked up at him, smirking. "I think you've filled out fine."

He gave her a lingering look, his eyes softening, before clearing his throat and flipping quickly through a couple more pages. "More police stuff, more police stuff, and . . . here."

Emma's eyes widened as the photos became images of places she recognized—the square, the little harbor, some of Seth's friends hanging around in Tony's garage drinking cheap beer and laughing. And finally, the two of them together—one was a silly picture Brynn had taken of her on the back of Seth's motorcycle, pretending to scream and hang on for dear life; another was a shot of them at the party he'd helped her with, arms around each other, smiling at the camera. And then, one Sam must have taken without her knowledge at the cookout—this last photo captured a brief moment when Seth had slung an arm around her and she'd rested her head against his chest, looking as though there was nowhere she'd rather be.

Because there wasn't.

Emma looked up to find Seth watching her intently. "You wanted to know who I am. All of it. This seemed like a pretty good start. Everything that mattered to me. That matters to me." He took her hand, threaded his fingers through hers, and looked down for a moment, almost shy. "I love you, Emma. I didn't know where I belonged, and you came along and showed me that this was exactly where I needed to be. There were things I worried I'd lost, but they just needed waking up. They needed you. I know you're afraid that—"

"No," Emma said, interrupting him with a gentle shake of her head, her heart so full it felt like it might burst. "I'm not afraid. I'm just not used to being completely, totally, madly in love with someone. But it's something I think I can get used to." His smile was beautiful. It was everything. "I love you, Seth. You brought chaos into my quiet little universe, and now I don't think I can live without it. So you're just going to have to stay."

Seth put the book aside, then tucked Emma's hair behind her ear, brushing his fingers down her cheek. "I'm not going anywhere," he said, lowering his mouth to hers. "As long as you're with me, I'm home."

Chapter Twenty-three

The Henry house hadn't seen so much activity in at least a hundred years.

Emma dashed through the downstairs, clutching a fistful of her skirt in one hand while her heels clicked on the floor. "Sam? Sam! The DJ's about to introduce you and Jake as husband and wife, and that's kind of hard to do if you're not out there! Sam?"

"I'm here! I'm here! What?" Sam emerged from the greenhouse, her cheeks bright pink, with Jake right behind her. A quick look told Emma that they hadn't mussed each other too badly, but the event coordinator in her couldn't let it slide.

"Outside! They're going to introduce you to everyone as man and wife. And stop touching each other! You live together. Can't you wait so you don't mess up your hair?"

Sam rolled her eyes, but she was laughing. "Emma, quit trying to work. It's my wedding! You're my maid of honor! Go with it! Feel the fun!"

"I'm feeling the fun."

"No, that's anxiety." Sam stepped forward and pressed a kiss to her sister's cheek. "Everything is perfect. This is the best day of my life, and you helped make it this way.

For free, even, which makes me love you more. But now, it's time to enjoy it."

As much as she wanted to nag, Emma felt herself melt. "It really is perfect," she agreed. "And you look beautiful."

Sam looked like she might have stepped out of a Jane Austen novel, and Emma couldn't imagine a dress that would have suited her more. It was a simple Empire waist, with sheer cap sleeves, a lace bodice, and a satin skirt with a lace overlay that split up the front. A blue ribbon tied beneath the bodice, the ends draping nearly to the floor. Her satin slippers peeked from beneath the skirt, and her pale hair was caught back in a simple tail, styled to fall in curls down past her shoulders. A silver headband was the finishing touch, having replaced her floor-length veil.

"I feel beautiful," Sam replied, "and ready to party."

"Sounds like the party's ready for us, too," Jake said. He put his arm around his wife's waist and grinned at Emma. She had to admit, the man wore a tuxedo as well as anyone she'd ever seen. And his hair had even decided to behave for the occasion. Mostly. She had a feeling her sister might have something to do with its current state of dishevelment.

At least the formal pictures were done.

"Okay," Emma said. "As the maid of honor, I command you! Go. Go, go!"

"We should have gotten you a bullhorn to go with the dress," Jake said. With a matching ribbon on it."

Sam's eyes widened. "Do you really want to give her that kind of power?"

"I already have the power," Emma said. "Like She-Ra." She shooed them outside while they teased her about

needing a sword, then watched as the two of them boo-
gied together onto the dance floor when they were for-
mally announced as Dr. and Mrs. Jake Smith. They looked
happy. All the guests laughing and chatting in the yard, or
dancing on the portable dance floor, looked happy, too.
Emma knew a successful wedding when she saw one, and
this was it.

"Excuse me, but have you seen my date? Gorgeous
brunette, wild look in her eyes, last seen chasing a pair of
seagulls away from the hors d'oeuvres?"

"Hmm. She sounds crazy. If I see her, I'll avoid her."
She turned to look at Seth, who didn't look so much like
a classic bad boy as he did just classic in a slim-cut black
suit and tie. He grinned at her, and her heart clenched
the way it always did. Now, though, it was all pleasure.
Because he loved her. He was hers.

"You're right," he said. "Maybe I should get a new
date. Are you free?"

"You're in luck," she said, and let him loop his arm
around her waist as they walked to the dance floor. Sam
and Jake were in the middle of their first dance, waltzing
to an old song Andi had played often when they were
growing up. She and Jake had even taken a few lessons
so they wouldn't step on each other's feet.

"Looks like they want the wedding party to join in,"
Seth said, giving her a nudge. "Hurry up so I can steal
you back."

Shane came out of nowhere to catch her hand, and
Emma found herself drawn into a surprisingly good
waltz with Jake's best man.

"Nobody told me you could dance," she said, looking
up at him. His hand at her waist was light, but he steered
her around the floor expertly. He looked down, a small
smile on his lips.

"I'm a man of many talents. I also owe you big. Larkin is a fun date. Not to mention she doesn't hate me."

"She is fun," Emma agreed. "And why should she hate you? You've been behaving, right?"

"Of course I'm behaving. I'm incredibly well behaved."

"You're definitely something."

"Thank you," he said, grinning as he looked around the dance floor. He looked good today, Emma thought. Everyone did, from the guests to the wedding party. She loved her own dress, an airy, Empire-waisted confection in the same blue as the ribbon on Sam's dress. She thought she'd likely shorten the dress to wear again, though for today, she loved how it swept around her legs. It wasn't often she got to feel like a princess, and she was thoroughly enjoying it.

Well, apart from those obnoxious seagulls. They'd taken a lot of convincing to get away from the food, but if there was one thing she could do, it was be convincing in a very loud voice.

Nearby, Zoe danced with Jake's friend Fitz, while the other two groomsmen danced together. It was sweet to see that Jake's old friend Ryan had finally let Aaron catch him, Emma thought. And a relief, since Aaron had been horribly moody while Ryan was playing hard to get. Not that she could blame Ryan. He seemed to still be getting comfortable with being out in the Cove. So far, though, with a couple of notable exceptions, the reaction had been very supportive.

The Cove took care of its own. It was one of the reasons she stayed. Nowhere was perfect, but this place, at least, was hers. And now it was Seth's, too.

The song changed, and Shane slipped away, back to his date. The other two bridesmaids, artist friends of

Sam's, twirled by her, laughing. That was when she recognized the song. She stood there, then turned to search the crowd for Seth. His expression was a dead giveaway.

"Really?" she asked. *"Really?"*

"This one was a special request—a group request, I might add—for Harvest Cove's own dancing queen and maid of honor, Emma Henry," the DJ said. There was plenty of laughing and hooting, but though she felt herself blushing, Emma only laughed and curtsied as "What a Feeling" from *Flashdance* began to play.

"Thanks a lot, guys!"

Seth came out to join her on the dance floor, sliding his arms around her as more people joined them, lots of them singing along as they danced.

"If anyone hands me a pitcher of beer, they're going to end up wearing it," Emma told him. He laughed, sweeping her around and then swaying smoothly to the beat.

"So, I ran into Brynn the other day," he said.

"Would this be the day you came in while I was out getting lunch? Because I heard about this."

"What, she ratted me out?"

"More like she was excited that you seemed to have an interest in the ins and outs of event planning. You made her day, asking about what she's doing for the Harding wedding. She's been on a high since Penny called her personally to tell her how much she loved what she'd put together." She kissed the tip of his nose. "You're pretty sweet for a tough guy."

"I try. I wasn't just being nice, though. I really did want to pick her brains about the Harding wedding."

Emma arched an eyebrow. "Really? Why?"

"I remember you telling me that you'd blown it by giving her your idea of a perfect wedding the first time around, and that Penny had wanted something different."

"Mmmhmm." She began to get the strangest feeling, a tingling awareness that she was about to have a moment. The kind that changed everything. The kind that led a lot of people to her door.

"She has a great memory. Even kept your original proposal, since she thought you might be able to use it for someone else. 'A perfect Harvest Cove wedding,' I think she called it."

"Mmmhmm." Why couldn't she talk?

"So I hope you don't mind," he said, "but I hired her."

"Hired her?"

Then he was pulling the ring from his pocket, a beautiful ring with an oval diamond the color of honey, set in a diamond oak-leaf basket. It flashed in the light, like a little drop of sunshine. "What do you say?" he asked, dropping to one knee. "Marry me? I'll make you happy, Emma. As happy as you make me."

He slipped the ring on her finger, and it fit her as perfectly as he did. So Emma pressed a kiss to his lips and said the only thing she could, her heart full of the promise of a life she'd once thought impossible—a life they would build together.

"You already have."

Continue reading for a special preview of
the next book in the Harvest Cove series,

ONE OF THESE NIGHTS

Available wherever books and e-books are
sold in September 2015 from Signet Eclipse.

"Mom, really, it's okay. No, no, I'm happy to have you come for a visit, but a week is more than ... A month? You really don't need to.... Yeah, I know I'm going to need help for a while."

Jason sat on the couch and glared at his bum leg, immobilized in a clunky cast. His leg might have been the issue, but this whole thing was a giant pain in his ass. He adjusted the phone between his shoulder and his ear and listened to another dozen reasons why his mother was coming to take care of him, possibly forever, because he was just that bad at life. Her voice, calm and deceptively patient, continued to gently pummel him. People thought she was sweet. She was. Sometimes. But they tended to miss the steel underneath. He didn't, and he knew when he was in for it. This was one of those times.

"Honey, I know you don't like anyone fussing over you, but I remember what it was like when your father broke his arm falling off that ladder a few years ago. He needed a lot of help, and I'm sure you do, too. Are you eating? You never did cook; you're probably just living on cereal. Do you have any clean clothes? I know you don't, Jason Patrick Evans, and don't even think about lying to me. You're probably not even seeing anybody but your cousin and maybe a few backyard squirrels. I knew this was going to happen with that job of yours eventually." She sighed, a gusty, long-suffering breath. "Well, it doesn't matter right now. I'll be there on Sunday for as long as you need me, just like we planned."

"Like *you* planned," Jason muttered, which earned him a sharp snort from the woman who he had once been convinced kept the entire planet from spinning off its orbit and out into space through sheer force of will. He'd gotten his stubbornness from her. That was one reason why occupying the same enclosed space with her for an extended period of time filled him with dread. He loved his mother dearly, but he gave it a matter of hours before she was after him about everything from his holey old boxer shorts to his lack of a social life. Worse, she'd then start trying to *do something* about the multitude of items at which he was failing miserably. And right now, the state of his house wasn't going to help his cause.

Jason scanned the high-ceilinged great room, which encompassed most of the log home's living space, and winced. Dust swirled lazily in a sunbeam. Dishes sat haphazardly in the sink. Clothes were tossed over the furniture, left there because just getting them off was enough of a chore right now. The sight did nothing for his mood—he was a lot of things, but a slob wasn't one of them. Unfortunately, his powering through this with sheer orneriness wasn't working out that well so far.

"If I didn't do the planning, nothing would happen. You'd sit there and fester until your cousin called me out of desperation, and we'd be back at the same place." She sighed again, and guilt mixed with his frustration. He didn't want to upset her. He just wanted to crawl in a hole somewhere until his leg was better. Preferably in an undisclosed location where she couldn't find him.

"Sorry, Mom."

"Uh-huh. I'm used to it. You were never a treat when you were sick, kiddo. Always moody. Not like your brother. You know he still asks me to come make him soup when he gets a cold? He even says thank you."

Jason bit back a groan. This was one of the many reasons why he had to find a way to give this impending visit a definite end point, and the sooner, the better. He didn't want daily updates on the endless charms and delights of his baby brother, who had embodied perfection since birth. At least, according to the rest of the family. It wasn't that he didn't love Tommy. It was just that Tommy had never really seemed to need it. He got more than enough love from everybody else.

Story of his life.

"When your father gets back from this fishing trip they've got him going on for work—I don't think for a second it's not just an excuse for a bunch of them to escape onto the water and drink too much for a few days, but they're calling it work—he said he'd like to come out to stay for a bit, too, not just to get me and run. He has plenty of vacation time saved up. Maybe we can get your brother to come visit, too, at least for a weekend. What do you think? We haven't all been together since last Thanksgiving, and that was only for a couple of days. I miss the Cove this time of year. You know we love Florida, but it's hotter than hell right now, and I don't want to learn to fish, even if your Dad does keep after me about it. Oh, if we can get you up and around, maybe we can go to the field days! Think how fun that would be! I told Tammy and Paul I was coming into town, and they said . . ."

Her words washed over him, but Jason stopped hearing them. It all sounded like a rushing, rising wave of pure panic to him. He had to do something. Anything.

Otherwise, his small sanctuary in the woods was quickly going to become his idea of hell on earth. Unfortunately, in his current condition, running away until further notice wasn't a viable option.

It took a few seconds for the soft knocking at his door to register, and even then he might not have noticed but for the way the bundle of tan-and-white fur, which had been sleeping smashed up against his thigh, suddenly burst into motion, barking furiously as she flew off the couch and scrambled toward the door.

Her injuries sure haven't slowed her down any, Jason thought, ruefully amused.

"Oh, is somebody there?" his mother asked.

"Yeah, probably just Jake. He said he was going to swing by after work to make sure I hadn't impaled myself on my crutches, on purpose or otherwise." He covered the receiver for a minute to call out, "Come in!" over the wild barking before returning his attention to the conversation at hand.

"Your cousin is sweet to take time out of his day when he's so busy. I hope you appreciate what he's doing for you."

"Sure," Jason drawled. "He comes over. I verbally abuse him until I get tired. He plays with Rosie, and we both end the day happy. It works out."

"Jason."

He was in midsmirk when he heard the light tap of a bootheel on his floor. A familiar—and very feminine— voice reached his ears and rippled all the way through him. Just the way it always did.

"Hello?"

He took a breath, pushed aside his immediate instinct to whip his head around and start snarling at her out of complete mortification at what she must be seeing, but managed a reasonably civil "Hey" with a slight turn of his head. "I'll just be a . . . second."

Jason had to force the final word out, since his brain had tried to stall out the instant he caught sight of her. He was used to seeing Zoe Watson in what he thought of as her work uniform: long, loose shirt—sometimes a sweater—usually with an incomprehensibly tied scarf over leggings and a wide variety of boots. The woman seemed to have some weird riding-boot fetish. Not that there was anything wrong with that. But this was after work—the first time he'd ever actually seen her outside the gallery, he realized—and either she was deliberately messing with his head or there was a lot he didn't know about Zoe.

Probably both.

She was wearing one of those shirts that looked like a silky handkerchief that had been cleverly tied to her in a couple of key spots, along with a pair of skinny white pants cut a few inches too short, and some kind of strappy heels that made his mouth water despite the fact that they made no sense to him. Zoe was little, maybe five two, and he knew she had a great figure, but this evening she was showcasing her hourglass curves in a way he'd only imagined. Every inch of her, from her shapely long legs to the graceful neck she almost never showed off, was a feast for his eyes. Her mocha skin had a warm glow in the hazy light filtering in through the windows.

It took longer than it should have for him to realize she was watching him closely—curiously. However he'd been staring at her, she didn't seem to know quite what to do with it.

"Not a problem," Zoe said with a small smile. "I'll wait." Her big gray eyes regarded him with something like amusement before she shifted a potted plant she was carrying from one arm to the other and dropped into a crouch to fuss over Rosie. Jason tried to collect his thoughts, aware his mother was insistently repeating a few words. A question? Yeah, it was a question.

"Jason, *who is that*? Because if I didn't know any better, I'd say it was a woman."

Jesus, you'd think she just spotted a unicorn.

He readjusted the phone against his ear, listening to Zoe croon at his dog. He hadn't pegged her as a dog person. He hadn't really pegged her as an anything person, actually. He was usually too busy trying not to drool on himself while he was arguing with her. Her body might be heavenly, but her face, a perfect oval with a pert little nose and full lips she often painted some lickable shade of red—not to mention those *eyes*—was enough to knock any sane man on his ass. He'd been sure he was building up immunity, thanks to their regular arguments.

So much for that.

"Jason, are you still there? Who—"

A thought occurred to him then, just a wisp of an idea stamped THIS MIGHT WORK. He grasped at it like a drowning man confronted with the bobbing remnants of a shattered ship. It might not be enough to save him, and Zoe would probably kill him anyway, but what choice did he have?

"That's Zoe, Mom." He saw her look up sharply from where she was petting Rosie.

"Oh?" It was a loaded question, and he knew it. He could hear all the other questions running just beneath the surface of that single simple word. Zoe rose and came to stand before him, one hand on her hip in a stance he was well acquainted with by now. The arched eyebrow meant she was curious, but the hand on the hip? It didn't bode well for him.

Maybe she'd cut him some slack because he was injured. He was desperate. And so while Zoe stared at him, he told Molly Evans the biggest lie he'd conjured since she'd been on the front porch at two a.m. asking his seventeen-year-old self whether he'd been drinking. "Yeah, well, she's been helping me out. That's why I'm not sure about all these plans you've got going. . . . I mean, I'd love to have everybody here, but my place is pretty small and she's, you know" — he scrubbed a hand through his hair — "around a lot."

Zoe's mouth dropped open.

Yep, I'm dead.

To Zoe's credit, she didn't hurl the potted plant in her hands at his head. She looked like she wanted to, but she didn't. Instead, with her storm gray eyes full of fire, she mouthed, *I will kill you.*

There was a moment of dead silence. Then his mother spoke: "Well, *finally*!"

Her laugh held so much relief, that any hope of his relationship status ceasing to be a topic of interest in the family evaporated. They still talked about him — poor, lonely, brokenhearted Jason — because of course they did. Because of Sara. When the divorce had been finalized, he'd assumed she was gone for good. He hadn't known that just the idea of her would continue to give him problems five years on. And as hard as things had been at the end, he didn't think this was what Sara had intended either. She'd just wanted to go. In the end, he'd let her.

He just wished everybody else would, too.

As Zoe's jaw tightened and the hand at her hip clenched into a fist, Jason tried to tell himself that what he'd just done was no big deal. A girlfriend, even an imaginary one, would make his mother quit worrying and save him from weeks of having a social life forced upon him when all he really wanted to do was convalesce and brood. Zoe didn't even have to be around. Hell, he'd invent a different Zoe if he had to, and then send her on an imaginary vacation or . . . something. But no matter how he tried to sugarcoat it, he couldn't escape the fact that he'd just dragged the real Zoe into his life in a big way, without asking permission, and with a whole lot of potential ramifications that she seemed fully aware of. That was why she was going to kill him. He probably deserved it.

But that was still a more appealing thought than having his family pile in on him for a month.

Damn. This is a new low.

His mother's voice chirped happily in his ear, pulling him back into a conversation he had no idea how to participate in. Not with Zoe's death stare fixed on him. He held up one hand toward her, tried for an expression that he hoped was somewhere in the vicinity of pathetic, and mouthed the words, *Wait. Please.*

"Hey, Mom. Look, I've gotta go." Jason hoped he didn't sound as panicked as he felt. "Yep. See you Sunday." He was ready to hang up when she said the words that shoved a sliver of ice-cold fear directly through his heart.

"I can't wait to meet the mystery woman."

She was being perfectly sincere. She sounded happy, even, and Jason was sure she was. For now, at least. But as it tended to do on the rare occasions he slipped into panic, the verbal tic Jason had worked so hard to rid himself of when he was a child returned to tie his tongue in knots. "I-I-I-I'm sure she'll be h-happy to meet you too."

Nice. In front of Zoe, even. You're on a roll today, man.

Zoe's expression changed, ever so slightly, and Jason looked away. He had to. The last thing he needed was a dose of pity from a woman who was already way the hell out of his league. His mother clucked her tongue at him across the miles. "Oh, don't be nervous, honey. I'm sure

I'll love her. It's about time you found somebody who appreciates you. After all Sara put you through, you deserve it."

"Uh." It was the only response he could muster, but she didn't seem to mind.

"Love you. See you Sunday!" she chirped. "I'll call once Moira picks me up and we're on our way!"

His aunt Moira, Jake's mother. A woman who knew damn well he wasn't dating anyone. His spur-of-the-moment plan was already in flames, and he hadn't even hung up the phone. Maybe he ought to have been glad he now had an epic fail like this to hold up as the ultimate proof that he really just needed to give up on having a social life. Forever.

"Bye," Jason said, his voice barely a growl, and hung up. He tossed the phone to the side, where it landed between a couple of couch pillows, and shoved his face into his hands. He didn't need to look at Zoe's face to know what must have been written all over it. There was a long moment of silence. And then, finally, in a voice that would have been as rich as cream but for the violence vibrating through it, Zoe spoke. Carefully. Deliberately.

Homicidally.

"What. Did. You. Just. Do?"

ALSO AVAILABLE FROM

KENDRA LEIGH CASTLE

FOR THE LONGEST TIME

The Harvest Cove Series

After a perfect storm of events leaves Sam high, dry, and jobless, she has to head home to Harvest Cove to regroup. Growing up, she was the town misfit, and a brief high school romance that resulted in heartbreak made her realize she was never going to fit in.

Life's been good to Jake Smith, but Sam's homecoming makes him question his choices. The sharp-tongued beauty was never a good fit for the small community, but he's never forgotten her—or how good they were together. While she makes it clear she's not about to repeat the past, Jake's determined to convince her to give him—and Harvest Cove—a second chance.

"Harvest Cove will wrap around your heart like a snuggly blanket on a chilly autumn day."
—*USA Today* bestselling author Katie Lane

Available wherever books are sold or at
penguin.com

LOVE
ROMANCE
NOVELS?

For news on all your favorite romance authors,
sneak peeks into the newest releases, book
giveaways, and much more—

"Like" Love Always on Facebook!

 LoveAlwaysBooks